The Shape of Forever

The People of Cedar Ridge, Book 3

Written by Diane Kann

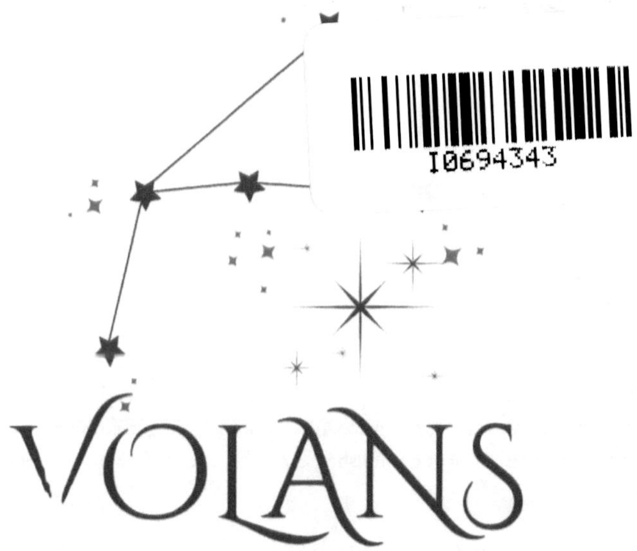

Brought to you by Volans Galaxy Press

© 2026 Diane Kann

All rights reserved.

No part of this publication may be reproduced, stored in a retrieval system, or transmitted in any form or by any means—electronic, mechanical, photocopying, recording, or otherwise—without prior written permission of the publisher, except in the case of brief quotations for review or educational use.

Published by Kannceptual Creations LLC

An imprint of Volans Galaxy Press

ISBN: 978-1-971356-51-8

Printed in the United States of America

First Edition, January 2026

Contents

Author's Biography

Diane Kann writes sweet romance stories that celebrate love, second chances, and the quiet moments that change everything. Her stories focus on emotional connection, gentle healing, and relationships built on trust, hope, and heart.

When she's not writing, Diane enjoys spending time in nature with her family and dogs, finding inspiration in peaceful landscapes and everyday moments, and dreaming up tender stories rooted in compassion.

Dedication

For the ones who have loved deeply—
and for those who learned that love does not always arrive loudly,
but settles in gently, through presence, patience, and choice.

For anyone who has rebuilt after loss,
who has guarded their heart carefully,
and who still dared to believe that something lasting could grow
from tenderness, trust, and time.

And for the souls who understand
that forever isn't a promise shouted into the future,
but a shape we create—
one ordinary, beautiful moment at a time.

— Diane Kann

Chapter One: The Rhythm of Cedar Ridge

The first blush of dawn was a shy painter, tentatively sketching soft hues of rose and gold across the eastern sky, its light finding its way through the large, mullioned windows of 'The Bound Page.' Inside, the air was already perfumed with the comforting, papery scent of a thousand stories waiting to be discovered, a fragrance Marisol Vega had come to associate with peace. Dust motes danced in the nascent sunlight, performing a silent ballet as she moved through the aisles, her fingertips trailing lightly over the spines of new arrivals. Her hands, perpetually dusted with the faint, dry scent of old paper, were a testament to her lifelong dedication to this haven of words.

Marisol cherished the quiet predictability of her mornings. It began with the ritualistic brewing of coffee, the rich aroma filling her small apartment above the shop, a prelude to the day ahead. Then, the descent into the hushed sanctity of 'The Bound Page,' where the scent intensified, mingling with the faint hint of lemon polish from the antique oak tables. Arranging the newly arrived novels was more than a task; it was a communion. She ran her fingers over the crisp covers, inhaled the distinct smell of fresh ink and paper, and felt a thrill of anticipation for the stories they held, stories that would soon find their way into the hands of Cedar Ridge residents.

Each book was a potential journey, a new perspective, a whispered secret waiting to be shared.

Her routine was a well-worn path, a comforting rhythm that had guided her life for years. From the moment the first cup of coffee was poured, through the gentle unlocking of the heavy oak door, to the final, lingering farewell to the last customer, her days unfolded with a gentle, almost pre-dictable grace. She knew the exact angle of the sun that would illuminate the reading nook by the bay window at precisely 10:17 AM, the subtle creak of the floorboard near the poetry section, and the distinct hum of the old radiator that offered a warm sigh on cooler mornings. This was her sanctuary, her kingdom, a space she had meticulously cultivated, much like a gardener tends to a beloved plot of land.

Cedar Ridge itself was a character woven into the fabric of Marisol's life, a town that breathed with a steady, unhurried pulse. Its familiar sights and sounds were as comforting as the worn armchair in her living room. The distant chime of the town hall clock marking the hours, the cheerful greetings exchanged between neighbors on Main Street, the rumble of the occasional truck delivering supplies to the local businesses – all these were the gentle melodies that composed the soundtrack of her existence. The town was a living, breathing entity, its rhythm syncing with her own, creating a sense of deep belonging.

She moved with a quiet efficiency, her movements fluid and practiced. Stacking the hardcovers with their striking jacket art, placing the paper-backs in neat rows, ensuring that the children's section was a riot of color and whimsy – each action was performed with a silent, deep satisfaction. It wasn't just about selling books; it was about connecting people with stories, about providing a refuge from the cacophony of the outside world. 'The Bound Page' was more than a business; it was a vital organ of Cedar Ridge, a place where minds could wander, hearts could be touched, and souls could find solace.

The town square, just a block away, was already stirring. She could hear the faint murmur of early risers, the clatter of the baker setting up his stall, the distant bark of a dog. These were the familiar sounds of a town waking up, of lives unfolding in predictable, comforting patterns. Marisol found a profound sense of peace in this ordinariness, in the knowledge that she was a part of this tapestry, a small but essential thread. Her life here was rich, not in grand adventures or dramatic turns, but in the quiet accumulation of shared moments, of predictable joys, of a life lived with purpose and intention.

Yet, beneath the surface of her organized contentment, a subtle, almost imperceptible yearning stirred. It wasn't dissatisfaction, not by any means. She loved her life, her bookstore, her town. But sometimes, as she arranged the books, her gaze would drift towards the window, and she would catch sight of couples walking hand-in-hand, their easy intimacy a silent question. Their shared smiles, the casual touch of their hands, the unspoken understanding that passed between them – these were glimpses into a world of declared connection that sometimes felt just out of reach.

She would pause, a book held loosely in her hand, and watch them. It was a quiet observation, devoid of envy, more a gentle contemplation. She wondered about the unspoken promises that undergirded such visible affection, the shared dreams that fueled their shared smiles. It was a feeling as subtle as the scent of old paper, a whisper of longing that hinted at a desire for something more tangible, something that resonated with the depth of the feelings she held within her own heart, even if they remained unspoken.

The bookstore was a space of endless possibilities, a world where heroes embarked on quests and lovers found their happily ever afters. Marisol was surrounded by these narratives of enduring love and bold declarations, and it was natural that a part of her would internalize their themes. The stories she curated and sold were filled with characters who, in their own ways, sought and found a definitive form of love, a commitment that was openly acknowledged and celebrated. This constant exposure to tales of romantic fulfillment, while inspiring, also served to highlight the quiet ambiguity that characterized her own deeply cherished relationship.

She traced the embossed title of a new romance novel, its cover depicting a couple in a tender embrace. Her fingers lingered on the raised letters, a silent acknowledgment of the narrative contained within. These stories offered a blueprint, a suggestion of what love could look like when it was boldly expressed and openly embraced. They were a constant reminder that while comfort and companionship were wonderful, there was a certain magic, a profound security, in knowing that your love was seen, acknowledged, and declared for all the world to witness.

The rhythm of Cedar Ridge was a soothing balm, a gentle hum that underscored her days. But sometimes, in the quiet stillness of the morning before the first customer arrived, when the sunlight slanted just so through the windows, Marisol felt a faint dissonance. It was the quiet hum of a question that had yet to be asked, the silent anticipation of a future that had yet to be fully defined. It was the quiet longing that lay just beneath the surface of her organized, content life, a gentle current pulling her towards an unknown horizon.

She admired the way the morning light, in its relentless pursuit of illuminating every corner of the room, cast a warm glow upon the worn leather of a favorite armchair, highlighting the subtle cracks and creases that spoke of countless hours of quiet companionship. It was a testament to endurance, to a love that had weathered time and use. And in that light, a thought, as delicate as a cobweb, began to form: that perhaps, just as the light found its way into every nook and cranny of her beloved bookstore, her own love deserved to be brought into the full, radiant light of acknowledgment.

The scent of brewing coffee was a promise of a new day, and the arrangement of books, a silent symphony of stories. Marisol Vega, immersed in the comforting embrace of 'The Bound Page,' felt the gentle pulse of Cedar Ridge around her, a town that was both her anchor and her stage. Her days were a testament to the quiet beauty of routine, the deep satisfaction of a life lived with purpose. Yet, as the sun climbed higher, its golden rays illuminating the dust motes in their ceaseless dance, a subtle, unspoken question began to bloom within her, as tender and persistent as a seedling pushing through rich soil.

It was a question whispered on the morning breeze, a longing for the clear, bright light of a future fully declared, a future that mirrored the vibrant stories she held within her hands. The predictable rhythm was her comfort, but a soft yearning for a new cadence, a more resonant chord, began to stir, a prelude to a melody yet to be composed, a testament to the quiet hope that even in the most cherished routines, love's greatest chapters are often yet to be written.

The afternoon sun, a warm, benevolent eye, streamed through the high windows of Theo Hart's carpentry shop, transforming the motes of saw-dust dancing in the air into a shimmering, golden haze. The scent that permeated the space was a rich, complex perfume: the sharp, clean aroma of freshly cut pine, the deeper, resinous perfume of oak, and the subtle, sweet undertones of linseed oil and beeswax polish.

It was a smell that spoke of transformation, of raw potential coaxed into being by skilled hands. Theo's hands, broad and strong, with a roadmap of fine lines and calluses etched into their surfaces, were currently guiding a smooth block of maple across the bed of his planer. The machine whirred to life, a steady, resonant hum that vibrated through the concrete floor, and the wood emerged a fraction thinner, its surface now impossibly smooth, catching the light with a silken sheen.

Theo was a man of quiet rhythms, his life as deliberately measured as the strokes of his hand plane or the steady beat of his hammer. His workshop was his sanctuary, a testament to his solitary dedication to the craft of woodworking. Here, amidst the organized chaos of planks, tools, and half-finished projects, he found a profound sense of peace. Each piece of wood held a story, a unique grain and character that whispered its secrets to him as he worked. He didn't just shape wood; he listened to it, allowing its inherent qualities to guide his design, his touch gentle yet firm, respectful of the material's natural beauty.

He moved with an economy of motion, his tall frame surprisingly agile as he navigated the space between his workbench and the lumber racks. The shop wasn't large, but every inch was utilized. Shelves overflowed with various species of wood – the pale, creamy hue of birch, the deep, rich mahogany, the warm, inviting tones of cherry.

Tools hung in neat rows on pegboards, their polished metal surfaces reflecting the sunlight: chisels of varying sizes, hand saws with teeth honed to a razor's edge, planes of cast iron and wood, their blades gleaming. There was a deliberate order to it all, a system only Theo truly understood, a testament to years of practice and an intuitive grasp of his trade.

He picked up a length of cedar, its aromatic fragrance immediately filling his nostrils, a scent that always reminded him of the wild forests from which it came. This piece was destined to become part of a custom-built hope chest, a piece commissioned by a young couple in town. He ran his thumb along the edge, feeling the slight roughness of the grain, imagining the finished product: a sturdy, beautiful vessel, a repository for dreams and memories. He found a deep satisfaction in creating objects that would be cherished, that would hold stories of their own. It was a different kind of storytelling than Marisol's, a silent, tangible narrative woven into the very fibers of the wood.

His focus was absolute when he was in the zone. The world outside the shop's thick wooden doors seemed to recede, its demands and complexities fading into a muted backdrop. Here, the only requirements were precision, patience, and a deep understanding of his materials. He could lose himself for hours, the rhythmic rasp of sandpaper, the steady tap-tap-tap of a chisel, the low hum of the dust collection system forming a familiar, comforting symphony.

It was a solitary existence, by choice. He thrived in this self-contained universe, where the only conversations were with the wood and the tools, and where the outcomes were tangible, measurable, and wholly his own.

He remembered, with a slight, inward smile, the time Marisol had visited the shop, her eyes wide with a mixture of curiosity and slight trepidation. She'd picked up a finished piece, a small, intricately carved wooden bird, its wings poised as if in mid-flight. She'd held it gently, her fingers tracing the delicate lines he'd painstakingly carved. "It's beautiful, Theo," she'd said, her voice soft, almost reverent. "It feels... alive." He'd merely nodded, a warmth spreading through him at her appreciation, but he hadn't elaborated on the hours of sanding, the frustration of a misplaced chisel stroke, the quiet triumph of finally capturing the essence of flight in inanimate wood. He hadn't explained the solitary journey of its creation, the moments of doubt and the eventual surrender to the process.

That was Theo, wasn't it? He poured his heart and soul into his work, but he rarely spoke of the emotions that fueled it. His passion was expressed through his hands, through the flawless execution of his craft, not through eloquent declarations. He found it easier to communicate through the language of wood, through the smooth finish of a tabletop, the sturdy joinery of a cabinet, the delicate curve of a chair leg. These were his words, his feelings made manifest.

He picked up a different piece of wood now, a slab of dark walnut, its grain swirling like a miniature storm. This was for a commissioned desk, a substantial piece for a writer who wanted a surface that would inspire creativity. Theo understood that. He knew the power of a well-crafted environment to foster a particular state of mind. He imagined the writer sitting there, the smooth wood cool beneath their forearms, the scent of walnut a subtle companion to their thoughts. He felt a connection to all those who would use the things he made, a silent partnership that spanned the distance between his workshop and their lives.

His relationship with Marisol was a different kind of creation, one he approached with a similar quiet dedication, but with a layer of complexity that often left him fumbling for the right materials. He loved her, that was as certain as the grain in any piece of wood he'd ever worked. He loved her quiet strength, her unwavering passion for her books, the way her eyes lit up when she spoke of a particularly beloved story. He cherished the gentle rhythm of their shared life, the comfortable silences, the shared meals, the way she fit into his world as seamlessly as a well-made dovetail joint.

But Theo was a man who built things, who solved problems with tangible solutions. Love, he was discovering, was far more abstract, far less predictable. It wasn't something you could plane smooth or sand to a perfect finish. It was a living, breathing thing, prone to shifts and changes, requiring a different kind of skill, a vulnerability he wasn't always sure he possessed. He could build a house that would withstand the fiercest storm, but he sometimes felt adrift when it came to navigating the subtle currents of Marisol's heart, or indeed, his own.

He remembered their early days, when he'd first brought her one of his carved birds. He'd presented it to her almost gruffly, a gesture of affection disguised as a casual offering. She'd held it, her smile radiant, and he'd felt a surge of something powerful, something akin to the deep satisfaction of completing a particularly challenging piece. But he hadn't known how to articulate that feeling, how to translate it into words that matched the depth of the emotion. He'd simply retreated into the familiar comfort of his workshop, letting the sawdust and the scent of wood polish absorb his unspoken words.

He paused in his work, leaning his forearms on the edge of his workbench. The late afternoon sun cast long shadows across the floor, and the sounds of Cedar Ridge, usually a distant murmur, began to filter in – the cheerful clang of the bell above the ice cream parlor door, the rumble of a pickup truck on Main Street, the laughter of children playing in the park. He was aware of Marisol, just a few blocks away, immersed in her own world of stories. He pictured her there, surrounded by the comforting scent of paper and ink, her fingers tracing the spines of books. They were two halves of a whole, he thought, each inhabiting their own carefully crafted space, their lives intertwined yet distinct.

He picked up a small block of maple and a sharp chisel. He began to carve, his movements slow and deliberate. A small, smooth stone, the kind you might find nestled in a creek bed. He found a certain solace in the repetitive nature of the task, the way the wood yielded under the pressure of the blade. It was a way to process, to think without speaking, to channel the swirling thoughts and feelings that often eluded his verbal grasp. This was his language, his method of understanding, of connecting with the world on his own terms.

He knew Marisol deserved more than just the quiet gestures of his affection, more than the tangible objects he created. She deserved to hear the words, to feel the certainty of his love declared aloud, not just implied in the smooth finish of a piece of furniture or the steady presence of his hand. He wrestled with it, this need to articulate, this unfamiliar terrain of emotional expression. It was like trying to work with a wood he'd never encountered, its properties unknown, its challenges daunting.

He continued to carve, the small stone taking shape under his skilled hands. He imagined giving it to her, holding it out not as a gift of craftsmanship, but as a tangible representation of something he found difficult to say. A promise of solidity, of enduring beauty, of a love that, like the grain in the wood, ran deep and true, even if he struggled to voice its full depth. He was a builder, after all. And he was slowly, painstakingly, learning to build something more than just furniture. He was learning to build a bridge between his guarded heart and the woman who held its key.

The scent of pine and oak and cedar hung heavy in the air, a comforting blanket of familiarity. Theo Hart, a craftsman by trade and by nature, worked on, his hands shaping wood, his mind wrestling with the far more complex art of expressing love. The rhythm of his workshop was a steady, reliable beat, a solitary song that echoed the quiet determination of a man building not just objects, but a life, piece by carefully considered piece, with a woman who understood the profound beauty of unspoken stories, and who, he hoped, would also come to understand the words he was slowly, surely, learning to speak.

He finished the stone, its surface smooth and cool to the touch, a small, silent testament to the vast, complex emotions that simmered beneath his quiet exterior, a prelude to the conversations that lay ahead, a promise whispered in the language of wood.

The aroma of freshly brewed coffee, a rich, dark counterpoint to the lingering scent of old paper and new ink, wafted from the kitchen. Marisol poured two mugs, the ceramic warm against her palms, and carried them to the small table tucked beside the window overlooking Main Street. Theo was already there, his broad back to her, wrestling with the morning newspaper, its rustle a familiar sound in the quiet of their shared home. He looked up as she approached, his eyes, the color of a clear summer sky, softening as they met hers.

"Morning," he said, his voice a low rumble, like distant thunder.

"Morning," she replied, placing his mug before him and settling into the chair opposite. The newspaper was spread between them, a silent, comfortable barrier, or perhaps a shared space, depending on how one looked at it. Marisol loved these moments, the quiet unfolding of their day, the easy companionship that had become the bedrock of their life together. It was a rhythm she'd come to cherish, as predictable and comforting as the turning of pages in a well-loved book.

Their days were a gentle ebb and flow, a dance choreographed by mutual respect and an unspoken understanding of each other's needs. Mornings began with coffee and the paper, a shared ritual before they went their separate ways for the day. Theo would retreat to his workshop, the scent of sawdust and wood a stark contrast to the papery perfume of her bookstore, 'The Storyteller's Nook,' nestled just a few doors down. Marisol would unlock the shop's creaky door, the scent of aged paper and leather bindings a welcome embrace, ready to greet the day's customers, her world populated by characters and narratives.

Yet, their lives were not entirely separate. Evenings were often spent together, sometimes at the bookstore, Marisol arranging displays of new arrivals while Theo, with his carpenter's eye for structural integrity and aesthetic balance, would offer his quiet, insightful suggestions. Other nights, they'd be at home, the comforting aroma of a meal simmering on the stove filling the air. These were the times when their worlds truly merged.

Marisol would find herself describing the intricate plot of a new historical fiction novel, her voice animated, her hands sketching invisible diagrams in the air. Theo, in turn, would talk about the challenges of a particularly tricky dovetail joint or the unique grain pattern of a newly acquired piece of cherry wood, his descriptions surprisingly vivid, his passion for his craft evident in the subtle shifts of his expression.

Their conversations were a curious blend of their two worlds. Marisol would pepper her descriptions of literary heroines with analogies to sturdy oak or elegant maple, while Theo would speak of the "story" a piece of wood held, its history etched into its very fibers, much like a character's life experiences shaped their personality. He'd describe the 'voice' of a particular wood, its inherent qualities that spoke to him, guiding his hands. Marisol, in turn, recognized that silent communication in his craft, the way he coaxed beauty and function from raw material. She saw the same quiet dedication in his work that she poured into curating her book selections, a deep-seated desire to connect, to share something meaningful with the world.

They had built a life together that was, in many ways, a testament to the beauty of shared spaces. The bookstore, though primarily Marisol's domain, had Theo's subtle imprint all over it. He'd built the sturdy, elegant bookshelves that lined the walls, each one a testament to his skill and his understanding of how best to display Marisol's beloved books. He'd crafted the cozy reading nooks with their plush cushions and the polished wooden counter where Marisol tallied sales and offered recommendations. He'd even designed and built the charming window display cases, their clean lines and warm wood making the books within seem all the more inviting.

Their home, a quaint Victorian cottage on the edge of town, was a similar blend of their personalities. Marisol's love for comfort and warmth was evident in the overflowing bookshelves, the plush rugs, and the collection of eclectic art that adorned the walls. Theo's touch was there in the sturdy, hand-built furniture, the meticulously maintained garden, and the subtle, practical improvements he'd made to the house, always with an eye for both form and function. It was a home that felt lived-in, loved, and distinctly theirs, a testament to their shared life.

There were evenings when they would sit in comfortable silence, Marisol lost in the pages of a novel, Theo perhaps sketching designs in his workshop or simply enjoying the quiet stillness of their shared space. These silences weren't empty; they were filled with a deep sense of contentment, a quiet acknowledgment of their shared journey. They understood each other without the need for constant dialogue, a skill honed through countless shared meals, late-night conversations that drifted from literature to the mundane details of daily life, and the simple act of being present in each other's lives.

Marisol knew Theo's routines, the subtle shift in his posture when he was lost in thought, the way his brow furrowed when he encountered a particularly challenging woodworking problem. She could tell, just by the sound of his footsteps, whether he was returning from his workshop with satisfaction or a touch of frustration. And Theo, she suspected, knew her just as well. He'd learned the subtle cues of her mood by the way she arranged the books on her shelves, the quickness of her smile, the slight tilt of her head when she was deep in contemplation.

Their partnership in 'The Storyteller's Nook' was another facet of their shared existence. While Marisol was the heart and soul of the business, the driving force behind its literary offerings, Theo was its silent, steadfast support. He didn't just provide the physical structure of the store; he offered a steadying presence, a calming influence during busy holiday seasons or when Marisol felt overwhelmed. He'd often pop in during his lunch break, bringing her a thermos of coffee or a small, perfectly crafted wooden bookmark, a gesture that always brought a smile to her face.

He rarely offered unsolicited advice about the books themselves, respecting Marisol's expertise implicitly. But he was a keen observer of their customers, and his quiet insights were often surprisingly astute. He'd notice, for instance, the way a particular customer lingered over the poetry section, or how another seemed drawn to stories of adventure, and he'd subtly point these observations out to Marisol, who would then use them to offer a more tailored recommendation. It was a collaboration built on mutual trust and a shared desire to create a welcoming space for the community.

Their shared meals were a testament to this comfortable rhythm. Whether it was a simple weeknight dinner or a more elaborate Sunday roast, the act of preparing and sharing food was a cherished ritual. Marisol often found herself drawn to recipes that echoed the warmth and comfort of their home, while Theo, with his appreciation for precision and balance, had a knack for creating surprisingly delicious dishes. These were moments of connection, where the day's events were discussed, not in detail, but in broad strokes, the essence of their experiences shared over steaming plates and quiet conversation.

Marisol would recount a particularly memorable customer interaction, the joy of finding the perfect book for someone, or the quiet satisfaction of recommending a story that resonated deeply. Theo would speak of a project nearing completion, the beauty of a finished piece, or the quiet satisfaction of seeing his craft bring joy to others. They were two artists, in their own ways, each contributing to the tapestry of Cedar Ridge, and their shared life was a testament to the beauty of that interwoven existence.

Yet, amidst this comfortable harmony, there were unspoken needs, gentle nudges towards something more, something less defined by the tangible and the immediate. Marisol, a woman of words, sometimes found herself yearning for a deeper verbal expression of their connection. She loved Theo's quiet strength, his unwavering presence, the way he made her feel safe and cherished. But there were moments, often late at night when the world outside their cottage had fallen silent, when a question, unasked but deeply felt, would surface: did he truly see her, beyond the comfortable routine, beyond the shared spaces?

She knew, intellectually, that he loved her. His actions spoke volumes – the way he always ensured her favorite tea was stocked, the thoughtful gifts he would surprise her with, the quiet pride in his eyes when she spoke of the bookstore's success. But Marisol, steeped in the language of stories, was accustomed to the overt declarations, the grand gestures, the explicit articulation of emotion that filled the pages of her beloved novels. Theo's love, while deeply felt, was often expressed in a quieter, more understated language, a language of action and presence rather than eloquent pronouncements.

She remembered one evening, after a particularly successful book signing event at the store. The air had been buzzing with excitement, Marisol's heart brimming with a potent mix of exhaustion and elation. Theo had been there, a steady presence amidst the crowd, his quiet support a comforting anchor. Later, as they were cleaning up, he had simply looked at her, a rare, unguarded smile on his face, and said, "You were amazing tonight, Marisol." It was a simple sentence, yet the sincerity in his voice, the depth of genuine admiration in his gaze, had sent a warmth spreading through her. But even then, she'd found herself wishing for more, for the words to elaborate on what she'd seen in his eyes, for him to articulate the pride and love that she suspected lay beneath the surface.

Their shared home, their shared business, their shared lives – they were all tangible manifestations of their connection, solid and dependable. But Marisol sometimes wondered if these shared spaces, while comforting and secure, might also be creating a subtle barrier, a comfortable enclosure that prevented deeper emotional exploration. The familiarity, while cherished, could also breed a certain complacency, a reliance on the unspoken that, while often effective, could also leave certain emotional needs unmet.

She found solace in the stories she sold, in the passionate declarations of love and commitment that filled their pages. These narratives offered a contrast to the quiet reserve that often characterized Theo's expressions of affection. She adored his steadiness, his grounded nature, the way he seemed to possess an unshakeable inner calm. But sometimes, a part of her, the part that lived and breathed stories, yearned for a more overt, more vocal manifestation of his love. It was a subtle yearning, a gentle whisper beneath the surface of their comfortable existence, a desire for the unspoken to be spoken, for the tangible to be accompanied by the lyrical.

Theo, in his own way, was a man of rituals and routines. He found comfort in the predictable, the measurable, the tangible. His workshop was a testament to this, a meticulously organized space where every tool had its place, every project had a clear beginning and end. Their shared life in Cedar Ridge was much the same, a well-ordered existence built on mutual respect and understanding. The bookstore, though Marisol's creative hub, was a space he helped maintain, a physical structure that housed her dreams. Their home was a sanctuary they had built together, a physical manifestation of their shared commitment.

He found deep satisfaction in these shared spaces, in the quiet rhythm of their days. He loved the ease with which they moved through their lives together, the comfortable silences that spoke volumes. He saw the bookstore as a thriving entity, a testament to Marisol's passion and hard work, and he took quiet pride in his contribution to its success. He found joy in their shared evenings, in the simple act of being present with her, whether they were discussing a new literary find or simply enjoying the quiet companionship of a shared meal.

But Theo, too, sensed the unspoken. He saw the way Marisol's eyes sometimes held a hint of yearning, a subtle plea for something more than the comfortable routine they had established. He understood that while his actions spoke of his love, his words often failed to convey the depth of his emotions. He was a man who expressed himself through his hands, through the solid, enduring creations that emerged from his workshop. He was still learning the language of the heart, a language that required a different kind of precision, a vulnerability that felt as raw and unfamiliar as a freshly planed piece of wood.

He noticed how Marisol's smile would brighten, just a fraction, when he offered a compliment that went beyond the practical, a compliment that acknowledged her spirit, her creativity, her very essence. He saw the way she sometimes looked at him, a flicker of something unarticulated in her eyes, and he knew that while their shared spaces were filled with comfort and security, there were still separate hearts within those spaces, each with its own unique rhythm, its own unspoken desires.

The harmony they had created was beautiful, a testament to their shared life, but it was a harmony that, Theo suspected, was still evolving, still seeking a deeper resonance, a more complete expression of their intertwined souls. He was a builder, and he was slowly, tentatively, beginning to build bridges within his own heart, bridges that would, he hoped, lead to a more profound understanding, a more vocal articulation of the love that resided there, waiting to be truly heard.

The late afternoon sun cast long, golden shadows across the cobblestone street, painting Cedar Ridge in hues of honey and amber. Marisol, leaning against the cool glass of her bookstore window, watched the familiar rhythm of the town unfold. Couples ambled past, their hands clasped, their laughter weaving through the gentle murmur of evening life. Mr. Henderson, with his perpetually rosy cheeks, walked his terrier, the dog's tail a blur of happy anticipation. The Peterson twins, now young women with dreams as vast as the prairie sky, shared an ice cream cone, their heads bent close in secret conversation. It was a tableau of enduring affection, of lives intertwined, and with each passing pair, a quiet question, a gentle ache, bloomed in Marisol's chest.

It wasn't dissatisfaction that stirred within her, not a whisper of regret for the life she shared with Theo. Their existence was a tapestry woven with threads of comfort, security, and a deep, abiding affection. Theo was her anchor, her steady north star in the sometimes-turbulent seas of life. His quiet strength, his unwavering presence, the sheer solidity of him – these were the foundations upon which she had built her happiness. But lately, amidst the comforting predictability of their days, a new question had begun to surface, a soft, persistent whisper of 'what if.' What if this contented coexistence, as beautiful and fulfilling as it was, wasn't a final destination but a picturesque resting point on a longer journey?

She traced a pattern on the condensation of the windowpane, her gaze lingering on a young couple sharing a park bench across the street. They were so earnest, so openly affectionate, their conversation punctuated by stolen glances and the gentle brush of hands. It was a public display of a private bond, a small, beautiful declaration of their commitment to one another. Marisol felt a pang, not of envy, but of a gentle longing. She and Theo had their quiet moments, their shared smiles that spoke volumes, their comfortable silences that were rich with understanding. But Cedar Ridge, in its charming, unassuming way, offered a constant reminder of the more overt expressions of love, the tangible symbols of a future deliberately built, brick by loving brick.

She thought of Sarah Jenkins, who had married her childhood sweetheart last spring, their wedding a vibrant testament to years of shared dreams. She saw them still, walking hand-in-hand to the farmer's market, their love a palpable thing, woven into the very fabric of their shared routine. Then there were the Millers, who had celebrated their fortieth anniversary with a town-wide picnic, their enduring partnership an inspiration to all. These were not grand, sweeping romances from the novels she sold, but the quiet, persistent bloom of love in the everyday, a love that had been consciously nurtured, openly acknowledged, and visibly solidified over time.

Marisol sighed, the sound barely audible above the gentle rustle of turning pages within the bookstore. It wasn't that she needed grand pronouncements or theatrical displays. Theo's love was evident in the sturdy bookshelves he'd built for her store, in the perfectly brewed coffee he always had waiting, in the way his eyes crinkled at the corners when she made him laugh. But lately, she found herself yearning for something more concrete, something that spoke of a shared future deliberately planned, a future that extended beyond the comfortable present. She yearned for the quiet certainty that came with knowing their lives were not just intertwined, but intentionally, irrevocably bound.

Her mind drifted to a conversation she'd overheard earlier that week at the post office. Mrs. Gable, her voice a conspiratorial whisper, had been recounting the details of her granddaughter's engagement. "They're already looking at houses," she'd enthused, her eyes sparkling. "Such a sensible young couple, planning their whole lives together. It's so reassuring, isn't it, to know they're building something solid." Marisol had felt a prickle of something akin to envy. Planning. Building. Solid. These were words that resonated deeply with her, words that spoke of intention and permanence.

She loved Theo. She loved their life in Cedar Ridge. She loved the comforting rhythm of their days, the predictable cadence of their shared existence. But the 'what ifs' had begun to gather, like dust motes dancing in a sunbeam, subtle yet undeniably present. What if their comfortable rhythm was a gentle lullaby that soothed them into a state of perpetual contentedness, preventing them from reaching for something more profound? What if the unspoken understanding that had served them so well for so long was, in fact, a subtle barrier to a deeper, more explicit declaration of their commitment?

She imagined a future where their love was not just a present reality, but a promised one. A future where the quiet understanding between them was amplified by spoken words, by shared plans, by the visible construction of a life intentionally built for two, forever. It was a dream she held close, a tender seedling of hope that she nurtured in the quiet corners of her heart. She wasn't looking for an ultimatum, not a demand that would disrupt the harmony they had so carefully cultivated.

Rather, it was a gentle yearning, a natural progression of love, a desire to translate the deep, unspoken affection she felt into a language that acknowledged its enduring power and its intended permanence.

Marisol turned from the window, her gaze sweeping over the shelves filled with stories of every kind. Tales of epic quests and quiet domestic dramas, of passionate love affairs and enduring friendships. Each book held within it a narrative, a journey, a testament to the complexities of the human heart. And within her own heart, a new narrative was beginning to unfold, a story that whispered of 'what if,' a story that yearned for the quiet courage to ask for a future that was not just lived, but deliberately, beautifully, and permanently built. The rhythm of Cedar Ridge was a comforting melody, but Marisol was beginning to wonder if there was a deeper, more resonant song waiting to be sung, a song of a love that was not just felt, but openly declared and eternally promised.

She picked up a worn copy of a classic romance, its pages softened by countless readings, and for a moment, she allowed herself to be swept away by the eloquent declarations of love, the unwavering devotion, the certainty of a happily ever after. It was a momentary escape, a brief indulgence in a fantasy that mirrored her own burgeoning desires, a desire for her own quiet story to find its own lasting cadence.

Theo found Marisol's presence a balm to his often-frayed nerves. Her laughter, a light, lilting sound that could cut through the densest silence, was the soundtrack to his life in Cedar Ridge. It was a sound he'd grown accustomed to, a sound he cherished in the quiet solitude of his workshop, surrounded by the scent of sawdust and varnish. He saw the way she moved, a graceful fluidity that spoke of quiet confidence, and felt a profound sense of gratitude for her steady warmth. She was the color in his monochrome world, the vibrant hue that transformed the ordinary into something extraordinary.

He'd built those bookshelves for her, each plank meticulously planed and sanded, each joint fitted with the precision of a seasoned craftsman. It was his way of contributing, of adding to the foundation of her dream. The bookstore, a haven of stories and whispered secrets, was her passion, and he was content to be a silent, steady supporter, the unseen force that held it all together. He loved the way her eyes lit up when a customer discovered a forgotten gem on her shelves, the way her brow furrowed in concentration as she recommended a new read. These were the moments that solidified his appreciation for her, the small, intimate glimpses into the heart of the woman he loved.

Yet, beneath the surface of their comfortable coexistence, a different current flowed, a subtle undercurrent of caution that Theo rarely acknowledged, even to himself. The specter of his past loomed, a persistent shadow that dictated his pace, his perspective. He'd loved once before, with a fierce, all-consuming passion that had left him utterly shattered. The loss had been a physical blow, a gaping wound that had taken years to even begin to scab over. And in the raw aftermath of that grief, Theo had erected walls, sturdy and seemingly insurmountable, around his heart.

He found solace in routine, in the predictable rhythm of his days. The scent of aged wood, the satisfying heft of a perfectly balanced tool, the quiet satisfaction of bringing order to chaos – these were the anchors that kept him grounded. Marisol, with her bright spirit and her infectious enthusiasm, had chipped away at those walls, not with force, but with gentle persistence. Her warmth had seeped into the cracks, her laughter had echoed in the empty spaces, and he found himself slowly, tentatively, allowing her in. He loved her, he truly did. His love for her was a deep, quiet wellspring, a constant presence that sustained him.

But the memory of what he had lost was a constant reminder of the fragility of happiness. The idea of entanglement, of weaving his life so completely with another's that any unraveling would cause catastrophic damage, sent a tremor of fear through him. He'd experienced that unraveling, and the scars ran deep. He saw the way Marisol looked at him sometimes, a soft, hopeful gaze that asked for... more. More than he was ready to give, more than he felt he could safely offer. He saw the unspoken desires in her eyes, the gentle yearning for a future that was explicitly, undeniably theirs.

He admired her ability to dream, to envision a shared path forward. It was a bravery he no longer possessed. His own dreams had been scaled down, adapted to the landscape of his grief. He was content with the present, with the warmth Marisol brought into his life, with the comfortable rhythm they had established. To push for more, to demand overt declarations and concrete plans, felt like tempting fate, like inviting the very possibility of loss he so desperately sought to avoid.

He remembered conversations with friends, their easy discussions of futures planned, of rings exchanged and houses bought. He'd listened, offering polite nods and manufactured smiles, while a knot of anxiety tightened in his chest. Their openness felt reckless, their vulnerability a stark contrast to his own guardedness. It wasn't that he doubted Marisol's love, or his own. It was a deeper, more primal fear of the pain that such profound connection could inflict if it were ever severed.

He often found himself watching her from across the bookstore, a ghost in the periphery of her vibrant world. He saw the way she interacted with customers, her genuine interest, her innate kindness. He saw the spark of excitement in her eyes when she spoke about a new author, the way she handled books with reverence, as if they held precious secrets. These were the things he loved about her, the tangible proof of her beautiful spirit. But when her gaze met his, and he saw that flicker of longing, a quiet panic would rise within him.

He would retreat, not in anger, but in a quiet, self-preservation mode. He would busy himself in his workshop, the familiar scent of wood a comforting shield. He'd lose himself in the intricate work of carving, letting the steady rhythm of his hands distract him from the unspoken questions that hung in the air between them. He knew Marisol deserved more than a love that was perpetually held at arm's length, a love that was hesitant to step fully into the light. He knew she deserved a partner who could openly embrace the future, who could paint their shared path with bold, confident strokes.

But the weight of his past was a heavy burden, a constant reminder of the devastating consequences of loving too deeply, of investing too much. He couldn't shake the feeling that he was perpetually on thin ice, that any significant shift, any overt declaration of commitment, could send him crashing through. He saw the way she sometimes lingered by the window, her gaze drifting towards couples walking hand-in-hand, and a pang of guilt would pierce him. He knew he was holding her back, unintentionally, but irrevocably.

His appreciation for her was immense, a silent, steadfast devotion. He valued her companionship, her understanding, her ability to bring light into his life. But the fear of loss, the deeply ingrained caution born from profound grief, was a formidable barrier. He wasn't trying to hurt her, not by any stretch of the imagination. He simply didn't know how to reconcile the depth of his feelings for her with the terror of experiencing such a devastating loss again.

He was a man caught between the comfort of the present and the paralyzing fear of a future that mirrored his painful past. He found himself wishing, with a silent, desperate ache, that he could simply forget, that he could unburden himself of the memories that kept him tethered to a place of perpetual caution. But the past, he knew, was an unyielding master, and its grip on his heart was still undeniably strong. He offered Marisol the quiet constancy of his presence, the steadfastness of his affection, but the overt promises, the visible building of a shared future, remained just beyond his reach, shrouded in the mists of his past sorrow.

Chapter Two: Echoes of Loss

The scent of aged wood was Theo's constant companion, a comforting, familiar aroma that clung to his clothes and permeated his workshop. It was a scent that spoke of history, of quiet creation, of a life lived by the steady rhythm of his own making. But today, the familiar olfactory tapestry was overlaid with a faint, almost forgotten perfume – the delicate whisper of dried flowers, the dusty, papery breath of time itself. It emanated from the old wooden box he'd unearthed from beneath a stack of reclaimed lumber, a box he hadn't opened in years, a repository of memories he'd consciously kept locked away.

He'd stumbled upon it while searching for a specific type of chisel, a rare tool he'd only use for the most delicate of carvings. The lid, warped with age and bearing the scars of countless moves, creaked in protest as he lifted it. Inside, nestled amongst bundles of letters tied with faded ribbon and a small, tarnished silver locket, lay a single, creased photograph.

His breath caught in his throat. It was her. Elara.

The woman in the photograph, bathed in the soft, sepia tones of a bygone era, was a vision of vibrant life. Her eyes, even in the faded image, sparkled with an effervescence that Theo remembered as if it were yesterday. A wide, uninhibited smile played on her lips, a smile that promised adventure, laughter, and an unshakeable zest for living. Her hair, a cascade of dark curls, framed a face that held a youthful exuberance, a radiant beauty that had once been the sun around which his world had revolved. The background was indistinct, a blur of green that suggested a park or a garden, a place of easy joy.

Theo's fingers, usually so steady and sure as they held his tools, trembled slightly as he reached for the photograph. The paper felt thin and brittle, a stark contrast to the solid, enduring nature of the wood he worked with daily. He traced the outline of her smile, a phantom touch that sent a jolt of emotion through him, a visceral echo of a happiness so profound it had once threatened to consume him.

This wasn't just a photograph; it was a portal. It flung him backward, not to a gentler time, but to a time of intense, all-encompassing love, a love that had been so potent it had irrevocably altered the landscape of his soul. He remembered the day this picture was taken. They'd been picnicking by the lake, a rare indulgence on a lazy summer afternoon. Elara had insisted on capturing the moment, her infectious energy bubbling over. He'd been reluctant, always more comfortable behind the lens than in front of it, but her bright eyes and insistent cajoling had won him over. He could almost hear her voice, light and teasing, urging him to "just smile, Theo, it won't kill you!"

The memory was so vivid, so real, it was as if he were standing there again, the warmth of the sun on his skin, the scent of freshly cut grass in the air, the sound of Elara's laughter echoing through the trees. He remembered the way she'd tilted her head, her smile widening as he'd finally managed a crooked grin. That smile, captured forever in this faded print, was a testament to a joy he hadn't felt since, a joy he'd buried deep within the rubble of his grief.

The weight of that grief, a crushing, suffocating force, pressed down on him now. It wasn't a gentle ache, a lingering sadness. It was a raw, gaping wound that had never truly healed, merely scabbed over, perpetually threatening to reopen. He remembered the immediate aftermath of her loss, the sheer disbelief, the agonizing void she'd left behind. Cedar Ridge, once a place of shared dreams and whispered promises, had become a town of ghosts, each corner holding a memory, each familiar face a painful reminder of what was no longer.

He'd retreated then, into the silent, solitary world of his workshop. Wood had become his confidante, his therapist. The meticulous work of shaping and joining, of bringing order to raw material, had been his only solace. He'd poured his pain, his anger, his despair into every piece, his hands moving with an almost desperate precision. It was in that space, amidst the sawdust and the varnish, that he had begun to rebuild himself, one splintered plank at a time.

But rebuilding had meant constructing walls. Thick, high walls designed to keep out any possibility of such profound pain ever again. He'd learned the brutal lesson that love, when it was as deep and as absolute as his had been for Elara, carried with it the terrifying potential for equally absolute devastation. The higher you built your hopes, the further you had to fall.

He looked at Marisol's picture again, the bright, innocent smile mocking his caution. Marisol, with her warmth and her vibrant spirit, had managed to chip away at those walls, not with force, but with a gentle, persistent kindness. Her laughter, her easy joy, her unwavering belief in the good of the world – these were the forces that had begun to erode the fortress he'd built around his heart. He loved her, he truly did. His feelings for her were a quiet, steady flame, a warmth that had begun to thaw the icy grip of his past.

But then he would see that flicker of longing in her eyes, the unspoken question about a shared future, about a tangible commitment, and the old fear would surge. It would rise like a tidal wave, threatening to drown the fragile seedling of hope that Marisol had planted. He would see Elara's smile, bright and carefree in the photograph, and remember the shattering force of her absence. He would remember the absolute certainty he'd once felt, the belief that their future was a solid, unshakeable entity, only to have it snatched away in a cruel twist of fate.

The fear wasn't about Marisol's love. He didn't doubt her feelings for a moment. It was about his own capacity to withstand another such cataclysm. He felt like a man who had survived a terrible earthquake, his home reduced to rubble. Now, even the slightest tremor sent him into a panic, convinced the ground beneath him would give way again. He couldn't bear the thought of witnessing such destruction a second time. The scars ran too deep.

He placed the photograph back in the box, the faint scent of dried flowers and old paper clinging to his fingertips. It was a scent that spoke of endings, of things that had once been vibrant and alive, now preserved in a state of gentle decay. It was a poignant reminder of the fragility of life, of the ephemeral nature of happiness.

He closed the lid, the click echoing in the quiet workshop. He couldn't forget Elara, not entirely. She was a part of him, woven into the very fabric of his being. But he couldn't let her memory, or the pain of her loss, dictate his entire future, holding him prisoner to a fear he couldn't quite shake.

He looked towards the window, the afternoon sun casting long shadows across the floor. Marisol was probably at the bookstore, her vibrant presence filling that space with life and laughter. He pictured her recommending a book, her eyes alight with passion, her smile warm and genuine. He loved those moments. He loved watching her, a quiet observer in her luminous world.

But the question remained, a persistent whisper in the back of his mind: could he offer her the kind of future she deserved? A future that wasn't shadowed by the specter of past loss, a future built on unwavering certainty and bold declarations? He didn't know. The walls were still high, the fear still potent. The faded photograph, a tangible artifact of a love that had been both glorious and devastating, was a constant reminder of the risks involved, a silent testament to the profound truth that sometimes, the greatest act of love is the courage to risk everything, even when your heart still bears the indelible marks of a past heartbreak. He knew Marisol deserved that courage, but for now, he was still grappling with how to find it within himself, how to bridge the chasm between the man he had become and the man he wanted to be for her.

The word 'forever' was a fragile thing in Theo's lexicon, a word whispered with caution, like a secret entrusted to the wind, easily scattered and lost. It wasn't that he doubted the existence of enduring love; he had lived it, breathed it, built his world around its incandescent glow. But he had also witnessed its brutal, unceremonious end, a cataclysm that had left him irrevocably altered. The intensity of his past commitment, the absolute certainty he'd once held, had only amplified the crushing weight of his loss. It was a stark, painful lesson etched into his very being: the deeper the roots of love, the more agonizing the uprooting.

He found himself returning to this thought with a frustrating regularity, a relentless echo in the quiet chambers of his mind. It was a paradox that gnawed at him. He loved Marisol, a deep, steady affection that had bloomed unexpectedly in the barren landscape of his heart. Her presence was a gentle warmth, a balm to wounds he hadn't realized were still so raw. Yet, the very idea of pledging himself to her, of uttering those seemingly innocuous words that promised an eternity, sent a shiver of dread down his spine. It wasn't a conscious rejection of her, or of the concept of lasting love, but rather a deep-seated instinct for self-preservation. He had already experienced the ultimate heartbreak, the agonizing severing of a bond he'd believed unbreakable. To invite that possibility again, to voluntarily place himself in the path of such devastating potential, felt like madness.

His workshop, usually a haven of focused solitude, had become the arena for this internal wrestling match. Here, amidst the familiar scent of sawdust and wood polish, with the rhythmic rasp of his tools a comforting counterpoint to the storm within him, he would unravel these tangled thoughts. He'd run his hands over the smooth grain of a half-finished chair, the cool, solid wood a grounding presence. It was in these moments of quiet contemplation, surrounded by the tangible evidence of his craft, that the abstract nature of his fears became almost physically manifest. The wood, in its resilience and enduring nature, was everything he wished his own heart could be, and yet, it was also the very material that had once housed his deepest joy, only to become a stark reminder of its absence.

He didn't believe love was absent from his life. Marisol was proof of that. Her laughter was a melody he'd grown to cherish, her insightful observations a light that illuminated his own often-darkened world. He loved the way she saw the beauty in the mundane, the way her enthusiasm was infectious, her kindness a constant, gentle force. He loved the quiet comfort of her presence, the ease with which they could simply exist in each other's company, a rare and precious gift. But this love, this burgeoning affection, felt different from what he'd known before. It was less a fiery conflagration and more a steady, warming hearth. And perhaps, he mused, that was its strength. Perhaps its very lack of overwhelming intensity made it more sustainable, less prone to the explosive combustion that had characterized his past.

Yet, the specter of the past loomed large. He remembered the sheer, unadulterated certainty he'd felt with Elara. There had been no doubt, no hesitation, no room for fear. Their future had seemed as solid and as real as the oak trees in the town square. And then, in a blink, it had all dissolved, leaving him adrift in a sea of grief. That experience had fundamentally rewired his understanding of commitment. He had learned, in the harshest of ways, that the more you invested in permanence, the more you stood to lose. The pain of that loss wasn't a distant memory; it was a living presence, a shadow that stretched long and deep, cast by the sun of his past love.

He found himself strategizing, almost unconsciously, ways to mitigate the risk. It was a subtle dance, a delicate avoidance of the very things that might lead to an irretrievable heartbreak. He didn't push for grand declarations, for pronouncements of undying devotion. He contented himself with the quiet joys, the shared moments, the comfortable silences. He believed, in a twisted sort of way, that by not demanding forever, by not anchoring himself to an absolute future, he was in fact protecting the love he did have. It was a fragile shield, he knew, one that relied on not provoking the very forces that had once shattered him. If love was a delicate bloom, he reasoned, then perhaps it was best not to transplant it into soil that had already proven treacherous.

This perspective meant he often held back, a subtle restraint in his interactions with Marisol. He would feel a pang of guilt when he saw the unspoken questions in her eyes, the yearning for a deeper commitment that he knew she deserved. But the fear was a powerful adversary, a voice that whispered insidious warnings in his ear. It reminded him of the sharp edges of loss, of the gaping void that had once consumed him. It told him that building a future, brick by painstaking brick, only made the eventual collapse all the more devastating.

He poured these anxieties into his work. When he planed a piece of wood, smoothing out its imperfections, he felt as though he were attempting to smooth out the rough edges of his own emotional landscape. When he joined two pieces together, creating a strong, cohesive structure, he longed for that same sense of unwavering solidity in his own life, in his own heart. But the wood, no matter how perfectly shaped, could always splinter. It could be consumed by fire, or decay, or simply break under immense pressure. And so, he understood, could love.

He would often find himself in his workshop late into the night, the only light the soft glow of his workbench lamp, the rest of Cedar Ridge slumbering peacefully. In that quiet, he would trace the lines of his own grief, not to wallow, but to understand. He recognized that his fear wasn't an indictment of Marisol, or of love itself, but a consequence of his own lived experience. He was a survivor, and survivors often carried the invisible scars of their battles. His was a battle against loss, and the lasting impact was a profound wariness of anything that promised permanence.

He didn't want to live a life devoid of love. That would be an unbearable penance. He wanted the warmth, the connection, the shared laughter. But he wanted it on terms that felt safe, terms that acknowledged the inherent fragility of human happiness. He believed that the truest form of love might be one that didn't demand an eternal guarantee, but rather found its strength in the present, in the day-to-day affirmation of affection, in the quiet understanding that even the most beautiful things are often fleeting. This was his philosophy, forged in the crucible of heartbreak, and it was a philosophy that made committing to a forever with Marisol feel like walking a tightrope over a bottomless chasm.

He was still learning to trust his own footing, to believe that the ground beneath him wouldn't give way again. And in the quiet of his workshop, surrounded by the silent witnesses of his craft, he grappled with the immense courage it would take to even attempt such a crossing. He knew Marisol deserved a love that was sure, that was bold, that promised forever without flinching. But the man who had once offered such a love had been broken, and the pieces, though slowly being reassembled, were still too fragile to risk another catastrophic fall. He believed in the enduring power of love, but he also believed in the brutal reality of loss, and the two, for him, were inextricably, terrifyingly linked.

The worn, comfortable armchair seemed to sigh as Marisol settled into its familiar embrace, the floral chintz a testament to years of welcoming embraces. Aunt Clara's kitchen was a sensory balm, a stark contrast to the knot of unease that had been tightening in Marisol's chest. The air was thick with the comforting, yeasty perfume of baking bread, a scent that always conjured images of warmth, abundance, and Clara herself, her hands dusted with flour, her eyes crinkling at the corners with a perpetually good-natured humor.

"There you are, dearie," Aunt Clara's voice, a rich, melodious contralto, cut through the quiet hum of the refrigerator. She emerged from the pantry, a dusting of flour clinging to her floral apron, a smile that could melt glaciers on her face. Her hug was a full-bodied affair, arms like strong, supportive branches wrapping around Marisol, anchoring her for a moment in a world that suddenly felt less precarious. "You look like you've got the weight of the world on your shoulders. Come, sit. I've just pulled a fresh loaf from the oven, and there's still some of that good strawberry jam we made last summer."

As Clara bustled about, expertly slicing the still-warm bread, Marisol watched her, a sense of profound gratitude washing over her. Aunt Clara wasn't just an aunt; she was Cedar Ridge's unofficial matriarch, a woman whose life was a testament to enduring love and quiet strength. Her marriage to Uncle George, a partnership that had weathered sixty years of storms and sunshine, was the stuff of local legend, a beacon of stability in a world that often felt tempestuous.

"I've been thinking a lot, Aunt Clara," Marisol began, her voice a little shaky as she accepted a thick slice of bread, still steaming gently. The crust yielded with a satisfying crackle under her knife.

Clara nodded, her gaze steady and knowing as she poured them both mugs of steaming herbal tea. "That's a good thing, child. Thinking is how we sort the wheat from the chaff, isn't it? What's been occupying that busy mind of yours?"

Marisol hesitated, the words catching in her throat. She wanted to articulate the confusion, the longing, the fear that had taken root after her last conversation with Theo. She wanted to explain the beautiful, tentative bloom of affection she felt for him, and the terrifying chasm that seemed to lie between her desires and his willingness to bridge it.

"It's about... commitment," Marisol finally managed, the word feeling heavy and fraught. "About what it means. And about... whether it's always a good thing."

Aunt Clara took a slow sip of her tea, her eyes never leaving Marisol's. There was no judgment in her gaze, only an open invitation to speak. "Ah, commitment. A tricky word, for some. For me, and for your Uncle George, it was always about building something together. Like this house," she gestured around the warm, cluttered kitchen, the heart of their home. "It didn't just spring up overnight, you know. It took planning, hard work, sometimes disagreements, but always, always the understanding that we were in it together. That we were building a future, not just for ourselves, but for whatever came next."

She set down her mug, her movements deliberate. "You see, love isn't like a wild vine that just takes over everything on its own, Marisol. Not the kind of love that lasts, anyway. It's more like a garden. You have to choose what you want to plant, clear the ground, prepare the soil. You have to water it, weed it, tend to it when it's struggling. And sometimes," she admitted with a soft chuckle, "you have to be prepared for the occasional pest or blight."

Marisol listened intently, the metaphor sinking in. It was so different from the often-dramatic, almost overwhelming visions of love she'd sometimes encountered in books or movies. Clara's perspective was grounded, practical, and yet, deeply romantic in its own quiet way.

"But what if you're afraid of the tending, Aunt Clara?" Marisol whispered, the question tumbling out before she could stop it. "What if you've seen what happens when the garden gets overgrown, or when the weeds choke out the flowers?"

Aunt Clara's hand, warm and surprisingly strong, covered Marisol's. "Oh, dearie, haven't we all? Life has a way of throwing curveballs. But fear... fear is a powerful weed itself, isn't it? If you let it take root, it can choke out all the good things before they even have a chance to bloom. Your Uncle George and I, we had our share of troubles. There were times when I wasn't sure we'd make it through. But we talked. We listened. And we always, always remembered why we started in the first place. The love we had for each other, the life we wanted to build."

She picked up the jam jar, its ruby-red contents glinting in the afternoon light. "You see this jam? It's made from strawberries, but you can't just throw a bunch of strawberries into a pot and expect jam. You have to cook them, add sugar, stir them for hours. It takes time and effort. But the result? A taste of summer, a sweet reminder of abundance. Love is like that. The commitment, the tending, the effort – it's the cooking, the stirring. It's what transforms the raw ingredients into something truly special, something that can be savored and shared."

Marisol spread a generous dollop of the sweet jam onto her bread, the tartness a welcome counterpoint to the bread's sweetness. She thought of Theo's workshop, the scent of sawdust and wood polish. He was a craftsman, a builder. He understood the value of careful construction, of building something solid and enduring. Why, then, was he so hesitant to build a future with her?

"But Aunt Clara," Marisol said, her brow furrowed, "what if the person you're building with... what if they're afraid the structure will collapse? What if they've seen it fall before, and they're so terrified of it happening again that they won't even pick up the hammer?"

Aunt Clara's eyes softened with understanding. She knew Marisol. She knew her heart, her tendency to be fiercely loyal and deeply invested. And she also knew, from hushed town whispers and Marisol's own guarded admissions, about the loss that had shadowed her niece's life years ago.

"Ah, Theo," Aunt Clara murmured, a knowing smile playing on her lips. "He's a good man, that one. A good, steady man. But I suspect he's carried a heavy burden for a long time, haven't you, dear?"

Marisol's cheeks flushed. "He's... he's been through a lot."

"We all have, Marisol. We all have our scars. But the trick is not to let those scars dictate your future. Your Uncle George, he had a bad fall from a ladder when he was young. Broke his leg something awful. For years, he wouldn't go up on the roof, wouldn't even look at a ladder. I thought we'd never get the gutters cleaned again!" She winked. "But eventually, he had to. We needed to. And he did. He was careful, yes. He always checked his footing. But he didn't let the memory of that one fall stop him from climbing when it was necessary."

She reached for another slice of bread, her movements slow and deliberate. "Theo's fear, it's understandable. It's a protective instinct. But sometimes, dearie, the best protection is to build something stronger, something that can withstand the storm. And that takes courage. It takes a leap of faith, yes, but it also takes a willingness to put in the work. To show the other person that this time, it's different. That the foundation is solid."

She looked at Marisol, her gaze penetrating. "And you, my dear, you have so much to offer. You have a heart full of love, a spirit that shines brighter than any star in Cedar Ridge. Don't let anyone dim that light because of their own past shadows. Sometimes, the bravest thing you can do is to be the one who holds up the hammer, who offers the steady hand, who believes in the future even when the other person can't quite see it yet."

The words settled over Marisol like a warm blanket, chasing away the chill of her anxieties. Aunt Clara's wisdom wasn't about grand pronouncements or sweeping declarations; it was about the quiet, consistent act of nurturing, of building, of believing. It was about understanding that commitment wasn't a cage, but a garden, and that the tending, though sometimes challenging, was what made the bloom so beautiful.

"So, you think it's worth the risk?" Marisol asked, her voice barely a whisper.

Aunt Clara smiled, a broad, reassuring smile that crinkled her eyes. "My dear Marisol, what in life is truly worth having that doesn't involve a little risk? The sun rises every morning, but there's always a chance of a storm. We choose to believe in the dawn, though, don't we? And we choose to build our lives, our gardens, our futures, on that belief. Theo needs to see that you believe. And he needs to believe that you believe in him, too. That you'll be there, with your watering can and your trowel, ready to tend to whatever grows between you."

She reached out and gently squeezed Marisol's hand. "Love, the enduring kind, it's not about avoiding the storms, child. It's about learning to dance in the rain together. And sometimes," she added, a twinkle in her eye, "it's about making a really good loaf of bread to share afterwards."

Marisol felt a lightness settle over her, a sense of clarity she hadn't had in weeks. Aunt Clara's words, grounded in a lifetime of love and wisdom, had offered a different perspective, a gentle but firm reframing of her fears. Commitment wasn't a burden; it was a choice, an active, ongoing process of creation. And Theo, with his craftsman's hands and his wounded heart, was capable of building something beautiful, if only he could be shown that the soil was fertile and that she, Marisol, was willing to be the gardener by his side.

She ate the rest of her bread slowly, savoring each bite, the sweetness of the jam mingling with the quiet hope that was beginning to bloom within her. The aroma of baking bread, once a simple comfort, now felt like a promise – a promise of warmth, of nourishment, and of a future that, with care and intention, could indeed be as rich and as enduring as Aunt Clara's legendary strawberry jam. The conversation had been a gentle recalibration, a reminder that love, like a well-tended garden, required patience, dedication, and an unwavering belief in the power of growth, even in the face of past frosts. She would talk to Theo again, she decided, not with fear, but with the quiet confidence that came from understanding that the tending, the building, the commitment, was not an end, but a beginning.

The garden. The word echoed in Marisol's mind, a quiet counterpoint to the insistent thrum of her own anxieties. Aunt Clara's analogy had taken root, much like the persistent little wildflowers that always seemed to find a way through the cracks in the old stone patio. It wasn't just a pretty metaphor; it was a blueprint, a starkly beautiful, and slightly terrifying, articulation of what Marisol felt was missing.

She stirred her tea, the spoon clinking softly against the ceramic mug. A garden, Aunt Clara had said, didn't just happen. It was an act of will, a deliberate choice. You didn't simply scatter seeds to the wind and hope for a riot of color. No, you had to choose the seeds. You had to clear the ground, break up the soil, turn it over with honest effort. You had to coax life from dormancy, offering it the sustenance it needed to push through the dark earth and unfurl its tender leaves towards the sun. And then, the constant vigilance: the watering, the feeding, the patient, relentless work of weeding. Weeds, Aunt Clara had implied with a knowing glint in her eye, were inevitable. They were the doubts, the fears, the distractions that could choke the life out of even the most promising bloom if left unchecked.

Marisol traced the rim of her mug, her gaze drifting out the window to where Aunt Clara's own garden, a riot of organized chaos, spilled over its borders. Roses, carefully pruned and trained, climbed trellises, their velvety petals unfurling in shades of crimson and blush. Lavender bushes, their fragrant spires buzzing with bees, stood sentinel. And nestled amongst the more formal blooms were pockets of wilder beauty – clusters of daisies, patches of forget-me-nots, their tiny blue eyes gazing upwards. It was a testament to years of dedicated care, a living, breathing chronicle of effort and love.

This, Marisol realized with a growing sense of urgency, was what she craved with Theo. Not just the potential for a bloom, but the process of cultivation. She wanted to feel the damp earth between her fingers, to choose the seeds of their shared future, to water them with unwavering affection and weed out the doubts that threatened to stifle them. She wanted to build something with him, not just exist alongside him in a state of suspended anticipation.

The silence in the kitchen, once a comforting balm, now felt charged with unspoken possibilities. She pictured Theo's workshop, the organized clutter of tools, the sawdust that coated every surface like a gentle snowfall. He understood creation. He understood the meticulous planning, the careful measurements, the patient application of skill that turned raw materials into something beautiful and functional. He built furniture that would last generations, sturdy and elegant. Why, then, was he so hesitant to apply that same craftsmanship to something as fundamental as a relationship?

"It's not enough to just hope for a garden, is it?" Marisol murmured, the words a soft breath against the quiet. She looked at Aunt Clara, her eyes seeking confirmation, understanding. "You can have the most fertile soil, the most perfect weather, but if you never plant anything, if you never tend to it, it just... stays fallow. Or worse, it gets overrun by weeds. It becomes wild and untamed, not in a beautiful way, but in a neglected way."

Aunt Clara nodded slowly, her gaze steady. "Precisely, dearie. A wild patch of land can be beautiful, in its own way. But a garden... a garden is a collaboration. It's a partnership. It's where you choose what you want to grow, and you nurture it. You give it the best of what you have to offer, and in return, it gives you beauty, sustenance, and a sense of accomplishment. It's the shared effort, the shared vision, that makes it truly thrive."

Marisol leaned back, the worn armchair creaking slightly in response. She thought of the quiet weekends they'd spent together – walking along the river, exploring the little antique shops in town, sharing meals. There was a natural ease between them, a comfortable rhythm that felt like a well-worn path. But it was a path that seemed to lead only to the present moment, never venturing into the uncharted territory of a shared future. There were no designated plots, no plans for what to sow. It was a beautiful, unstructured wilderness, and Marisol was beginning to fear that she was the only one who felt the urge to cultivate it.

"I think," she began, choosing her words carefully, "that Theo sees the potential. He sees the fertile ground, perhaps. But he's... he's afraid to pick up the trowel. He's afraid to get his hands dirty with the commitment of it all. He's seen gardens before, Aunt Clara, that have been choked out by blight. He's seen the hard work of tending them go to waste. And I think that fear makes him hesitant to even begin."

Aunt Clara reached out, her hand a comforting weight on Marisol's arm. "And you, my dear, you're standing there with a basket full of seeds, ready to plant. You see the potential for beauty, for abundance. You're willing to put in the work, to nurture what grows. But if you stand there too long, with your seeds clutched tight, they'll start to wither. The moment for planting will pass."

The imagery was so potent, so clear. Marisol, the hopeful gardener, standing at the edge of a vast, waiting field, her hands full of potential, while Theo, the craftsman who understood the value of building, hesitated at the gate, paralyzed by the memory of past demolitions.

"But how do you convince someone to start digging," Marisol asked, her voice tinged with a plea, " when they're convinced the ground is cursed? When they believe that anything they try to grow will inevitably be destroyed?"

"You don't convince them," Aunt Clara said softly, her voice firm yet gentle. "You show them. You start planting your own seeds, Marisol. You start tending your own little corner of the garden with fierce dedication. You show them that it's possible to create beauty, to cultivate life, even in the face of past storms. You demonstrate the resilience of growth. You water your seeds with unwavering affection, you nourish them with consistent kindness, and you weed out the doubts with patience and understanding."

She paused, her gaze holding Marisol's. "And you also show them that you are there, by their side. That you are not just planting for yourself, but for the shared space you hope to create. You offer your hand, not just to hold a trowel, but to help steady theirs when they finally decide to pick it up. You let them see that this time, the tending will be a joint effort. That you are committed to the harvest, whatever it may be."

Marisol closed her eyes, picturing it. A small, carefully tended patch of ground, bursting with vibrant life. Marigolds for protection, sunflowers reaching towards the sky, perhaps some herbs, fragrant and useful. A tiny Eden, born from her own determined effort. And Theo, watching from the periphery, his craftsman's eye drawn to the meticulous care, the evident growth.

"So, I have to be the one to start the garden?" Marisol asked, the question heavy with the weight of responsibility. "Even if he's the one with the blueprints for a whole estate?"

Aunt Clara chuckled, a warm, melodious sound. "My dear, a beautiful estate is built, stone by stone, seed by seed. Sometimes, the most magnificent structures begin with a single, well-tended flower bed. Your Theo has the vision, the skill to build grand things. But he needs to see that there's someone willing to dig the first hole, to offer the first drop of water. He needs to see that the desire to cultivate is as strong, if not stronger, than the fear of decay."

Marisol thought of the conversations they'd had, the tentative explorations of what could be. Theo's walls had always been high, his explanations for his reticence wrapped in layers of logic and past trauma. He spoke of the fragility of happiness, the inevitability of loss, the danger of investing too much in something that could be so easily taken away. He saw commitment as a vulnerability, a doorway through which pain could enter.

But Aunt Clara's garden offered a different perspective. It was a place of vulnerability, yes, but also a place of profound strength. It was about embracing the cycle of life, the inevitable challenges, and finding beauty and resilience in the process. It was about understanding that even after the harshest winter, spring would eventually return, and new life could emerge.

"It's about showing him," Marisol said, the realization dawning with a quiet power, "that the risk of a withered garden is far greater than the risk of planting. That the pain of not trying, of letting potential lie dormant, is a deeper wound than the possibility of a failed harvest."

"Exactly," Aunt Clara confirmed, her smile radiant. "You can't force someone to bloom, Marisol. But you can create the most beautiful, nurturing environment for them to do so. You can be the sunshine, the rain, the steady hand that pulls the weeds. You can demonstrate, through your own actions, that love, when tended with care and commitment, is not a fragile thing destined to wilt, but a resilient force capable of extraordinary growth."

Marisol felt a wave of quiet determination wash over her. The fear hadn't vanished entirely, but it had receded, replaced by a sense of purpose. The garden analogy wasn't just about the effort required; it was about the profound reward. The vibrant colors, the sweet scents, the satisfaction of watching something beautiful flourish under your care. It was the promise of a shared space, a sanctuary built not just on shared moments, but on shared effort, shared dreams, and a shared commitment to nurturing what they had.

She imagined the future, not as a precarious structure that could crumble, but as a vibrant, evolving garden. A place where she and Theo, hand in hand, would choose what to plant, would water it with their affection, and would patiently weed out any doubts that dared to sprout. It would require work, undoubtedly. There would be challenges, perhaps even seasons of drought or unexpected pests. But the reward – a shared space, alive with the beauty of their commitment – would be worth every drop of sweat, every moment of tending.

"So," Marisol said, her voice imbued with a newfound steadiness, "I need to start planting. I need to show him that I'm ready to get my hands dirty."

Aunt Clara beamed, her eyes sparkling with a mixture of pride and wisdom. "That's my girl. You have a beautiful heart, Marisol. Don't let anyone convince you that it's too vulnerable to be worth risking. Tend to it, nurture it, and let it bloom. And when you're ready, offer him a trowel. The rest, well, that's for the garden to decide."

Marisol took a deep breath, the scent of baking bread and the lingering fragrance of Aunt Clara's herbs filling her lungs. The metaphor had done its work. It had shifted her perspective, transforming her fear of commitment into an eager anticipation of cultivation. The garden wasn't a symbol of vulnerability; it was a testament to the power of intentional creation, a vibrant promise of the beauty that could flourish when love was not merely allowed to happen, but was actively, lovingly, tended.

She would talk to Theo again, not with the hesitant anxiety of someone waiting for a seed to sprout by chance, but with the quiet confidence of a gardener ready to transform a plot of earth into something truly extraordinary. The work would be demanding, but the vision of that thriving garden, watered by their shared effort, was a prospect that made every challenge seem not just surmountable, but profoundly worthwhile. It was time to dig in.

The clink of cutlery against porcelain was the only sound that punctuated the comfortable quiet of their dinner. Marisol watched Theo from across the table, the soft glow of the pendant lamp above casting a warm light on his features. They'd been through this before, in a way – the unspoken distances that sometimes stretched between them, the careful navigation of topics that felt too raw, too fragile to touch. But tonight, spurred by Aunt Clara's garden analogy and her own quiet resolve, Marisol felt a gentle pull, an urge to understand the roots of Theo's hesitancy. It wasn't about prying; it was about cultivating a deeper soil for their own nascent garden.

"You know," she began, her voice soft, almost tentative, "Aunt Clara was telling me about her rose garden today. How some of them just... didn't make it one year. A particularly harsh winter, she said." She stirred the pasta on her plate, her eyes not quite meeting his, giving him an easy out if he needed one. "She said it was hard, seeing something she'd put so much effort into just... fade."

Theo paused, his fork halfway to his mouth. He was a man of quiet observation, his reactions often subtle, like the shift of light on a polished surface. He didn't flinch away from the mention of loss, but his gaze held a distant quality, as if he were peering into a landscape only he could see. "Winters can be brutal," he offered, his voice a low murmur, almost an echo of the sentiment.

Marisol took a sip of water, a small, deliberate action. "She said it felt like a personal failure, at first. But then she remembered that you can't control the weather, and you can't always predict everything that will go wrong. But you can choose to replant. You can choose to learn from what happened and try again, maybe in a different spot, or with a different variety." She met his eyes then, her own filled with an open question. "Did you ever... have something like that? Something you put your heart into, that didn't survive?"

The silence that followed was different from their usual comfortable quiet. This was a loaded silence, heavy with unspoken history. Theo set his fork down, his movements precise, deliberate. He looked at his plate for a long moment, the shadows playing across his face. He wasn't avoiding her gaze; he was gathering himself.

"There was someone," he began, his voice raspy, as if he hadn't used these words in a long time. "A long time ago. Before... before I came here." He chose his words with the same care he applied to selecting the right wood for a joint, each one measured for its weight and impact. "Someone I loved very much. We... we had plans. Not a garden, not exactly, but... a life. A future we were building, piece by piece. Like a house."

Marisol's breath caught in her throat. This was it. The fault line she'd sensed, the underlying tremor beneath his carefully constructed stability. She remained still, her gaze unwavering, offering him the silent assurance that she was listening, truly listening, without judgment.

"It was unexpected," he continued, his voice gaining a quiet, mournful cadence. "A sudden illness. One moment, everything was there, solid, real. The next... gone. Like a gust of wind that knocks down a meticulously built structure, leaving only scattered debris." He ran a hand over his jaw, a gesture of quiet frustration, or perhaps pain. "The emptiness that followed... it was absolute. A silence so profound it felt like a physical presence."

He looked up then, and Marisol saw a depth of sorrow in his eyes that stole her breath. It was the quiet ache of a wound that had never truly healed, merely scarred over. "When you've poured everything you have into something, when you've laid the foundation, built the walls, imagined the roof... and then it's just... gone. Reduced to nothing by something you couldn't see coming, couldn't fight." He let out a slow breath, a sigh that seemed to carry the weight of years. "It makes you... cautious. It makes you question the wisdom of building anything at all."

Marisol's heart ached for him. She saw not just the stoic craftsman, but the man who had experienced a loss so profound it had reshaped his view of the world. She understood now, with a clarity that was both heartbreaking and clarifying, why he was so hesitant to invest, to commit, to truly build. He had built a life, a house, with someone, and watched it crumble without warning. The fear wasn't just about weeds; it was about catastrophic collapse.

"I'm so sorry, Theo," she whispered, the words inadequate, yet all she had. She reached across the table, her hand covering his, her touch gentle. His skin was warm beneath hers, a steady, grounding sensation. He didn't pull away. Instead, he turned his hand over, his fingers loosely interlacing with hers, a silent acknowledgment, a small, hesitant acceptance of her comfort.

"It was a long time ago," he said, his voice softer now, the sharpness of the memory blunted by time, but the ache still present. "But it leaves a mark. It teaches you that... that things are fragile. That even the strongest wood can split, the most solid stone can crack. And when you've seen that happen... you tend to look for the flaws before you even begin to build."

"And you see flaws in us," Marisol stated, not as an accusation, but as a quiet observation. "You see the potential for things to break."

He squeezed her hand gently. "I see the potential for pain, Marisol. And I've learned that sometimes, the pain of loss outweighs the joy that came before it. I've learned that putting your heart into something means you risk having it broken. And I... I'm not sure I'm willing to risk that again."

The honesty hung in the air between them, a delicate, precious thing. It wasn't the defiant withdrawal she might have expected, but a quiet admission of vulnerability. He wasn't saying he didn't care; he was saying he was afraid to care too much, for fear of losing too much.

"Aunt Clara said that sometimes, the fear of a withered garden makes you miss the beauty of the one you could have. That the risk of not planting, of not tending, is also a kind of loss." Marisol's voice was barely audible, but Theo heard it. He studied her face, his thumb gently stroking the back of her hand.

"I understand her analogy," he said slowly. "I understand the effort, the care, the constant vigilance. And I respect that. I build things, Marisol. I know what it takes to create something that lasts. But what I learned, with... with her... was that even the most carefully constructed things can be undone in an instant. And the foundation of that life, the emotional foundation, was shattered. I don't know if I have the strength to rebuild that kind of foundation again, knowing how easily it can be broken."

He released her hand then, and Marisol felt a pang of disappointment, but also a profound sense of understanding. He wasn't pushing her away; he was sharing the burden of his past, a past that had taught him to build walls rather than gardens.

"It's not just about the building, Theo," she said, her voice firm but gentle. "It's about the tending. It's about the choosing of the seeds, the watering, the weeding. It's about knowing that there will be challenges, but choosing to face them together. It's not about building something that will last forever, untouched by time or storm. It's about building something that evolves, that weathers the storms together, and that grows stronger because of it."

He was quiet for a long moment, his gaze distant again, lost in thought. "I suppose," he said finally, his voice low, "that's a different way of looking at it. I've always seen the potential for destruction. You see the potential for resilience."

"I see the potential for us," Marisol said, her voice a soft plea. "I see that you've been hurt, deeply hurt. And I can't erase that. I can't undo the loss you experienced. But I can offer you... a different kind of space. A space where we can try to build something new, not as a replacement, but as a continuation. A space where the foundation is strong not just because of its construction, but because of the commitment to repair it, together, if it ever shows cracks."

She paused, letting her words settle. "It's not about pretending the past didn't happen, Theo. It's about acknowledging it, and choosing to move forward, even with the scars. It's about understanding that vulnerability isn't just about the risk of pain, but about the possibility of connection. And I... I want to connect with you. I want to share this space, this life, with you. And I'm willing to put in the work. I'm willing to get my hands dirty."

Theo looked at her, a flicker of something unreadable in his eyes – a mixture of pain, curiosity, and perhaps, a nascent hope. "You're not afraid?" he asked, the question raw and direct.

Marisol smiled, a gentle, knowing smile. "I'm not fearless, Theo. But I am hopeful. And I believe that some things are worth the risk. I believe that love, when tended with honesty and commitment, can be a resilient force. And I believe... that we could be something beautiful, if we're both willing to plant the seeds."

He held her gaze for a long moment, the silence between them no longer heavy with unspoken fears, but filled with the quiet hum of possibility. He didn't offer a grand declaration, no sudden commitment. But in the way his shoulders relaxed, in the slight softening of his gaze, Marisol saw a small opening, a chink in the armor he'd so carefully constructed. It was the first tentative seed, planted in the quiet soil of their shared home, watered with the gentle rain of honesty and understanding. And for now, that was more than enough. It was a start. A very real, very hopeful start.

Chapter Three: Cedar Ridge's Embrace

The air in Cedar Ridge was turning crisp, carrying the sweet, earthy scent of decaying leaves and the distant promise of woodsmoke. It was the kind of scent that settled deep into your bones, a comforting reminder of seasons past and seasons yet to come. And this year, more than any other, Marisol felt that scent clinging to her, a tangible manifestation of the burgeoning warmth that had begun to bloom within her, intertwined with the quiet understanding she'd found with Theo.

The Annual Harvest Festival was on the horizon, a beacon of communal joy that transformed Cedar Ridge into a kaleidoscope of autumn hues and neighborly spirit.

From her vantage point behind the counter of "The Gilded Acorn," Marisol watched the town square slowly morph into a festive wonderland. It was a familiar sight, one she'd witnessed countless times as a resident, but this year held a new significance. This year, she and Theo, as proprietors of its two most prominent businesses – her cozy bakery and his robust woodworking shop – were not just spectators, but integral threads in the vibrant tapestry of the festival's creation.

The pumpkin stalls, usually simple wooden crates, were being meticulously crafted by Theo and his team, their sturdy frames destined to cradle gourds of every size and hue. Bunting, in shades of burnt orange, deep crimson, and golden yellow, was being unfurled from lampposts, each strand a whisper of the coming celebration. Twinkling fairy lights, reserved for this special occasion, were being carefully strung between the ancient oaks that ringed the square, promising a magical glow once twilight descended.

The festival wasn't merely an event; it was the beating heart of Cedar Ridge. It was the day when the lines between farmer and shopkeeper, young and old, newcomer and lifelong resident, blurred into a shared experience of gratitude and connection. It was a testament to the town's enduring spirit, a reminder that even in a world that seemed to spin faster and faster, some traditions held firm, anchoring the community in a common purpose. This year, for Marisol, it felt like more than just a tradition; it was a reflection of her own evolving life, a new chapter being written under the warm glow of autumn's embrace, with Theo by her side.

The planning committee meetings, once held in hushed tones and with polite deference, had taken on a new rhythm. Marisol, with her innate knack for organization and her infectious enthusiasm, had quickly become a central figure, her suggestions often met with nods of approval. Theo, though quieter, was a formidable presence, his practical insights and steady hand invaluable. He'd overseen the construction of the main stage where local musicians would perform, ensuring its structural integrity with the same precision he applied to his furniture. He'd also volunteered his team to set up the children's craft tents, their sturdy, child-sized benches and tables a testament to his craftsmanship.

One blustery afternoon, while wrestling with a particularly stubborn roll of burlap meant to drape the sides of the farmer's market stalls, Marisol found herself in the middle of the square, a slight frown creasing her brow.

The wind tugged at the fabric, threatening to send it tumbling. Just as she was about to concede defeat, a shadow fell over her.

"Having trouble there?" Theo's voice, a low rumble that always seemed to resonate with the steady beat of a hammer, cut through the wind. He was holding a coil of strong, weather-resistant rope.

Marisol looked up, a smile immediately chasing away the frustration. "A little. This wind has a mind of its own today."

He didn't say anything, but simply took the burlap from her, his strong fingers deftly securing it with a few quick, expert knots. The rope cinched the fabric tight, holding it firmly in place against the playful gusts. He then handed her the end of the rope, a silent offer of partnership.

"Thanks, Theo," she said, her voice tinged with genuine appreciation. "You're a lifesaver. Or at least, a burlap-saver."

He offered a rare, small smile, his eyes crinkling at the corners. "Just doing my part. Wouldn't want the pumpkins to go unprotected."

They worked in comfortable silence for a few moments, securing the rest of the burlap. The physical act of working together, of moving in sync, felt surprisingly natural. Marisol found herself stealing glances at him, observing the controlled power in his movements, the way his brow furrowed in concentration, the subtle grace in his hands as they manipulated the rope. It was a different kind of intimacy than the quiet conversations they'd shared, a communication spoken through shared effort and mutual understanding.

"It's going to be a good one this year," Marisol said, breaking the silence. "The energy feels... different."

Theo nodded, his gaze sweeping across the bustling square. "People are ready. Ready for something to celebrate. Something that brings us all together." He paused, then added, his voice softer, "Like this town. It's good at that."

Marisol felt a warmth spread through her, a feeling that had nothing to do with the autumn chill. "It is," she agreed. "And you're a big part of that, Theo. You and your... solid creations." She gestured to the sturdy scaffolding of the stalls, the perfectly aligned wooden beams. "They're like the bones of the festival."

He met her gaze, a flicker of something that might have been pride, or perhaps just quiet acknowledgment, in his eyes. "Someone has to make sure it doesn't fall apart," he said, his characteristic pragmatism surfacing. But there was a gentleness in his tone that softened the practicality.

As the days ticked closer to the festival, the preparations intensified. Marisol's bakery was a whirlwind of activity, her ovens working overtime to produce the pies, tarts, and cookies that would be a staple of the harvest spread. The scent of cinnamon, apples, and spiced pumpkin wafted from her kitchen, a fragrant invitation to the coming festivities. She found herself thinking of Theo more often than usual, wondering if he was taking breaks, if he was eating properly. The quiet understanding that had bloomed between them was subtly shifting, deepening into a more conscious awareness of each other.

One evening, after a particularly grueling day of baking, Marisol found herself walking through the town square, the fairy lights now strung and ready to be illuminated. The skeletal frameworks of the stalls stood sentinel, waiting for their autumnal adornments. She stopped by the base of the main stage, running her hand over the smooth, polished wood. It was strong, beautiful, and utterly dependable. Just like Theo.

As if summoned by her thoughts, Theo emerged from the shadows of his workshop, a blueprint rolled under his arm. He looked surprised to see her, but his surprise quickly softened into a welcoming smile.

"Couldn't sleep?" he asked, his voice a low murmur that seemed to blend with the rustling leaves.

"Just wanted to see it," she replied, gesturing around the square. "It looks... magical. Even before the lights come on."

He joined her by the stage, his presence a comforting anchor. "The final coat of varnish on the benches is drying now. Should be ready for the kids' craft tent tomorrow." He unrolled the blueprint, and they both studied the intricate drawings, his finger tracing the lines of support beams and decorative carvings.

"You really are an artist, Theo," Marisol said, her voice filled with genuine admiration. "Not just with wood, but with... planning. With bringing something solid and beautiful into being."

He looked at the blueprint, then back at her, a thoughtful expression on his face. "It's about building something that lasts," he said, his voice quiet. "Something that can withstand the elements, the wear and tear of time. It's about creating a foundation that can support... well, everything."

The word "everything" hung in the air between them, a soft echo of their previous conversations, of the unspoken depths they were slowly, carefully, exploring. Marisol felt a familiar pull, a desire to bridge the remaining distance, to connect with the man behind the craftsman.

"And what happens," she asked, her voice barely a whisper, "when the foundation itself is shaken? When something unexpected happens that no amount of planning can prevent?"

Theo's gaze drifted, his eyes focusing on a distant point beyond the square. The easy warmth that had settled between them seemed to recede, replaced by a familiar shadow of reserve. He was silent for a long moment, and Marisol's heart gave a small, anxious lurch. She knew this territory, the landscape of his past losses, the cautious defenses he'd built.

Finally, he spoke, his voice lower than before, almost a confession. "Then... then you learn how fragile even the strongest foundations can be. You learn that some things... some things can be lost, no matter how much you try to hold onto them. And that knowledge... it makes you want to build differently. More cautiously. With stronger walls, perhaps, to keep the storms out."

Marisol reached out, her hand finding his on the blueprint. His fingers were warm, calloused, and steady. "But sometimes," she said, her voice gentle but firm, "the strongest walls can also be the loneliest. And sometimes, the storms are meant to be weathered together, not shut out."

He turned his hand, his fingers interlacing with hers, a small, hesitant gesture of connection. His thumb brushed lightly over her knuckles, a silent acknowledgment of her words, of her presence. "I'm learning that," he admitted, his gaze meeting hers. There was a vulnerability in his eyes that tugged at her heart, a raw honesty that spoke volumes. "It's... a process."

"And I'm here for the process, Theo," Marisol said, her voice unwavering. "Whatever it takes. I believe in building things that last, too. But I also believe in building them with someone. Together."

The town square, bathed in the pale moonlight, felt like a sanctuary. The unfinished stalls and the unlit lights seemed to hold a promise, a potential for joy and connection that mirrored the tentative hope blossoming between them.

The Annual Harvest Festival, in all its autumnal splendor, was more than just a celebration of the season; it was becoming a testament to the quiet, steady growth of their own shared story, a story rooted in the strong, fertile ground of Cedar Ridge, and tended with a growing, shared understanding. The air, once just crisp with autumn, now felt charged with possibility, a prelude to the magic that was about to unfold, not just in the square, but in the deepening connection between two hearts finding their way home.

The air in Cedar Ridge, even with the festive decorations beginning to festoon the town square, still held that particular autumn crispness, carrying the scent of damp earth and distant woodsmoke. It was a scent Marisol had always found comforting, a tangible reminder of the cyclical nature of life and the steady rhythm of the seasons.

This year, however, the scent seemed to weave itself into a new narrative, one that held the burgeoning warmth of her burgeoning feelings for Theo, a quiet understanding that had slowly, surely, taken root. The Annual Harvest Festival was just around the corner, an event that transformed Cedar Ridge into a vibrant tableau of autumn colors and an outpouring of communal spirit.

From her perch behind the counter of "The Gilded Acorn," Marisol watched the town square come alive. It was a scene she'd witnessed countless times, but this year, it felt different. This year, she and Theo, as the owners of two of the town's most prominent businesses – her beloved bakery and his sturdy woodworking shop – weren't just observers; they were integral parts of the festival's creation. Theo and his team were constructing the pumpkin stalls, their robust frames designed to cradle gourds of every shape and size.

Bunting in hues of burnt orange, crimson, and gold was being unfurled, each strand a promise of the celebrations to come. And the twinkling fairy lights, reserved for this special occasion, were being carefully strung between the ancient oaks that embraced the square, ready to cast a magical glow as twilight descended.

The festival was more than just a date on the calendar; it was the very soul of Cedar Ridge. It was the day when the distinctions between farmer and shopkeeper, young and old, newcomer and lifelong resident, dissolved into a shared experience of gratitude and connection. It was a testament to the town's enduring spirit, a reaffirmation that even in a world that often felt chaotic and hurried, some traditions remained steadfast, anchoring the community in a common purpose. For Marisol, this year's festival felt like a reflection of her own evolving life, a new chapter unfolding under the warm embrace of autumn, with Theo a constant, grounding presence.

The planning committee meetings had shed their previous formality, now humming with a new energy. Marisol, with her innate organizational skills and infectious enthusiasm, had quickly become a central figure, her ideas met with eager acceptance.

Theo, though a man of fewer words, possessed a quiet authority. His practical suggestions and steady demeanor were invaluable. He'd personally overseen the construction of the main stage, ensuring its structural integrity with the same meticulous care he applied to his finest furniture. He'd also volunteered his team to build the children's craft tents, their charmingly sturdy benches and tables a testament to his craftsmanship, designed to withstand the enthusiastic energy of Cedar Ridge's youngest residents.

One blustery afternoon, as Marisol wrestled with a particularly uncooperative roll of burlap intended for the farmer's market stalls, she found herself in the middle of the square, a frustrated sigh escaping her lips. The wind, a mischievous force, tugged at the fabric, threatening to whisk it away. Just as she was about to admit defeat, a shadow fell over her.

"Having trouble there?" Theo's voice, a deep resonance that always reminded her of the steady beat of a hammer, cut through the wind's bluster. He held a coil of sturdy, weather-resistant rope in his hands.

Marisol looked up, her frustration instantly melting into a smile. "A little. This wind has a mind of its own today."

Without a word, he took the burlap from her, his strong fingers deftly securing it with a few swift, expert knots. The rope cinched the fabric taut, holding it firm against the playful gusts. He then offered her the end of the rope, a silent invitation to partnership.

"Thanks, Theo," she said, her voice filled with genuine gratitude. "You're a lifesaver. Or at least, a burlap-saver."

A rare, small smile touched his lips, crinkling the corners of his eyes. "Just doing my part. Wouldn't want the pumpkins to go unprotected."

They worked in a comfortable silence for a few moments, securing the rest of the burlap. The shared effort, the effortless rhythm of their movements, felt surprisingly natural. Marisol found herself stealing glances at him, observing the controlled power in his actions, the focused intensity in his brow, the quiet grace of his hands as they worked the rope. It was a different kind of intimacy than their quiet conversations, a communication conveyed through shared tasks and mutual understanding.

"It's going to be a good one this year," Marisol ventured, breaking the silence. "The energy feels... different."

Theo nodded, his gaze sweeping across the square, already buzzing with activity. "People are ready. Ready for something to celebrate. Something that brings us all together." He paused, then added, his voice softer, "Like this town. It's good at that."

A warmth spread through Marisol, a feeling entirely unrelated to the autumn chill. "It is," she agreed. "And you're a big part of that, Theo. You and your... solid creations." She gestured to the sturdy framework of the stalls, the perfectly aligned wooden beams. "They're like the bones of the festival."

He met her gaze, a fleeting expression that might have been pride, or perhaps simply quiet acknowledgment, in his eyes. "Someone has to make sure it doesn't fall apart," he said, his characteristic pragmatism surfacing. But there was a gentleness in his tone that softened the practicality.

As the days counted down to the festival, the preparations in Cedar Ridge intensified. Marisol's bakery was a hive of activity, her ovens working overtime to churn out the pies, tarts, and cookies that were essential components of the harvest spread.

The comforting aroma of cinnamon, apples, and spiced pumpkin wafted from her kitchen, a fragrant promise of the coming festivities. She found herself thinking of Theo with a frequency that surprised her, wondering if he was taking breaks, if he was remembering to eat. The quiet understanding that had begun to bloom between them was subtly shifting, deepening into a more conscious awareness of each other.

One evening, after a particularly demanding day of baking, Marisol found herself wandering through the town square. The fairy lights were now strung, awaiting illumination, and the skeletal frames of the stalls stood like silent sentinels, ready for their autumnal adornments. She paused by the base of the main stage, her fingers tracing the smooth, polished wood. It was strong, beautiful, and utterly dependable. Much like Theo.

As if summoned by her thoughts, Theo emerged from the shadows of his workshop, a rolled blueprint tucked under his arm. He seemed surprised to see her, but his surprise quickly softened into a welcoming smile.

"Couldn't sleep?" he asked, his voice a low murmur that seemed to blend with the rustling leaves overhead.

"Just wanted to see it," she replied, gesturing around the square. "It looks... magical. Even before the lights come on."

He joined her by the stage, his presence a comforting anchor in the twilight. "The final coat of varnish on the benches is drying now. Should be ready for the kids' craft tent tomorrow." He unrolled the blueprint, and they both studied the intricate drawings, his finger tracing the lines of support beams and decorative carvings.

"You really are an artist, Theo," Marisol said, her voice laced with genuine admiration. "Not just with wood, but with... planning. With bringing something solid and beautiful into being."

He looked at the blueprint, then back at her, a thoughtful expression clouding his features. "It's about building something that lasts," he said, his voice quiet. "Something that can withstand the elements, the wear and tear of time. It's about creating a foundation that can support... well, everything."

The word "everything" seemed to hang in the air between them, a soft echo of their previous conversations, of the unspoken depths they were slowly, cautiously, exploring. Marisol felt a familiar pull, a desire to bridge the remaining distance, to connect with the man behind the skilled craftsman.

"And what happens," she asked, her voice barely a whisper, "when the foundation itself is shaken? When something unexpected happens that no amount of planning can prevent?"

Theo's gaze drifted, his eyes focusing on a distant point beyond the square. The easy warmth that had settled between them seemed to recede, replaced by a familiar shadow of reserve. He was silent for a long moment, and Marisol's heart gave a small, anxious lurch. She knew this territory, the landscape of his past losses, the cautious defenses he had erected.

Finally, he spoke, his voice lower than before, almost a confession. "Then... then you learn how fragile even the strongest foundations can be. You learn that some things... some things can be lost, no matter how much you try to hold onto them. And that knowledge... it makes you want to build differently. More cautiously. With stronger walls, perhaps, to keep the storms out."

Marisol reached out, her hand finding his on the blueprint. His fingers were warm, calloused, and steady. "But sometimes," she said, her voice gentle but firm, "the strongest walls can also be the loneliest. And sometimes, the storms are meant to be weathered together, not shut out."

He turned his hand, his fingers interlacing with hers, a small, hesitant gesture of connection. His thumb brushed lightly over her knuckles, a silent acknowledgment of her words, of her presence. "I'm learning that," he admitted, his gaze meeting hers. There was a vulnerability in his eyes that tugged at her heart, a raw honesty that spoke volumes. "It's... a process."

"And I'm here for the process, Theo," Marisol said, her voice unwavering. "Whatever it takes. I believe in building things that last, too. But I also believe in building them with someone. Together."

The town square, bathed in the pale moonlight, felt like a sanctuary. The unfinished stalls and the unlit lights seemed to hold a promise, a potential for joy and connection that mirrored the tentative hope blossoming between them. The Annual Harvest Festival, in all its autumnal splendor, was more than just a celebration of the season; it was becoming a testament to the quiet, steady growth of their own shared story, a story rooted in the strong, fertile ground of Cedar Ridge, and tended with a growing, shared understanding.

The air, once just crisp with autumn, now felt charged with possibility, a prelude to the magic that was about to unfold, not just in the square, but in the deepening connection between two hearts finding their way home.

The following morning, the town square was a vibrant hub of activity, a testament to the collective spirit of Cedar Ridge. Marisol, having delivered a fresh batch of her signature apple cider donuts to the festival committee, found herself navigating the bustling throng. The scent of roasted nuts mingled with the sweet perfume of late-blooming chrysanthemums, creating an intoxicating autumnal bouquet.

She spotted Mayor Thompson, a man whose booming laugh and perpetually cheerful demeanor were as much a fixture of Cedar Ridge as the old clock tower, deep in conversation with a group of farmers. As she drew closer, he waved her over, his eyes twinkling.

"Marisol, my dear! Just the person I wanted to see," he boomed, clapping her on the shoulder with a force that nearly sent her staggering. "Heard from Theo that your bakery is going to be providing enough pies to feed an army! Excellent work, excellent work." He then turned his attention to the nascent bookstore that had opened its doors on Main Street just a few months prior. "And what about that little bookshop of yours? Any special Harvest Festival promotions in the works? We need to keep our visitors entertained between pumpkin-patch visits, you know."

Marisol smiled, feeling a familiar warmth spread through her. "We're running a special on local history books, Mayor," she replied, her voice carrying easily over the cheerful din. "And I've put together a small display of cozy reads, perfect for a crisp autumn evening. Theo's even crafted some charming little book stands for them." She glanced towards Theo's workshop, a silent acknowledgement of his contributions, and a flicker of pride warmed her chest.

"Wonderful! Simply wonderful," Mayor Thompson declared, already turning his attention to a passing delivery truck. "That's the spirit of Cedar Ridge! Everyone pitching in."

As she continued her walk, weaving through the crowd, a familiar voice called out her name. "Marisol, dear!"

She turned to see Mrs. Gable, her silver hair pulled back in a neat bun, holding a steaming pie dish. Mrs. Gable, the undisputed queen of Cedar Ridge baking, had been honing her craft long before Marisol had even dreamed of opening "The Gilded Acorn." Yet, there was no hint of competition between them, only a shared passion and a deep respect.

"Mrs. Gable! What a lovely surprise," Marisol said, her eyes falling on the golden-brown crust of the pie. "Is that...?"

"My famous apple pie, dear," Mrs. Gable announced, a proud smile gracing her lips. "Still warm from the oven. I made a few extra, and I thought you and Theo might enjoy a slice. You two have been working so hard on the festival." She pressed the dish into Marisol's hands. "It's the least I can do. It's important for folks to see you two working together. It shows the town that we can all come together, no matter our... different talents." She winked, a knowing glint in her eyes.

Marisol accepted the pie, the warmth seeping through the dish into her hands. "Thank you, Mrs. Gable. That's incredibly kind of you. Theo will be so pleased." She paused, looking at the pie, then back at Mrs. Gable. "It really is a wonderful thing, isn't it? This town. How everyone... supports each other."

Mrs. Gable nodded, her gaze sweeping across the animated scene. "That's the beauty of Cedar Ridge, dear. We've all got our quirks, our struggles. But when it comes down to it, we're all here for each other. And seeing you and Theo... well, it's a good sign. A sign that even after storms, things can grow strong again."

As she walked away, the weight of the pie a comforting presence in her hands, Marisol felt a deep sense of gratitude for the simple, honest interactions that defined life in Cedar Ridge. The easy camaraderie of the townsfolk, their genuine warmth and unwavering support, was a stark contrast to the internal complexities she and Theo were navigating. Yet, it was precisely this gentle constancy, this unwavering embrace of the community, that provided a steadying force, a reminder of what truly mattered. Theo, despite his guarded nature, had come to appreciate this about Cedar Ridge, this unspoken pact of mutual support that allowed even the most reserved hearts to feel a sense of belonging. And in this bustling, festive square, surrounded by the familiar faces and cheerful greetings, Marisol felt that belonging, not just for herself, but for the hesitant, hopeful partnership she was building with Theo, brick by sturdy, wooden brick.

The air in Cedar Ridge, even with the festive decorations beginning to festoon the town square, still held that particular autumn crispness, carrying the scent of damp earth and distant woodsmoke. It was a scent Marisol had always found comforting, a tangible reminder of the cyclical nature of life and the steady rhythm of the seasons.

This year, however, the scent seemed to weave itself into a new narrative, one that held the burgeoning warmth of her burgeoning feelings for Theo, a quiet understanding that had slowly, surely, taken root. The Annual Harvest Festival was just around the corner, an event that transformed Cedar Ridge into a vibrant tableau of autumn colors and an outpouring of communal spirit.

From her perch behind the counter of "The Gilded Acorn," Marisol watched the town square come alive. It was a scene she'd witnessed countless times, but this year, it felt different. This year, she and Theo, as the owners of two of the town's most prominent businesses – her beloved bakery and his sturdy woodworking shop – weren't just observers; they were integral parts of the festival's creation. Theo and his team were constructing the pumpkin stalls, their robust frames designed to cradle gourds of every shape and size.

Bunting in hues of burnt orange, crimson, and gold was being unfurled, each strand a promise of the celebrations to come. And the twinkling fairy lights, reserved for this special occasion, were being carefully strung between the ancient oaks that embraced the square, ready to cast a magical glow as twilight descended.

The festival was more than just a date on the calendar; it was the very soul of Cedar Ridge. It was the day when the distinctions between farmer and shopkeeper, young and old, newcomer and lifelong resident, dissolved into a shared experience of gratitude and connection.

It was a testament to the town's enduring spirit, a reaffirmation that even in a world that often felt chaotic and hurried, some traditions remained steadfast, anchoring the community in a common purpose. For Marisol, this year's festival felt like a reflection of her own evolving life, a new chapter unfolding under the warm embrace of autumn, with Theo a constant, grounding presence.

The planning committee meetings had shed their previous formality, now humming with a new energy. Marisol, with her innate organizational skills and infectious enthusiasm, had quickly become a central figure, her ideas met with eager acceptance. Theo, though a man of fewer words, possessed a quiet authority.

His practical suggestions and steady demeanor were invaluable. He'd personally overseen the construction of the main stage, ensuring its structural integrity with the same meticulous care he applied to his finest furniture. He'd also volunteered his team to build the children's craft tents, their charmingly sturdy benches and tables a testament to his craftsmanship, designed to withstand the enthusiastic energy of Cedar Ridge's youngest residents.

One blustery afternoon, as Marisol wrestled with a particularly uncooperative roll of burlap intended for the farmer's market stalls, she found herself in the middle of the square, a frustrated sigh escaping her lips. The wind, a mischievous force, tugged at the fabric, threatening to whisk it away. Just as she was about to admit defeat, a shadow fell over her.

"Having trouble there?" Theo's voice, a deep resonance that always reminded her of the steady beat of a hammer, cut through the wind's bluster. He held a coil of sturdy, weather-resistant rope in his hands.

Marisol looked up, her frustration instantly melting into a smile. "A little. This wind has a mind of its own today."

Without a word, he took the burlap from her, his strong fingers deftly securing it with a few swift, expert knots. The rope cinched the fabric taut, holding it firm against the playful gusts. He then offered her the end of the rope, a silent invitation to partnership.

"Thanks, Theo," she said, her voice filled with genuine gratitude. "You're a lifesaver. Or at least, a burlap-saver."

A rare, small smile touched his lips, crinkling the corners of his eyes. "Just doing my part. Wouldn't want the pumpkins to go unprotected."

They worked in a comfortable silence for a few moments, securing the rest of the burlap. The shared effort, the effortless rhythm of their movements, felt surprisingly natural. Marisol found herself stealing glances at him, observing the controlled power in his actions, the focused intensity in his brow, the quiet grace of his hands as they worked the rope. It was a different kind of intimacy than their quiet conversations, a communication conveyed through shared tasks and mutual understanding.

"It's going to be a good one this year," Marisol ventured, breaking the silence. "The energy feels... different."

Theo nodded, his gaze sweeping across the square, already buzzing with activity. "People are ready. Ready for something to celebrate. Something that brings us all together." He paused, then added, his voice softer, "Like this town. It's good at that."

A warmth spread through Marisol, a feeling entirely unrelated to the autumn chill. "It is," she agreed. "And you're a big part of that, Theo. You and your... solid creations." She gestured to the sturdy framework of the stalls, the perfectly aligned wooden beams. "They're like the bones of the festival."

He met her gaze, a fleeting expression that might have been pride, or perhaps simply quiet acknowledgment, in his eyes. "Someone has to make sure it doesn't fall apart," he said, his characteristic pragmatism surfacing. But there was a gentleness in his tone that softened the practicality.

As the days counted down to the festival, the preparations in Cedar Ridge intensified. Marisol's bakery was a hive of activity, her ovens working overtime to churn out the pies, tarts, and cookies that were essential components of the harvest spread.

The comforting aroma of cinnamon, apples, and spiced pumpkin wafted from her kitchen, a fragrant promise of the coming festivities. She found herself thinking of Theo with a frequency that surprised her, wondering if he was taking breaks, if he was remembering to eat. The quiet understanding that had begun to bloom between them was subtly shifting, deepening into a more conscious awareness of each other.

One evening, after a particularly demanding day of baking, Marisol found herself wandering through the town square. The fairy lights were now strung, awaiting illumination, and the skeletal frames of the stalls stood like silent sentinels, ready for their autumnal adornments. She paused by the base of the main stage, her fingers tracing the smooth, polished wood. It was strong, beautiful, and utterly dependable. Much like Theo.

As if summoned by her thoughts, Theo emerged from the shadows of his workshop, a rolled blueprint tucked under his arm. He seemed surprised to see her, but his surprise quickly softened into a welcoming smile.

"Couldn't sleep?" he asked, his voice a low murmur that seemed to blend with the rustling leaves overhead.

"Just wanted to see it," she replied, gesturing around the square. "It looks... magical. Even before the lights come on."

He joined her by the stage, his presence a comforting anchor in the twilight. "The final coat of varnish on the benches is drying now. Should be ready for the kids' craft tent tomorrow." He unrolled the blueprint, and they both studied the intricate drawings, his finger tracing the lines of support beams and decorative carvings.

"You really are an artist, Theo," Marisol said, her voice laced with genuine admiration. "Not just with wood, but with... planning. With bringing something solid and beautiful into being."

He looked at the blueprint, then back at her, a thoughtful expression clouding his features. "It's about building something that lasts," he said, his voice quiet. "Something that can withstand the elements, the wear and tear of time. It's about creating a foundation that can support... well, everything."

The word "everything" seemed to hang in the air between them, a soft echo of their previous conversations, of the unspoken depths they were slowly, cautiously, exploring. Marisol felt a familiar pull, a desire to bridge the remaining distance, to connect with the man behind the skilled craftsman.

"And what happens," she asked, her voice barely a whisper, "when the foundation itself is shaken? When something unexpected happens that no amount of planning can prevent?"

Theo's gaze drifted, his eyes focusing on a distant point beyond the square. The easy warmth that had settled between them seemed to recede, replaced by a familiar shadow of reserve. He was silent for a long moment, and Marisol's heart gave a small, anxious lurch. She knew this territory, the landscape of his past losses, the cautious defenses he had erected.

Finally, he spoke, his voice lower than before, almost a confession. "Then... then you learn how fragile even the strongest foundations can be. You learn that some things... some things can be lost, no matter how much you try to hold onto them. And that knowledge... it makes you want to build differently. More cautiously. With stronger walls, perhaps, to keep the storms out."

Marisol reached out, her hand finding his on the blueprint. His fingers were warm, calloused, and steady. "But sometimes," she said, her voice gentle but firm, "the strongest walls can also be the loneliest. And sometimes, the storms are meant to be weathered together, not shut out."

He turned his hand, his fingers interlacing with hers, a small, hesitant gesture of connection. His thumb brushed lightly over her knuckles, a silent acknowledgment of her words, of her presence. "I'm learning that," he admitted, his gaze meeting hers. There was a vulnerability in his eyes that tugged at her heart, a raw honesty that spoke volumes. "It's... a process."

"And I'm here for the process, Theo," Marisol said, her voice unwavering. "Whatever it takes. I believe in building things that last, too. But I also believe in building them with someone. Together."

The town square, bathed in the pale moonlight, felt like a sanctuary. The unfinished stalls and the unlit lights seemed to hold a promise, a potential for joy and connection that mirrored the tentative hope blossoming between them. The Annual Harvest Festival, in all its autumnal splendor, was more than just a celebration of the season; it was becoming a testament to the quiet, steady growth of their own shared story, a story rooted in the strong, fertile ground of Cedar Ridge, and tended with a growing, shared understanding. The air, once just crisp with autumn, now felt charged with possibility, a prelude to the magic that was about to unfold, not just in the square, but in the deepening connection between two hearts finding their way home.

The following morning, the town square was a vibrant hub of activity, a testament to the collective spirit of Cedar Ridge. Marisol, having delivered a fresh batch of her signature apple cider donuts to the festival committee, found herself navigating the bustling throng. The scent of roasted nuts mingled with the sweet perfume of late-blooming chrysanthemums, creating an intoxicating autumnal bouquet.

She spotted Mayor Thompson, a man whose booming laugh and perpetually cheerful demeanor were as much a fixture of Cedar Ridge as the old clock tower, deep in conversation with a group of farmers. As she drew closer, he waved her over, his eyes twinkling.

"Marisol, my dear! Just the person I wanted to see," he boomed, clapping her on the shoulder with a force that nearly sent her staggering. "Heard from Theo that your bakery is going to be providing enough pies to feed an army! Excellent work, excellent work." He then turned his attention to the nascent bookstore that had opened its doors on Main Street just a few months prior. "And what about that little bookshop of yours? Any special Harvest Festival promotions in the works? We need to keep our visitors entertained between pumpkin-patch visits, you know."

Marisol smiled, feeling a familiar warmth spread through her. "We're running a special on local history books, Mayor," she replied, her voice carrying easily over the cheerful din. "And I've put together a small display of cozy reads, perfect for a crisp autumn evening. Theo's even crafted some charming little book stands for them." She glanced towards Theo's workshop, a silent acknowledgement of his contributions, and a flicker of pride warmed her chest.

"Wonderful! Simply wonderful," Mayor Thompson declared, already turning his attention to a passing delivery truck. "That's the spirit of Cedar Ridge! Everyone pitching in."

As she continued her walk, weaving through the crowd, a familiar voice called out her name. "Marisol, dear!"

She turned to see Mrs. Gable, her silver hair pulled back in a neat bun, holding a steaming pie dish. Mrs. Gable, the undisputed queen of Cedar Ridge baking, had been honing her craft long before Marisol had even dreamed of opening "The Gilded Acorn." Yet, there was no hint of competition between them, only a shared passion and a deep respect.

"Mrs. Gable! What a lovely surprise," Marisol said, her eyes falling on the golden-brown crust of the pie. "Is that...?"

"My famous apple pie, dear," Mrs. Gable announced, a proud smile gracing her lips. "Still warm from the oven. I made a few extra, and I thought you and Theo might enjoy a slice. You two have been working so hard on the festival." She pressed the dish into Marisol's hands. "It's the least I can do. It's important for folks to see you two working together. It shows the town that we can all come together, no matter our... different talents." She winked, a knowing glint in her eyes.

Marisol accepted the pie, the warmth seeping through the dish into her hands. "Thank you, Mrs. Gable. That's incredibly kind of you. Theo will be so pleased." She paused, looking at the pie, then back at Mrs. Gable. "It really is a wonderful thing, isn't it? This town. How everyone... supports each other."

Mrs. Gable nodded, her gaze sweeping across the animated scene. "That's the beauty of Cedar Ridge, dear. We've all got our quirks, our struggles. But when it comes down to it, we're all here for each other. And seeing you and Theo... well, it's a good sign. A sign that even after storms, things can grow strong again."

As she walked away, the weight of the pie a comforting presence in her hands, Marisol felt a deep sense of gratitude for the simple, honest interactions that defined life in Cedar Ridge. The easy camaraderie of the townsfolk, their genuine warmth and unwavering support, was a stark contrast to the internal complexities she and Theo were navigating. Yet, it was precisely this gentle constancy, this unwavering embrace of the community, that provided a steadying force, a reminder of what truly mattered.

Theo, despite his guarded nature, had come to appreciate this about Cedar Ridge, this unspoken pact of mutual support that allowed even the most reserved hearts to feel a sense of belonging. And in this bustling, festive square, surrounded by the familiar faces and cheerful greetings, Marisol felt that belonging, not just for herself, but for the hesitant, hopeful partnership she was building with Theo, brick by sturdy, wooden brick.

As the afternoon waned, casting long shadows across the bustling town square, Marisol found herself drawn towards the newly illuminated gazebo, a whimsical structure Theo had meticulously crafted. It stood as a beacon of the festival's nascent magic, its fairy lights twinkling like captured stars against the deepening twilight sky. The air was alive with the murmur of excited chatter, the laughter of children, and the irresistible, intoxicating scents of roasted nuts and warm, spiced cider, a fragrant symphony that promised an evening of enchantment. Families meandered, their faces alight with the simple joy of the occasion, while children, their energy seemingly boundless, darted through the fading light, chasing the ephemeral glow of fireflies that danced like tiny, living lanterns.

Marisol found a quiet spot near the gazebo's base, a welcome pocket of calm amidst the cheerful chaos. She watched Theo, his broad shoulders silhouetted against the warm glow of a nearby food stall, as he engaged in a brief, animated conversation with one of the festival organizers. Even from this distance, she could see the steady competence in his movements, the subtle charm he possessed when he chose to let it show.

A small, almost involuntary smile touched her lips. He was so undeniably himself, a man of quiet strength and deep integrity, and in that moment, surrounded by the vibrant tapestry of the festival, she felt a profound sense of peace, a quiet contentment that settled deep within her.

He turned then, his gaze sweeping across the square, and his eyes met hers. A subtle shift occurred in his expression, a softening that always made her heart give a little flutter. He excused himself from the conversation and began to make his way towards her, his strides long and purposeful.

"Couldn't resist the call of the fairy lights?" Theo asked as he reached her, his voice a low rumble that seemed to blend with the gentle hum of the evening. He stood beside her, his presence a solid, comforting anchor.

Marisol leaned her head back slightly, gazing up at the twinkling lights strung through the gazebo's latticework. "They're beautiful, Theo. You've outdone yourself."

He followed her gaze, a faint smile playing on his lips. "Just trying to make the town square a little more magical for everyone."

They stood in comfortable silence for a few moments, the shared appreciation for the twinkling lights, and for the atmosphere they helped to create, a silent testament to their burgeoning connection. The scent of roasted chestnuts, their earthy aroma mingling with the sweet spice of the cider, filled the air, grounding them in the sensory richness of the moment. Marisol watched as a young couple, their arms intertwined, walked past, their laughter light and carefree. Nearby, a group of children squealed with delight as they chased fireflies, their small hands cupped, trying to capture the elusive sparks.

"It's moments like these, isn't it?" Marisol murmured, her voice soft, almost lost in the general hubbub. "These small, simple pockets of joy. They're what make a place feel like home."

Theo nodded, his gaze also fixed on the scene unfolding before them. "There's a purity to it," he agreed, his voice deeper than usual. "Uncomplicated happiness. It's... good to see." He paused, then added, "Especially now."

His words, though simple, held a weight that resonated with Marisol. She knew he was referring not just to the festival, but to the undercurrent of their own lives, the underlying tensions that still lingered between them, despite the growing warmth. The "now" he spoke of was a precarious space, filled with the promise of their developing feelings, but also shadowed by past hurts and unspoken fears.

"It is good to see," she echoed, turning to look at him. The fairy lights cast a soft, almost ethereal glow on his face, softening the sharp angles of his jaw and highlighting the quiet strength in his eyes. "It's a reminder of what matters."

Theo met her gaze, and for a fleeting moment, the carefully constructed walls he so often maintained seemed to crumble. There was a vulnerability in his eyes, a silent question, a yearning that mirrored her own. It was in these unguarded glances, these shared moments of quiet reflection, that Marisol felt the most profound connection to him. The underlying issues between them, the deep-seated anxieties that had kept them at arm's length for so long, were still very much present, lurking just beneath the surface of their conversations. Yet, in this shared space, bathed in the gentle glow of the festival lights, those complexities seemed to recede, replaced by a simpler, more immediate reality: the quiet comfort of their shared presence.

"You know," Marisol began, her voice a little lighter now, trying to capture the easy joy of the scene, "I never thought I'd be this excited about a harvest festival. But seeing everyone come together like this... it's really something."

"It's Cedar Ridge," Theo replied, a small, genuine smile touching his lips. "It's what we do. We build things. Things that last. And we come together when it matters." He gestured vaguely towards the bustling stalls, the animated crowds. "This is one of those times."

Marisol felt a familiar warmth spread through her at his words. It was a simple statement, but it held a profound truth, a recognition of the town's enduring spirit, and perhaps, she dared to hope, a subtle acknowledgement of the foundation they were slowly, carefully, building between themselves.

"I saw Mrs. Gable earlier," Marisol shared, a smile playing on her lips as she recalled the interaction. "She brought me a pie. An apple pie. Still warm."

Theo's smile widened. "Of course she did. She's been baking that pie for fifty years, she'll tell you. And she'll also tell you that it's best shared." He paused, his gaze returning to the families enjoying the evening. "She's right, you know. About sharing. About making sure things don't fall apart. Not just the festival, but... everything."

The unspoken hung heavy in the air between them, a familiar dance of veiled emotions and hesitant admissions. Marisol felt a pang of longing, a desire to push past the comfortable ambiguity, to step fully into the shared space they were creating. But for now, this quiet companionship, this shared moment under the twinkling lights, felt like a precious gift. The scent of roasted nuts, now more pronounced as the evening deepened, filled her senses, a comforting, earthy aroma that spoke of harvest and home. And the spiced cider, offered freely by volunteers at a nearby stand, warmed her from the inside out, a sweet and spicy balm against the lingering chill of uncertainty.

"It's a beautiful night, Theo," Marisol said softly, her gaze drifting from the fireflies to his face. The glow of the fairy lights seemed to catch the light in his eyes, making them sparkle with an intensity that sent a shiver down her spine.

"It is," he agreed, his voice a low murmur that held a warmth that had nothing to do with the autumn air. He turned his body fully towards her, his posture shifting from that of a casual observer to one of focused attention. "And it's good to share it with you, Marisol."

The sincerity in his voice, the quiet admission, felt like a gentle unfolding, a careful step forward on the path they were navigating. Marisol's heart swelled with a hope that was both fragile and tenacious. The challenges between them remained, the deep-seated fears that had shaped Theo's past and influenced his present were not easily erased. But in this shared moment, under the romantic spell of the illuminated gazebo, surrounded by the simple joys of the Harvest Festival, a different kind of truth was being revealed.

It was the truth of shared appreciation, of quiet comfort, and of a burgeoning connection that felt as steady and as enduring as the ancient oaks that framed the town square. The fairy lights, like the small, unspoken hopes they were beginning to share, cast a warm, inviting glow, promising a future that, while perhaps uncertain, was undeniably luminous.

The flickering gas lamps lining the perimeter of the town square cast a warm, inviting glow, their soft light mingling with the bolder sparkle of the fairy lights adorning the gazebo and the eaves of the surrounding buildings.

Cedar Ridge, usually a town that cherished its quiet dignity, had shed its reserve for the Harvest Festival, transforming into a lively, vibrant entity. Marisol found herself drawn to the periphery of the main throng, a contented observer, her senses saturated with the symphony of the evening: the cheerful din of conversations, the infectious peals of children's laughter, the distant strumming of a folk band, and the pervasive, comforting aromas of cinnamon, roasted nuts, and mulled cider.

She watched a familiar couple, the Millers, their silver hair a testament to decades spent together, moving through the crowd with a practiced, unhurried grace. Mr. Miller, his arm a steady presence around his wife's shoulders, leaned in to whisper something that elicited a soft chuckle from her. It was a quiet intimacy, a comfortable understanding that had been forged in the fires of shared joys and weathered sorrows. Marisol felt a gentle ache in her chest, a yearning for that kind of settled certainty, that visible, enduring partnership. She'd always believed in the power of commitment, but seeing it embodied so effortlessly, so naturally, in the people of Cedar Ridge, gave her abstract notions a tangible form.

Her gaze then drifted to a younger family, their two small children a whirlwind of delighted energy, chasing each other around the base of Theo's newly constructed pumpkin-stacking display. The mother, her eyes crinkling with amusement, kept a watchful gaze on her boisterous brood, while the father, his hand firmly clasped around his son's small fingers, steered them towards the face-painting booth. Theirs was a different kind of rhythm, a vibrant, slightly chaotic energy that pulsed with the promise of a future built together. It was a testament to the strength found in shared endeavors, in the willing embrace of both the mundane and the magical moments of life.

These observations, simple yet profound, wove themselves into Marisol's thoughts, a quiet counterpoint to the lively scene around her. The festival, she realized, wasn't just a celebration of the harvest; it was a living testament to the very fabric of Cedar Ridge. It was a tapestry woven with countless threads of partnership, of shared lives, of people who had chosen to build their futures side-by-side. The ease with which couples moved, the collaborative spirit evident in every corner of the square – from the shared effort in setting up stalls to the collective pride in the town's traditions – all spoke to a deeply ingrained understanding of what it meant to be a community.

Marisol thought of her own bakery, "The Gilded Acorn," a place built from her dreams and nurtured with her hard work. It was a solo endeavor, a testament to her independence. But lately, her thoughts had begun to drift towards the idea of building with someone, not just for herself. The hesitant tenderness she felt for Theo, the quiet understanding that had bloomed between them, felt like the first shoots of something that could, with time and care, grow into something as steadfast and as beautiful as the partnerships she witnessed all around her. The festival, in its joyous exuberance, seemed to amplify that nascent hope, holding up a mirror to the kind of lasting connection she craved.

She remembered a conversation she'd had with Mrs. Gable just that morning, amidst the flurry of last-minute preparations. Mrs. Gable, her hands dusted with flour even as she surveyed the bustling town square, had a way of cutting through pretense with gentle, knowing observations. "You know, dear," she'd said, her voice a warm hum, "this festival, it's more than just pumpkins and pies. It's about seeing everyone out here, shoulder to shoulder.

It's about the quiet understanding that passes between folks who've seen each other through thick and thin. It's the heart of Cedar Ridge, really. And it's good to see new hearts finding their way into that rhythm, too." The implication, the subtle nod to Marisol and Theo's evolving relationship, had brought a blush to her cheeks. But beneath the blush, there was a profound sense of validation. Cedar Ridge, it seemed, recognized and celebrated the building of these connections, offering a nurturing environment for them to flourish.

Marisol watched Theo from a distance, his steady presence a comforting constant amidst the festive chaos. He was speaking with a group of farmers, his hands gesturing with a quiet authority as he discussed the placement of some newly carved wooden signage. Even from across the square, she could see the respect he commanded, the genuine appreciation that flowed between him and the townsfolk. It wasn't just his skill as a craftsman that people valued; it was his inherent integrity, his quiet dependability. He was a pillar of the community, someone people trusted implicitly, someone who, like his furniture, was built to last.

The idea of shared building, of constructing a life with another person, resonated deeply within her. It wasn't just about the grand gestures; it was about the everyday acts of partnership, the silent agreements, the mutual support that sustained relationships through the inevitable challenges.

The vision of the Millers' easy companionship, the young family's vibrant energy, and Mrs. Gable's quiet wisdom all converged in her mind, painting a picture of what true community, and by extension, true partnership, looked like. It was a commitment to show up, not just for the celebrations, but for the quiet days, the unexpected storms, and the everyday hum of life.

She saw Mrs. Henderson, the town librarian, meticulously arranging a display of children's books near the story-telling tent. Next to her, Mr. Henderson, a man of few words but impeccable carpentry skills, was adjusting a small, sturdy easel to showcase some of her hand-painted illustrations. Their collaboration was a quiet ballet of shared passions, a testament to how different talents could intertwine to create something beautiful.

Marisol recognized that same silent collaboration beginning to unfold between herself and Theo, a delicate dance of shared ideas and complementary strengths. His sturdy creations provided the framework, the dependable structure, while her bakery offered the warmth, the comforting sweetness.

The collective spirit of the festival wasn't merely a superficial display of camaraderie; it was the embodiment of Cedar Ridge's soul. It was the unspoken agreement to lift each other up, to celebrate shared successes, and to offer solace in times of need. This was the foundation upon which lasting relationships were built, a foundation that Marisol found herself increasingly drawn to. The certainty that came with belonging to such a community, the knowledge that you weren't alone in your endeavors, was a powerful draw. It was a feeling that seeped into the very air, a subtle but pervasive reassurance that wherever you stood in Cedar Ridge, you were part of something larger, something enduring.

As the evening deepened, and the stars began to emerge in the inky sky, Marisol felt a profound sense of gratitude. The Harvest Festival, with its vibrant energy and its palpable sense of connection, had provided her with more than just a backdrop for the burgeoning feelings she harbored for Theo. It had served as a gentle, yet powerful, reminder of the profound beauty of shared lives, the enduring strength of community, and the quiet, unwavering promise of commitment.

She looked at Theo again, his silhouette now clearly defined against the warm glow of the festival lights, and a quiet certainty settled within her. She was ready to embrace that rhythm, to build something lasting, something real, within the heart of Cedar Ridge, and perhaps, with the right partner, to build it together.

The boisterous energy of the Harvest Festival, a joyful cacophony of laughter, music, and excited chatter, swirled around Marisol. She was lost in her observations, the ebb and flow of the crowd a fascinating study in human connection, when a sudden surge of people moved through the square.

A group of revelers, their voices loud and their movements less than graceful, veered too close, their path intersecting with hers and Theo's. It happened in a flash, a blur of movement and noise. But Theo, his senses always attuned, reacted instantly. Before Marisol could even register the potential for collision, she felt the firm, warm pressure of his hand settle on the small of her back.

It was a subtle, almost unconscious gesture, yet it resonated with a profound depth. The touch was a bulwark, a silent declaration against the encroaching chaos. His palm rested there, a steady anchor, guiding her subtly out of the path of the jostling crowd.

The contact was brief, no more than a fleeting second as the group swept past, but the impact on Marisol was anything but fleeting. It was a silent testament to his awareness, his inherent protectiveness that seemed to hum beneath his reserved exterior. He didn't need to speak; his actions spoke for him, translating a language of care that he often struggled to find words for.

In that instant, amidst the vibrant swirl of the festival, Theo's touch became a silent affirmation of their burgeoning connection. It wasn't a grand declaration, no public display of affection, but a quiet, intimate act that spoke volumes. It was the unspoken promise of someone who would stand between her and any potential harm, someone who was instinctively looking out for her well-being. Marisol felt a warmth spread through her, not just from the physical contact, but from the emotional weight it carried.

It was a reassurance, a grounding presence in the midst of the festival's energetic pulse. She felt seen, protected, and, in a way that was both comforting and exhilarating, cherished.

Theo, for his part, barely registered the conscious thought behind his action. It was pure instinct, a primal urge to shield Marisol from any discomfort or potential harm. His gaze had flickered, his eyes catching the unwieldy momentum of the approaching group, and his hand had moved without deliberation. It was the same instinct that guided his woodworking, that ensured the stability of his furniture, that made him meticulous in his craft. He saw a potential disruption, a momentary threat to Marisol's peace, and he responded. The feel of her form beneath his palm, the slight shift of her weight as he guided her, was a familiar sensation, one that had become increasingly pleasant and, he'd grudgingly admit to himself, sought-after.

He watched the group pass, their boisterousness thankfully receding, and then withdrew his hand. He didn't look at Marisol immediately, his attention already shifting back to the task at hand, to the subtle adjustments needed for the town square's festive décor. But beneath the surface of his outward calm, a quiet satisfaction settled within him. He had protected her, in his own quiet way, and that was enough. It was a small victory, a silent affirmation of the growing bond between them.

He often found himself struggling to articulate the complex emotions Marisol stirred within him. Words felt clumsy, inadequate, when faced with the profound shift she represented in his life. But his actions, these small, instinctive gestures, seemed to speak more truthfully than any carefully chosen phrase ever could.

Marisol, however, wasn't ready to let the moment pass so easily. She turned her head, her eyes meeting Theo's, a soft question lingering in her gaze. The flicker of a smile played on her lips, a silent acknowledgment of his gesture. She saw the subtle flush that rose on his cheeks, the way his gaze briefly faltered before returning to hers, and she understood. He might not be one for grand pronouncements, but his protectiveness was a language she was beginning to understand, a language spoken in the steady strength of his hand, the unwavering focus of his eyes, the quiet attentiveness he offered her.

"Thank you," she murmured, her voice barely above a whisper, yet carrying the weight of her gratitude. "That was... thoughtful."

Theo offered a slight nod, his gaze holding hers for a beat longer than strictly necessary. "Just making sure you didn't get bowled over," he replied, his voice a low rumble, a hint of amusement in its tone. He wanted to say more, to explain the feeling that had propelled his action, the sudden surge of possessiveness he'd felt at the prospect of her being jostled. But the words caught in his throat, tangled with a hundred other unspoken sentiments. Instead, he shifted his weight, his gaze flicking back to the intricate string of fairy lights he was adjusting.

But Marisol saw the underlying message, the unspoken layer beneath his casual response. She saw the awareness in his eyes, the subtle tightening of his jaw as the group had passed, and the gentle, almost hesitant way his hand had rested on her. It was a profound intimacy, a silent agreement forged in the shared space of that fleeting moment. The warmth of his touch had lingered on her skin, a physical reminder of his presence, his care. It was a comfort that seeped into her bones, a quiet reassurance that, even in the midst of a bustling crowd, she was not alone.

She continued to watch him, captivated by the quiet intensity he brought to even the simplest of tasks. He was a man of action, not words, and in his actions, she was finding a depth of emotion that surprised and delighted her. His protectiveness wasn't aggressive or overbearing; it was a quiet, steady presence, a subtle offering of support and security. It was the kind of protection that came not from a need to control, but from a genuine desire for her well-being.

The incident, though minor, served as a tangible confirmation of what she had been sensing between them. There was a growing foundation of trust, a mutual understanding that was being built, piece by painstaking piece. Theo's instinctive protectiveness was a cornerstone of that foundation, a silent promise that he would always have her back. And in return, Marisol found herself wanting to offer him the same unwavering support, the same quiet reassurance.

As they continued to navigate the lively festival grounds, Marisol found herself more aware than ever of Theo's presence beside her. Each brush of his arm against hers, each shared glance, felt imbued with a new significance. His protectiveness wasn't an overt display, but a constant, subtle current running beneath their interactions. It was in the way he steered her around obstacles, the way his eyes would scan the crowd when they were momentarily separated, the way he instinctively positioned himself to shield her from any potential discomfort. These were small gestures, easily overlooked by others, but to Marisol, they were monumental.

She remembered how, earlier that evening, while they were admiring the intricately carved wooden pumpkins displayed near the town hall, a child had darted past, almost knocking over a delicate display of hand-painted gourds. Theo's arm had shot out, not to grab the child, but to steady the display, his reflexes honed by years of working with delicate materials. He'd then offered the startled child a gentle, reassuring smile, a silent lesson in spatial awareness without a hint of reprimand. It was that same gentle, thoughtful protectiveness that he'd extended to her, a quiet assurance that he was looking out for her in all the ways that mattered.

The warmth of his touch on her back, though brief, had settled deep within her. It was a physical manifestation of a deeper emotional connection, a silent acknowledgment of their shared journey. He might not be a man of effusive declarations, but his actions spoke a language of devotion that Marisol was learning to read fluently. The festival, with its vibrant tapestry of community and connection, was proving to be the perfect backdrop for their evolving relationship, allowing these subtle, yet profound, demonstrations of affection to unfold naturally.

The protective instinct, she realized, wasn't just about warding off physical danger; it was about nurturing a sense of safety, of belonging, that allowed a heart to truly open. And with Theo, she felt that safety, that growing sense of belonging, more profoundly than she ever had before.

Chapter Four: Unspoken Fears

The scent of pine and dried leaves, still clinging to her from the festival, seemed to amplify the quiet intimacy of the evening. Back in the familiar comfort of her home, the lingering buzz of the town square faded, replaced by the gentle murmur of the wind outside and the rhythmic ticking of the grandfather clock in the hall. Marisol found herself drawn to her small writing desk, a sanctuary of sorts, where thoughts often coalesced under the soft glow of the lamp. Her journal, its leather cover worn smooth with use, lay open, an invitation to unpack the swirling emotions that had taken root within her.

She picked up her favorite pen, its weight familiar and comforting in her hand. The scratch of its nib against the crisp paper was a soothing sound, a counterpoint to the unspoken dialogue that had been unfolding between her and Theo all evening. His quiet presence, his subtle gestures of protection, they were eloquent in their own way, but they also left a void, a space where words should have been. She longed for an acknowledgment, a vocalization of the feelings that seemed to hum between them, a confirmation that what she felt was real and reciprocated in a way that transcended instinct and habit.

October 18th, she began, the date a simple anchor in the flow of her thoughts. Another day, another step closer, or so it feels. The festival was...

magical. And Theo was there, a steady presence in the midst of it all. He's so… him. So grounded, so sure of himself when he's working, building, creating. But when it comes to us, to what's between us, he's like a ship without a rudder, adrift in a sea of unspoken things. Tonight, when those people were pushing through, his hand on my back… it was more than just a physical act. It was a shield. A promise. A silent, powerful statement that he's got my back. And my heart just… swells. But then, the moment passes, and he's back to adjusting lights, his gaze sliding away, and I'm left with the echo of his touch, a beautiful, aching question mark.

She paused, her pen hovering above the page. The lamplight cast a warm, golden hue across her face, illuminating the faint furrow of her brow. The desire for Theo's explicit commitment was a growing ache, a yearning that had become more pronounced with each passing day. She knew he cared. She saw it in the way his eyes would linger on her for a fraction too long, in the way he'd instinctively step closer when they were in a crowd, in the almost imperceptible softening of his expression when she smiled at him. But these were whispers, and her heart craved a declaration, a clear statement that would solidify their connection.

It's like we're building this beautiful house together, she continued, the metaphor flowing effortlessly from her mind to the page. Every shared moment, every stolen glance, every act of kindness is a brick, meticulously placed. The foundation is strong, built on mutual respect and a shared sense of… something deep and true. But we don't have the deed. There's no official document, no signed contract that says this house is ours, that this love is ours. And I'm terrified that one day, someone will come along and claim it, or that it will simply crumble because it wasn't properly secured. Without that acknowledgment, without him saying the words, I worry that this love, this beautiful thing we're nurturing, might just fade away, like a forgotten song.

Her hand trembled slightly as she wrote the word "fade." It was a raw fear, one she hadn't fully allowed herself to articulate until now. She understood Theo's reticence. His past had clearly left him guarded, wary of vulnerability. But Marisol's heart, while strong, was also open and yearning for a love that was not just felt, but also expressed. She envisioned their relationship as a sturdy oak, its roots deep and intertwined, its branches reaching towards the sky. But even the strongest oak needed sunlight and rain to thrive, and for their love, that meant words, spoken truths, and a commitment that could withstand any storm.

I've tried to be patient, she wrote, her voice in her head taking on a pleading tone. I've told myself that actions speak louder than words, and Theo's actions are a symphony. He fixed my leaky faucet without me even asking. He remembered I loved those little lemon cookies and brought me a whole tin. He's so thoughtful, so incredibly kind. But still... there's this silence. This vast, echoing silence where his feelings should be. And it's starting to feel like a chasm. I see how he looks at me sometimes, and it's as if he's seeing something precious, something he's afraid to break. But isn't love meant to be embraced, not guarded so fiercely that it can't breathe?

She imagined Theo, in his workshop, meticulously sanding a piece of wood, his brow furrowed in concentration. That was the Theo she knew, the skilled craftsman, the quiet observer. But there was another Theo, a more hidden one, who surfaced in fleeting moments – the one who held her gaze a moment too long, who offered that small, almost shy smile. She wanted to reach that hidden Theo, to coax him out of his shell and into the light of open affection.

My biggest fear is that I'll wake up one morning, and this feeling will have somehow evaporated, she confessed, the ink bleeding slightly on the page as a stray tear fell. That the magic of this small town, the shared glances, the quiet companionship, will all amount to nothing more than a beautiful chapter in a book that never gets a sequel. I want to be more than just a companion, Theo. I want to be the one. The one you choose, every single day, not just by instinct, but by deliberate, spoken intent. Is that too much to ask?

She closed her eyes, picturing his strong hands, the calloused palms that were so adept at shaping wood into art. She imagined those hands reaching for her, not to steady her, not to guide her, but to hold her, to intertwine with hers. She yearned for the feeling of his fingers splayed against her skin, a conscious, deliberate act of claiming, of cherishing. It was a yearning that went beyond the physical, a deep-seated need for emotional security, for the knowledge that she was loved and wanted, not just in passing moments, but in the quiet stillness of everyday life.

I worry that my own unspoken fears are also creating a barrier, she admitted, shifting her focus inward. Am I reading too much into his gestures? Am I projecting my own desires onto his actions? He's not like me. He doesn't dissect every feeling, every interaction. He just... is. And I admire that in him, his authenticity. But it makes this path forward so uncertain. I don't want to push him, to scare him away. But I also can't keep living in this beautiful, fragile limbo, where every shared smile feels like a potential promise and every averted gaze feels like a quiet rejection.

She paused, taking a deep, fortifying breath. The silence in the room seemed to amplify the thrumming of her own heart. She knew Theo wouldn't force her to love him, and she wouldn't force him to say the words before he was ready. But the waiting, the constant anticipation, was taking its toll. It was a delicate dance, a tightrope walk between hope and apprehension.

The house without a deed, she wrote, circling back to her earlier metaphor. That's what this feels like. A magnificent structure, full of warmth and light, but without the legal ownership. What happens when a storm hits? Or when a new owner, with more confidence and a clearer claim, comes knocking? I want to feel secure, Theo. I want to know that this love, this beautiful, burgeoning love, is ours, to build upon, to defend, to cherish. I want to be able to say, with absolute certainty, that you are mine, and I am yours. Not just in our hearts, but in our words, too.

She imagined writing it all down, handing him the journal, letting him read her deepest anxieties and her most fervent hopes. But that wasn't her way, not yet. She needed to find the courage within herself first. She needed to explore these feelings, to understand them, before she could even begin to articulate them to him. The journal was her confidante, her safe space to be utterly, devastatingly honest.

He's a good man, Theo. A truly good man. And I'm falling for him, harder and faster than I ever thought possible. I'm falling for his quiet strength, his gentle hands, his unwavering integrity. But I'm also falling for the man who's just out of reach, the man who hides behind a shield of reserve. I want to break through that shield, not with force, but with patience, with love, and maybe, just maybe, with a few well-chosen words of my own. The silence is deafening, Theo. And I'm starting to fear what it might mean for us.

She underlined the last sentence, the ink darkening the paper. The scratch of her pen had been the only sound in the room for what felt like hours, a steady rhythm of confession and introspection. The lamp cast long shadows, and the world outside had long since settled into slumber. But Marisol's mind was wide awake, her heart aflutter with a mixture of vulnerability and a nascent resolve. The fear was real, a persistent whisper in the back of her mind, but beneath it, a stronger current was beginning to form – the desire to build not just a beautiful house, but a home, a sanctuary, that was undeniably, irrevocably theirs. And that, she knew, would require more than just silent gestures. It would require the courage to speak the unspoken.

The soft glow of the desk lamp seemed to cast a spotlight on her inner turmoil. The words "just friends" had been a casual, almost dismissive phrase tossed around by others, particularly by Mrs. Gable at the bakery, who, despite her kind eyes, possessed a disconcerting knack for nudging conversations in potentially awkward directions. Each time it was uttered, it landed like a pebble in the otherwise placid waters of Marisol's heart, sending ripples of unease through her. Just friends. The words felt like a cage, a neat, tidy box that didn't encompass the sprawling, vibrant landscape of her feelings for Theo. They were a dismissal of the unspoken intimacy that hummed between them, the shared glances that held a universe of meaning, the quiet comfort of his presence that felt more profound than mere camaraderie.

She traced the rim of her coffee mug, the warmth seeping into her fingertips, a stark contrast to the chill that crept into her soul whenever that phrase resurfaced. They lived under the same roof, shared meals, navigated the everyday rhythms of life in Cedar Ridge together. He was the first person she saw in the morning, the last she spoke to at night. He knew her moods, anticipated her needs, and offered a silent, unwavering support that had become as essential to her as the air she breathed. How could any of that be reduced to "just friends"? It felt like calling a masterpiece a mere sketch, a symphony a simple jingle. The very idea was an insult to the depth and complexity of what was growing between them.

Marisol's pen hovered over the page again.

It's the unspoken that's the heaviest, she wrote, the ink flowing with a sense of urgency. We've built this life, brick by careful brick, and it's sturdy, it's beautiful, it's ours. But the foundation, the legal deed, the official title – that's what's missing. And every time someone mentions "friends," it feels like a reminder that the whole structure might be built on shaky ground. It's like we're living in a magnificent house, but it's perpetually on the market, waiting for a buyer who's willing to make a commitment, to sign the papers.

She chewed on the end of her pen, her mind replaying a recent interaction with Eleanor Vance, the town's resident socialite, a woman whose sharp tongue was matched only by her equally sharp fashion sense. Eleanor had cornered her at the farmer's market, her eyes twinkling with a blend of curiosity and veiled judgment. "Marisol, dear," she'd purred, her voice like expensive silk. "You and Theo are quite the pair, aren't you? Always together. It's so lovely to see such a strong friendship blossoming in this town. You two are practically inseparable." The word "friendship" had hung in the air, thick and suffocating. Marisol had managed a polite smile, a noncommittal hum, but inside, her stomach had clenched.

Friendship. It was the polite, acceptable term, the one that kept things safely within the bounds of what society deemed appropriate. But it wasn't the truth of it, not the vibrant, soul-deep connection she felt.

The danger, I think, is that if we don't define it, if we don't acknowledge it, it will eventually define itself, she continued writing, her thoughts gathering momentum. And 'just friends' is such a narrow definition. It implies a lack of deeper feeling, a casualness that doesn't exist between us. It implies a boundary that we've already long since crossed, without even realizing it. It's the polite fiction we're living under, and I'm starting to feel suffocated by it.

She envisioned Theo, his hands busy with some intricate piece of woodworking, his brow furrowed in concentration. He was a man of action, of quiet competence. He expressed himself through his craft, through the tangible results of his labor. And she admired that, truly she did. It was one of the many things that drew her to him. But the emotional landscape, the realm of spoken declarations and explicit affirmations, seemed to be a territory he navigated with extreme caution, if at all. It was as if he feared that by naming their connection, by giving it a label, he would somehow break it, or worse, be compelled to commit to something he wasn't ready for.

But isn't that the nature of love, Theo? she asked the empty room, her voice a soft whisper. Isn't it meant to be named? To be celebrated? To be spoken aloud so that the world knows, and so that we ourselves are anchored in its reality? This 'just friends' label is like a polite way of saying 'we're not quite there yet.' But where is 'there'? And what happens if we never get there? What happens if we just… linger in this comfortable in-between, too afraid to take the next step, too content to risk the unknown?

The fear of being misunderstood, of being seen as pushy or demanding, warred with her desire for clarity. She didn't want to pressure him, to make him feel cornered. But the ambiguity was a constant, low-grade ache. It was the persistent hum of a question left unanswered, a melody without its final, resolving chord. She found herself overanalyzing every interaction, searching for clues, for signs that he felt as deeply as she did. Was the way he brushed her hair from her face more than just a gesture of kindness? Was the lingering touch of his hand on her arm a subconscious declaration? Or was she simply projecting her own hopes onto his actions, weaving a narrative of romance from threads of simple affection?

I'm afraid of the 'what ifs,' she confessed to her journal, the words spilling onto the page in a rush. What if he's happy with things just as they are? What if he doesn't see this as anything more than a convenient, comfort- able arrangement? What if my desire for more scares him away? What if 'just friends' is his way of protecting himself from the pain of a past love, and I'm just a temporary balm? These questions loop endlessly in my mind, and the silence where his answers should be is deafening.

Cedar Ridge, with its tight-knit community and penchant for gossip, felt like both a blessing and a curse in this regard. On one hand, the warmth and familiarity of the town provided a stable backdrop for their burgeoning feelings. On the other hand, the constant undercurrent of observation, the subtle inquiries, the well-meaning but often intrusive questions, made the lack of a defined relationship all the more conspicuous. It was as if the entire town was waiting, watching, for them to either solidify their bond or retreat back into the comfortable confines of platonic affection.

I see other couples, Marisol, she wrote, her hand beginning to ache with the intensity of her writing. Couples who walk hand-in-hand, who steal kisses on the street, who openly express their affection. And I feel a pang of envy, a longing for that same uninhibited display of love. We have that potential, I know we do. But the fear of the unknown, the fear of rejection, the fear of shattering this comfortable equilibrium, it holds us back. And the phrase 'just friends' becomes a convenient excuse, a way to maintain the status quo, to avoid the vulnerability that comes with a declared love.

She thought about the way Theo looked at her when he thought she wasn't watching. There was a softness there, a depth that went beyond mere friendship. It was a gaze that held a nascent longing, a quiet admiration, and sometimes, a flicker of something that looked suspiciously like… tenderness. But these were fleeting glimpses, quickly masked by his usual stoic demeanor. It was like trying to catch moonlight in her hands; beautiful, ethereal, but ultimately elusive.

The weight of 'just friends' is the weight of unspoken potential, she mused, tapping her pen against the paper. It's the acknowledgment that something more exists, but the refusal to give it form. It's the comfortable cage that prevents us from truly soaring. It's the polite dismissal of a love that's too powerful, too real, to be contained within such a simple, ordinary word. I want to break free from that cage, Theo. I want us to be more than just friends. I want us to be… everything.

She paused, rereading the last sentence. It was bold, honest, and a little terrifying. But it was also true. The comfortable life they had built together in Cedar Ridge, the quiet mornings, the shared laughter, the easy companionship – it all felt like a prelude to something greater. And the longer they remained in the undefined space, the more the specter of "just friends" loomed, threatening to relegate their beautiful, evolving connection to a footnote in their lives.

She knew, with a certainty that resonated deep within her soul, that she wanted more. And the first step, she realized, was to acknowledge, even just to herself, the sheer, undeniable weight of that desire. The silence was no longer just a lack of words; it was a tangible presence, a heavy cloak that threatened to smother the very love she so desperately wanted to nurture.

The familiar strum of an acoustic guitar, a melody as worn and comfortable as an old armchair, drifted from the dashboard speakers. It was a song Theo hadn't heard in years, one that had faded into the background noise of his life, yet as the opening chords swelled, a forgotten scene flashed behind his eyes, vivid and sharp as broken glass. The air in his truck seemed to thicken, the sunlight slanting through the windshield suddenly feeling accusatory. He gripped the steering wheel, knuckles white, as the memory, unbidden and unwelcome, took hold.

He was younger, so much younger. His hands, less calloused then, were clasped around a much smaller hand, a hand that felt impossibly fragile. The setting was a dusty park, the kind with chipped paint on the swings and a lone, gnarled oak tree offering scant shade. He remembered the desperation in the eyes of the person before him, a desperate plea that had felt like a physical weight on his young shoulders. And he remembered the words that had tumbled out of his own mouth, a torrent of well-intentioned but ultimately hollow assurances. "I promise," he'd said, the words tasting of naivete and bravado. "I promise I won't let anything happen to you. I promise I'll always be here."

The music swelled, and with it, the crushing reality of how thoroughly he had failed. The promise, so easily made, had been as ephemeral as a soap bubble, bursting under the slightest pressure. He'd been a boy, ill-equipped and ill-prepared, and the consequences had been... catastrophic. He saw the aftermath again, the hollowed-out grief, the blame that had settled on him like a shroud, the silent accusation in the eyes of those he'd tried to protect. It wasn't just his own failure he remembered, but the irreparable damage it had inflicted on others. The weight of that broken vow had been a burden he'd carried in secret for years, a silent testament to his own fallibility.

He'd learned a hard lesson that day, a lesson etched into his very being: promises were not solid ground. They were treacherous illusions, glittering on the surface but hollow within. For Theo, a promise had become synonymous with a potential point of failure, a guaranteed path to disappointment, and a breeding ground for pain. It was a gamble with impossibly high stakes, and the only rational response, he'd concluded, was to refuse to play.

Why willingly walk into a situation where he was almost certain to falter, to disappoint, to cause hurt? It was simpler, safer, to keep his own counsel, to guard his words, and to offer only what he knew, with absolute certainty, he could deliver: his presence, his effort, his quiet steadfastness. But never a promise. Never a vow that could be broken, no matter how pure the intention.

The song faded, replaced by the drone of traffic. Theo blinked, forcing himself back into the present. The memory, though painful, offered a stark clarity. It explained the hesitation he felt whenever Marisol's hopeful gaze met his, searching for something he was loath to give. It explained his quiet discomfort when conversations veered towards future plans, towards commitments that felt too much like a gilded cage. He wasn't cold or indifferent; he was terrified. Terrified of repeating the mistakes of his past, of causing another person the kind of pain he'd witnessed and, in a way, inflicted.

He remembered the hushed tones of his mother's voice, laced with a grief he'd never truly understood as a child. He remembered the way his father had withdrawn, his silence more damning than any spoken word. They had been a family, once, bound by love and laughter. But that one broken promise, that one failure to uphold his word, had fractured something fundamental, leaving behind only the echo of what had been lost. He'd been too young to grasp the nuances, to understand that circumstances could conspire against even the best intentions. All he'd known was the searing pain of failure, the gnawing guilt of letting someone down when they had needed him most.

That experience had shaped him in profound ways. It had instilled in him a deep-seated aversion to definitive pronouncements, to anything that suggested an unshakeable certainty about the future. He'd learned to live in the present, to focus on the tangible, the immediate. He could build a chair that would last a lifetime, carve a bird so lifelike it seemed ready to take flight, or fix a leaky faucet with unerring precision. These were things he could control, things whose success or failure was determined by his skill and effort, not by the fickle hand of fate or the unpredictable nature of human emotions.

But words, especially words of commitment, felt different. They were volatile, prone to misinterpretation, subject to the whims of time and circumstance. He'd seen too many people, his own parents included, get caught in the tangled web of spoken promises, their lives twisted and broken when those promises inevitably faltered. It was a dangerous dance, one he had resolved to sit out.

He thought about Marisol again, about the way her eyes would sometimes soften when she looked at him, a quiet question simmering beneath the surface. He knew she was looking for more than just companionship, more than the comfortable routine they had established. He saw the unspoken desires, the hopes she carefully nurtured, and a knot of anxiety would tighten in his chest. He wanted to give her what she deserved, but the ghost of that broken promise loomed, a constant, chilling reminder of his own limitations.

He remembered the specific moment, the exact words he'd used that day in the park. He'd been trying to comfort a younger cousin, a child who was terrified of being left alone. Their parents were going through a bitter separation, and the child clung to Theo, his small body trembling. Theo, eager to soothe the young boy's fears, had blurted out the words, "I promise I'll always be here. You can always count on me." It had felt so easy, so natural, to offer that reassurance. He'd meant it, with every fiber of his being. He'd wanted to be that steadfast figure, that unwavering rock.

But then, a few weeks later, an unexpected opportunity had arisen for his family, a chance to relocate for his father's work. It was a move that offered financial stability, a fresh start. But it meant leaving behind the familiar, including his young cousin. He'd tried to explain, to soften the blow, but the child's innocent face had crumpled, the unspoken accusation more potent than any shouted word. The image of that heartbroken child, his trust shattered, was seared into Theo's memory. He hadn't just broken a promise; he had broken a child's spirit, or at least, he felt responsible for having done so.

This trauma had created a deep-seated fear within him. A fear that any commitment he made would inevitably lead to pain for someone else. He equated promises with potential harm, with the risk of leaving someone vulnerable and exposed when he inevitably failed to deliver. It was a self-imposed exile from the realm of explicit emotional pledges. He offered his time, his loyalty, his practical support, because those were things he could quantify, things he could control. But the words "I promise," with their inherent weight and expectation, felt like a trap, a beautifully constructed snare designed to catch him in his own fallibility.

He found himself analyzing his interactions with Marisol through this lens. Every shared laugh, every comfortable silence, every moment of quiet understanding was tinged with his underlying fear. He wanted to recip-rocate the warmth he felt from her, the burgeoning affection that was as undeniable as the sunrise. But the specter of his past prevented him from articulating it, from giving it a name that might require a commitment he wasn't sure he could sustain without causing unintended damage.

He recalled a conversation he'd had with his Uncle David years ago, a man who had a knack for seeing straight through Theo's carefully constructed defenses. David had been a musician, a free spirit who had often spoken of the ephemeral nature of life and the importance of embracing the present. He'd seen Theo wrestling with his internal conflict, the war between his growing feelings for Marisol and his deep-seated fear of commitment.

"You're afraid, Theo," David had said, his voice gentle but firm. "You're afraid of making a promise because you think it means you'll be chained to it forever, that you'll be held responsible for every variable that life throws your way. But a promise isn't a chain, son. It's a guidepost. It's an intention. And sometimes, even when you try your best, things don't work out the way you planned. That doesn't make you a failure. It makes you human."

Theo had nodded, absorbing the words, but they hadn't fully penetrated the armor he'd built around his heart. The pain of that childhood expe-rience had been too raw, the lesson too harsh. He'd internalized the idea that failure to keep a promise was a fundamental character flaw, a betrayal of trust that could never be truly forgiven or forgotten.

He looked at Marisol's journal, the pages filled with her elegant script, her thoughts laid bare for him to see. He knew she was grappling with their ambiguous relationship, with the "just friends" label that felt like a cage to her. And he understood her frustration, her longing for clarity. But his own internal landscape was a minefield, littered with the debris of past regrets. How could he offer her the security she craved when he himself was haunted by the fear of his own potential to disappoint?

His aversion to promises wasn't born of malice or a lack of affection. It was a shield, a protective mechanism forged in the fires of past trauma. He wanted to be worthy of Marisol's trust, of her burgeoning love, but the echo of that broken promise whispered a constant warning: be careful, Theo. Don't offer what you can't guarantee. Don't build a future on foundations that might crumble. And so, he remained in a state of quiet observation, offering what he could, hoping it was enough, while wrestling with the unspoken fear that it might never be. The memory, triggered by a simple song, had once again solidified his resolve to tread carefully, to avoid the precipice of spoken vows, and to protect himself, and perhaps Marisol, from the devastating consequences of a promise broken.

The silence in the truck was no longer just an absence of noise; it was a tangible entity, heavy with unspoken anxieties. Theo felt the weight of it pressing down on him, mirroring the burden he carried within. He'd always believed that the sharpest sting of pain wasn't the initial hurt, but the agonizing aftermath of what could have been, the bitter taste of dashed hopes. And in his world, explicit commitments, those grand declarations of intent, were the architects of such profound disappointment.

They were carefully constructed castles built on the shifting sands of human fallibility, destined to crumble and leave behind only ruins and regret. He looked at Marisol, her profile softened by the afternoon sun filtering through the dusty windshield, and a familiar ache tightened his chest. It wasn't that he didn't feel a deep, burgeoning affection for her; it was the terrifying certainty that his own inherent limitations, his capacity for error, could one day shatter the delicate bloom of her trust. He was convinced that by offering her a promise, any concrete promise, he was essentially handing her a loaded gun and telling her to aim it at him, because eventually, inevitably, he would fail to live up to it.

This fear wasn't about a lack of love, he told himself. It was a desperate, albeit misguided, attempt at protection. He envisioned himself as a surgeon, tasked with a delicate operation. He wouldn't guarantee a complete recovery; that would be irresponsible, a reckless overestimation of his abilities against the unpredictable nature of the human body. Instead, he would promise to do his utmost, to apply his skill and knowledge with unwavering dedication, to monitor the patient's progress with vigilant care.

Anything more would be a betrayal of the truth, a setting of expectations so high they would inevitably lead to a fall. And Marisol, with her open heart and her unwavering belief in the possibility of a happy ending, deserved better than to be subjected to his own potential for failure. He saw her hopeful gaze, the way her eyes would linger on his a moment too long, seeking an assurance he couldn't, or rather, wouldn't, give. It was like watching a wilting flower, knowing he held the watering can but fearing that even his best efforts might not be enough to prevent its eventual decline.

He recalled a conversation with his Aunt Clara, a woman whose life had been a tapestry woven with both vibrant joys and profound sorrows. She had once told him, in her wise, crinkled-eyed way, that "expectations are just pre-written heartbreaks, Theo. The more you expect, the more you leave yourself open to be wounded." He'd taken her words to heart, perhaps too much so. He'd seen how his uncle's unwavering faith in the stock market had left him devastated after the crash.

He'd witnessed his own mother's quiet despair when a dream business venture, one she'd poured her heart and soul into, had collapsed. These weren't small disappointments; they were life-altering ruptures, and they had all stemmed, in his young mind, from the dangerous act of expecting something to be more than it was, or to last longer than it did.

Marisol, he knew, expected a future. Not necessarily a white picket fence and a dog named Buster, but a progression, a deepening, a sense of security that their relationship was moving forward, solidifying, becoming more. And he, Theo, the carpenter who built things to last, the mechanic who could coax life back into dying engines, found himself paralyzed by the prospect of building a future with her. How could he build something so profoundly emotional, so inherently unpredictable, when his very nature recoiled from the precipice of potential failure? His hands, so skilled with wood and metal, felt clumsy and inept when it came to navigating the intricate landscape of her heart.

He imagined the words, the ones that might appease her, that might bridge the growing chasm of unspoken needs between them. "I love you." Simple, yet loaded with the weight of a thousand potential futures. "I see a future with you." A declaration that promised permanence, a commitment that felt akin to setting his own future in stone, only to risk having the chisel slip and shatter the entire edifice. He saw himself on a tightrope, high above a cheering crowd. He could walk it, yes, with skill and focus. But if he were to look down, to acknowledge the height, to imagine the fall, the tremor in his legs would be enough to send him plummeting. And Marisol was the crowd, her hope a potent force that, if he failed her, would transform into a crushing wave of disappointment.

His internal monologue was a relentless cycle of "what ifs." What if he promised to be there for her daughter's graduation, only to be called away on an emergency out of state? What if he vowed to always be her confidant, only to be so consumed by his own internal struggles that he became distant and unfeeling? What if he offered her the quiet comfort of a shared life, only to discover, down the line, that he wasn't the man she truly needed, that his own ingrained fears had built a wall between them that love, no matter how strong, couldn't surmount? Each scenario played out in his mind with agonizing clarity, a preview of the heartache he was so desperate to avoid inflicting.

He understood, on an intellectual level, that Marisol wasn't asking for an impossible guarantee. She was asking for reassurance, for a sign that he was invested, that she wasn't just a temporary distraction or a convenient companion. But his past experiences had so thoroughly ingrained in him the fragility of human connection and the devastating impact of broken promises that he couldn't separate her genuine desires from the potential for his own failure. He was trapped in a paradox: he cared for her deeply, and precisely because he cared, he was terrified of being the instrument of her pain.

It was easier to be the steady, reliable presence. To fix the leaky faucet, to offer a listening ear without offering definitive solutions, to be the dependable friend who was always there, but never quite all in. This was a space he understood, a territory where his capabilities were clearly defined, and the risks of failure were manageable. He could offer his hands, his time, his skills. But the words, the spoken promises that bound two souls together, felt like a foreign language he hadn't quite mastered, a language fraught with peril.

He felt a pang of guilt, a sharp jab that he was withholding something so fundamental from her. He knew, deep down, that this protective shell he'd built around himself, while shielding him from perceived harm, was also creating a distance that was slowly, subtly, eroding the very connection he was trying to preserve. He was so focused on avoiding the possibility of causing her pain that he was inadvertently causing her a different kind of hurt – the slow ache of uncertainty, the quiet frustration of not being able to fully connect with the man she was growing to love. His attempt to guard her from the storm was, ironically, trapping her in a perpetual state of unease.

The peril of his unfulfilled expectations wasn't just about his potential failure to meet a promise; it was about the expectation she held, the quiet hope that he might be capable of more, an expectation he was actively trying to dismantle before it even had a chance to bloom. He was trying to prevent a future heartbreak by ensuring there was no future to be had, a twisted logic that gnawed at him with every mile they drove, with every silent moment they shared.

The scent of roasted chicken and herbs, usually a comforting aroma that filled Marisol's small kitchen, now felt heavy, almost suffocating. The dinner table, set with the mismatched but cherished plates they'd accumulated, was usually a haven of easy conversation and shared laughter. Tonight, however, it was an arena where silence waged a more potent war than any argument could. Each clink of a fork against ceramic, each soft scrape of a knife, seemed to echo with an amplified intensity in the charged atmosphere.

Marisol watched Theo across the table, her gaze lingering on the way his jaw tensed with each bite, the almost imperceptible tightening around his eyes. He was physically present, his hands steady as he navigated his meal, but his mind, she suspected, was miles away, lost in the labyrinthine corridors of his own making.

She remembered the ease of their earlier meals, the way they could talk about anything and everything – the absurdities of small-town gossip, the latest project at the school, the quirky habits of their neighbors. They'd found a rhythm, a comfortable cadence that had woven itself into the fabric of her life, a welcome counterpoint to the quiet solitude she'd grown accustomed to. But lately, that rhythm had faltered, replaced by a stilted awkwardness that felt like a dissonant chord in an otherwise harmonious melody. It was as if an invisible wall had sprung up between them, not of malice or anger, but of something far more insidious: unspoken fears, unmet expectations, and the growing chasm of their differing perspectives on what commitment truly meant.

Theo, for his part, felt the weight of her gaze like a physical presence. He tried to focus on the food, on the familiar taste of the rosemary-infused chicken that Marisol had prepared with her usual culinary care. He admired her thoughtfulness, her quiet dedication to making their shared moments feel special. It was these very qualities that both drew him to her and terrified him. Her earnestness, her capacity for deep feeling, her quiet assumption that life, and love, was meant to be built upon a foundation of unwavering trust – these were things he felt perpetually unqualified to offer.

He found himself resorting to a kind of internal fencing, deflecting any direct engagement with the emotional undercurrents that swirled around them. He would offer a noncommittal nod, a brief, generalized comment about the food, anything to avoid the potential for deeper introspection, to sidestep the very precipice of expectation that Marisol, perhaps unknowingly, stood at.

He caught her eye for a fleeting moment, and in the brief exchange, he saw a flicker of something that pierced his carefully constructed defenses – a quiet plea, a searching question that he couldn't, or wouldn't, answer. Her eyes, usually so expressive, held a trace of apprehension, a vulnerability that twisted in his gut. He quickly averted his gaze, focusing instead on the condensation forming on his water glass, as if the simple act of observing it could somehow absorb the unspoken tension that permeated the air between them.

He understood, on a fundamental level, that she deserved more than this silent dance of avoidance. She deserved clarity, a sense of security, a clear indication that their shared present was building towards a shared future. But the words, the promises that would offer her that security, felt like dangerous currency, too easily devalued by the unpredictable fluctuations of human nature.

Marisol, sensing his withdrawal, let out a soft, almost imperceptible sigh. It wasn't a sigh of frustration, but one of gentle melancholy, a quiet acknowledgment of the growing distance. She understood Theo's hesitations, the ingrained caution that seemed to govern his approach to life. She saw the kindness in his actions, the quiet dependability he offered in a thousand small ways – fixing a squeaky hinge, offering a warm jacket on a chilly evening, simply being present.

These were not insignificant gestures. They were the solid, tangible expressions of a man who was, in his own way, deeply caring. But she also sensed the unspoken, the carefully guarded corners of his heart that remained just beyond her reach. It was as if he were offering her a beautifully crafted, sturdy wooden box, but keeping the key to its most precious contents locked away.

The comfortable routine of their shared meals, which had once been a source of solace and connection, now felt like a fragile illusion, a temporary respite from the underlying currents of unease. The soft glow of the kitchen lamp, which had always cast a warm, inviting light, now seemed to highlight the shadows lurking in the corners of their unspoken fears. Marisol found herself analyzing every gesture, every nuance of Theo's expression, searching for clues, for reassurances that he wasn't pulling away entirely. She wondered if he felt the same growing chasm, if he was aware of the subtle shift in the atmosphere between them. Or was he so lost in his own internal battles that he was oblivious to the quiet longing in her heart?

She recalled a conversation they'd had a few weeks prior, a casual discussion about future plans, about the possibility of a summer trip. Theo had responded with his usual measured approach, acknowledging the idea but carefully sidestepping any definitive commitment. He'd spoken about needing to see how things played out, about the unpredictability of his work schedule. At the time, Marisol had accepted his response at face value, attributing it to his practical nature. But now, in the quiet aftermath of their unspoken dinner, she began to see it as a pattern, a consistent theme of cautious reservation that underscored his reluctance to embrace anything that felt too... permanent.

The silence stretched, punctuated only by the soft ticking of the wall clock, each second a small testament to the unspoken words that hung heavy in the air. Marisol toyed with a stray crumb on her plate, her mind replaying snippets of their interactions, searching for a rationale, a comforting explanation for Theo's guardedness. She knew he was a good man, a fundamentally decent soul. But goodness, she was learning, didn't always translate to the kind of emotional openness that fostered a truly deep and lasting connection.

His fear of future disappointment, she suspected, was a formidable fortress, one he had built brick by careful brick over years of perceived failures and dashed hopes. And she, in her own quiet way, was beginning to feel the chill emanating from its formidable walls.

Theo cleared his throat, the sound startlingly loud in the stillness. "The chicken was great, Marisol," he offered, his voice a little rough. It was a genuine compliment, a true reflection of his appreciation for her cooking, but it felt like a well-worn shield, designed to deflect any further inquiry into the emotional landscape of their shared evening. He watched her closely, searching for any sign of irritation, of disappointment. He wanted to offer more, to bridge the gap that he felt widening between them, but the words themselves felt like treacherous stepping stones across a churning river.

What if he said "I love you," and in a week, a month, a year, he couldn't live up to the weight of those words? What if he vowed to build a life with her, only to discover that his own internal demons made him incapable of being the partner she deserved? The potential for failure loomed, a specter that haunted his every interaction, his every burgeoning feeling.

Marisol offered a small, polite smile. "Thank you, Theo." Her voice was soft, betraying none of the turmoil churning within her. She understood his need to keep things light, to maintain a semblance of normalcy. But the normalcy felt increasingly fragile, like a thin sheet of ice over deep, dark water. She found herself longing for a moment of genuine, unvarnished vulnerability from him, a simple admission that he felt the strain, that he recognized the growing distance. But he remained resolutely guarded, his reserve a palpable barrier between them.

He noticed the way she pushed a piece of chicken around her plate, her appetite seemingly diminished. A pang of guilt, sharp and unwelcome, shot through him. He was the cause of this, wasn't he? His inability to articulate his feelings, his deep-seated fear of commitment, was creating this palpable tension, this uncomfortable silence that was slowly but surely eroding the warmth that had once defined their shared meals.

He wished he could offer her the simple reassurance she seemed to crave, the verbal affirmation that would cement their connection and dispel her quiet doubts. But the words caught in his throat, tangled with the complex web of his own anxieties. He was a man who could meticulously plan the construction of a sturdy cabin, who could diagnose the intricate workings of a faulty engine, but when it came to the architecture of the human heart, he felt utterly lost, a novice architect facing a blueprint he couldn't comprehend.

He pushed his plate away, the gesture signaling the end of the meal, and with it, perhaps, the end of any hope for a deeper conversation tonight. "I should probably start cleaning up," he offered, his voice a little too casual, a little too eager to escape the charged atmosphere. It was a practical suggestion, a way to regain a sense of control, to revert to the familiar territory of shared chores. But Marisol knew, with a sinking heart, that the true mess wasn't on the dinner plates, but in the unspoken anxieties that lay between them, a far more complex and daunting challenge to clean up.

She watched him as he began to clear their plates, his movements efficient and practiced. There was a quiet dignity in his actions, a testament to his inherent good nature. But beneath the surface, she sensed a deep well of unexpressed emotion, a reluctance to delve into the messy, complicated realities of human connection. She wondered if he saw their relationship as just another project, something to be maintained, perhaps, but not something to be truly embraced, to be fully invested in. The thought was a cold, unwelcome one, and she pushed it away, clinging to the hope that his caution was a temporary phase, a lingering shadow from a past he couldn't quite shake.

As they worked side-by-side, the familiar rhythm of their shared domesticity returned, but it was a hollow echo of what it had once been. The clatter of dishes, the swish of the dishcloth, the murmur of the running water – these sounds, usually a comforting backdrop to their evenings, now seemed to underscore the vast expanse of their unspoken thoughts. Marisol found herself observing Theo's hands, the strong, capable hands that could build and repair, but that seemed so hesitant to offer the simple, heartfelt touch that could bridge the growing distance between them.

She longed for him to reach out, to simply take her hand, to offer a silent acknowledgment of the unspoken tension, to let her know that he wasn't alone in his struggle. But his hands remained busy with their tasks, his focus seemingly fixed on the tangible, the immediate.

The silence, which had once felt comfortable and companionable, now felt like a vast, empty space, filled with the ghosts of conversations that had never happened, of feelings that had never been expressed. Cedar Ridge, usually a place of quiet charm and familiarity, suddenly felt like a landscape where their unspoken fears had taken root, growing like weeds in the fertile ground of their shared home. Marisol wondered if Theo truly understood the toll this emotional withholding was taking. It wasn't just about the absence of grand declarations; it was about the slow, insidious erosion of intimacy, the gradual dimming of the light that had once shone so brightly between them.

Theo, as he scrubbed a stubborn spot of gravy from a plate, felt a wave of melancholy wash over him. He saw the quiet resignation in Marisol's posture, the slight slump of her shoulders as she wiped down the counter. He knew he was disappointing her, not through any deliberate act of malice, but through his own ingrained caution, his deep-seated fear of causing her pain. He yearned to tell her that he cared, that she meant more to him than he could easily articulate, but the words felt like foreign objects in his mouth, ill-fitting and potentially damaging.

He was trapped in a paradox of his own making: the more he cared, the more he feared his own capacity for error, and the more he feared his own capacity for error, the more he withdrew, creating a distance that only amplified her unspoken questions.

He finished drying the last dish, his movements slower now, heavier. He leaned against the counter, watching Marisol as she put away the last of the silverware. Her profile was etched against the dim light, a picture of quiet strength and unspoken longing. He wanted to reach out, to pull her into his arms, to tell her that he was trying, that he was fighting his own demons, that her presence was a balm to his weary soul. But the words remained locked away, prisoners of his own self-imposed silence. He had built so many walls around his heart, protecting it from perceived threats, that he was now a prisoner within his own fortifications, unable to fully embrace the warmth and light that Marisol offered.

The silence in the kitchen, once a comforting presence, had morphed into something heavy, something oppressive. It was the silence of unspoken fears, of differing desires, of a love story that was teetering on the precipice of misunderstanding. Marisol finally turned, her gaze meeting his across the small space. There was a quiet sadness in her eyes, a gentle acknowledgment of the chasm that had opened between them. Theo could see the question there, the unspoken plea for understanding, for connection.

And in that moment, he felt the full weight of his own inadequacy, the profound challenge of bridging the gap between his carefully guarded heart and her open, hopeful spirit. The comfortable routine of their shared meals, which had once felt like an anchor, now served only to highlight the disquieting drift that had begun to pull them apart.

Chapter Five: The Event Horizon

The notice, plastered on the bulletin board outside Miller's General Store and tacked to the door of the post office, was stark in its brevity and dire in its implications. "URGENT TOWN HALL MEETING: The Future of the Cedar Ridge Public Library." Below, in slightly smaller but no less significant font, was the date and time, and the location: the community hall, a building that had witnessed countless town gatherings, from bake sales and election debates to holiday pageants and the occasional wedding reception. This, however, promised to be a different kind of assembly. The Cedar Ridge Public Library, a sturdy brick structure with ivy creeping up its walls, a silent sentinel of knowledge and community gathering for generations, was in peril.

Marisol saw the notice first. She was on her way to pick up some fresh produce, her mind already running through the ingredients for her grandmother's famous apple pie, a recipe she was planning to perfect for the upcoming fall festival. The familiar sight of the notice stopped her mid-stride. Her heart gave an uncomfortable lurch. The library. It wasn't just a building; it was the repository of her childhood dreams, the quiet sanctuary where she'd first discovered the magic of faraway lands and the solace of other people's stories.

It was where she'd spent countless afternoons poring over books, its hushed aisles a comforting balm to her sometimes-lonely childhood. It was also where she'd spent many evenings with Theo, curled up on the worn leather sofa in the reading nook, sharing quiet companionship amidst the scent of aging paper and polished wood. The thought of it being in danger sent a ripple of anxiety through her.

She stood there for a long moment, the breeze rustling the leaves overhead, the usual cheerful hum of the town seeming to recede. The library was more than just books; it was a cornerstone of Cedar Ridge, a place that represented continuity, a link to the past and a vital resource for the future. It was where children learned to read, where adults found new skills and a connection to the wider world, where seniors found community and quiet solace. Its closure would leave a gaping hole in the heart of their small town, a wound that might never truly heal. She knew, with a certainty that settled deep in her bones, that she would be there. And she suspected Theo would be too, though his involvement in such public forums was usually more reserved.

Theo saw the notice later that day, as he was leaving the hardware store. He'd been picking up supplies for a small repair job he was doing for Mrs. Gable down on Elm Street. The same notice, in the same stark font, felt like a shadow cast over his usual pragmatic thoughts. He understood the practicalities of budgets and funding. He knew that institutions, even beloved ones, often struggled to stay afloat in the face of financial realities. But he also understood the intangible value of a place like the Cedar Ridge Public Library. He'd seen the quiet dedication of the librarians, the way they knew every patron by name, the way they curated the shelves with care and consideration.

He'd seen the eager faces of children attending story time, their eyes wide with wonder. And he'd seen the quiet comfort it offered to those who sought refuge within its walls. He remembered, years ago, finding solace in its quiet corners himself, a place where he could escape the pressures of his own young life, where the weight of expectation felt a little lighter. The thought of that sanctuary being lost felt like a significant loss, not just for the town, but for the very fabric of Cedar Ridge's identity.

The community hall, when Marisol arrived, was already beginning to fill. The air inside was thick with a nervous energy, a palpable sense of shared concern. The usual friendly chatter was subdued, replaced by hushed conversations and worried glances. Old Mrs. Gable, her back still slightly stooped from years of gardening but her spirit as bright as ever, was already holding court by the refreshment table, a plate of her famous gingerbread cookies offering a small, albeit delicious, distraction.

Young families, their children clutching worn teddy bears or brightly colored picture books, huddled together, their faces etched with a mixture of anxiety and a fierce determination to protect a place that held so much meaning for them. The older residents, the pillars of the community who had seen Cedar Ridge through decades of change, sat in their usual spots near the front, their expressions solemn, their presence a quiet testament to their long-standing commitment to the town.

Marisol spotted Theo near the back, leaning against the wall, his arms crossed. He looked as she'd expected, a quiet observer, his gaze sweeping over the assembled crowd with a thoughtful intensity. He met her eyes and offered a small, almost imperceptible nod, a flicker of acknowledgment that spoke volumes in the charged atmosphere. She made her way towards him, navigating through the maze of concerned townsfolk.

"Quite a turnout," she murmured, her voice a little louder than necessary to cut through the low hum of voices.

Theo shifted his weight, his gaze still scanning the room. "Expected, I suppose. It's not every day your town's library is on the chopping block." His tone was measured, devoid of overt emotion, yet Marisol sensed the undertow of his own concern. He understood the practicalities, the financial constraints, but he also recognized the symbolic weight of this institution.

"It's more than just a building, isn't it?" Marisol said, her voice tinged with a plea for understanding, for him to articulate what she already felt.

He finally turned his full attention to her, his gaze steady. "For many, it's the heart of the town. A place of learning, of escape, of... possibility." He paused, his eyes lingering on hers for a beat longer than usual. "And a lot of memories."

The mayor, Mr. Henderson, a man whose usual jovial demeanor was replaced by a sober seriousness, stood up at the podium. The murmuring in the room subsided, replaced by an expectant silence. He cleared his throat, his voice amplified by the microphone, resonating through the hall.

"Thank you all for coming out tonight," he began, his voice carrying a weight of responsibility. "As you know, we've called this urgent meeting to discuss a matter of grave importance to our community: the future of the Cedar Ridge Public Library." He paused, letting the gravity of his words sink in. "As many of you are aware, the library has been facing significant funding challenges for some time now. We've explored every avenue, sought grants, implemented cost-saving measures, but unfortunately, we've reached a critical juncture. The current financial situation makes it increasingly difficult, if not impossible, to sustain its operations at the level we all expect and deserve."

He looked out at the sea of faces, his expression a mixture of regret and resolve. "The town council has been presented with a difficult decision. We have been given a proposal to significantly reduce the library's operating budget, which would effectively mean a drastic reduction in services, hours, and potentially, staff. Or, in the most dire scenario, the outright closure of the facility."

A collective gasp rippled through the hall. A few people murmured amongst themselves, their voices laced with disbelief and dismay. Marisol's hand instinctively went to her chest, her heart giving another heavy thud. Theo remained beside her, his jaw set, his gaze fixed on the mayor, a silent observer absorbing the unfolding drama.

"We understand the deep affection and reliance this community has on its library," Mayor Henderson continued, his voice softer now. "It has served us faithfully for over a century. It's a testament to our town's commitment to education, to culture, and to shared community spaces. But we must also face the fiscal realities. The town's budget is not unlimited, and we have other essential services that require funding."

He gestured towards a table laden with charts and graphs, the visual representation of the town's financial woes. "These figures paint a stark picture. We are facing a deficit that impacts all aspects of town services. The library, while a vital institution, has seen a decline in usage over the past few years, and its operational costs remain significant."

A woman from the front row, a familiar face from the Friends of the Library committee, stood up. Her voice, though trembling slightly, was firm. "Mayor Henderson, with all due respect, 'decline in usage' is not the story I see. I see our children discovering new worlds on those shelves. I see our seniors finding companionship in book clubs. I see students using the computers for homework because not everyone has reliable internet at home. Our library is a lifeline!"

Another voice, this one from a younger man who Marisol recognized as a recent transplant to Cedar Ridge, chimed in. "I moved here precisely because of the charm and community spirit. A strong library is a hallmark of a town that values its residents. Closing it would be a step backward, not forward."

The hall erupted into a chorus of voices, a cacophony of concern, protest, and impassioned pleas. It was clear that this was not a matter that would be easily dismissed or decided. The deep emotional connection the residents of Cedar Ridge had to their library was evident in every raised voice, every furrowed brow.

Theo watched the scene unfold with a quiet intensity. He saw the passion, the genuine distress, and the unwavering commitment of his neighbors. He understood the mayor's predicament, the difficult balancing act between fiscal responsibility and community well-being. But he also recognized the danger of making decisions based solely on spreadsheets, of failing to account for the immeasurable value that institutions like the library brought to a town.

He saw Marisol, her eyes alight with a fierce conviction, ready to speak, her passion for literature and community radiating from her. He knew she would articulate the intangible, the emotional core of what the library represented, in a way that numbers could never capture. He felt a stirring within him, a sense of shared purpose, even as his own nature inclined him towards a more measured, less vocal approach. He understood the importance of standing together, of voicing support for something that was intrinsically good, even if the path forward was uncertain.

As the discussion continued, it became clear that the immediate problem wasn't a lack of appreciation for the library, but a desperate need for creative solutions. People began to offer suggestions, some practical, others more idealistic. A retired accountant proposed a dedicated fundraising drive, complete with a detailed breakdown of how much each household could contribute annually. A local artist offered to organize a series of art auctions featuring local talent, with proceeds going to the library. The librarian herself, a kind woman named Eleanor who had dedicated thirty years of her life to the institution, stood up and spoke with quiet dignity about the essential services the library provided, services that often went unnoticed but were crucial for many residents.

"We offer computer access and training," she said, her voice clear and steady. "We provide a safe and supervised space for children after school. We host workshops on everything from resume writing to local history. We are not just a place for books; we are a hub for lifelong learning and community engagement."

Marisol waited for her moment, observing the ebb and flow of the debate. She saw the genuine efforts being made, the outpouring of support. But she also sensed a pervasive undercurrent of fear, a feeling that even with the best intentions, the financial reality might be insurmountable. When a lull fell over the room, she knew it was her turn. She took a deep breath, her gaze sweeping over the faces of her neighbors, her friends, her community.

"I know we're all looking at the numbers," she began, her voice strong and clear, carrying a resonance that commanded attention. "And I understand that budgets are real, and difficult decisions have to be made. But I think we're missing a crucial element in this equation – the heart of what the library represents." She paused, letting her words settle. "For me, and I suspect for many of you, the library is more than just a building filled with books. It's a sanctuary. It's a place where imagination takes flight, where knowledge is accessible to everyone, regardless of their background or their bank account. It's where we come to learn, to grow, to connect with stories that shape our understanding of the world and of ourselves."

She looked directly at Mayor Henderson. "When I was a child, feeling a bit lost and lonely, it was the library that became my refuge. It was there that I discovered worlds beyond Cedar Ridge, that I found characters who became my friends, that I learned that there was a vast universe of possibilities waiting to be explored. And it's not just me. I see it every day. I see the children discovering the joy of reading, the teenagers finding quiet study spaces, the adults seeking new skills or simply a peaceful place to escape the stresses of daily life. This isn't just about preserving a building; it's about preserving a vital piece of our community's soul."

She moved her gaze to Theo, who was watching her intently, a rare flicker of something akin to pride in his eyes. "We can't put a price on the impact the library has had on generations of Cedar Ridge residents. We can't quantify the inspiration it has sparked, the dreams it has nurtured, the connections it has fostered. To lose our library would be to lose a part of ourselves. It would be to diminish the very essence of what makes Cedar Ridge a special place to live."

She stepped away from the microphone, her voice filled with conviction. "We need to find a way. We need to be creative, to rally together, to show that this community values this institution enough to fight for it. I believe in the power of this town, in the collective will of its people. Let's not let fear or financial spreadsheets dictate the fate of something so precious."

A wave of applause followed her words, a spontaneous eruption of support that filled the hall with a renewed sense of hope. Theo watched her, a quiet admiration dawning in his expression. Her passion was infectious, her words resonating with a truth that transcended mere practicality. He understood her connection to the library, the way it had shaped her, and he knew that her voice was a powerful force for good in this community.

The meeting continued for another hour, the initial despair giving way to a more constructive energy. Ideas were tossed around, committees were formed, and a tentative plan began to emerge. There would be a series of fundraising events, starting with a town-wide yard sale organized by the Friends of the Library. There would be a petition circulated throughout the town, a public demonstration of support to present to the town council. And there would be a renewed effort to explore grant opportunities, with a dedicated team of volunteers tasked with researching and writing applications.

As the meeting began to wind down, a sense of cautious optimism settled over the room. The threat of closure hadn't vanished entirely, but it no longer felt like an insurmountable inevitability. Instead, it felt like a challenge, a call to action that had galvanized the community.

Theo found Marisol by the exit, her face alight with a mixture of exhaustion and exhilaration.

"You were amazing," he said, his voice low, cutting through the lingering murmur of departing townsfolk.

Marisol turned, a grateful smile gracing her lips. "We all were. It's easy to feel overwhelmed when you're facing something like this alone, but when you see everyone coming together… it makes you believe that anything is possible."

Theo nodded, a rare warmth softening his features. "You're right. It does." He hesitated for a moment, then reached out, his fingers brushing lightly against her arm. "You spoke for all of us tonight, Marisol. You put into words what many of us were feeling but couldn't articulate."

His touch sent a small, pleasant jolt through her. It was a simple gesture, but in the context of their recent unspoken tensions, it felt significant. It was a bridge, however tentative, across the silent divide that had begun to form between them.

"We'll need to keep this momentum going," she said, her gaze steady on his. "It's not just about one meeting. It's about sustained effort."

"I know," Theo replied, his eyes holding hers. "And I'm willing to help. Whatever you need."

The words, simple as they were, carried a weight that surprised Marisol. It was more than just a general offer of support; it was a commitment, a promise of tangible involvement. In the context of their recent dinner, it felt like a significant step, a sign that he was willing to engage, to invest.

As they stepped out into the cool night air, the stars beginning to pepper the inky sky above Cedar Ridge, Marisol felt a sense of hope that had been absent for weeks. The town hall meeting had been a stark reminder of the challenges they faced, both as a community and as individuals navigating their own complex relationships. But it had also been a powerful affirmation of their shared resilience, their capacity to come together and fight for what they believed in.

And in Theo's quiet offer of support, she saw a glimmer of that same resilience, a willingness to step forward and engage, even when his own reservations might have held him back. The future of the library was still uncertain, but for the first time in a long time, Marisol felt a surge of optimism, a belief that together, they could weather any storm. The fight for the library had begun, and in its own quiet way, it was also a fight for the heart of Cedar Ridge, and perhaps, for the heart of their own unfolding story.

The buzz in the community hall, though slightly diminished from its initial uproar, still hummed with a nervous energy. The proposal from the town council was on the table, stark and unyielding in its financial logic, but Marisol's words had planted seeds of a different kind of understanding. She'd stepped away from the microphone, her heart still thrumming with the adrenaline of her plea, and found herself momentarily caught in a current of approving nods and quiet murmurs of agreement. People who had been hesitant to voice their own feelings, perhaps intimidated by the weight of fiscal responsibility, now felt emboldened. Eleanor, the librarian, approached her, her eyes shining with a mixture of gratitude and renewed determination.

"That was beautifully said, Marisol," Eleanor whispered, her voice thick with emotion. "You captured what so many of us feel but struggle to express. It's not just about books; it's about the soul of this town."

Marisol offered a weak smile, feeling the weariness seep into her bones now that the immediate surge of emotion had passed. "I just... I couldn't stand by and let it happen. The library is too important. It's woven into the fabric of who we are here."

Theo materialized beside her, his presence a quiet anchor in the lingering disarray. He hadn't moved far from where she'd last seen him, his arms still crossed, but the intensity of his gaze had shifted. It was no longer merely observant; it held a new layer of contemplation, a recognition of the powerful sentiment Marisol had articulated. He didn't offer effusive praise, but his quiet nod, the subtle inclination of his head, spoke volumes. "You articulated it well," he said, his voice low, a deep resonance that seemed to cut through the residual noise. "The intangible value. It's not easily quantifiable, but it's undeniably there."

Marisol turned to him, a flicker of surprise at his direct acknowledgment. "Thank you, Theo. I know it's easy to get lost in the numbers, but some things... some things are worth more than their price tag." She looked around the hall, at the faces etched with concern, with a newfound sense of purpose. "This library... it's been a quiet witness to so many chapters of our lives. My childhood was filled with its hushed aisles, with the scent of old paper and the promise of adventure waiting on every shelf.

It was my escape, my sanctuary. I learned about courage from brave knights, about kindness from unlikely friends, about the vastness of the world from tales spun by far-off lands. It wasn't just about reading; it was about understanding. It was about seeing myself reflected in stories, about finding solace when things felt overwhelming."

She gestured vaguely towards the front of the hall, where the charts and graphs still lay on display, a stark reminder of the fiscal challenges. "And it wasn't just me. I see the children now, their faces alight with wonder during story time. I see the teenagers, hunched over textbooks, finding a quiet space to focus away from the distractions of home. I see the seniors, their eyes bright as they discuss the latest novel in their book club, finding connection and shared experience. This library is a living, breathing entity. It adapts, it evolves, it serves. It provides internet access for those who can't afford it, job-seeking resources for those in need, a safe haven for children after school. To close it would be to sever vital lifelines, to silence a chorus of voices that contribute to the symphony of Cedar Ridge."

She met Theo's gaze again, a silent acknowledgment of the unspoken history between them, the shared moments within those library walls that now felt even more poignant. "It's like... like preserving a cherished relationship," she continued, her voice softening, her words weaving a tapestry of emotion. "You don't let go of something precious just because it requires effort, or because there are moments of difficulty. You work through it. You find solutions. You invest in it because the connection, the shared history, the sheer joy it brings, is invaluable. Our library is that kind of relationship for Cedar Ridge. It's a legacy. It's a promise to future generations that knowledge and community will always be accessible, that the stories of our past will continue to inspire the dreams of our future."

The mayor, Mr. Henderson, who had been speaking with some of the council members, approached them, his expression still serious but tinged with a flicker of weary hope. "Marisol," he said, his voice low, "your words were... powerful. You gave voice to a sentiment that has been simmering beneath the surface all evening. We hear you. We understand the emotional connection. But the financial reality remains a formidable hurdle."

"I know," Marisol replied, her gaze unwavering. "And I'm not suggesting we ignore the numbers. But perhaps we need to look at those numbers differently. Perhaps we need to consider the return on investment not just in dollars, but in community well-being, in educational attainment, in civic engagement. The library is an investment, Mayor Henderson, not an expense. And it's an investment that pays dividends far beyond any spreadsheet." She turned back to Theo, a subtle invitation in her eyes, a silent question. He saw it, and a subtle shift occurred within him.

Her passion was undeniable, her conviction a force that had genuinely moved him. He understood the pragmatism of the council's position, the burden of fiscal responsibility. But Marisol had reminded him of something equally important: the human element, the intangible value that often got overlooked in the cold calculus of budgets.

He thought about his own relationship with the library, not as a child lost in stories, but as a young man seeking refuge from the complexities of his own life. The quiet corners, the vastness of knowledge at his fingertips – it had offered him a sense of order, a calm in the storm of his adolescent years. And he'd seen the quiet dedication of the librarians, their tireless efforts to curate not just books, but opportunities. He'd witnessed firsthand the impact of their outreach programs, the way they supported local business-es by providing resources, the way they fostered a sense of belonging for newcomers. Marisol's plea wasn't just about sentimentality; it was about the very soul of their town, a soul that was richer and more vibrant because of the library's presence.

"She's right," Theo said, his voice cutting through the low murmur of the receding crowd. His tone was measured, devoid of the emotional fire that Marisol possessed, but it carried the weight of reasoned conviction. "The immediate cost of maintaining the library might seem high, but the long-term cost of losing it would be far greater. We're talking about losing a critical resource for education, for personal development, for community cohesion. That's not something you can simply budget for in the short term. It's an erosion of the town's very foundation."

He looked at Mayor Henderson, his gaze steady. "There has to be a way to re-evaluate the budget, to find creative solutions. Perhaps a dedicated endowment fund, a stronger push for grants with tangible community benefits attached, or even a scaled-down but still functional model that prioritizes essential services."

Marisol felt a surge of warmth at Theo's words. It was a quiet endorsement, a powerful affirmation that resonated more deeply than any boisterous cheer. His willingness to engage, to lend his pragmatic mind to the emotional plea, felt like a significant step forward. It wasn't just about saving the library; it was about bridging the growing distance between them, about finding common ground in their shared love for Cedar Ridge.

The meeting began to break up then, the attendees dispersing with a renewed sense of purpose, a shared mission to tackle the impending crisis. Marisol lingered, watching Theo as he spoke quietly with Mr. Henderson, his brow furrowed in concentration, his hands gesturing as he outlined a point. It was a side of him she rarely saw, this engaged, proactive problem-solver, and it was undeniably attractive. Her speech had been a plea for preservation, for the enduring legacy of stories and connections.

It was a reflection of her own deep-seated belief that meaningful bonds, whether with people or with institutions, were worth fighting for, that they possessed a permanence that transcended fleeting challenges. And in Theo's unexpected advocacy, she saw a potential for a similar enduring connection, a relationship that, like the library, was worth investing in, worth nurturing, worth saving. The future of the library, and perhaps her own future, felt a little less uncertain, a little more hopeful, bathed in the soft glow of the community hall's fluorescent lights.

The buzz in the community hall began to settle, the initial storm of impassioned speeches and heartfelt pleas gradually subsiding into a more focused, yet still charged, atmosphere. Mayor Henderson, a man whose tie seemed perpetually loosened by the end of any town meeting, cleared his throat. "Alright, alright," he said, his voice carrying a weary authority. "Marisol, your words have certainly given us all a great deal to consider. And Theo," he glanced towards Theo, who stood a few feet away, his arms now uncrossed, his gaze fixed on the charts still displayed at the front of the hall, "your input is always valued, especially on matters of structure and... well, substance."

He gestured towards a series of rolled-up blueprints lying on a side table, guarded by a stern-faced council member named Agnes Periwinkle, whose pursed lips suggested she was already calculating the cost of every line drawn on those papers. "We've had preliminary architectural assessments done," Mayor Henderson continued, "looking at the current state of the library. It's an old building, as we all know. Solid, in its way, but showing its age. The roof needs significant work, the electrical system is... let's just say 'vintage,' and the foundation has some settling issues that need addressing before we even think about a full renovation."

Agnes unrolled one of the larger blueprints with a snap, the paper crackling loudly in the relative quiet. It depicted the current layout of the library, a familiar maze of shelves and reading nooks, but overlaid with red lines and annotations marking areas of concern. "Here," Agnes pointed with a sharp fingernail, her voice precise and unwavering. "The west wing foundation. We're seeing a sag of nearly three inches. And the wiring in the children's section... it's a fire hazard waiting to happen, frankly.

Replacing all of this, bringing it up to code, adding any modern amenities – improved accessibility, better insulation, perhaps even a small community meeting room – it's a substantial undertaking. The estimates we've received are... considerable." She let the numbers hang in the air, heavy and unwelcome.

A collective sigh rippled through the remaining attendees. The abstract fear of closure had, for many, been replaced by the concrete dread of exorbitant repair costs. Marisol watched Theo, her heart thumping a nervous rhythm against her ribs. She'd seen him study blueprints before, during his work on various construction projects around town, but this felt different. This was about more than just a building; it was about preserving a piece of their shared history, a place that held so many of their individual stories.

Theo approached the table, his movements deliberate. He didn't rush, but there was an undeniable pull drawing him in, a gravitational force emanating from the lines and measurements on the paper. He nodded to Agnes, a polite acknowledgement, and then his eyes scanned the annotations, his lips moving slightly as he read the technical jargon. He wasn't just looking; he was absorbing, analyzing, deconstructing the problem from a perspective no one else in the room possessed with quite the same depth.

He pointed to a section near the back, where the blueprint indicated a load-bearing wall. "This main support beam," he said, his voice a low rumble that immediately captured everyone's attention, cutting through Agnes's financial pronouncements. "It's original timber, isn't it? Cedar, by the looks of the grain. It's held up remarkably well, but it's been stressed by the shifting foundation, particularly in this corner. The sag isn't just cosmetic; it's a sign that the load distribution is compromised."

Agnes huffed, a sound like a deflating bellows. "We are aware of the structural integrity issues, Mr. Thorne. The architects have outlined them in detail. The cost of reinforcing and replacing compromised elements is precisely what we are discussing."

Theo ignored Agnes's thinly veiled impatience, his focus entirely on the blueprint. He traced a line with his index finger. "But the solution isn't simply to shore up what's there. This whole section needs to be re-evaluated. You're looking at underpinning the foundation for at least ten feet around this corner, carefully lifting the beam, and then installing a new, stronger support system. It's... extensive." He paused, a thoughtful frown creasing his brow. "And the wiring... Agnes, are these plans showing the original knob-and-tube installation in the west wing?"

"Of course, it's original," Agnes stated with an air of exasperated superiority. "As is most of the plumbing and the... the general ambiance of the building."

Theo's gaze shifted from the blueprint to the worn, yet still grand, façade of the community hall. He could picture the library as it stood, its sturdy brickwork and arched windows, a familiar landmark that had witnessed generations of Cedar Ridge residents pass through its doors. He remembered, with a sudden clarity, the late afternoons he'd spent there as a teenager, not reading, but simply existing in the quiet. He'd found a strange sense of peace in the hushed aisles, a refuge from the storm of his own adolescent anxieties.

The scent of aging paper, the soft scuff of shoes on the wooden floor, the gentle rustle of turning pages – it had been a symphony of calm. He'd watched Marisol there, a blur of motion and youthful exuberance, her face lit by the glow of a computer screen as she helped someone navigate the online catalog, or lost in the pages of a book, her brow furrowed in concentration. The library, for him, had been a place of quiet observation, a place where he could disappear without being noticed. But Marisol had always seemed so present within those walls, so connected to the very essence of the place.

"That original timber," Theo continued, his voice regaining a touch of its earlier warmth, "it's part of the building's character. It's not just a structural element; it's a piece of the town's history. To simply replace it with modern steel... it loses something. Something vital." He looked at Marisol, his gaze softening almost imperceptibly. He saw the flicker of hope in her eyes, the quiet plea that echoed in her earlier speech. He knew he wasn't just a carpenter who could fix a beam. He understood, in a way he hadn't before, the value of what Marisol was fighting for. It wasn't just about preserving a building; it was about preserving a feeling, a sense of continuity, a connection to the past that anchored them in the present and guided them toward the future.

"There are ways," Theo said, his voice gaining conviction, "to reinforce that beam, to incorporate it into a new support structure without sacrificing its integrity or its aesthetic. It would require careful bracing, custom metalwork to secure it, and... yes, significant labor. But it's possible. And it would be the right way to do it. To honor the original craftsmanship while ensuring the building's longevity." He traced another line on the blueprint. "And this electrical system... it's not just about replacing it. It's about upgrading it to meet modern needs. More outlets, better lighting, but also integrating new systems – better Wi-Fi infrastructure, perhaps even provisions for future technological advancements."

He looked around the room, his gaze sweeping over the faces of his neighbors. He saw the lingering doubt, the practical concerns, but also a dawning sense of possibility. "I can do that," he said, his voice steady and clear. "I can oversee the structural work, the reinforcement, the integration of the old with the new. I can source the materials, manage the team... I can ensure that the building is not just sound, but that it retains its soul." He met Marisol's gaze directly, a silent promise passing between them.

He knew his own history with commitment, with the fear of permanence. But looking at the library, at Marisol's unwavering belief in its importance, he felt a shift within himself. This wasn't about him; it was about Cedar Ridge. It was about building something that would last, something that would serve as a beacon for generations to come.

"I'm not an architect," Theo continued, acknowledging the expertise of the professionals who had drawn the plans. "But I understand how buildings come together. I understand the stresses, the strains, the subtle ways they communicate their needs. I've spent years building things that are meant to stand the test of time. And this library... this building deserves that kind of care. It deserves to be more than just a line item on a budget. It deserves to be a legacy."

He then looked directly at Mayor Henderson. "I'm willing to contribute my time, my expertise, my crew's labor, to the structural and renovation aspects of this project. Not for free, mind you," he added, a hint of his usual pragmatic realism returning, "but at a significantly reduced rate, structured as a community investment. We can work out the details, but I want to be involved in ensuring this building is not just saved, but truly restored. And, if we're going to do it right, we need to think long-term. This isn't a quick fix; it's an investment in the heart of our town."

The air in the hall seemed to crackle with a renewed energy. Theo's offer was unexpected, a bold statement of commitment from a man known for his guarded nature. It wasn't just about saving money; it was about investing his skill, his passion, his very essence into the preservation of a community cornerstone. Marisol felt a warmth spread through her, a quiet triumph that had nothing to do with the applause that was starting to swell around them. Theo wasn't just acknowledging the library's importance; he was actively choosing to be a part of its future.

Mayor Henderson, his initial weariness momentarily forgotten, looked at Theo with a mixture of surprise and genuine appreciation. "Theo," he said, his voice imbued with a new kind of hope, "that's... that's a remarkable offer. A truly remarkable offer. It speaks volumes about your commitment to Cedar Ridge."

Agnes, though still clutching the blueprints with proprietary fierceness, seemed momentarily taken aback. The sheer practicality and expertise of Theo's pronouncements had a way of cutting through her budget-driven anxieties. "It would certainly help to offset some of the labor costs," she conceded, her tone still reserved, but with a faint hint of reluctant admiration. "But the material costs, the engineering assessments, the permitting... those remain significant."

"And we will address those," Marisol interjected, stepping forward again, her voice imbued with the same passion that had ignited the hall earlier. "Theo's contribution changes the equation. It makes a full renovation not just a pipe dream, but a tangible possibility. We can launch a dedicated fundraising campaign, focus on grants that specifically support historical preservation and community infrastructure. We can ask for material donations from local suppliers.

This isn't just about cutting costs; it's about pooling our resources, our talents, our collective will." She looked at Theo, a grateful smile gracing her lips. His contribution was more than just practical; it was a gesture of profound connection. He was offering not just his carpentry skills, but a piece of himself, a willingness to invest in something permanent, something that would outlast fleeting fears and personal reservations.

Theo met her smile, a subtle nod of acknowledgement. He understood the unspoken message. He was stepping out of the shadows of his own past, embracing the possibility of a shared future, not just with Marisol, but with the town of Cedar Ridge itself. The library, with its worn shelves and echoing halls, had always represented a kind of permanence, a steadfast presence in a world of flux. And now, he was actively choosing to be a part of that permanence, to lend his strength and skill to ensure its continued existence.

It was a profound shift, a quiet declaration that he was ready to build something more than just houses and furniture; he was ready to build a legacy. The event horizon of the library's potential closure was still a daunting prospect, but now, bathed in the warm glow of Theo's unexpected contribution, a pathway forward, however challenging, had begun to illuminate. The blueprints, once symbols of daunting expense, now represented a canvas of possibility, a testament to the enduring power of community and the quiet strength of shared purpose.

The community hall buzzed with a different kind of energy now. It was no longer the frantic hum of desperation or the sharp sting of disagreement, but a deeper, more resonant vibration—the palpable thrum of a town collectively holding its breath, teetering on the precipice of a significant decision. The library, that steadfast sentinel of knowledge and memory, stood at a crossroads, and with it, Cedar Ridge itself. Marisol felt it in her bones, a subtle shift in the air, a collective leaning forward, as if the very act of shared deliberation was shaping the future.

Mayor Henderson, his usual weariness momentarily banished by the un-expected turn of events, stood by the table, his gaze sweeping over the faces in the room. Agnes Periwinkle, while still a picture of fiscal prudence, had unclasped her hands, a sign of grudging acknowledgement, if not outright agreement.

Theo's offer had been more than just a practical solution to a complex renovation; it was a profound act of faith, a public declaration of com-mitment from a man not known for such displays. It had been the spark that ignited a new kind of hope, transforming the daunting mountain of repair costs into a navigable slope. Marisol watched him, a silent observer in the midst of the nascent murmurs of agreement and the thoughtful questions that now arose. He stood a little straighter, his usual guarded posture softened by an almost imperceptible sense of purpose. He had stepped out of the realm of individual projects and into the shared space of community building, and the weight of that choice seemed to settle on him not as a burden, but as an anchor.

"So," Mayor Henderson began, his voice finding a new clarity, "Theo's proposition changes things. Significantly. We're not just talking about patching up a building anymore; we're talking about a restoration. A true commitment to preserving its character, its history, while making it functional for the next century." He gestured towards the blueprints Agnes still guarded, but now they seemed less like a ledger of expenses and more like a roadmap. "Agnes, from a purely financial perspective, Theo's willingness to contribute his crew's labor and his own expertise at a reduced rate is... immense. It brings the projected costs down considerably, making other avenues, like grant applications and focused fundraising, far more viable."

Agnes nodded slowly, her sharp eyes still scrutinizing the numbers she held in her mind. "It does indeed, Mayor. It alleviates a substantial portion of the labor overhead. However, the material costs, specialized engineering consultations, permits, and contingency funds remain significant. We are still looking at a figure that will require a substantial town effort." She paused, her gaze flicking to Theo, a flicker of something akin to respect crossing her stern features. "But it is, as you say, a game-changer. It makes the 'impossible' a little more... within reach."

A ripple of quiet discussion spread through the room. The initial shock of Theo's offer had settled, and now, the practical implications began to take root. People looked at each other, not with the usual suspicion or individual agendas that sometimes surfaced at town meetings, but with a shared sense of possibility. They saw the library not just as a building that was falling into disrepair, but as a symbol of their collective identity, a vessel that held the stories of their lives, from childhood learning to quiet contemplation, from town meetings to cherished local history archives.

Marisol felt a surge of emotion, a profound gratitude for Theo, for the town, for this unexpected convergence. Her fight for the library had felt like a solitary battle, a lone voice crying in the wilderness of budget cuts and practical concerns. But Theo's intervention had amplified her voice, given it substance, and, more importantly, had brought others into the chorus. She saw Mrs. Gable, a lifelong resident whose memory stretched back to the library's very construction, her eyes glistening. She saw young Liam, who had spent countless hours there devouring fantasy novels, his face alight with the promise of continued access. She saw Mr. Henderson, the retired history teacher, nodding thoughtfully, perhaps already envisioning the revitalized archives.

"This is our chance," Marisol said, her voice clear and steady, cutting through the growing hum of conversation. "Theo's offer has opened a door. Now, it's up to us to walk through it. This isn't just about saving the library from closure; it's about reaffirming what Cedar Ridge stands for. We are a town that values its past, that invests in its future, and that believes in the power of shared spaces. The library is more than just books; it's a community hub, a place where connections are forged, where knowledge is shared, and where memories are made. Letting it crumble would be a disservice not only to ourselves but to the generations to come."

She looked at Theo, a silent acknowledgment of his pivotal role. His willingness to put his skills, his reputation, and his time on the line was a testament to a deeper change within him, a willingness to invest in something beyond himself, something that would endure. It was a brave step, especially for someone who had always seemed to guard his heart so carefully. And in that moment, Marisol felt a new layer of connection forming between them, a bond forged not just in shared glances and whispered conversations, but in the shared endeavor of building something meaningful.

"We can do this," she continued, her gaze sweeping across the room, meeting as many eyes as she could. "We can launch a comprehensive fundraising campaign. We can apply for historical preservation grants. We can reach out to local businesses for material sponsorships. We can organize volunteer workdays for the less structurally intensive tasks. Every contribution, no matter how small, will matter. This is Cedar Ridge's library. And it deserves to be saved, not just maintained, but revitalized. It deserves to be a vibrant heart of our community for years to come."

Mayor Henderson listened intently, his hand resting on the table. "Marisol's right," he said, his voice firm. "This is a pivotal moment. We have the opportunity to come together and achieve something significant. Theo's offer is a remarkable act of generosity, and it's our responsibility, as a community, to rise to the occasion. Agnes, can you work with Theo and the architectural team to refine the updated cost estimates, factoring in his contribution? We need a clear, actionable plan."

Agnes, with a sigh that held a surprising undertone of resolve, nodded. "I will begin that process immediately, Mayor. We'll need a detailed breakdown of Mr. Thorne's proposed contributions and how they integrate with the overall project scope."

Theo, who had been listening intently, stepped forward. "I'm happy to work with Agnes and the architects. I have a good sense of the material requirements for the structural work, and I can provide estimates for the labor hours my team will contribute. We can also explore sourcing reclaimed materials where appropriate, to further enhance the historical integrity and potentially reduce costs." His voice was calm and measured, a stark contrast to the emotional undercurrents that still flowed through the room. He was practical, grounded, but his words carried the weight of a deeper commitment.

As the meeting began to shift into smaller, more focused discussions, Marisol found herself beside Theo, a comfortable silence settling between them. The blueprints, once a symbol of overwhelming expense and potential loss, now felt like a blueprint for their shared future, for the future of Cedar Ridge.

"You really mean it, don't you?" Marisol asked, her voice barely a whisper, her gaze fixed on the intricate lines of the architectural drawings. "You're willing to put that much of yourself into this."

Theo turned to her, his expression unreadable for a moment before a small, genuine smile touched his lips. "It's not just about the building, Marisol," he said, his voice low. "It's about what it represents. And... it's about recognizing that some things are worth fighting for. Worth building. And worth... staying for."

The last phrase hung in the air, a quiet revelation. For Theo, who had always seemed to be on the verge of leaving, to suggest "staying" was a profound declaration. The library, with its enduring presence, its tangible history, was offering him, and the entire town, a chance to define what it meant to be rooted, to be committed.

"I know you've always been... a builder, Theo," Marisol continued, her voice catching slightly. "But this feels different. This is building something that lasts, something that connects people. Something that's more than just wood and nails."

"It is," Theo agreed, his gaze meeting hers, and for the first time, Marisol saw a vulnerability in his eyes that mirrored her own. "It's about legacy. About what we leave behind. And I think... I think this library deserves a good one. And maybe," he added, a trace of his usual wry humor returning, "maybe Cedar Ridge deserves one too. One that we build together."

The prospect of a full renovation, once a distant dream overshadowed by financial realities, now shimmered with the possibility of becoming a tangible reality. The library's event horizon was still a point of concern, the potential for closure a lingering shadow, but now, illuminated by Theo's unwavering commitment and the collective will of Cedar Ridge, a clear and hopeful path forward had emerged. The blueprints, meticulously detailed and once daunting, now represented a canvas of shared purpose, a testament to the enduring power of community and the quiet, yet profound, strength that arises when individuals choose to invest in something larger than themselves.

The fate of the library had become inextricably linked with their own, a shared challenge that was forcing introspection about what truly mattered, about the legacies they wished to build, and the enduring commitment they were willing to make to the heart of their town. The unity, though still a work in progress, was undeniable, a testament to Cedar Ridge's resilience and its capacity to rally around the values that defined it. The library, in its quiet way, was becoming a crucible, forging stronger bonds and illuminating the path ahead for both the town and for Marisol and Theo.

The air in the community hall, once thick with the tension of impending closure and the sharp edges of financial worry, had begun to soften. It was a subtle shift, like the gentle warming of the earth after a long frost, a thawing of anxieties replaced by the nascent bloom of possibility. Marisol felt it not just in the hushed conversations and the thoughtful nods exchanged across the room, but deep within her own chest, a resonance that echoed Theo's unexpected declaration. His offer to lead the renovation, to lend his expertise and his team's labor, wasn't just a financial lifeline for the library; it was a profound gesture that spoke volumes about a man she was only beginning to understand.

She watched him now, standing slightly apart from the clusters of people, his usual guarded demeanor softened by an almost imperceptible glow. It was the quiet satisfaction of purpose, a man who had found a solid footing in a cause larger than himself. This wasn't the transient nature of his past projects, the quick builds and swift departures; this was an investment, a tangible commitment to Cedar Ridge, to its history, and to its future. For Marisol, who had poured so much of herself into the fight to save the library, his involvement was a beacon, a confirmation that the battle wasn't solitary. It was a shared endeavor, an anchor in the sometimes-turbulent waters of community life.

Theo's engagement with the library's renovation was more than just a practical solution to a daunting problem; it was an offering, a silent acknowledgment that Cedar Ridge, and perhaps the people within it, held a value that transcended his carefully constructed walls of self-preservation. Marisol had seen glimpses of his inherent kindness, his quiet generosity that he tried so hard to keep hidden beneath a veneer of gruff independence. But this, this was different. This was a public declaration, a willingness to be seen, to be invested, in something that would endure long after the final nail was hammered and the last coat of paint had dried. It was a brave step for a man who had always seemed to tread so lightly, so carefully, as if afraid of leaving too deep a footprint.

As the discussions continued, coalescing into practical next steps, Marisol found herself drawn to Theo's side. The blueprints, once a symbol of overwhelming despair, now seemed to represent a shared canvas, a roadmap not just for restoring a building, but for building a future, together. The weight of his commitment, the sheer scope of what he was undertaking, was palpable. He was not just donating his time and skill; he was donating a piece of himself, his reputation, his belief in the value of shared spaces.

"You really mean it, don't you?" Marisol asked, her voice barely a whisper, her gaze tracing the intricate lines of the architectural drawings spread across the table. The questions that had swirled in her mind for weeks – about his intentions, his fears, his capacity for permanence – seemed to coalesce into this one simple, heartfelt inquiry. She looked at him, her eyes searching for an answer beyond the words. "You're willing to put that much of yourself into this."

Theo turned to her, and for a fleeting moment, a flicker of vulnerability softened his features, a glimpse into the guarded depths she had only occasionally touched. Then, a slow, genuine smile curved his lips, a smile that reached his eyes and chased away the shadows. "It's not just about the building, Marisol," he said, his voice low, carrying a quiet sincerity that resonated with her own passion. "It's about what it represents. And... it's about recognizing that some things are worth fighting for. Worth building. And worth... staying for."

The last phrase hung in the air between them, a delicate, almost fragile offering. For Theo, a man who had always seemed poised for departure, whose presence in Cedar Ridge had felt both solid and yet somehow temporary, the word "staying" was a profound revelation. It spoke of a burgeoning connection to the town, a willingness to put down roots, to become a part of the fabric of its ongoing story. The library, in its steadfast and enduring presence, its tangible history etched into its very walls, was offering him, and the entire town, a chance to define what it truly meant to be rooted, to be committed.

Marisol's heart gave a small, hopeful leap. She had always known Theo was a builder, his hands skilled, his mind adept at envisioning and creating. But this project, this commitment to the library, felt different. It was about building something that would outlast him, something that would connect generations, something that was imbued with the spirit of community, not just the strength of wood and nails. "I know you've always been... a builder, Theo," she continued, her voice catching slightly, a testament to the emotion that surged within her. "But this feels different. This is building something that lasts, something that connects people. Something that's more than just wood and nails."

"It is," Theo agreed, his gaze meeting hers, and in that shared look, Marisol saw a reflection of her own deep-seated hope, a shared understanding of the profound significance of their collective endeavor. "It's about legacy. About what we leave behind. And I think... I think this library deserves a good one. And maybe," he added, a hint of his characteristic wry humor returning, a familiar comfort in its presence, "maybe Cedar Ridge deserves one too. One that we build together."

The notion of building a shared legacy, of investing in the enduring spirit of Cedar Ridge, settled over Marisol like a warm embrace. It was a prospect that transcended the immediate crisis of the library's potential closure. It was about weaving their own stories into the larger tapestry of the town, about becoming active participants in its ongoing narrative. Theo's willingness to embrace this communal responsibility chipped away at the fear of permanence that had always seemed to keep him at arm's length.

He was discovering that investing in something lasting, something that would benefit many, could be a source of strength, not just a potential vulnerability. The shared concern for the library, this quiet, powerful force, had indeed become a bridge between them, a foundation upon which something deeper and more meaningful could be built.

As the meeting dispersed into smaller, more focused conversations, Marisol and Theo remained by the table, a comfortable silence settling between them. The blueprints, once a daunting symbol of an insurmountable challenge, now represented a tangible vision of hope, a shared commitment etched in ink and paper. The library's event horizon, the point of no return that had loomed so ominously, was now receding, replaced by the radiant glow of a revitalized future. The town, spurred by Theo's unexpected generosity and Marisol's unwavering advocacy, was stepping forward, united by a common purpose.

Theo's contribution was more than just a financial infusion; it was a powerful statement of intent, a quiet but resounding affirmation of his growing connection to Cedar Ridge. Marisol felt a renewed sense of optimism, not just for the library, but for what this shared endeavor might signify for her own burgeoning relationship with Theo. He was no longer just the enigmatic builder who had arrived in town; he was becoming an integral part of its story, a man willing to invest his skills, his time, and his heart in its preservation.

The library, in its own quiet way, was becoming a crucible, forging stronger bonds not only within the community but between two individuals who were slowly, tentatively, finding their way towards each other. The act of saving the library was becoming an act of building something far more enduring: a shared sense of purpose, a commitment to a legacy, and perhaps, a future together.

The initial shock of Theo's offer had given way to a determined momentum. The practicalities of fundraising, grant applications, and volunteer coordination began to take shape, each element a testament to the town's collective will. Marisol, observing the flurry of activity, felt a profound sense of gratitude for the way Theo's singular act of generosity had galvanized the entire community. It was as if his willingness to commit had given everyone permission to believe, to invest, and to participate.

She found herself drawn to the library, no longer with the heavy heart of impending loss, but with a growing sense of anticipation. The dusty shelves, the worn carpets, the faint scent of old paper and beeswax – these were not signs of decay, but whispers of history, of countless lives touched by the quiet magic within these walls. She imagined Theo's crew here, their sturdy hands and focused minds at work, carefully restoring the grandeur of the original architecture, breathing new life into the beloved old building. She envisioned him overseeing the process, his keen eyes assessing each detail, his commitment to quality evident in every decision.

Later that week, as Marisol walked through the nearly empty library, the silence amplified the echo of her own footsteps. She ran her hand along the smooth, cool surface of a mahogany table, a silent testament to craftsmanship and durability. It was in moments like these, surrounded by the tangible history of Cedar Ridge, that she felt most connected to its soul.

And it was in these moments, too, that she thought of Theo, of his quiet strength, his unexpected depth.

She remembered his words from the town meeting, "It's about what it represents... and... worth staying for." The simplicity and sincerity of his statement had resonated deeply. It wasn't just about a building; it was about belonging, about investing in something that offered a sense of permanence, a connection to a place and its people. For Theo, who had always seemed to carry an invisible suitcase, ready to depart at a moment's notice, this project was a significant step towards finding that sense of belonging. He was choosing to build, not just structures, but a connection, a commitment.

As if summoned by her thoughts, a familiar figure appeared in the doorway, silhouetted against the late afternoon sun. Theo. He paused, taking in the scene, his gaze sweeping over the rows of books, the quiet dignity of the space. When his eyes met Marisol's, there was a soft warmth there, a recognition of the shared purpose that now bound them.

"Thinking about the future?" he asked, his voice a low rumble that seemed to fit the quiet sanctity of the library.

Marisol smiled, a genuine, heartfelt smile. "Something like that. Just... imagining it. Imagining it full of life again. And imagining you... here, making it happen."

He walked towards her, his gait steady, his presence filling the space with a quiet confidence. He stopped beside her, their shoulders almost brushing, and for a moment, they simply stood together, absorbing the atmosphere of the library.

"It's going to be a lot of work," he said, his gaze distant, as if already seeing the scaffolding, the dust, the transformation. "More than just the physical labor. It's about honoring the history, about making sure we preserve its character while making it functional for the next generation."

"I know," Marisol replied softly. "But you're the one to do it. You have that vision. And you have... a commitment to it now." She hesitated, then added, "I've seen it."

Theo turned to her, his eyes holding hers. There was a quiet intensity in his gaze, a willingness to be vulnerable that Marisol found herself increasingly drawn to. "You've seen me build things before, Marisol. Small towns, big cities. But this feels... different. This is about building something that matters beyond the bottom line. Something that will be here for a long time." He paused, a thoughtful expression on his face. "It's like... a point of no return, in a good way. You step over that threshold, and you can't go back to who you were before."

Marisol understood. The library, a place that had always been a cornerstone of Cedar Ridge, was now serving as a catalyst for personal transformation. For Theo, it was an opportunity to shed the fear of permanence, to embrace the idea that commitment could be a source of strength, not a liability. He was stepping over his own personal event horizon, moving from a life of transience to one of enduring connection.

"And what do you see on the other side of that threshold, Theo?" she asked, her voice barely a whisper, her heart beating a little faster.

He looked at her, his expression open, unguarded. "I see... a community that's stronger. A place that's worth investing in. And... I see the possibility of finding my own place here, too. A place where I belong." He reached out, his fingers gently brushing a stray strand of hair from her cheek. The touch was light, tentative, yet it sent a jolt of warmth through her. "I think... I think this library is giving me that. It's showing me that building something for the long haul, something that connects people, can be the most rewarding construction of all."

In that quiet moment, surrounded by the silent stories of Cedar Ridge, Marisol felt a profound sense of hope bloom within her. Theo's journey towards permanence, his embrace of community, was mirroring her own journey of finding her voice and her purpose. The library, once a symbol of what they stood to lose, was now a testament to what they could gain, together. The shared endeavor had woven a thread between them, a quiet understanding that promised a future as rich and enduring as the stories held within the library's walls. The event horizon was no longer a point of dread, but a radiant dawn, illuminating a path forward for Cedar Ridge, and for them.

Chapter Six: Declarations and Doubts

The lingering buzz from the community hall meeting still hummed in the air, a vibrant counterpoint to the quietude of Marisol's living room. Outside, the twilight deepened, painting Cedar Ridge in hues of lavender and charcoal. Inside, the lamplight cast a warm, honeyed glow, softening the edges of the antique furniture and creating an intimate haven. Theo sat across from her, a mug of tea cradled in his hands, the familiar lines of his face relaxed in a way Marisol rarely saw outside of these hushed, private moments. The shared victory, the palpable shift in the town's collective spirit, had undeniably cracked open a door between them, allowing a gentler, more open conversation to flow.

Marisol took a slow sip of her own tea, the warmth spreading through her. She had spent the drive home replaying Theo's words, his quiet declaration of commitment to the library echoing in her mind. It wasn't just his expertise or his resources; it was the underlying sentiment, the suggestion that Cedar Ridge, and perhaps she herself, had become something worth building for. The thought had settled in her chest, a quiet, persistent warmth. But as with all things between them, a sliver of doubt, a residue of past hurts, always lingered.

"It was... incredible, wasn't it?" Marisol began, her voice soft, carefully gauging the atmosphere. "Seeing everyone come together like that. Your offer... Theo, it really changed everything." She watched him, searching for a flicker of recognition, a confirmation that he understood the magnitude of his gesture, not just for the library, but for them.

Theo's gaze met hers, and he offered a small, almost shy smile. "It was good to see," he admitted, his voice a low murmur. "I didn't expect... that kind of response. It felt like the right thing to do."

"The right thing," Marisol echoed, letting the words settle. The phrase felt loaded with unspoken meaning. For Theo, who had always projected an image of detached pragmatism, 'the right thing' seemed to carry a weight that went beyond mere civic duty. It hinted at a deeper connection, a nascent sense of belonging. "It was more than just the right thing, Theo. It was... brave. And it was generous. And it meant a lot to me."

She let that hang in the air for a moment, the unspoken 'you' at the end of that sentence a palpable presence. She didn't want to demand anything, not after months of carefully navigating the minefield of his guarded nature. But she craved honesty, a clarity that extended beyond the immediate, tangible goal of saving the library.

"When you said that thing about... about 'staying'," Marisol continued, her fingers tracing the rim of her mug. "That really struck me. I've always felt like you were... on the verge of leaving. Like Cedar Ridge was just a temporary stop for you. And maybe, you know, I was too." She offered a faint, self-deprecating smile, hoping he wouldn't take it as an accusation. "It's just... the way you are. Building things, and then moving on. It's what you do."

Theo stirred, shifting in his seat. The lamplight caught the subtle tension in his shoulders, a familiar reflex. But he didn't pull away, didn't retreat. Instead, he leaned forward, his gaze steady. "I know what I project, Marisol.

And maybe, for a long time, that's all I was. Someone who moved on." He paused, choosing his words with care. "But Cedar Ridge... and you... you've made me stop and think about what 'moving on' actually means. And what I might be leaving behind if I do."

This was it. The opening she had been waiting for, a direct acknowledgment of the uncertainty that had shadowed their tentative connection. "And what do you think about that?" she asked, her voice barely a whisper. "About leaving things behind? About... about staying?"

The silence that followed wasn't awkward; it was charged with anticipation. Theo's eyes, usually so difficult to read, seemed to soften, revealing a vulnerability that sent a tremor through her. "I think," he said, his voice low and resonant, "that for the first time in a long time, the idea of staying doesn't feel like a trap. It feels like... a choice. A good choice." He took a deep breath. "And the library... seeing how much it means to this town, how much it means to you... it's made that choice feel more real. More solid."

Marisol's heart fluttered. He was speaking her language, the language of tangible commitments, of building something that endures. "I want that, Theo," she said, her voice thick with emotion. "I want this... us... to feel as solid as that library is going to be. I want it to be something people can see, can rely on. Not just a whispered possibility. Not just a quiet feeling between us."

She looked at him, her gaze unwavering. "I need... I want more than just stolen moments and hesitant glances. I want... I want us to be a visible thing, Theo. Like the library. Something that's part of the fabric of this town. Something that's not afraid to be seen."

Theo met her gaze, and in his eyes, she saw a reflection of her own yearning. The shadows of his past, the wounds that had made him so fiercely self-protective, seemed to recede, pushed back by the gentle light of the present. "You're asking me to be visible," he stated, not a question, but an observation.

"Yes," Marisol confirmed, her voice firm but gentle. "I am. And I know that's hard for you. I know you've been hurt, and I know you've built walls for a reason. But those walls... they keep out the bad, yes, but they keep out the good too. And I want to be good, Theo. I want to be a good thing for you. A good thing for us."

He reached out, his hand covering hers on the table. His touch was firm, grounding. "You are good, Marisol," he said, his voice rough with emotion. "You're more than good. You're... resilient. And you're kind. And you see things in me that I try my best to hide." He squeezed her hand. "Asking me to be visible... it's not a demand, is it? It's a hope."

Tears pricked at Marisol's eyes. "It is," she whispered. "It's a deep, deep hope. I don't want to feel like I'm waiting for you to leave. I want to feel like we're building something together, something that has roots, something that can withstand storms. Like the library."

"The library," Theo mused, his thumb gently stroking the back of her hand. "It's a good metaphor, isn't it? Strong foundations. Walls that have seen generations. A roof that protects." He looked at her, his expression open and earnest. "I want that for us, Marisol. I want to build that. And I want to be seen building it with you."

The honesty in his words was breathtaking. It was a confession, a promise, all wrapped into one. Marisol leaned forward, her heart swelling with a mixture of relief and a fierce, burgeoning joy. "And I want to be seen with you," she said, her voice trembling slightly. "I want to stand beside you, not in the shadows. I want our story to be as clear and as strong as the renovated library will be. No more hiding, Theo. No more pretending that this is just... convenient."

He brought her hand to his lips, his gaze never leaving hers. The gesture was tender, reverent. "It's never been just convenient, Marisol," he said, his voice husky. "Even when I tried to tell myself it was." He paused, a flicker of that familiar self-doubt crossing his features before being replaced by a resolute determination. "The library needs a strong foundation. And I think... I think we do too. A foundation of honesty. Of visibility."

"And of trust," Marisol added softly. "Trust that we're both in this, for the long haul. That we're not going to disappear when things get difficult, or when the shine wears off."

"The shine on a library doesn't wear off," Theo countered, a gentle smile touching his lips. "It only deepens. It becomes richer with history, with stories." He cupped her face, his thumbs brushing away a stray tear. "And that's what I want for us. A richness that comes from sharing the quiet moments, the difficult ones, and the triumphs. I want our story to be one that can be read, not whispered."

Marisol closed her eyes for a moment, savoring the feel of his touch, the sincerity in his words. The fear that had been her constant companion, the fear of loving someone who might leave, felt significantly diminished. The shared purpose of the library had been the catalyst, but their willingness to be open, to be vulnerable, was the true mortar that was binding them together.

"So," she began, opening her eyes to find him watching her with an intensity that made her breath catch, "what happens now? Now that we've declared our intentions, both to the town and... to each other?"

Theo's smile deepened, a genuine, radiant thing that reached his eyes. "Now," he said, his voice filled with a quiet certainty, "we build. We build the library, stone by stone, beam by beam. And we build our story. Openly. Honestly. Together." He leaned in, his lips meeting hers in a kiss that was both tender and profound. It wasn't a kiss of conquest or fleeting passion, but a kiss of commitment, a silent promise of a future built on shared purpose and unwavering visibility.

In that embrace, bathed in the warm glow of the lamplight, Marisol felt the last vestiges of doubt dissolve, replaced by a quiet confidence, a certainty that they were, finally, building something that would last. The shadows of their past had not vanished entirely, but they were no longer defining their present. They were simply part of the backdrop, the textured history against which their visible, enduring love story would unfold.

Marisol drew a slow, steadying breath, the echo of Theo's words still resonating in the quiet room. His affirmation, the gentle admission that 'staying' no longer felt like a trap, had been a revelation, a balm to a part of her that had long ached with uncertainty. But now, with the shared victory of the library meeting still a warm ember between them, a new thought had taken root, a gentle insistence that she needed to articulate. It wasn't about controlling Theo, or forcing his hand. It was about defining what their 'together' could, and should, look like.

"Theo," she began, her voice soft but carrying a new resonance, a quiet strength that had been building within her. She met his gaze, the lamplight catching the earnestness in her eyes. "When I talk about wanting this... wanting us... to be visible, to be solid like the library, I don't mean it as a way to tie you down. Not at all." She paused, choosing her words with care, acutely aware of his past wounds, the invisible barriers he'd erected. "For me, it's about creating a sense of shared permanence. It's about building something tangible, something that we can both look at and know that it's real, that it's ours, and that it's here."

She gestured vaguely around the cozy living room, then towards the window, as if encompassing the whole of Cedar Ridge. "Think about the library. Its value isn't just in the books on its shelves, or the programs it offers. It's in the fact that it's always been here. It's a landmark, a constant.

People know where to find it. They know it's a part of their lives, of this town's story. And that permanence, that deep-seated knowing, it provides a kind of security, doesn't it? A peace of mind."

Marisol leaned forward slightly, her hands clasped in her lap. "That's what I'm reaching for, Theo. Not a cage, but a cornerstone. I want us to be a cornerstone in each other's lives, and in this community. I want our relationship to be a place where we both feel safe, where we know we're not going to be uprooted by the next passing breeze or the next big opportunity that might pull you away." She offered a small, wry smile. "I know that's a fear you've lived with for a long time, the fear of being tied down. And I've certainly felt that in the past, like I was always waiting for the other shoe to drop, for the inevitable departure."

She met his eyes again, her gaze unwavering. "But what I'm saying now is that I want to choose to put down roots. I want to choose this life, with you, in this town. And I want that choice to be reflected in something solid, something that isn't just a feeling in our hearts, but something that's visible, acknowledged, and secure. Like the library's new wing. It's not just a concept anymore; it's a structure that will stand for generations. It's a testament to what we can build when we invest our time, our energy, and our belief in something."

Theo listened intently, his expression thoughtful. He hadn't pulled away, hadn't retreated into his usual guarded silence. Instead, he seemed to be absorbing her words, his brow furrowed slightly in concentration. This was good. This was progress.

"So, when I say I want us to be visible," Marisol continued, her voice gaining a little more conviction, "it's not about putting on a show for the town. It's about us having a shared space, a shared future, that we both feel completely comfortable and confident in. It's about being able to say, without hesitation, 'this is my life, and this is who I share it with.' It's about the comfort that comes from knowing that this connection isn't transient, that it's built on a foundation of mutual choice and a commitment to the future. It's about feeling anchored."

She traced the pattern on her teacup with her fingertip. "I understand that for you, 'permanence' might have always felt like a burden, something that restricts or confines. But for me, it's the opposite. It's a source of strength. It's the quiet assurance that even when things get tough, and they will get tough, we have something solid to hold onto. We have a shared history we're building, and a shared future we're working towards. It's the difference between a fleeting spark and a steady flame."

Marisol looked at Theo, her heart aching with the sincerity of her own need. "I don't want to spend another day feeling like I'm living in the prologue of a story that might never get fully written. I want us to be in the middle chapters, actively living, actively building. And that requires a certain level of visibility, of commitment, that goes beyond hushed conversations and stolen moments. It's about creating a life together that's as robust and as enduring as the library you're helping to rebuild. A place that people can point to and say, 'Look at what they've built. Look at what they have.' Not out of nosiness, but out of a shared appreciation for what it means to create something lasting."

She took another sip of her tea, letting the warmth settle her nerves. "It's about the peace of mind that comes from knowing that we are choosing each other, consistently, every single day. That we are not just passengers on a journey, but architects of our own shared destination. The library, in its own way, is a symbol of that. It's a commitment to the intellectual and cultural heart of this town, a commitment that will serve generations to come. And I want that same kind of enduring commitment for us. A commitment that says, 'We are here. We are choosing to be here. Together.'"

The idea of permanence, Marisol realized, wasn't about being possessive. It was about creating a shared sanctuary, a space where vulnerability was not a risk, but a foundation. It was about a conscious decision, made with open eyes and open hearts, to weave their lives together into something more substantial than fleeting feelings. It was about creating a narrative that was not defined by what might be lost, but by what was being actively, joyfully, and visibly created.

"I've spent so long guarding my heart," she admitted, her voice dropping to a softer register, more personal now. "I've learned to be independent, to rely only on myself. And there's a strength in that, I know. But it can also be a lonely strength. And what I'm discovering with you, Theo, is that there's a different kind of strength to be found in choosing to be vulnerable with someone, in choosing to build something with them. And that choice needs to be visible, not just to us, but to ourselves, so we can see the tangible proof of our commitment."

She met his gaze, her expression open and hopeful. "I want to be able to say, with absolute certainty, that I'm building a life here. A life that includes you, deeply and unequivocally. And for that to feel truly secure, truly real to me, it needs to be more than just a promise whispered in the dark. It needs to be a structure, solid and visible, like the library. A testament to our shared journey, a beacon of our chosen permanence in Cedar Ridge." The words hung in the air, a heartfelt articulation of her deepest desires, a plea for a future built not on fleeting moments, but on enduring foundations.

Theo's gaze had remained fixed on Marisol, even as she spoke. He'd absorbed her words, each carefully chosen phrase about permanence and visibility landing like stones in a still pond, sending ripples of understanding, but also of a deep, familiar unease. He saw the earnestness in her eyes, the genuine desire for a foundation, for an anchor in the often-turbulent seas of life. And he felt a pang, sharp and unexpected, at the thought of causing her pain, of failing to meet this fundamental need. He understood her analogy to the library, the enduring symbol of community and commitment that was so central to Cedar Ridge. He understood the desire for something tangible, something that would stand the test of time, a testament to a love shared.

But beneath the surface of his attentive listening, a battle raged. The scent of pine, fresh and earthy from his work at the lumber mill earlier that day, seemed to cling to him, a constant reminder of the transient nature of things, of wood that was felled, shaped, and eventually weathered or consumed. It was a scent that spoke of change, of impermanence, and in that moment, it felt like a physical manifestation of his own internal landscape. He could feel Marisol's earnest desire for a solid structure, a visible commitment, and a part of him yearned to give it to her. He wanted to be that structure, that visible commitment. But the ghost of past losses, of promises broken and futures unfulfilled, loomed large, casting long shadows over his own capacity to build something that would truly last.

He shifted slightly in his seat, the worn leather creaking softly. "Marisol," he began, his voice a low rumble, tinged with a weariness that had nothing to do with physical exertion and everything to do with the internal conflict he was grappling with. He met her gaze, his own eyes, usually so clear and direct, clouded with a familiar uncertainty. "I... I hear you. I do. And I understand what you're saying about wanting something solid. Something that feels real, and... and permanent." He paused, searching for the right words, the words that wouldn't shut her down, but that wouldn't betray his own deep-seated fears.

"It's just..." He ran a hand through his hair, the rough texture of it a familiar comfort. "When you talk about building something visible, something that's 'ours' in a way that everyone can see... my first instinct is to... to pull back a little." He admitted, the honesty of it making his chest tighten. "It's not about you, or about what you're offering. It's about... what happens if it doesn't work? What happens if we build this grand structure, and then... and then it crumbles?"

He looked down at his hands, his fingers tracing the grain of the wooden armrest. The ingrained fear, a constant companion since childhood, resurfaced with a vengeance. Loss had been a recurring theme in his life, a specter that haunted his every endeavor. He'd learned, through painful experience, that the more you invested, the more you promised, the deeper the wound when things inevitably fell apart. And his greatest fear was causing Marisol that same kind of devastating pain.

"My dad," he started, his voice barely above a whisper, as if speaking the name aloud would summon the memories with greater force. "He was always promising us the world. Big vacations, a new house, a better life. And he meant it, I think. He truly believed he could deliver. But life... it has a way of interfering. And when those promises couldn't be kept, the disappointment... it was crushing. Not just for him, but for all of us. For me." He could still feel the weight of that inherited disappointment, the burden of watching dreams turn to dust.

He looked back up at Marisol, his gaze earnest. "And then there was... Sarah." The name hung in the air, a ghost from his past, a reminder of a love that had been declared, celebrated, and ultimately, lost. "We had plans, Marisol. Big plans. We talked about forever, about a life built together. And I poured everything I had into that. My heart, my future, my belief. And when she left... when it all fell apart... it felt like a part of me had been ripped away. And the pain of that loss was magnified because of all the promises, all the public declarations we'd made. It was like I had to not only grieve the loss of her, but also the loss of the future we'd so boldly proclaimed."

Theo sighed, the sound heavy with the weight of his history. "So, when you talk about making us visible, about building something permanent... I get scared. I get scared that if we put too much emphasis on the external, on the declarations, we'll be setting ourselves up for an even bigger fall. It's like... if we're too loud about it, too sure of it, the universe will feel the need to prove us wrong." He managed a wry, self-deprecating smile. "It sounds crazy, I know, but that's how it feels. It's like a magnet for disaster."

He paused, letting his words settle, watching for any flicker of disappointment on Marisol's face. He hated that his own internal struggles were creating a barrier between them, a hurdle that he wasn't sure he had the strength to overcome. He wanted to be the man who could offer her that solid ground, that unwavering commitment, but his past had left him with a profound wariness, a deep-seated understanding that even the strongest foundations could be shaken.

"And there's another thing," he continued, his voice softer now, more intimate. "The pressure. If we make it all official, all public, there's a pressure to maintain it, isn't there? A pressure to always be what everyone expects us to be. And I... I'm not always good at that. I have my moods, my days where I just want to be quiet, to be left alone with my thoughts. And if I feel like I'm constantly under a microscope, like I have to perform for the sake of the 'visible' relationship, I think... I think I'd start to resent it. And I would never want to resent you, or us."

He looked at her, his eyes pleading for understanding. "Right now, what we have feels... pure. It feels like it's just for us. It's in the quiet moments, the shared glances, the stolen conversations. It's built on trust, on a connection that's growing organically. And I'm terrified that if we try to formalize it too quickly, to make it too concrete, we'll suffocate it. We'll kill the very thing that makes it so special, so... precious."

The scent of pine seemed to intensify, or perhaps it was just his heightened awareness of it. He remembered the feel of the rough bark, the sharp, invigorating scent as he'd worked. It was a world away from the delicate, complex emotions Marisol was navigating, but it was his world, a world of tangible things, of things that could be measured and understood. This emotional landscape, however, was a foreign country, one he was still fumbling his way through, armed with only the blunt tools of his own experiences.

"I don't want to make a promise I can't keep," he said, the words laced with a raw vulnerability that he rarely showed. "I don't want to build a house of cards and then be the one to watch it tumble down, taking you with it. I've seen enough of that. I've lived enough of that." He took a deep breath, the air filling his lungs with the familiar scent of home, of Cedar Ridge, but also tinged with the unspoken anxieties that had followed him for so long.

"When I say I want to stay," he clarified, meeting her gaze directly, his eyes holding a depth of emotion he couldn't quite articulate, "I mean it. I'm not looking for an escape route anymore. This town, this life... it's starting to feel like home in a way I never thought possible. And you... you are a huge part of that." He paused, searching for the right emphasis. "But that doesn't mean I've suddenly shed all my old fears, all my old conditioning. The fear of loss, of things not lasting... it's deeply ingrained. It's like a scar that's always there, just beneath the surface. And the more you try to smooth it over, the more you risk reopening the wound."

He leaned back, the movement deliberate, as if trying to create a small distance between himself and the intensity of the conversation. "I want us to be strong, Marisol. I want us to be real. But I also want us to be kind to ourselves, and to each other. And I worry that by rushing to make everything 'permanent' and 'visible,' we're putting ourselves under undue pressure. Pressure that could, ironically, make us more vulnerable to the very thing we're trying to avoid – the breakdown of what we have." He looked at her, his heart aching with the truth of his own confession. He wanted to be able to offer her the unwavering certainty she deserved, but the shadows of his past held him captive, whispering cautionary tales of inevitable heartbreak.

Marisol listened, her gaze steady, absorbing Theo's confession. She understood his fear, the protective instinct that urged him to shield their burgeoning connection from the potential for loss. It was a valid fear, born of a lifetime of disappointment and hurt. But as he spoke of the dangers of making promises, of the fragility of visible commitments, a different kind of unease began to stir within her. It wasn't the sharp, immediate fear of a shattered structure, but a slow, creeping dread, like the subtle shift of the earth beneath one's feet, imperceptible until it's too late.

She reached out, her fingers tentatively brushing against his, a silent offering of comfort and understanding. "Theo," she began, her voice soft, yet imbued with a newfound firmness. "I hear you. I truly do. And I appreciate your honesty, more than you know. Your father, Sarah… those are deep wounds. And I would never ask you to disregard them, or to pretend they don't exist." She paused, gathering her thoughts, her mind sifting through metaphors, seeking the one that could best articulate the subtle erosion she feared. The library, with its enduring shelves and meticulously cataloged stories, felt like a symbol of permanence, but it also represented something else: stories that were loved, read, and cherished. Stories that were actively kept alive.

"But what if," she continued, her gaze holding his, "what if the greatest danger isn't in the promise itself, but in the silence that surrounds it? What if, by avoiding the declarations, by keeping our love in the quiet, unspoken spaces, we're actually allowing it to… to fade?" She hesitated, searching for the right words, the ones that wouldn't sound accusatory, but that would convey the depth of her concern. "It's like," she offered, a gentle smile touching her lips, "it's like a beloved book. You love it, you cherish it, you know it's there on your shelf. But if you never open it, if you never read it again, if you never share its story with anyone, does its magic truly endure?"

Theo's brow furrowed slightly, the analogy clearly resonating with him, though perhaps not in the way she'd intended. He understood the idea of a book, of a tangible object. But the 'reading' of it, the active engagement, that was where their perspectives diverged. For him, the act of reading was akin to making a declaration, to shining a spotlight on something that might be vulnerable. For her, it was about nurturing, about keeping the story alive.

"I'm not talking about grand pronouncements," Marisol clarified, sensing his hesitation. "I'm not talking about a public declaration of undying love to the entire town. What I'm afraid of, Theo, is the slow erosion of intimacy that can happen when things are left unsaid, unacknowledged. When we're so focused on protecting ourselves from the pain of potential loss, we can inadvertently starve the very thing we're trying to protect." She took a breath, her voice softening. "Love, to me, needs to be tended. It needs to be watered, given sunlight, and sometimes, it needs to be spoken aloud. It needs affirmation. It needs to know it's seen, and heard, and valued."

She leaned forward slightly, her hands now resting on the worn wooden table between them. "Think about it. We have this beautiful, profound connection. We share laughter, we share vulnerabilities, we share dreams. And I know, in my heart, that you care for me. But Theo, what happens when that connection is tested, as all connections are? What happens when doubts creep in, or when life throws its inevitable curveballs? If we haven't built a foundation of explicit affirmation, of spoken promises – not to the world, but to each other – will we have the strength to weather those storms?"

Her own fear, so different from Theo's, yet equally potent, began to surface. It was a fear of the slow, silent disappearance of what they had. The fear that one day, she would wake up and realize that the vibrant connection they shared had become a faded memory, a story left unread on the shelf of their lives. "It's not about the risk of demolition," she explained, her voice gaining a quiet intensity. "It's about the risk of... of neglect. Of love slowly, almost imperceptibly, losing its luster because it's not being actively nurtured. It's like a plant that's left in a dark corner, not because anyone intends to harm it, but simply because it's forgotten, or because tending to it feels like too much effort, too much of a commitment."

She looked at his hands, strong and capable, hands that built and shaped wood. She longed for him to see that emotional vulnerability, the tending of a relationship, also required a similar kind of strength, a different kind of dedication. "When you talk about the fear of crumbling structures," she said, her voice laced with a tender vulnerability, "I understand. But my fear is that an unspoken love, however precious, is like a foundation built on sand. It might hold for a while, it might even seem solid in fair weather, but without the cement of explicit commitment, without the regular reinforcement of spoken affirmation, it's susceptible to the subtle currents, the gentle tides that can, over time, wear it away until it's no longer there."

She offered a small, sad smile. "I want us to be a book that's read and reread, Theo. A story that's shared and cherished, not just existing in quiet solitude. I want us to have the courage to acknowledge the depth of what we feel, not as a dare to the universe, but as a testament to ourselves, and to each other. Because," she admitted, her voice dropping to a near whisper, "the thought of this fading away, of us simply drifting apart because we never truly anchored ourselves in words... that's a deeply frightening prospect for me. It's a quiet kind of heartbreak that I'm not sure I could bear." She met his gaze, her eyes earnest, seeking a flicker of understanding, a recognition of her own deeply held, quiet fear.

The silence that followed was not one of comfortable understanding, but of two deeply held, opposing fears circling each other. Theo's fear of the overt declaration, the public promise, was a shield, a way to preempt the pain of loss. Marisol's fear was the opposite: the quiet dissolution, the slow fading of a love left unacknowledged, unvoiced. Her vulnerability in expressing this fear, so different from his own deeply ingrained anxieties, hung in the air, a poignant counterpoint to his own deeply held beliefs about protecting what he cherished.

"I… I've seen it happen," she confessed, her voice barely above a whisper, revealing a personal experience that underscored her fear. "In my own life, with people I've loved. Not in a grand, dramatic way, but in a slow, subtle drift. Conversations became shorter. Shared moments, fewer. It wasn't anyone's fault, exactly. It was just… a lack of intention. A lack of active engagement with the relationship itself. We were like two ships passing in the night, content in our shared space for a while, but never quite finding a way to dock. And eventually, the currents pulled us apart, not with a crash, but with a quiet, almost imperceptible separation."

She traced a line on the wooden table with her fingertip. "It's the absence of 'us' as a declared entity, Theo. It's the lack of saying, 'This is ours. This is important. We are building this, together.' And without that spoken acknowledgment, it's too easy to let life happen to us, instead of actively shaping our shared life. It's too easy to let assumptions fill the space where direct communication should be." She looked up at him, her eyes filled with a raw plea. "I don't want to wake up one day and realize that what I believed to be a strong, vibrant love has simply… evaporated, because we were too afraid to name it, to claim it, to actively tend to it."

She understood his reluctance. She saw the genuine fear in his eyes, the ghosts of past betrayals that haunted his every move. But her own fear was a different beast. It was the fear of a slow, silent death, of a love that withered not from a sudden storm, but from a prolonged drought of affirmation. It was the fear of being comfortable enough to neglect the active tending, the consistent nurturing that love, in her experience, required to truly flourish and endure.

"For me," she continued, her voice a gentle murmur, "the visibility, the declaration, isn't about inviting disaster. It's about building resilience. It's about creating a shared history, not just in our hearts, but in our spoken words, in our intentional actions. It's about having something concrete to hold onto when the abstract feelings become clouded by doubt or difficulty. It's about having a 'yes' we can look back on, a 'we' that we've actively chosen and affirmed, again and again." She offered him another soft smile, a wistful one this time. "I don't want us to be a beautiful story that was never fully told, Theo. I want us to be a saga, a testament to a love that was brave enough to be acknowledged, to be nurtured, and to endure."

The weight of their differing fears settled between them, a palpable presence in the quiet room. Theo, protective of what he held dear, feared the vulnerability of open declaration. Marisol, equally protective, feared the slow decay of unspoken affection. The space between them, once filled with the promise of connection, now held the echo of their divergent anxieties, each a valid counterpoint to the other, a silent testament to the complexities of love, and the enduring challenge of truly understanding another's heart. Her vulnerability, in sharing this quiet dread, added a poignant depth to their conversation, a counterpoint to his own loudly proclaimed, yet deeply rooted, fears of loss.

The air in the room, thick with unspoken anxieties, began to soften. The sharp edges of their differing fears, so starkly defined moments before, blurred into a more nuanced landscape. Theo watched Marisol, his gaze no longer guarded but filled with a dawning realization. He saw the genuine hurt that flickered in her eyes, not a judgment, but a quiet sorrow born of her deeply held belief in the active cultivation of love. Her fear wasn't of a dramatic fall, but of a slow, silent fading, a gradual dimming of a light he'd only just begun to appreciate.

It was a vulnerability that resonated, a different kind of fragility he hadn't fully grasped until she laid it bare with such earnestness. He saw, with a clarity that was both humbling and disarming, that his protective measures, intended to preserve their nascent connection, were inadvertently creating the very distance she dreaded. His silence, his refusal to articulate their bond, was a void she feared would be filled by neglect, not by the devastation he braced himself against.

Marisol, in turn, met his gaze. The knot of apprehension in her chest loosened as she recognized the shift in him. The guardedness, the almost imperceptible tension in his shoulders, eased as he absorbed her words, as he truly saw her fear. It wasn't about pushing him into anything he wasn't ready for, but about conveying the depth of her own needs, her own understanding of what it took for love to not just survive, but to thrive. She saw the ghosts that still clung to him, the echoes of past pain that made him instinctively build walls.

His reticence wasn't a rejection of her, but a deeply ingrained defense mechanism, a response to a history of perceived betrayals. And in that moment, amidst the lingering tension, a fragile bridge began to form between their seemingly disparate viewpoints. It wasn't a bridge of agreement, not yet, but a bridge of acknowledgment, a shared space where their individual truths could coexist, even if they hadn't yet reconciled.

A shared, soft look passed between them. It was a silent acknowledgment, a wordless conversation that spoke volumes. In Theo's eyes, Marisol saw not just his fear, but a flicker of understanding, a recognition of the genuine pain his reticence had caused. He saw, perhaps for the first time, the emotional cost of his deeply ingrained caution. And in Marisol's gaze, Theo saw not a demand, but an offering of empathy, an understanding of the deep-seated fears that governed his reactions.

She wasn't asking him to be someone he wasn't, but to consider the impact of his carefully constructed defenses on the delicate bloom of their connection. The shared silence in their living room, once a charged space of conflict and misunderstanding, now felt different. It wasn't the tense quiet of two people at odds, but a shared, contemplative pause, a moment of mutual reflection where the echoes of their individual battles began to subside, replaced by a quiet recognition of each other's humanity.

He reached out, not to grasp, but to gently rest his hand on hers, which still lay on the table. His touch was a question, a tentative exploration of the newfound understanding that had settled between them. "I... I didn't realize," he began, his voice rough with an emotion he rarely allowed himself to express. "I didn't see that my... my hesitation felt like neglect to you. That's the last thing I ever wanted." He paused, his thumb stroking the back of her hand, a small, grounding gesture. "My fear is about losing you entirely. About the whole structure coming down. I didn't understand that... that your fear was of it crumbling away, piece by piece, without even realizing it was gone."

Marisol squeezed his hand, a silent reassurance. "And I didn't understand," she murmured, her voice still soft, "that your fear was so profound, so rooted in your past. I know you wouldn't intentionally hurt me, Theo. But sometimes, the things we do to protect ourselves can have unintended consequences. For me, love needs to be seen, to be acknowledged, to be actively nurtured. It's not about proving anything to anyone else; it's about building something strong and vibrant between us." She met his gaze, her own eyes reflecting a gentle understanding. "Your past is a part of you, Theo, and I respect that. But I also believe that we can build a new future, one that honors our present, and doesn't let the shadows of the past dictate every step forward."

He turned his hand over, lacing his fingers with hers. The contact was electric, not with the spark of passion, but with the quiet hum of mutual recognition. It was a simple act, yet in that simple gesture lay a world of unspoken acknowledgment. He saw the quiet strength in her, the resilience that allowed her to articulate her fears so openly, even when they differed so starkly from his own. He saw the genuine affection in her eyes, an affection that sought not to conquer his fears, but to understand them, and to offer a different path forward. "I'm not... I'm not good with words, Marisol," he admitted, his gaze drifting to their joined hands. "Not with the kind of words you're talking about. The declarations, the promises. They feel... precarious. Like they could shatter so easily."

"I know," she replied, her voice a soothing balm. "And I don't expect you to suddenly become someone you're not. But perhaps... perhaps we can find a middle ground. A way to acknowledge what we have, without feeling like we're walking a tightrope. Perhaps it's in the small things. The way you look at me when you think I'm not watching. The way you still bring me that specific blend of coffee, even though you know I don't always ask for it. Those are affirmations, Theo. Those are small, quiet declarations of care." She smiled, a genuine, warm smile that reached her eyes. "And maybe, when we're ready, it can be more. Not a grand pronouncement, but a simple statement. 'I choose this. I choose you.' Something that anchors us, not to the world, but to each other."

Theo held her gaze, a flicker of something akin to hope igniting within him. He hadn't considered those small gestures as declarations, but seeing them through her eyes, he began to understand. They were the quiet seeds of affirmation, the subtle tendrils of connection that he unconsciously nurtured. Her ability to find meaning in the understated, to see the potential for strength in the everyday, was a revelation. He had been so focused on the potential for catastrophe that he had overlooked the steady, quiet accumulation of moments that built a foundation.

The shared silence between them was no longer a battlefield of opposing fears, but a sanctuary of newfound understanding. It was a space where the raw edges of their individual anxieties could begin to heal, softened by the gentle light of mutual acknowledgment and the quiet promise of a future where their truths could coexist. He tightened his grip on her hand, a silent commitment to explore that middle ground, to try and build the bridge, plank by careful plank, towards a shared understanding.

Chapter Seven: The Language of Presence

Theo's hands. He'd always taken them for granted, these calloused, strong instruments that had learned their trade from his father, and his father before him. They were the tools of his life's work, capable of coaxing beauty from raw timber, of erecting structures that stood against the elements, of mending what was broken. They were practical, efficient, and, until this moment, had never been the subject of his introspection in quite this way. Now, as he sat in his workshop, the late afternoon sun slanting through the dusty panes, casting long shadows across the workbench, he found his gaze drifting to them. They were flecked with sawdust, stained with varnish, bearing the faint, indelible lines of countless hours spent shaping wood. These were the hands of a carpenter.

Marisol's words, spoken with such earnest conviction in the quiet of their living room just hours before, echoed in his mind.

"Love needs to be seen, to be acknowledged, to be actively nurtured. It's not about proving anything to anyone else; it's about building something strong and vibrant between us." He'd confessed his difficulty with grand declarations, his fear of words that felt precarious, liable to shatter. She hadn't dismissed his struggle; instead, she'd pointed to the small things, the quiet affirmations, the everyday gestures that spoke of care. "The way you look at me when you think I'm not watching. The way you still bring me that specific blend of coffee, even though you know I don't always ask for it. Those are affirmations, Theo. Those are small, quiet declarations of care."

And then she'd added, with a gentle hope that had settled deep within him, "And maybe, when we're ready, it can be more. Not a grand pronouncement, but a simple statement. 'I choose this. I choose you.' Something that anchors us, not to the world, but to each other."

He flexed his fingers, the rough skin protesting slightly. He had always seen his work as simply that – work. A means to provide, a profession he was good at, a legacy he carried. But Marisol's perspective was shifting something within him, a subtle recalibration of his understanding of 'declaration.' His commitment, his love for her, wasn't just in the words he struggled to find, but in the very fabric of his daily existence, woven through the actions he performed with these very hands.

He looked at the half-finished rocking chair on the workbench. The wood was cherry, its grain swirling with a natural elegance. He'd been sanding the curves of the armrests, smoothing them until they felt like velvet under his touch. This wasn't just about creating a piece of furniture; it was about creating something for her. He pictured her sitting in it, reading a book, the gentle sway a quiet comfort. He was building it with a conscious intention now, each stroke of sandpaper imbued with a thought of her. His presence in this workshop, his dedication to his craft, the long hours he put in – it wasn't just about his own satisfaction. It was a testament. A quiet, consistent declaration of his commitment to the life they were building together.

The scent of freshly cut oak from a recent project, a sturdy workbench destined for the local community center, hung heavy and sweet in the air. For years, it had been just the honest aroma of his livelihood. Now, it felt different. It was the smell of his labor, his dedication, a tangible representation of his ability to build, to create, to provide. He realized with a sudden, surprising clarity that Marisol's understanding of love, her need for active nurturing, didn't solely reside in grand romantic gestures or effusive verbal affirmations. It was also present in the steadfastness of his presence, the unwavering rhythm of his days spent working, providing, and creating a stable foundation.

He picked up a chisel, its worn wooden handle fitting perfectly into his palm. He'd used this same chisel to carve the intricate detailing on the mantelpiece at the old Miller house, a project that had taken weeks of meticulous work. He remembered Marisol visiting him there, bringing him lunch, her presence a bright spark in the dusty, echoing rooms. She had watched him work then, not with the impatient expectation of a dramatic unveiling, but with a quiet appreciation for the process. He saw it now, the parallel between his craft and their relationship. Both required patience, skill, and a deep understanding of the materials. Both could be damaged by haste or carelessness.

His hands weren't just tools; they were conduits. They translated his intentions, his desires, his unspoken affections into something tangible, something real. He'd always been a man of action, not words. When he felt something deeply, he did something. He fixed the leaky faucet, he mended the broken fence, he built the sturdy bookshelf. These were his love languages, the ways he expressed his care and devotion. Marisol, in her own beautifully articulated way, was helping him recognize the profound significance of these silent acts.

He ran his thumb over the rough wood of a workbench leg. He thought about the time the old oak tree in their backyard had been struck by lightning, its mighty branches split and splintered. While others had debated the cost of removal, Theo had spent days carefully salvaging the wood, his hands moving with a practiced reverence. He'd planed it, dried it, and then, over the next few months, transformed it into a beautiful, rustic dining table – a centerpiece for their home. That table, born from an act of destruction, was now a symbol of resilience, of transformation, of his ability to create something lasting and beautiful from what might have been lost. He hadn't needed to say, "I love you, and I will make something beautiful from this brokenness." His hands had spoken the truth for him.

He picked up a block of pine, its scent clean and fresh. He began to shave off thin curls of wood, the sharp blade biting cleanly. This was a small piece, destined to become a part of a larger structure, just as his own contributions were part of the larger architecture of their life together. He consciously focused on the sensation, the resistance of the wood, the smooth glide of the blade. He was no longer just performing a routine task. He was imbuing it with meaning. Each shaving that fell was like a small, silent word, a whispered affirmation.

I am here. I am building this with you. I am committed.

He remembered a particularly difficult winter, when a fierce storm had threatened to damage the roof of the small cottage they'd rented before buying their current home. Theo had spent a cold, biting night on the roof, his hands numb, securing loose shingles, reinforcing weak points. He hadn't complained; he'd just done what needed to be done. Marisol had brought him hot chocolate, her concern a silent comfort, her belief in his capability a steady reassurance. He hadn't needed her to praise his bravery, only to know that he was protecting their home, their shared space. His efforts then, driven by a primal need to protect and provide, were a declaration of his commitment to her, to their future.

He looked at the stack of lumber waiting to be milled. Each plank, each beam, represented potential. Potential for a bookshelf, a cradle, a porch swing. Potential for comfort, for utility, for beauty. And each piece, shaped by his hands, would carry a whisper of his dedication. He realized that Marisol's desire for acknowledged love wasn't a demand for constant verbal validation, but a need for assurance that the love was actively being built, being tended to, being made visible in the tangible world. His hands, in their tireless work, were doing just that. They were demonstrating his commitment, his care, his enduring affection, not with flowery prose, but with the solid, undeniable language of creation.

He ran his calloused thumb over a knot in the wood. He'd always seen knots as imperfections, things to be worked around or disguised. But Marisol had a way of finding beauty in unexpected places, in the unique character of things. Perhaps these knots, like the imperfections in any relationship, weren't things to be hidden, but rather features that added depth and character. His hands, capable of both smoothing away rough edges and highlighting the natural grain, could learn to embrace these nuances, both in his work and in their relationship. He could learn to see the "knots" in their shared journey not as flaws, but as opportunities for deeper connection, for a more resilient bond.

He picked up a piece of sandpaper, coarser this time, and began to work on a slightly rougher patch of wood. The friction was more pronounced, requiring a firmer hand. This felt akin to the moments of doubt and disagreement they had navigated. It wasn't always smooth, and sometimes it required more effort, more deliberate action, to bring things to a polished state. But the goal remained the same: to create something strong, something beautiful, something enduring. His hands, skilled in the art of sanding, were learning a new lesson – that true commitment, true love, wasn't about avoiding the rough patches, but about working through them with intention and care.

He thought of the way Marisol looked at him when he was engrossed in his work, that soft, appreciative gaze that spoke volumes. It wasn't just admiration for his skill; it was an acknowledgment of the effort, the dedication, the quiet love that went into each piece. She saw the declarations in his work, even when he didn't articulate them.

She understood the language of his presence, the silent testament of his hands. And he, in turn, was beginning to understand that his presence, his dedication, his tireless work, were not just the acts of a carpenter, but the profound and unwavering expressions of a man deeply in love. He was building more than just furniture; he was building a life, plank by careful plank, nail by unwavering nail, with hands that had finally learned to speak the language of his heart.

The subtle shift in Theo's perspective wasn't a dramatic upheaval, but rather a quiet dawning, like the slow diffusion of dawn's light across the quiet hills surrounding Havenwood. He'd always been a man of action, his love expressed through the tangible results of his labor. But Marisol, with her gentle insistence on the seen and acknowledged nature of affection, had begun to illuminate the profound power of small, intentional gestures. It started with the mundane, the everyday annoyances that, left unattended, could chip away at contentment.

Marisol had mentioned, almost in passing weeks ago, a persistent drip from the kitchen faucet. It wasn't a torrent, merely a rhythmic plink, plink, plink that underscored the silence of their mornings. Theo, caught in the usual rhythm of his workshop, had filed it away. But now, remembering Marisol's quiet plea for a love that was actively nurtured, he found himself reaching for his toolbox before even finishing his morning coffee.

He'd moved through their small house with a newfound attentiveness, his gaze lingering on details he'd previously overlooked. The faucet, with its stubborn drip, became his first deliberate act. He tightened the valve, replaced a worn washer, and within minutes, the steady plink was replaced by the quiet hum of their refrigerator. It was a small victory, almost insignificant in the grand scheme of his woodworking projects, but as he watched Marisol's subtle smile when she noticed the silence, he felt a warmth bloom in his chest, a silent affirmation that resonated deeper than any shouted declaration.

His attention soon extended beyond their home to the place where Marisol poured her passion and intellect: The Havenwood Pages. He'd found himself making detours on his way to and from the lumberyard, his truck rolling past the inviting storefront. He'd observed her there, a quiet observer from his driver's seat, noting the way she navigated the narrow aisles, her brow furrowed in concentration as she helped a customer find a specific title. He began to understand that her work, her sanctuary, deserved his consideration too. One crisp afternoon, he found himself inside the bookstore, ostensibly looking for a woodworking manual.

He found himself scanning the floor, noting the occasional misplaced book, the slight clutter near the checkout counter. He remembered Marisol's meticulous nature, her inherent desire for order and beauty. Without a word, he began to straighten a stack of returned novels, gently nudging a display of new releases into perfect alignment. He cleared a small pathway that had become obstructed by a cart of new arrivals, ensuring a smooth, unobstructed passage. These weren't tasks that demanded his carpentry skills, but they were tasks that spoke of respect, of care for her space.

He started bringing her tea. Not just any tea, but the specific blend she favored – a calming chamomile with a hint of lavender, the one she often reached for when lost in thought or feeling overwhelmed. He'd started noticing her subtle cues, the way her shoulders tensed after a long day, the slight weariness in her eyes. He'd began to make it a habit to have it ready, a steaming mug waiting on the counter when she returned, or a thermos packed for her lunch break at the bookstore. He didn't announce it, didn't seek praise. It was simply an offering, a silent acknowledgment of her needs, a small act of service designed to bring a moment of comfort into her day. It was his way of saying, I see you, and I want to make your day a little easier.

These weren't grand gestures designed to impress or to solicit a dramatic response. They were, as Marisol might put it, intentional acts of service.

Each one was a tiny brick laid in the foundation of their shared life, a deliberate choice to nurture what they were building. He began to see their home and the bookstore not just as physical locations, but as extensions of their shared existence, spaces that reflected their joint efforts and mutual respect.

He found himself looking at the worn armchair in their living room, not just as a piece of furniture, but as a place where Marisol curled up to read, a place he could ensure was always comfortable and inviting. He saw the garden path, a simple dirt track leading to their back door, as a route she took daily, and he took it upon himself to ensure it was free of tripping hazards, perhaps even scattering a few smooth stones to make it more pleasant underfoot.

His actions were a quiet rebellion against his own ingrained reticence with words. He was a man who built, who fixed, who provided. His instincts were to do. And Marisol was teaching him that doing could be a language of love, a powerful and enduring form of communication. The leaky faucet, the clear path in the bookstore, the perfectly brewed tea – these were his declarations, spoken not in sonnets, but in the quiet, consistent rhythm of his care. He was learning to translate his feelings into tangible acts, building permanence not through grand pronouncements, but through the steady, unwavering dedication of his presence and his efforts. He was slowly but surely mastering the language of intentional service, a language that spoke directly to the heart of the woman he loved.

The woodworking guild's annual charity auction was approaching, a significant event in Havenwood that drew artisans from across the county. Theo had always contributed a piece, usually a functional item – a sturdy workbench, a set of elegant serving trays. This year, however, felt different. Marisol had been talking about the literacy program the guild was supporting, her eyes alight with passion as she described the impact it had on young minds. He found himself drawn to the idea of creating something that held not just practical value, but also a deeper meaning, a direct connection to her cause.

He began sketching designs in his workshop, the scent of sawdust and wood polish filling the air. He considered a child-sized rocking horse, a classic piece that evoked a sense of nostalgia and joy. But he wanted something more unique, something that spoke to the magic of reading itself. He settled on a bespoke bookshelf, intricately carved with motifs inspired by classic fairy tales – a climbing vine of enchanted roses, a tiny, mischievous pixie peeking from behind a stack of books. He spent weeks on it, each detail a testament to his growing understanding of Marisol's heart. He chose a warm, inviting maple wood, its grain smooth and inviting, perfect for the delicate carvings.

He wasn't just building a bookshelf; he was building a vessel for stories, a monument to the power of imagination that Marisol championed. He meticulously sanded every curve, ensuring a silken finish. He carved the tiny details of the fairy tales with a precision that bordered on reverence, imagining the children who might one day discover them, their fingers tracing the contours of a story brought to life. He even incorporated a small, hidden drawer at the base, a secret compartment for a special note or a cherished bookmark, a nod to the hidden wonders found within every book.

During this intensive period of creation, Theo found his attention to the small, domestic details of their life increasing. He made sure Marisol's car had a full tank of gas before she left for work each morning, a practical act born from knowing she often ran errands for the bookstore. He started leaving little notes tucked into her lunch bag – not elaborate declarations, but simple affirmations like "Hope your day is wonderful" or "Thinking of you."

He even took on the task of sorting and folding the laundry, a chore he'd previously found tedious, finding a quiet satisfaction in creating neat piles, ensuring her favorite sweaters were handled with care. These were the small, consistent efforts that, he was learning, truly built permanence. They were the quiet whispers of his love, spoken in the silent, steadfast language of service.

One evening, Marisol returned home, looking particularly weary. She'd been dealing with a challenging shipment delay at the bookstore, and the stress was evident in the slump of her shoulders. Theo, who had just finished applying the final coat of varnish to the fairy tale bookshelf, greeted her with a warm hug. He didn't bombard her with questions or offer unsolicited advice. Instead, he gently steered her towards the living room, where he'd laid out her favorite plush blanket on the sofa and had a mug of her chamomile tea waiting.

He then sat beside her, not demanding conversation, but simply offering his presence. He didn't talk about the bookshelf; he knew that would feel like an imposition when she was clearly overwhelmed. He just sat there, a steady, grounding force, his hand resting lightly on her knee.

After a long silence, punctuated only by the gentle ticking of the grandfather clock in the hall, Marisol sighed, a sound of release rather than exhaustion. "You know," she said softly, her voice a little rough, "sometimes, just knowing you're here... it makes all the difference." She turned to him, her eyes softer than he'd seen them in days. "And this," she gestured vaguely towards the kitchen, "the quiet. I noticed. Thank you."

Theo's heart swelled. It wasn't about the grand gesture of the bookshelf, though he knew she would be touched when she saw it. It was about the quiet, consistent acts that had paved the way for her comfort. He realized that his focus on these small, intentional acts was building something far more significant than just a charitable contribution. He was building trust, deepening their connection, and creating a sense of effortless care that permeated their shared life.

He was, in his own quiet way, actively nurturing their love, making it visible not just in grand projects, but in the subtle, everyday kindnesses that spoke volumes. He was building permanence, one small, deliberate act at a time.

The dedication of the bookshelf at the charity auction was a moment of quiet triumph. Marisol had been overcome with emotion when she saw it, her hand flying to her mouth as she traced the carved details. She'd spoken to the attendees about the importance of fostering a love for reading in children, her words flowing with her characteristic eloquence and passion. And when the auctioneer announced that the bookshelf had sold for a significant sum, far exceeding expectations, Marisol had met Theo's gaze, her eyes shining with a profound gratitude that needed no words. He saw in her expression not just appreciation for the donation, but a deep understanding of the love and intention he had poured into its creation.

His contribution to the auction was more than just a wooden artifact; it was a tangible representation of his commitment to Marisol's values, a testament to his willingness to actively support what mattered to her. It solidified the idea that his efforts, even the small, seemingly insignificant ones, had a ripple effect, contributing to the larger tapestry of their shared life and their community.

He was no longer just a carpenter in Havenwood ; he was a partner, a supporter, a man who understood that love was built not just in grand declarations, but in the consistent, intentional acts of service that made life smoother, brighter, and more meaningful. He was building permanence, not just in wood, but in the very fabric of their relationship, with every carefully considered action, every silently offered comfort, every loving detail he brought into their shared existence.

Marisol watched Theo with a quiet intensity, her gaze sweeping over him as he moved through their shared life. It wasn't a critical scrutiny, but rather a deep, appreciative observation, akin to how she'd study the cover of a newly acquired first edition, searching for the subtle clues that hinted at its true value. She saw the almost imperceptible hesitation before he'd reach for his toolbox to silence the persistent drip of the kitchen faucet, the way his brow furrowed for a fleeting moment as he recalled her casual mention of it weeks prior.

It was in that brief pause, that flicker of recollection and subsequent action, that she recognized the blossoming of a new language between them. He wasn't just fixing a leaky faucet; he was acknowledging her words, her unspoken discomfort, and actively choosing to alleviate it. This was Theo, the man of steadfast action, weaving a new thread into the fabric of their relationship, a thread spun from intentionality.

The small, almost inconsequential tasks Theo began undertaking around The Havenwood Pages were not lost on her. She'd arrive in the mornings to find a stack of returned books neatly aligned, their spines perfectly flush with the edge of the shelf, a small testament to his recent visit. Sometimes, a misplaced literary journal would be tucked back into its rightful place, or the small table near the window, often cluttered with patrons' forgotten belongings, would be cleared and wiped clean.

These were not the grand gestures of a man trying to impress, but the quiet, consistent efforts of someone who cared deeply about her space, her work, and by extension, her well-being. It was the silent affirmation that her world, the one she had so carefully curated within the walls of her beloved bookstore, mattered to him. Each straightened book, each cleared surface, felt like a whispered assurance: I see this. I care.

And the tea. Oh, the tea. She'd discovered the thermos tucked into her bag on more than one occasion, its contents still warm, the familiar aroma of chamomile and lavender a gentle embrace in the midst of a busy workday. There were mornings she'd find a steaming mug waiting on the kitchen counter, precisely brewed to her liking, before she'd even had a chance to think about making it herself. Theo, who had always been more inclined to practicality than pronouncements, was speaking a language she understood intimately, a language of comfort and consideration. It was a language spoken through the simple act of ensuring she had a moment of warmth and peace in her day, a silent acknowledgment that she might be tired, that she might need that small, restorative pause. It was his way of saying, I'm thinking of you. I'm looking after you.

Marisol found herself cataloging these gestures, not with the detached analysis of a critic, but with the warm appreciation of a reader discovering a beloved character's hidden depths. She saw the way he'd linger in the aisles of her bookstore, his eyes not just scanning for books, but observing the flow of customers, noting where a slight obstruction might impede their movement, or where a display might benefit from a touch of his innate sense of order. It was as if he were silently auditing her space, not to criticize, but to subtly enhance it, to make it more welcoming, more functional, more hers.

She remembered his quiet presence during the charity auction, the immense pride that had radiated from him as he spoke about the bookshelf he'd crafted. It wasn't just about the auction itself, or the funds raised; it was about him pouring his skill, his time, and his affection into something that directly supported her passion for literacy. That bookshelf, with its intricate carvings of fairy tale motifs, was more than just wood and varnish; it was a tangible representation of his understanding of her heart, a masterpiece sculpted from empathy.

She began to see the quiet thoughtfulness infused into their everyday routines. The way he'd ensure her car was fueled up, a small act of preventative care that saved her time and potential frustration. The almost imperceptible straightening of the rug in the hallway, a minor adjustment that prevented a potential trip hazard. These weren't things he announced or sought acknowledgment for. They were simply woven into the fabric of his day, subtle acts of service that demonstrated a profound level of attentiveness.

Her own communication style was often steeped in words, in eloquent descriptions and considered prose. But she was discovering that Theo's language was one of consistent, unwavering presence, of practical demonstrations of care that spoke volumes without uttering a single syllable.

Her observant heart recognized the profound shift. It wasn't just about Theo performing chores; it was about the intention behind them. It was about the conscious choice he made to see her needs, to anticipate them, and to act upon them. She saw the way he'd now instinctively know when a quiet evening was what she needed most after a particularly demanding day at the bookstore, offering not advice or solutions, but simply his steady presence, a silent anchor in the storm.

He'd learned to read the subtle cues in her posture, the tension in her shoulders, the slight weariness around her eyes, and he would respond not with words, but with a perfectly brewed cup of tea, a comforting blanket, or simply the quiet solidarity of his hand resting on hers. This was his way of saying, I understand. I'm here.

She understood that while her words might paint vivid pictures, his actions were building the solid, enduring framework upon which those pictures could be hung. He was communicating his commitment not through grand pronouncements, but through the steady, reliable rhythm of his care. The gentle rustle of pages turning in her beloved bookstore seemed to echo her growing understanding. Each turn of the page was a step forward in their shared narrative, a deepening of their connection.

She saw the quiet devotion in his eyes when he looked at her, a devotion that didn't need to be spoken aloud because it was so clearly reflected in his deeds. He was learning to speak her language, not by mimicking her words, but by translating his own deep affection into the universal dialect of thoughtful action. Her heart, so accustomed to the lyrical flow of stories, was finding a new, equally compelling narrative in the quiet, consistent language of Theo's presence.

She reflected on the myriad ways love could manifest, how it could be as varied and intricate as the stories she curated. Theo's love wasn't the effusive, declaration-filled romance of the novels on her shelves. It was something quieter, more grounded, yet no less profound. It was the steady hand that tightened a loose screw, the thoughtful gesture that brewed a comforting cup of tea, the silent acknowledgment of her presence that spoke volumes. It was the understanding that commitment wasn't always found in dramatic pronouncements, but often resided in the small, consistent acts of service that made life a little smoother, a little brighter, a little more bearable.

Marisol found herself cherishing these unspoken affirmations. They were the quiet footnotes to the grand narrative of their lives, the subtle details that added depth and resonance. She saw Theo's efforts not as mere chores, but as deliberate acts of love, carefully chosen and consistently delivered. They were his unique way of expressing the depth of his feelings, a language of action that spoke directly to her heart. The rhythm of their days in Cedar Ridge, once a solitary melody for each of them, was slowly but surely harmonizing, creating a duet of shared care and mutual understanding. Her observant heart recognized the profound beauty in this unspoken devotion, appreciating the quiet strength of a love built not on eloquent speeches, but on the solid foundation of intentional kindness.

She understood that Theo's reticence with words didn't diminish the depth of his feelings; it simply meant he expressed them differently. His love was a craftsman's love, built with precision, care, and an unwavering commitment to quality. He showed his affection through the enduring strength of his actions, the thoughtful detail in his efforts, and the quiet consistency of his presence. Marisol, whose life was dedicated to the power of narrative, was learning to read a new kind of story, one written not in ink, but in the language of presence and service. And this story, she realized, was one of the most beautiful she had ever encountered.

The quiet hum of their shared life was punctuated by these small, meaningful gestures, each one a testament to Theo's growing understanding of her, and his unwavering commitment to their shared future. Her heart, attuned to the subtlest nuances, recognized the profound significance of these acts, understanding that they were the building blocks of a love that was both enduring and deeply resonant.

The quiet hum of their shared life in Cedar Ridge had begun to resonate with a new kind of melody, one that Theo found himself not just hearing, but actively composing. For a long time, his vision of their future had been akin to a delicate glass sculpture, beautiful but easily shattered, something to be admired from a distance, with a constant, underlying fear of its fragility. It was a promise held with bated breath, a whispered hope that he dared not disturb too forcefully. But Marisol, with her gentle yet persistent presence, her unwavering belief in their burgeoning connection, had begun to chip away at that ingrained caution. She had inadvertently handed him a different set of tools, not to protect a fragile object, but to construct something solid, something enduring.

He found himself looking at their shared existence not as a precarious arrangement, but as a project demanding his active participation, a structure to be built brick by brick. The small repairs he'd made around Marisol's home, the organized shelves at The Havenwood Pages, the thermos of tea appearing at just the right moment – these were no longer just acts of consideration; they were the foundational elements, the raw materials being meticulously laid.

He'd catch himself staring at the kitchen faucet, not just seeing a minor inconvenience, but visualizing the seamless flow of water, a small but significant detail in the overall blueprint of their domestic peace. Each perfectly aligned book spine was a well-placed stud, each cleared table a smoothly plastered wall. He was no longer just reacting to Marisol's needs; he was anticipating them, integrating them into the evolving design of their life together.

This shift was subtle, a quiet recalibration of his internal compass, but its impact was profound. The idea of permanence, which had once loomed like a formidable, unscalable cliff face, now presented itself as a collaborative construction site. He started to see it not as a terrifying commitment, but as an exciting endeavor, a shared project where their individual contributions would interlock, creating something stronger and more beautiful than either could achieve alone. The library project, with its meticulous planning and shared vision, had been a tangible precursor to this deeper understanding.

He recalled the days spent poring over blueprints, discussing structural integrity, and the sheer satisfaction of seeing a concept materialize from scattered ideas into a tangible reality. He recognized that his relationship with Marisol was, in many ways, a far grander and more intricate project, one that required not just blueprints, but heart and soul, not just mortar, but unwavering affection.

He began to internalize this builder's mentality. When Marisol mentioned a book she was searching for, it wasn't just a fleeting request; it was a potential addition to their collective library, a new section to be carefully curated. When they discussed their weekends, it wasn't just about filling empty hours, but about strategically allocating time for shared experiences, for reinforcing the walls of their connection.

He found himself sketching out ideas, not on graph paper, but in the quiet moments of reflection – how to make their shared living space more functional, how to carve out dedicated corners for their individual pursuits within their shared home. He imagined their future not as a delicate vase on a mantelpiece, but as a sturdy, well-built house, weathered by time but standing firm against any storm, its rooms filled with laughter, warmth, and the comfortable silence of shared understanding.

The fear of loss, that ever-present shadow that had often clouded his interactions with Marisol, began to recede, replaced by a growing sense of purpose. He was no longer simply holding his breath, hoping for the best. He was actively engaged in making the best happen. He understood that building something substantial required consistent effort, an unwavering commitment to the process, and a willingness to address any potential weaknesses before they compromised the entire structure.

He started to see himself not as a mere participant, but as a co-architect, a craftsman pouring his skills and his heart into creating a shared edifice. This perspective transformed the weight of commitment from a burden into a source of pride and motivation.

He remembered the feeling of accomplishment after completing the book shelf for the charity auction. The way the wood had yielded to his tools, the satisfaction of seeing the intricate carvings take shape, the sheer joy of presenting something that was not only functional but also beautiful, and that directly supported something Marisol held dear. That project had been a revelation, a tangible demonstration of his capacity to build something lasting and meaningful. Now, he was applying that same principle to their relationship.

The library was a testament to their shared passion for stories, a public declaration of their collaborative spirit. But the true masterpiece, he was beginning to understand, was the private world they were constructing, brick by careful brick, in the quiet spaces of their everyday lives.

This internal shift manifested in his actions. He found himself taking initiative more readily, not waiting to be asked, but seeing what needed to be done and doing it. He'd surprise Marisol with a perfectly organized pantry, knowing how much she valued order and efficiency in her own domain. He'd research and suggest practical solutions for minor household issues, not to assert dominance, but to contribute to the smooth functioning of their shared home. Each completed task, each problem solved, felt like another brick laid firmly in place, another reinforcement of the foundation they were building. He was learning to speak Marisol's language, not through flowery words, but through the steady, reliable rhythm of his contributions, through the tangible evidence of his care and commitment.

He started to see their shared future not as a fragile tapestry that could be unraveled by a single misplaced thread, but as a robust, multi-layered structure, capable of enduring the inevitable stresses of time and life. He envisioned the laughter of future generations echoing within its walls, the quiet comfort of companionship filling its rooms, the sturdy permanence of a love that had been deliberately and lovingly constructed. This was no longer a distant dream; it was a tangible blueprint, and he was actively laying the groundwork.

He understood that building a shared future wasn't about grand pronouncements or romantic declarations, but about the consistent, often unglamorous, but ultimately profoundly rewarding work of laying one solid brick upon another, with patience, with intention, and with an unwavering belief in the enduring strength of what they were creating together. The quiet strength of Theo's presence was transforming from a comforting reassurance into a powerful force, a testament to his evolving understanding of love as a verb, an action, a constant, deliberate act of building.

The aroma of freshly brewed coffee, rich and dark, had become the olfactory signature of their mornings. It wasn't a grand gesture, not a sweeping declaration of affection, but it was a consistent, comforting presence that spoke volumes. Theo, a man often more comfortable with the tactile language of wood and paper, had discovered a new dialect in the simple act of preparing Marisol's morning beverage. He'd learned her preference for a splash of almond milk, the exact temperature that warmed her without scalding, the specific shade of amber that meant the brew was perfect. This ritual, performed with a quiet efficiency each day, was his silent reassurance, his tangible offering of love before the world outside their cozy cottage had fully awakened.

Marisol, still wrapped in the lingering tendrils of dreams, would often find him at the kitchen counter, the gentle hiss of the coffee maker a melodic counterpoint to the soft murmur of the morning news he'd already put on. She'd pad into the kitchen, her bare feet cool against the worn wooden floor, and lean against the doorframe, simply watching him. There was no need for words. The way his brow furrowed slightly in concentration as he measured the grounds, the quiet satisfaction that settled on his features when he poured the steaming liquid into her favorite mug – it was a symphony of unspoken affection. He was showing her, in his own deliberate way, that he was present, not just physically in their shared space, but emotionally invested in the rhythm of their days.

For Theo, these small acts were anchors, grounding him in a reality he had once feared to fully inhabit. The fragility he'd once perceived in their connection had begun to dissipate, replaced by the sturdy reality of shared routines. He remembered the early days, the tentative dance of their courtship, where every word felt charged with the potential for misunderstanding, every touch a risk. He'd been so afraid of saying the wrong thing, of pushing her away with an ill-chosen phrase, that he'd often retreated into silence, a silence that he now recognized could be misconstrued as indifference. But Marisol, with her innate understanding and her patient heart, had somehow seen past his reticence, recognizing the effort he was making, the silent language he was slowly, painstakingly learning.

Her own way of expressing care was so open, so effervescent, that it had initially intimidated him. Marisol wore her heart on her sleeve, her laughter like sunshine, her concerns voiced with a disarming honesty. He, on the other hand, had built his life around a more guarded exterior, a fortress of self-reliance forged in a past where vulnerability was a luxury he couldn't afford. Yet, Marisol had found the secret passage into his inner world, not by force, but by a gentle, persistent knocking. She didn't demand grand pronouncements; she seemed to understand the significance of the subtle shifts, the quiet affirmations.

The scent of coffee was more than just a morning ritual; it was a signal, a silent broadcast of his commitment. It was him saying, "I'm here. I'm thinking of you. I'm building this with you, one quiet morning at a time." He watched as Marisol would take her first sip, her eyes closing for a moment in pure, unadulterated pleasure. That small sigh of contentment, that faint smile that touched her lips, was his reward, a far more profound affirmation than any spoken word could ever be. It was the understanding that he was contributing to her happiness, to the quiet joy of their shared existence, and that was a powerful, deeply satisfying feeling.

This understanding extended beyond the kitchen. He'd find himself intuitively knowing when she needed a moment of quiet companionship, when a shared silence was more comforting than any conversation. He'd sit beside her on the porch swing as she sketched, the rhythmic creak of the chains a soft accompaniment to the scratch of her charcoal on paper. He wouldn't interrupt her creative flow, wouldn't demand her attention. Instead, he'd simply be there, a steady, grounding presence, a silent reassurance that she wasn't alone in her endeavors.

He was learning that presence wasn't about occupying space; it was about filling it with a sense of unwavering support, a quiet strength that said, "Whatever you're creating, whatever you're facing, I'm here, a steady hand on the tiller."

He remembered the time she'd been wrestling with a particularly challenging historical detail for her upcoming book. She'd been poring over dusty tomes in the back room of The Havenwood Pages, her frustration palpable. Theo, without a word, had simply brought her a warm blanket and a cup of chamomile tea, placing them gently on the table beside her. He'd then retreated to his own work, allowing her the space to concentrate, but his quiet presence in the adjoining room was a constant, unspoken offer of support. When she finally emerged, triumphant, her face alight with the thrill of discovery, he'd met her with a simple, knowing smile and a nod. It was a shared victory, born from his understanding of her needs and his silent way of meeting them.

Marisol, in turn, had become attuned to his unspoken needs. She understood his quietude wasn't a sign of disinterest, but a part of his nature. She'd learned to read the subtle shifts in his posture, the way his gaze would soften when he was content, the slight clench of his jaw when he was grappling with a problem. She'd learned that a shared meal, prepared by her hands and eaten in comfortable silence, could be as nourishing to him as a heartfelt conversation. She reciprocated his silent reassurances with her own brand of understanding, creating a reciprocal rhythm of care that fortified their bond.

The scent of coffee brewing wasn't just a smell; it was a feeling. It was the feeling of home, of safety, of belonging. It was Theo's quiet promise, whispered in the language of steam and aroma, that he was building a life with her, brick by careful brick, wordless affirmation by wordless affirmation. Marisol felt it deep in her bones, this growing sense of security. Theo's love, though it didn't often manifest in grand declarations, was as steady and reliable as the sunrise over Cedar Ridge.

It was a love that was etched into the very fabric of their shared days, a silent reassurance that resonated in the quiet hum of their home, in the gentle ritual of morning coffee, and in the enduring strength of his unwavering presence. He was her anchor, her quiet harbor, and in his silent devotion, she found a peace she had long sought, a love as profound and as comforting as the first warm breath of dawn. His presence was a constant, a reassurance that no matter the storms that might gather, they had built a shelter, and he was there, steadfastly, by her side, ready to face whatever came their way, together.

The act of brewing coffee was, in essence, his way of tending their shared garden, ensuring that even before the day had truly begun, a measure of warmth and comfort was always in bloom. This meticulous attention to detail, this dedication to a simple, yet significant, morning ritual, was the cornerstone of his unspoken vows, a testament to his growing understanding that true love was often found not in the grand pronouncements, but in the quiet, consistent acts of care that wove themselves into the tapestry of everyday life. He was proving, through his actions, that his commitment was not a fleeting emotion, but a deeply ingrained conviction, a foundation upon which their future was being steadily and lovingly constructed.

Chapter Eight: The Library's Future

The aroma of cinnamon and sugar, mingling with the earthy scent of aging paper, had become the unofficial perfume of Cedar Ridge over the past few weeks. It was a heady, optimistic fragrance, a testament to the town's collective heart beating in unison for the preservation of their beloved library. Marisol, her hands dusted with flour and her eyes sparkling with a determination that could rival any storm cloud, found herself at the epicenter of this burgeoning movement. The library, once a quiet sanctuary of hushed tones and dog-eared pages, had transformed into a bustling hub of activity, a testament to the power of community spirit.

The bake sale, held on a crisp Saturday morning under the benevolent gaze of the autumn sun, was the first significant salvo fired in their campaign. Tables overflowed with a dizzying array of homemade treats, each one a silent ambassador for the cause. Mrs. Gable's legendary apple pies, their crusts a golden lattice of perfection, were gone within the first hour. Young Timmy Peterson, usually more interested in chasing squirrels than civic duty, had proudly presented a batch of lopsided, but undeniably enthu-siastic, chocolate chip cookies that sold out just as quickly. Marisol herself had contributed a towering lemon meringue pie, its cloud-like topping a beacon of sugary hope.

The air buzzed with friendly chatter, the clinking of change, and the occasional excited squeal of a child clutching a cookie almost as big as their face. Laughter, genuine and unrestrained, rippled through the town square, a sound that felt as vital to their fundraising efforts as the dollars being dropped into the collection jars. It wasn't just about the money; it was about the connection, the shared purpose that knit them closer together with every transaction.

Following closely on the heels of the bake sale was the book drive. Marisol had spearheaded this initiative, meticulously crafting flyers that spoke of forgotten stories yearning to be rediscovered. She'd personally visited every shop and business, her plea both heartfelt and professional. The response was overwhelming. Stacks of well-loved paperbacks, children's picture books with crayon scribbles on their pages, and even a few sturdy hardcovers that bore the faint scent of their previous owners' homes began to accumulate in designated boxes outside the library.

She remembered standing amidst those towering piles, the sheer volume of donated books a powerful visual representation of the community's investment. Each volume represented a past reader, a shared experience, a whisper of the joy the library had brought into their lives. She'd run her fingers over the worn covers, imagining the hands that had held them, the minds they had opened, and felt a surge of gratitude for the tangible support.

Theo, who had initially observed the burgeoning fundraising efforts with a quiet, supportive presence, was now wading in with a more tangible contribution. His workshop, usually a haven for the meticulous crafting of custom furniture, was now intermittently filled with the scent of sawdust and the rhythmic tapping of his hammer. He'd offered his carpentry skills for building display stands for the upcoming craft fair, sturdy and elegantly simple structures that would showcase the local artisans' work without overshadowing it.

He'd also taken on a few small renovation projects within the library itself. Armed with his tools and a quiet efficiency, he'd repaired a creaky bookshelf that had been a minor nuisance for years, replaced a few loose floorboards in the children's section, and even reinforced a section of the wobbly staircase leading up to the archives. Marisol had watched him work, a profound sense of peace settling over her. His hands, usually so skilled at coaxing beauty from raw wood, were now lending their strength to the tangible infrastructure of their shared dream.

There was a quiet pride in his movements, a deep satisfaction in contributing to something so vital to the heart of their community. He wasn't one for grand speeches or public displays, but his actions spoke a language of devotion that resonated deeply with her. He built not just furniture, but foundations, both literally and figuratively, for their future.

The craft fair, held the following weekend on the library lawn, was a vibrant explosion of local talent. Hand-knitted scarves in a kaleidoscope of colors, intricate pottery glazed in earthy tones, delicate handcrafted jewelry that caught the sunlight, and whimsical wooden toys carved with loving care all vied for attention. Marisol, dressed in a simple dress that allowed her infectious energy to shine through, flitted between the stalls, her enthusiasm a contagious force.

She engaged with every vendor, her genuine admiration for their creations evident in her warm smiles and insightful questions. The scent of beeswax candles mingled with the sweet fragrance of lavender sachets, creating an olfactory tapestry as rich and varied as the crafts themselves. The fair wasn't just about selling goods; it was a celebration of the town's creative spirit, a tangible demonstration of the diverse talents that enriched Cedar Ridge. Each purchase, whether it was a delicate ceramic bird or a sturdy leather-bound journal, was another brick laid in the foundation of their revitalized library.

The collective energy of Cedar Ridge was palpable. It wasn't just the organized events; it was the impromptu conversations on the street, the shared glances of understanding at the grocery store, the children excitedly telling their parents about the library's upcoming "new adventures." There was a sense of ownership, a shared investment in the success of their endeavor. The library, which had once been a quiet repository of knowledge, had become a beacon, drawing people together, igniting a shared passion.

Marisol found herself marveling at the transformation. She'd always believed in the library, had always seen its potential, but witnessing the town rally around it with such fervor was a profoundly moving experience. It was a testament to the enduring power of communal spaces, to the idea that a shared resource could forge unbreakable bonds.

The local bakery, "The Daily Bread," had dedicated a special loaf of their signature sourdough to the library fund, its crust imprinted with a tiny, stylized book. The florist, "Petals and Posies," offered a bouquet of sunflowers, their cheerful faces a symbol of optimism, with a portion of the proceeds going directly to the library. Even the usually reserved mechanic, Mr. Henderson, had donated a fully serviced bicycle that was raffled off, its gleaming chrome a testament to his own quiet generosity. Every contribution, no matter how large or small, felt like a precious jewel added to a crown, each one contributing to the overall splendor of their collective effort.

Theo, his hands now smelling faintly of wood polish, would often find himself at the library after his day's work, not just to help with renovations, but simply to observe. He'd watch Marisol, her face flushed with excitement as she chatted with a donor, or her brow furrowed in concentration as she organized a shipment of donated books. He'd see the librarian, Mrs.

Gable, her usual stoic demeanor softened by the visible outpouring of support, her eyes shining with a gratitude that mirrored Marisol's own.

He'd seen the children, their faces alight with anticipation, tracing the progress of the new shelving Theo had helped install. He found a deep contentment in this shared purpose, a sense of belonging that was both novel and profoundly welcome. His work with his hands, a solitary pursuit by nature, had become interwoven with the very fabric of the town's collective effort, a silent contribution to a shared dream.

He realized that his love for Marisol wasn't just about their shared mornings and quiet evenings; it was about embracing her passions, about becoming a part of the world she cared so deeply about, and about contributing to the betterment of the community they now called home. The scent of coffee, once the sole olfactory marker of his affection, was now joined by the comforting aroma of baked goods, the sweet fragrance of flowers, and the ever-present, comforting scent of well-loved books, all of which symbolized the growing warmth and vibrancy of their shared life and the revitalized heart of Cedar Ridge.

Theo's workshop, typically a sanctuary of meticulously planned projects and the precise scent of freshly cut lumber, had taken on a new rhythm. The familiar hum of his table saw was now punctuated by the rhythmic tap-tap-tap of a hammer, the rasp of sandpaper, and the quiet scrape of a chisel. He'd always been a man of action, his communication often delivered through the language of wood and joinery rather than spoken words. But this project, this renovation of the Cedar Ridge library, had ignited a deeper, more profound purpose within him. It wasn't just about repairing; it was about rebuilding, about reinforcing the very foundations of a place that held so much meaning for his town, and for Marisol.

He'd started with the shelving. The old oak had served its purpose for decades, bearing the weight of countless stories, but time and overuse had left their mark. Gouges and scratches marred the once-smooth surfaces, and a few sections sagged precariously, threatening to spill their literary treasures onto the floor. Theo approached each damaged shelf with the reverence of an archeologist, carefully assessing the extent of the wear. He'd meticulously repaired the worst of the damage, not with a quick patch, but with a thoughtful infusion of new wood, seamlessly blending old and new so that the repairs themselves became a testament to the library's resilience.

He'd spent hours sanding down the worn edges, smoothing out the rough patches until his fingertips could glide over the wood without snagging. Each smooth sweep of the sandpaper felt like a prayer, an unspoken promise to preserve the stories held within those walls. He discovered a quiet satisfaction in the painstaking process, a deep-seated contentment that settled over him with each completed section. It was a stark contrast to the gnawing sense of impermanence that had sometimes haunted him in the past. Here, with every nail he hammered, every joint he secured, he was building something tangible, something that would endure.

Beyond mere repair, Theo's vision extended to creating new spaces, inviting nooks where the magic of reading could truly flourish. He envisioned quiet corners, bathed in the soft glow of natural light, where a reader could lose themselves for hours. He meticulously designed and constructed several of these reading alcoves, each one a testament to his skill and his understanding of how people interact with space.

He crafted low, sturdy benches upholstered in a durable, warm-toned fabric, designed to be both comfortable and inviting. Behind these benches, he built custom bookshelves, perfectly sized to hold a curated selection of new arrivals or perhaps a display of local authors. The wood he chose was a rich, warm cherry, its subtle grain adding a touch of elegance without being ostentatious. He paid attention to every detail: the gentle curve of the shelves, the precise angle of the backrests, the placement of each to ensure maximum light and a sense of peaceful seclusion.

He even incorporated small, built-in side tables, just large enough to hold a cup of coffee or a well-worn bookmark. He knew that these spaces, born from his own hands, would become as integral to the library's future as the books themselves. He imagined children curled up in these nooks, their faces illuminated by the adventure unfolding on the page, and a quiet smile would spread across his lips.

The structural integrity of the aging building was also a significant focus for Theo. He wasn't just a craftsman; he was a guardian of the library's physical form. He climbed into the dusty attic, his flashlight beam cutting through the gloom, to inspect the roof beams. He reinforced weakened joists, ensuring that the building could withstand the test of time and weather. He meticulously examined the staircase leading up to the archives, a section that had always felt a little wobbly underfoot.

With careful precision, he replaced a few of the older, more worn steps and reinforced the underlying support structure, ensuring that this often-forgotten corner of the library was just as safe and sound as the rest. He worked with an almost obsessive attention to detail, his mind focused solely on the task at hand. Each measured cut, each perfectly placed screw, was a silent declaration of his commitment. He understood that a library was more than just books on shelves; it was a sanctuary, a place of learning and community, and it deserved to be protected, to be nurtured.

His work often extended into the evenings, long after the sounds of Marisol's bakery had faded and the town square had settled into a quiet hush. He would find himself drawn to the library, not out of obligation, but out of a quiet compulsion. He'd sit on one of the new benches he'd built, the scent of wood polish and old paper filling the air, and simply observe. He'd watch the dim light filter through the large windows, casting long shadows across the newly laid floorboards he'd helped secure.

He'd trace the lines of the repaired shelving with his eyes, a sense of profound satisfaction washing over him. It was in these quiet moments of reflection that the true depth of his feelings for Marisol solidified. Her passion for this place, her unwavering belief in its potential, had become a part of him. His craftsmanship, once a solitary pursuit, was now imbued with a deeper meaning, an unspoken offering of his love and his commitment to her and to their shared life in Cedar Ridge.

He was building more than just furniture; he was building a future, piece by carefully crafted piece, right alongside the woman who had captured his heart. The library, once a symbol of what was at risk, was slowly transforming into a tangible testament to what they, as a community, could achieve, and Theo was proud to be a part of that transformation, his hands leaving an indelible mark on its hopeful new chapter.

Marisol's mind, ever a bustling nexus of ideas, had always found a particular kind of solace within the hushed reverence of the Cedar Ridge Library. Even in its current state of gentle disrepair, it was a place that pulsed with the quiet hum of possibility. But as Theo's tireless work began to weave a new tapestry of restoration and innovation, her own vision for its future unfurled with an almost breathtaking clarity. It was no longer about simply preserving what was, but about breathing vibrant new life into its very soul, transforming it into the beating heart of their beloved Cedar Ridge.

She stood at the threshold of the main reading room, the scent of Theo's wood polish mingling with the faint, comforting aroma of aged paper. The newly reinforced shelves, solid and gleaming, seemed to hold their breath, ready to embrace a fresh influx of stories. The reading nooks he'd meticulously crafted were more than just furniture; they were invitations. Invitations to linger, to dream, to discover. Her gaze swept over them, imagining them filled with the rustle of pages, the soft murmur of hushed conversations, the delighted giggles of children lost in a fantastical world.

This was the foundation, the sturdy scaffolding upon which her grander ambitions could now take flight.

"It's more than just books, isn't it, Theo?" she murmured, her voice a soft melody against the quiet backdrop. She hadn't needed to say the words aloud; he'd understood. His hands, calloused and strong, had not merely repaired wood; they had, in a way, repaired her faith in the enduring power of community spaces.

Her vision for the revitalized library was a kaleidoscope of activity, a testament to the belief that a library could be a dynamic, ever-evolving hub. It wouldn't just be a repository of stories; it would be a stage, a classroom, a gathering place. "I see author readings," she declared, her eyes alight with the possibilities, "local authors, yes, but also authors from further afield, bringing their unique perspectives and experiences right here to Cedar Ridge. Imagine the conversations we could spark, the new worlds we could open up for people just by having them share their journeys."

She gestured towards the large, sun-drenched bay window, where Theo had already installed a sturdy, built-in window seat, a perfect perch for observing the gentle ebb and flow of town life. "And for the children," she continued, her voice brimming with an infectious enthusiasm, "we need dedicated story hours. Not just for the little ones, but for all ages. Picture it: Theo's cozy nooks filled with children, their imaginations soaring with every word, their parents perhaps nearby, enjoying a quiet moment with a coffee or catching up on their own reading. We could even have themed story times, bringing characters to life with simple props and costumes."

But her aspirations didn't stop at the whimsical delight of childhood tales. Marisol saw the library as a crucial resource for lifelong learning. "Adult education workshops are essential," she stated with conviction. "Think about it: computer literacy classes for those who are still a little hesitant with technology, creative writing workshops for aspiring poets and novelists, even practical skills like basic bookkeeping or gardening advice from local experts. We have so much knowledge within Cedar Ridge itself, so many talented individuals who could share their expertise. The library can be the bridge that connects that knowledge with those who seek it."

She walked towards the old circulation desk, which Theo had thoughtfully reinforced and given a fresh, smooth surface. "This," she said, running her hand over the cool wood, "will be the heart of operations, of course. But it will also be a point of connection, a place where people can ask questions, get recommendations, and truly feel welcomed. We'll have a dedicated space for new arrivals, of course, prominently displayed, but also a curated section for local history, for books by Cedar Ridge authors, and even a 'staff picks' shelf that changes weekly, offering a personal touch."

Marisol's vision extended far beyond mere preservation; she saw the library as a living, breathing testament to the power of shared knowledge and sustained community effort. It was a concept she'd held close to her heart for years, a dream nurtured in quiet moments amidst the familiar scent of baking bread. Now, with Theo's tangible contributions, it felt as though the dream was finally taking root in solid ground.

"This isn't about just keeping the doors open," she explained, her gaze meeting Theo's, which was fixed on her with an attentive warmth that always made her heart flutter. "It's about ensuring the library continues to serve generations to come. It's about creating a legacy. Think about the children who will grow up coming here, the teenagers who will find refuge and inspiration within these walls, the adults who will discover new passions and skills. Their stories, their learning, their connections – they will all echo through Cedar Ridge's future, woven into the very fabric of this town."

Her eyes gleamed with a passionate intensity, reflecting the bright promise of the afternoon sun streaming through the windows. "We can host book clubs, film screenings, even small art exhibitions featuring local talent. We can collaborate with the historical society to digitize old town records, making them accessible to everyone. We can create a vibrant online presence, showcasing upcoming events and offering digital resources, extending the library's reach beyond its physical walls. The possibilities are truly limitless."

She paused, taking a deep, appreciative breath, absorbing the transformation already underway. "Theo, you're not just building shelves and alcoves. You're building possibilities. You're strengthening the foundations of something truly special, something that will nourish this community for years to come. When people walk in here, I want them to feel a sense of wonder, a sense of belonging, a sense of endless potential. I want them to feel that this space is theirs, a reflection of their own aspirations and their shared commitment to learning and growth."

She thought of the quiet corners, where the only sound might be the turning of a page. She envisioned these spaces becoming hubs of quiet contemplation, places where even the most introverted soul could find a welcoming embrace. "We could even have a 'quiet zone' clearly designated, for those who truly need absolute silence to focus. And then, perhaps a more communal area, where people can collaborate on projects or simply enjoy each other's company over a shared interest. It needs to be adaptable, responsive to the needs of our community as they evolve."

Marisol's thoughts then turned to the practicalities, the logistics that would bring these grand visions to fruition. "We'll need to establish a Friends of the Library group, a dedicated team of volunteers who can help with fundraising, event planning, and outreach. We'll need to actively seek grants and donations, of course, but a strong volunteer base will be our backbone. This is a community project, and it needs community ownership."

She picked up a stray, perfectly smoothed piece of wood Theo had left on a workbench, turning it over in her hands. "I see this library becoming a beacon, Theo. A place where everyone feels welcome, regardless of their background or their interests. A place where curiosity is celebrated, where knowledge is shared freely, and where the bonds of our community are strengthened. It's about more than just words on a page; it's about connection, about understanding, about building a brighter future together."

The gleam in her eyes intensified, a testament to the depth of her conviction. "We'll have a dedicated children's area, bright and cheerful, with comfortable seating and a wealth of age-appropriate books. We'll ensure it's a safe and stimulating environment, encouraging early literacy and a lifelong love of reading. And for the teenagers, a space that feels modern and relevant, perhaps with access to computers and study areas, a place where they can connect with each other and with the resources they need to succeed."

She continued, her voice gaining a melodic cadence, painting a vivid picture of the library's future. "Imagine, Theo, a space where community groups can meet, where knitting circles can gather, where seniors can find companionship and engage in stimulating activities. A space where new parents can find support and resources, where aspiring entrepreneurs can access business information, where anyone can come to learn, to grow, and to connect. This library will be the pulse of Cedar Ridge, a place that truly reflects the diverse interests and needs of our residents."

Her hand tightened slightly on the piece of wood. "And it will all be built on a foundation of shared vision and collaborative effort. Your hands are creating the physical space, but it's our collective spirit, our dedication to this town, that will truly bring it to life. This isn't just your project, or my project. It's our project, Cedar Ridge's project. And when people walk through those doors, I want them to feel that sense of shared ownership, that pride in what we have accomplished together. They should see it as a testament to what we can achieve when we work hand-in-hand, driven by a common purpose and a deep love for our community."

Marisol sighed, a contented sound. "It's a lot, I know," she admitted, a soft smile playing on her lips. "But I believe in this town, Theo. I believe in its people. And I believe that this library, revitalized and reimagined, can be a powerful force for good, a catalyst for connection and growth for generations to come. It will be a place where stories are not just read, but lived, shared, and created. A place that will continue to shape the narrative of Cedar Ridge long after we are gone, its spirit echoing through the laughter of children, the quiet hum of study, and the shared discoveries of our community." The passion in her voice was palpable, a vibrant testament to the enduring power of a well-loved, well-used community cornerstone.

The air in the Cedar Ridge Community Hall buzzed with an energy that was both hopeful and heavy with trepidation. It was an energy Marisol had felt building for weeks, a collective exhale and inhale that had punctuated every planning session, every whispered conversation about the library's future. Tonight, that energy coalesced, vibrating in the polished wooden floorboards beneath their feet and seeming to ripple through the assembled townsfolk.

Faces, familiar from the bakery, the hardware store, and the Friday night farmers' market, were turned towards the makeshift stage at the front of the hall, their expressions a mosaic of anticipation, concern, and unwavering support. This was it – the pivotal town meeting, the moment where the fate of the Cedar Ridge Library, a repository of memories and a beacon of potential, would be decided.

Marisol stood near the back, her heart thrumming a nervous rhythm against her ribs. Beside her, Theo's presence was a steady anchor. His hand rested lightly on her arm, a silent reassurance that spoke volumes. She could feel his own quiet anticipation, the shared weight of responsibility they both carried for the project they had poured so much of themselves into. Around them, the usual friendly chatter had subsided, replaced by a hushed expectancy. Empty chairs, scattered amongst the occupied ones, hinted at the town's willingness to invest time and space in this crucial discussion. The scent of old wood and the faint aroma of coffee from the refreshment table did little to dispel the palpable tension. It was the scent of commitment, of a community wrestling with its own legacy.

Mayor Thompson, a man whose kindly demeanor often masked a shrewd pragmatism, stood at the podium, his gaze sweeping across the room. He cleared his throat, the small sound amplified in the sudden stillness. "Good evening, everyone," he began, his voice carrying a resonance that commanded attention. "Thank you all for being here tonight. As you know, we've gathered to discuss the future of our beloved Cedar Ridge Library. This is a moment of significant consequence for our town, a moment that will define our commitment to education, culture, and the shared spaces that bind us together."

He paused, letting his words settle. "We've heard the passionate proposals, seen the tireless work of dedicated individuals like Marisol and Theo, and considered the various paths forward. Tonight, it's time to make a decision. It's time to decide not just on a building, but on the kind of community we aspire to be." He gestured to Marisol, who took a deep breath and stepped forward, her earlier nervousness giving way to a surge of conviction. The journey to this point had been a long one, filled with countless hours of planning, fundraising, and, most importantly, a shared belief in the library's vital role.

"Thank you, Mayor Thompson," Marisol began, her voice clear and steady, projecting to the far corners of the hall. "For years, the Cedar Ridge Library has been a quiet guardian of our town's stories, a sanctuary for curious minds. But like any cherished institution, it needs to evolve. It needs to adapt to the needs of our changing community, to embrace new technologies, and to offer more than just books. It needs to become a dynamic hub, a vibrant center for learning, connection, and growth."

She spoke of the proposals, detailing the plans for expanded programming – the author readings, the computer literacy workshops, the children's story hours that would ignite young imaginations. She painted vivid pictures of the revamped reading nooks, the accessible technology stations, and the community meeting spaces that would foster collaboration and shared experiences. Her words were imbued with a genuine passion, a deep-seated love for this town and its potential. She spoke of the library not as a relic of the past, but as a vital organ of the present, pumping knowledge and culture throughout Cedar Ridge.

"We envision a library that serves everyone," she continued, her gaze sweeping across the faces in the audience. "From our youngest learners taking their first steps into the world of reading, to our seniors seeking connection and lifelong learning opportunities. We see it as a place where teenagers can find a safe and inspiring environment to study and explore their interests, where aspiring entrepreneurs can access resources, and where families can connect and grow together. This isn't just about preserving a building; it's about investing in our people, in our collective future."

Theo then stepped up, his presence adding a quiet gravitas to Marisol's impassioned plea. He didn't speak in grand pronouncements; his language was one of tangible action, of skilled hands and determined effort. He spoke of the structural repairs already undertaken, the new shelves installed, the careful restoration of the historic architectural details. He presented a clear, concise breakdown of the budget, outlining the costs associated with the proposed renovations and the ongoing operational expenses. His presentation was a testament to meticulous planning and a realistic understanding of the resources required.

"We've assessed the structural integrity of the building," Theo explained, his voice calm and measured. "The foundation is solid, but the roof needs immediate attention, and the electrical and plumbing systems require comprehensive upgrades. The proposed renovations include creating a dedicated children's wing, modernizing the main reading area to accommodate more seating and technology, and establishing a versatile community room that can be used for various events and meetings. We've secured estimates for the materials and labor, and the projected costs are within a manageable range, provided we receive the necessary funding."

He held up a set of blueprints, larger than life on a projection screen. "This is not a pie-in-the-sky dream," he emphasized, his gaze meeting the eyes of those in the audience. "These are concrete plans, supported by detailed specifications and quotes from reputable contractors. We've also factored in accessibility upgrades, ensuring that our library will be a welcoming space for all members of our community, regardless of physical ability. The operational budget includes funds for new acquisitions, staffing, and essential maintenance, ensuring the library can thrive for years to come."

He then addressed the crucial aspect of funding. "We are proposing a two-pronged approach to secure the necessary capital. Firstly, a dedicated bond measure, which will allow us to finance the major renovation and upgrade costs. This bond will be repaid over twenty years, with a modest increase in property taxes, an investment that will yield immeasurable returns in community enrichment. Secondly, we are actively pursuing grants from state and national library foundations, and a robust 'Friends of the Library' fundraising campaign is already underway, demonstrating significant community buy-in and volunteer commitment."

He laid out the numbers with an unvarnished honesty. "The total projected cost for the renovation and initial operational buffer is $750,000. The bond measure, if approved, will cover $600,000 of this amount. The remaining $150,000 will be raised through grants and community donations. We are confident, based on current pledges and the enthusiastic response to our initial fundraising efforts, that we can meet this goal." He then opened the floor for questions, his steady presence a reassurance to anyone with doubts.

The questions began tentatively, then flowed with an increasing confidence. Mrs. Gable, a sprightly woman known for her sharp intellect and even sharper wit, raised her hand. "Theo, you mentioned a modest increase in property taxes. Can you give us a more concrete figure? For those of us on fixed incomes, every dollar counts."

Theo nodded, unfazed. "Absolutely, Mrs. Gable. For an average-sized home in Cedar Ridge, the projected increase would be approximately $25 per year, or roughly $2 per month. This is an investment in a resource that will serve our entire community, from our children to our elders, for decades to come."A young father, Mr. Henderson, spoke up. "Marisol, you talked about computer literacy classes. How will these be structured? Will they be accessible for people who have never even touched a computer before?"

Marisol's eyes lit up. "That's an excellent question, Mr. Henderson. We plan to offer beginner classes, tailored specifically for those who are new to technology. We'll have patient, skilled instructors, and the class sizes will be small to ensure individual attention. We also envision offering one-on-one tech support sessions, where individuals can bring their own devices and get personalized assistance. The goal is to empower everyone in our community to confidently navigate the digital world."

Another resident, a retired teacher named Mr. Davies, inquired about the impact on library hours and staffing. "Will this expansion mean longer operating hours, and will we need to hire more staff? And what about the volunteers – how will they be integrated into the new model?"

"Excellent points, Mr. Davies," Mayor Thompson interjected. "The plan includes extending library hours, particularly on weekends and evenings, to better serve working families and students. To accommodate this, we are proposing the addition of one full-time librarian position and two part-time assistants. As for our invaluable volunteers, they will be instrumental in running programs, assisting with circulation, and supporting various library activities. The 'Friends of the Library' group will play a crucial role in coordinating volunteer efforts and ensuring they are well-trained and supported."

The questions continued, probing into every aspect of the proposal – the potential for partnerships with local schools, the plans for cataloging and accessing digital resources, the timeline for the renovation, and the contingency plans for unforeseen issues. Marisol and Theo, with the Mayor acting as a skilled moderator, addressed each concern with thoughtful, comprehensive answers. They spoke with a united front, their shared vision and mutual respect evident in every exchange.

It became clear that this was not merely a debate about a building; it was a discussion about the soul of Cedar Ridge. It was about what the town valued, about its commitment to its residents, and about its willingness to invest in a future that embraced knowledge, community, and shared growth. The emotional weight of the moment was palpable. There were murmurs of agreement, nods of understanding, and the occasional spontaneous applause that broke through the formal proceedings.

Sarah Jenkins, a lifelong Cedar Ridge resident and a staunch supporter of the library, stood up. Her voice, though soft, carried the weight of years of observation. "I remember coming to this library as a child," she said, her eyes misting slightly. "It was my escape, my place of wonder. I've seen it struggle, seen its light dim. But I've also seen the passion in Marisol's eyes, the dedication in Theo's hands. This isn't just about fixing a building; it's about rekindling a spirit. It's about ensuring that the next generation of Cedar Ridge children have a place to dream, to learn, and to grow, just as we did." Her words resonated deeply, drawing a collective sigh of affirmation from the room.

The debate, while robust, was remarkably civil. It was a testament to the respect the townsfolk held for each other and for the shared goal they were working towards. There were no acrimonious exchanges, no personal attacks. Instead, there was a shared understanding that this decision would impact them all, and that a collaborative approach was essential.

As the discussion began to wind down, Mayor Thompson stepped forward once more. "We have heard your questions, your concerns, and your heartfelt sentiments. It is clear that the future of the Cedar Ridge Library is a matter of great importance to this community. Now, it is time to move forward. We will be holding a formal vote on the bond measure next month, and I urge each of you to consider what has been discussed here tonight. This is our opportunity to invest in a brighter future for Cedar Ridge, to ensure that our library remains a vibrant and essential cornerstone of our town for generations to come."

The meeting concluded with a sense of collective purpose. The air, once heavy with anticipation, now felt lighter, imbued with a renewed sense of optimism. Marisol and Theo stood together, a quiet satisfaction settling over them. They had presented their case, answered the questions, and, most importantly, they had ignited a spark of shared vision within the community. The path ahead would still require diligent effort, tireless advocacy, and continued community engagement. But tonight, they had taken a crucial step forward. The library's future, once a question mark, now seemed to glow with the promise of possibility, a testament to the enduring power of a community united by a common dream.

The hum of conversation that now filled the hall was different; it was no longer the sound of uncertainty, but the murmur of shared resolve, of plans being made, and of a future being built, together. The weight of responsibility hadn't vanished, but it was now a shared burden, carried with pride and a deep sense of accomplishment. The seed of an idea had been planted, nurtured, and now, on this pivotal night, it was beginning to truly take root in the heart of Cedar Ridge.

The quiet hum of conversation that followed Mayor Thompson's closing remarks was a symphony of progress and shared resolve. It wasn't just the clatter of coffee cups or the rustle of departing coats; it was the murmur of neighbors discussing figures, of parents envisioning their children at story time, of seniors planning their next book club meeting. This was the sound of a community actively investing in its own future, a future inextricably linked to the revitalized Cedar Ridge Library. Marisol, still buzzing with the residual energy of her presentation, felt a profound sense of accomplishment wash over her. She glanced at Theo, who stood beside her, his presence a steady, grounding force amidst the celebratory din.

Their partnership, forged in the crucible of countless planning sessions, late-night brainstorming, and shared anxieties, was no longer an unspoken understanding; it was a tangible entity, visible to everyone in the room. It was in the way they instinctively moved in sync, the subtle nod of agreement that passed between them, the shared smiles that spoke of a language only they truly understood. Theo's hand found hers for a fleeting moment, a firm, reassuring clasp that conveyed a depth of support far beyond mere professional collaboration. It was a silent endorsement, a profound affirmation of their shared journey.

Theirs was a partnership built not on grand declarations, but on the quiet strength of shared purpose. Marisol, the visionary, the one who painted the vibrant picture of possibility, and Theo, the pragmatist, the meticulous architect of that vision, the one who ensured the foundations were solid and the blueprints were sound. Together, they were more than the sum of their parts. They represented the best of Cedar Ridge: the aspiration and the execution, the dream and the dedication. Their united front in championing the library was a powerful testament to their commitment, not just to their beloved town, but to each other, a silent promise of a shared future that was still being carefully, deliberately navigated.

Even as the crowd began to thin, a small group gravitated towards Marisol and Theo, eager to express their support and ask follow-up questions. Mrs. Gable, her eyes sparkling with renewed conviction, approached them. "Marisol, Theo, that was truly inspiring," she said, her voice warm. "I can already see it, this library bustling with life. And Theo, your clarity on the financials... it's reassuring. We can do this." Theo offered a small, genuine smile. "Thank you, Mrs. Gable. It's the collective effort that will make it happen. We've got a solid plan, and with the community's backing, it's more than achievable."

Mr. Henderson, the young father who had been so concerned about the computer classes, joined them, his two children clinging to his legs. "I'm so glad we're doing this," he said, looking at Marisol. "My kids are going to love it. And for me, knowing there are classes where I can finally get a handle on this technology... it's a relief." He looked at Theo. "And the $25 a year? It's nothing, really, for what we're getting. A modern library, accessible to everyone. It's a steal."

Marisol knelt down to speak to his children. "And what do you think about a new, bright room just for you, with lots of new books and maybe even some fun activities?" The children's eyes widened, their excited murmurs a testament to the impact of her vision." They're already excited," Mr. Henderson chuckled. "You've got them hooked."

The conversation flowed easily, a natural continuation of the meeting. It wasn't just about the library anymore; it was about the shared fabric of Cedar Ridge, about the connections they were strengthening, about the common ground they were discovering and reinforcing. Marisol and Theo found themselves talking about the community garden project that had flourished last summer, about the annual harvest festival that always brought everyone together, about the small, independent businesses that formed the backbone of their town. They realized that the library was not an isolated entity; it was an integral part of a larger, vibrant ecosystem.

Theo, usually more reserved in public settings, found himself engaging more readily, his practical insights complementing Marisol's enthusiastic outlook. He spoke about the potential for the community room to host local artisan workshops, echoing Marisol's idea of the library as a hub for skill-sharing. He elaborated on the possibility of partnering with the local historical society, a long-standing but somewhat dormant organization, to create a digital archive of Cedar Ridge's past, accessible through the library's new technology stations.

"Imagine," Theo said, his voice gaining a quiet confidence, "a visitor could walk in, access our digital archives, and get a real sense of the town's history, its people, its stories. We could even incorporate oral histories, recorded by residents themselves. It would be a living history book."

Marisol's eyes lit up. "That's a brilliant idea, Theo! It ties into the idea of the library as a repository of more than just published works. It's about preserving our collective memory, our local narrative." She turned to the small group that had gathered. "And we're not talking about replacing the physical archives; this would be an expansion, a way to make our history more accessible and engaging."

The conversation then shifted to the practicalities of the fundraising campaign. Sarah Jenkins, whose earlier words had resonated so deeply, spoke up. "I've already spoken to a few people about forming a dedicated 'Friends of the Library' committee. We need to be organized, have clear roles, and set achievable goals. Marisol, your passion is infectious, and Theo, your meticulousness is reassuring, but we need a strong volunteer team to really drive this home."

Marisol nodded. "Absolutely, Sarah. We've been thinking about that too. We envision a committee that can manage different aspects – grant writing, event planning for fundraisers, community outreach, volunteer coordination. Theo and I can provide the framework and the overall direction, but the success of this campaign will truly depend on the dedication of our volunteers."

Theo chimed in, "We've prepared a draft of roles and responsibilities, based on similar successful campaigns in other towns. It includes positions like Fundraising Coordinator, Events Manager, Communications Lead, and Volunteer Coordinator. We can present it to anyone interested in forming the committee. The goal is to leverage everyone's talents and interests."

The exchange was a perfect illustration of their dynamic. Marisol presented the grand vision, while Theo laid the groundwork for its execution. They didn't compete for attention or try to outshine each other; they complemented, supported, and amplified each other's strengths. This wasn't just about the library anymore; it was about the quiet unfolding of their own personal story, a story woven into the fabric of Cedar Ridge, a story of two people finding common ground, common purpose, and perhaps, as the days and weeks unfolded, something even deeper.

As they continued to mingle, Marisol couldn't help but notice the subtle glances exchanged between Theo and some of the older residents, the easy camaraderie that belied his often reserved demeanor. He was a Cedar Ridge native, after all, his roots running as deep as the ancient oaks that dotted the landscape. He understood the town's rhythm, its quirks, its heart. And Marisol, the relative newcomer who had fallen head over heels for the town and its people, felt a growing sense of belonging, a feeling amplified by Theo's quiet presence beside her.

Later, as the last of the townspeople began to depart, leaving behind the lingering scent of coffee and the faint echo of their conversations, Marisol and Theo found themselves standing amidst the quietude of the community hall. The polished floorboards now reflected the dim overhead lights, and the empty chairs seemed to hold the ghosts of the evening's impassioned discussions.

"We did it, Theo," Marisol whispered, a sense of wonder in her voice.

Theo turned to her, a rare, unguarded smile gracing his lips. "We did. And it's just the beginning." He reached out, not to grasp her hand this time, but to gently tuck a stray strand of hair behind her ear. His gaze held hers, and in that quiet moment, the unspoken partnership that had been so evident to everyone else in the room felt like it was reaching a new, more personal, and profoundly intimate stage.

"You were... amazing tonight, Marisol," he said, his voice softer than usual. "You articulated everything I've been feeling, everything we've been working towards, with such clarity and passion. You make me believe in it even more."

Marisol's heart fluttered. "And you, Theo. Your presentation... it was so grounded, so real. You made it feel achievable, tangible. I couldn't have done this without you. Not this, not anything."

He stepped a little closer, the space between them charged with an unspoken tension. "I know," he said, his thumb brushing lightly against her cheekbone. "That's the thing, isn't it? We do it together."

The library, a symbol of their shared endeavor, had brought them together, forging a bond of mutual respect and admiration. But as they stood there, in the quiet aftermath of their collective triumph, it was clear that their partnership had transcended the blueprints and the budget projections. It was a partnership of the heart, still developing, still finding its voice, but undeniably present, a quiet promise whispered in the heart of Cedar Ridge, just like the future of the library they were both so determined to build. The road ahead would be paved with challenges, but for the first time, Marisol felt a profound certainty that no matter what lay ahead, they would face it, side by side, their unspoken partnership a silent, unwavering strength.

Chapter Nine: Defining the Future

The residual warmth from the community hall still clung to Marisol, a comforting embrace after the exhilarating whirlwind of the meeting. The cheers, the affirmations, the palpable sense of collective buy-in—it had all coalesced into a vibrant energy that pulsed beneath her skin. Beside her, Theo's presence was a steady anchor, his hand now resting loosely on the small of her back as they navigated the familiar, moon-dappled path leading away from the town square. The night air was crisp, carrying the faint scent of pine and damp earth, a welcome counterpoint to the lingering aroma of coffee and polite applause.

They hadn't spoken much since leaving the hall, a comfortable silence weaving itself between them. It was the kind of silence that arises after a significant shared experience, a silent acknowledgement of what had been accomplished and a gentle acknowledgment of the path that still lay ahead. The library, once a symbol of potential strife and uncertainty, now felt like a testament to their shared vision and the town's resilience. The anxieties that had often gnawed at Marisol, the fear of impermanence, of her efforts being swept away like so many fallen leaves by the capricious winds of change, had begun to recede, replaced by a quiet, deep-seated satisfaction.

As they approached the familiar wooden bridge spanning the Cedar River, the gentle, ceaseless murmur of the water below seemed to beckon them.

It was a sound that had always soothed Marisol, a constant rhythm in the sometimes-turbulent flow of life in Cedar Ridge. Theo slowed his pace, his gaze following the silvery ribbon of moonlight on the water's surface.

"It's beautiful tonight," he said, his voice a low rumble that blended seamlessly with the river's song.

Marisol nodded, a soft smile gracing her lips. "It always is. It's one of the things that makes Cedar Ridge so special, isn't it? This quiet beauty that's always here, no matter what else is going on."

They paused on the bridge, leaning against the sturdy wooden railing. The river flowed beneath them, unhurried, carrying its secrets downstream. It felt like a moment suspended in time, a breath held between the end of one chapter and the quiet anticipation of the next. The successful preservation of the library had, in a way, created a similar sense of flow between them. The unspoken tensions, the careful navigation of their evolving relationship, had been subtly smoothed, like stones worn down by the persistent caress of water.

"I still can't quite believe it," Marisol confessed, her voice barely a whisper. "That we actually did it. That the library is safe." She turned to Theo, her eyes reflecting the starlight. "Thank you, Theo. For everything. For believing in it, and for... for believing in me."

Theo met her gaze, his usual reserve softening into something far more tender. "You're the one who brought it to life, Marisol. You painted the picture so vividly, you made us all see what was possible. I just helped lay the foundation." His thumb brushed lightly against her hand where it rested on the railing, a small gesture that sent a jolt of warmth through her. "And I always believed in you. I just... needed to be sure you believed in us, too."

The words hung in the air, charged with an unspoken weight. It was the closest they had come to acknowledging the delicate dance they had been engaged in, the careful circling around the heart of the matter. The library, their shared project, had been the catalyst, the common ground upon which their individual aspirations had converged. But now, with that shared victory behind them, the landscape of their personal future felt as vast and as open as the river stretching out before them.

"Us," Marisol repeated, the word feeling both fragile and profound. "I always believed in us, Theo. I just... I wasn't sure if you did." The admission felt like a dam finally breaking, releasing a flood of pent-up emotion. "This town... and the library... it all felt so important, and I was so afraid of losing it all. And of... losing you in the process."

Theo's hand moved from her hand to gently cup her cheek, his touch sending a tremor through her. His eyes, usually so direct and analytical, were now filled with a depth of emotion that made her heart ache in the most beautiful way. "Marisol," he said, his voice rough with feeling, "you are the most vibrant part of this town. You breathe life into everything you touch. And losing you? That's not something I've ever considered. The library... it was a mountain we had to climb together. But it was always about more than just the building. It was about building something together."

The moonlight seemed to intensify, casting them in a soft, ethereal glow. The sound of the river, once a gentle murmur, now felt like a symphony, a soundtrack to this pivotal moment. Marisol leaned into his touch, her eyes closing for a fleeting second as she absorbed the sincerity of his words. The permanence she had craved for the library, she now realized, was something she was beginning to crave for their connection.

"I've been so focused on the library, on making sure it had a future," she admitted, her voice thick with emotion. "I think... I think I was so afraid of disrupting what we had, of pushing too hard, that I forgot to consider our own future. Our own story."

Theo's thumb traced the curve of her cheekbone, his gaze unwavering. "Our story is just beginning, Marisol. And it's going to be a good one. I've learned so much from you, about seeing the potential, about daring to dream big. And you've learned from me, about the grounding, the planning, the making sure the dream has solid foundations." He paused, a hint of a smile playing on his lips. "We balance each other. That much is clear."

"We do," she agreed, her voice gaining strength. "And I don't want to lose that balance. Or the strength it gives us." She took a deep breath, the cool night air filling her lungs. This was it. The moment she had both anticipated and dreaded. "Theo... what happens now? For us?"

He gently turned her to face him fully, his hands resting on her shoulders. The steady pressure was reassuring, grounding. "Now," he began, his voice firm yet gentle, "we stop thinking about 'what ifs' and start thinking about 'what nows.' The library is secure. We've built something significant for Cedar Ridge. But we've also built something significant between us."

He stepped closer, his gaze searching hers. "I don't want to go back to the way things were. I don't want to pretend this connection, this... partnership... is just about town projects. It's more than that. It has to be."

Marisol's heart pounded in her chest, a joyous rhythm that echoed the river's flow. "It is more, Theo. It has to be."

He finally closed the small distance between them, his lips meeting hers in a kiss that was both tentative and sure. It wasn't a kiss born of impulsive passion, but one of deep, abiding affection, of shared understanding, and of a future that was finally being embraced. It was a kiss that spoke of quiet mornings, of shared laughter, of building a life, not just a library. The moonlight, the river, the very air around them seemed to hold their breath, witnessing the quiet, profound unfolding of their love story.

As they broke apart, their foreheads resting against each other, Marisol felt a sense of peace settle over her, a profound contentment that resonated deeper than any public victory. "So, what are your 'what nows,' Theo?" she whispered, her voice husky.

He pulled back slightly, his eyes alight with a warmth that made her feel seen, cherished. "My 'what nows' involve a lot more time spent like this," he said, his gaze sweeping from her eyes down to her lips. "They involve making sure Cedar Ridge continues to thrive, and making sure we continue to thrive, together. They involve building a future, Marisol. A future that includes you, very prominently."

He cupped her face in his hands, his touch firm and possessive. "I want to be part of your future, Marisol. Not just as a co-conspirator in town projects, but as... as your partner. In everything."

Tears welled in Marisol's eyes, not of sadness, but of overwhelming joy. She had come to Cedar Ridge seeking a place to belong, and she had found it. She had found a community, a purpose, and in the most unexpected way, she had found a love that felt as steady and as enduring as the Cedar River itself.

"I want that too, Theo," she breathed, her voice thick with emotion. "More than anything."

He lowered his head, his lips brushing against hers again, a soft, lingering promise. "Then it's settled," he murmured against her skin. "We'll figure it out. Together."

They stood there for a long time, bathed in the moonlight, the river flowing on, a constant reminder of the gentle, persistent force of nature—and of love. The conversation had been a long time coming, a necessary step in defining not just the future of their beloved town, but the future of their own intertwined lives. The anxiety that had once defined Marisol's days had been replaced by a quiet confidence, a certainty that whatever challenges lay ahead, they would face them as they had faced everything else: side by side, their partnership a silent, unwavering strength, their love story now etched into the heart of Cedar Ridge, as enduring as the river that flowed beside them. The path forward, once shrouded in uncertainty, now felt illuminated by the promise of a shared horizon.

The air was cool and carried the rich, earthy perfume of late autumn. Marisol breathed it in, the scent a grounding balm after the exhilarating conversations of the past few days. The library's future, once a nebulous worry, now felt solid, a testament to their collective effort. But it was the future that lay beyond the polished shelves and hushed aisles that occupied her thoughts most keenly. Theo had been so open, so wonderfully present, and she felt a new sense of ease blossoming between them, a quiet confidence that allowed for deeper conversations.

They walked hand-in-hand, their steps falling into an easy rhythm on the path leading away from the river. The moonlight, a pale, ethereal wash, filtered through the skeletal branches of the oak trees, casting dancing shadows on the fallen leaves. Each crunch underfoot was a soft punctuation mark in the deepening quiet.

Marisol found herself glancing at Theo, her heart a gentle flutter against her ribs. He had spoken of their shared future, of building something together, and the sincerity in his eyes had resonated deep within her. But she knew, from years of navigating her own anxieties, that true security came not just from shared plans, but from shared dreams. She wanted to hear his dreams, not as a response to her anxieties, but as aspirations that pulsed with his own unique light.

"Theo," she began, her voice soft, a mere whisper against the rustle of leaves. She felt his fingers tighten almost imperceptibly around hers, a silent invitation to continue. "You know how much the library means to me. How much preserving that space, that history, means."

He turned his head, his profile etched against the dappled moonlight. "I do, Marisol. And I'm so glad we could make it happen. You were the driving force."

"But," she continued, choosing her words carefully, "it's not just about the buildings, is it? It's about what they represent. What they allow us to build. And I've been thinking a lot about that lately. About what we are building." She paused, letting the words settle. The scent of damp earth and decaying leaves, a scent that often signaled endings, now felt like the fertile ground for new beginnings.

Theo stopped walking, turning to face her fully. The shadows softened the sharp angles of his face, making him seem even more approachable. "What are you thinking about, Marisol?" His tone was open, devoid of any defensiveness, and she felt a surge of gratitude for his willingness to simply listen.

"I'm thinking," she said, her gaze meeting his, "about what you envision for us. Not just in terms of projects, or the town's progress, but for us. For you and me." She offered him a gentle smile, a silent reassurance that this was not an interrogation, but an invitation. "I've realized that for so long, my focus has been on what I'm afraid of losing. The library, my place here, connections… you." She admitted it with a quiet honesty, the words feeling less like a confession and more like a simple statement of fact. "But I don't want to approach our future from a place of fear anymore. I want to build it from a place of hope. Of what we want."

She reached out, her fingers tracing the line of his jaw, a touch as soft as the falling leaves. "So, I'm not going to ask you what you fear for us, Theo. Because I think we've both had our share of anxieties. Instead, I want to ask you… what do you dream of for us? What does a good future look like, in your eyes?"

She watched him, her heart open. The silence stretched between them, not an awkward void, but a space filled with anticipation. The faint murmur of the Cedar River, a constant, soothing presence, seemed to underscore the quiet intimacy of the moment. She saw a flicker of introspection in his eyes, a delving into thoughts he might not have articulated even to himself.

Theo's hand covered hers, his thumb gently stroking the back of her hand. His gaze was steady, and Marisol felt a profound sense of connection, a silent acknowledgment of the trust they had built.

"That's... a good question, Marisol," he said, his voice a low, thoughtful rumble. "And you're right. It's easy to get caught up in the 'what ifs,' in the potential pitfalls. But dreaming... that's different." He looked out at the moonlit landscape, a soft smile gracing his lips. "I see Cedar Ridge continuing to flourish, of course. The library is just the beginning. I see more community initiatives, more shared projects that bring people together. I see the kind of town where people feel connected, where they can put down roots and truly belong."

He turned back to her, his eyes holding a warmth that made her breath catch. "But for us?" he continued, his voice softening further. "I envision... continuity. A steady, unwavering presence in each other's lives. I see us sharing the everyday moments as much as the grand achievements."

Marisol leaned in slightly, eager to hear more. This was the language of her heart, the subtle weaving of lives that she craved.

"I imagine us having quiet mornings," Theo mused, his gaze drifting towards the faint lights of the town in the distance. "Coffee on the porch, the newspaper between us, the world just starting to stir. I imagine us tackling challenges, big or small, with that same sense of partnership we found with the library. Not as a team of two people working on a project, but as two people whose lives are intertwined, who support each other's individual growth as much as our shared path."

He shifted his weight, his free hand coming up to gently cup her cheek. His touch was feather-light, yet it sent a tremor of pure joy through her. "I dream of laughter, Marisol. Easy, unforced laughter that fills the silences. I dream of adventures, perhaps exploring the trails around Cedar Ridge more, or discovering new places together. I dream of a future where we don't have to ask 'what if' but can simply say 'this is'."

He paused, his thumb tracing a gentle arc on her skin. "I dream of a home," he admitted, his voice growing more personal, more intimate. "Not just a place to live, but a home that we build together, filled with shared memories, shared books, shared dreams. A place where we both feel completely, unequivocally ourselves, and completely, unequivocally loved."

Marisol's heart swelled. His words were a balm to her soul, a confirmation of the quiet hope that had been growing within her. She had felt it, had sensed their potential, but to hear him articulate it so beautifully, so sincerely, was a profound gift.

"And what about your own ambitions, Theo?" she asked, her voice a little husky with emotion. "Do you see them fitting into this picture? Or would they be separate?"

He met her question with a firm, unwavering gaze. "My ambitions are no longer separate, Marisol. They've evolved. They've become more... expansive. Working with you on the library, seeing your passion, your dedication... it's inspired me. It's shown me that I don't have to choose between my work and my personal life, between my own goals and building a life with someone. In fact, I've realized that a fulfilling personal life fuels my professional ambitions, and vice versa. I want to build something significant, yes, but I want to build it with you by my side. And I want to support you in building whatever it is you dream of, too. Your creativity, your vision... it's a force. I want to be a part of nurturing that, not dimming it."

He leaned closer, his forehead resting against hers. The scent of pine needles and damp earth was stronger here, a wilder fragrance that spoke of the untamed beauty of the surrounding landscape. "I envision us complementing each other, Marisol. You bring the color, the spark, the grand vision. I bring the structure, the planning, the grounding. Together, we can create something truly extraordinary. Something that lasts."

The word 'lasts' hung in the air between them, a promise whispered on the autumn breeze. It was the very word she had longed to hear, the anchor she had unknowingly been seeking.

"Theo," she breathed, her voice barely audible. Tears pricked at the corners of her eyes, not from sadness, but from an overwhelming sense of peace and belonging. "That... that is exactly what I dream of, too."

She pulled back slightly, her hands still cupping his face, her thumbs tracing the contours of his skin. "I was so afraid of being too much, or not enough. Of pushing you away by wanting too much for us. But hearing you say this... it makes me feel so seen. So understood."

He covered her hands with his, his grip firm and reassuring. "You are never 'too much,' Marisol. You are just... you. And that is more than enough. It's everything." His gaze was intense, filled with an emotion that mirrored her own. "I love the way you see the world, the way you inspire people, the way you make me see things differently. I love the passion you pour into everything you do. And I love the quiet strength that underpins it all."

He leaned in, his lips brushing against hers, a soft, hesitant kiss that spoke volumes. It was a kiss of affirmation, of shared dreams, of a future that was no longer a vague possibility, but a tangible reality they were actively creating.

"So," he murmured against her lips, his voice low and husky, "no more fear, then? Only dreams?"

Marisol's smile widened, a radiant, uninhibited expression of joy. "Only dreams," she confirmed, her voice filled with a newfound confidence. "And the determination to build them, together."

He kissed her again, a deeper, more certain kiss this time, one that promised commitment and a shared journey. The fallen leaves rustled around them, the river whispered its timeless song, and the moon, a silent witness, bathed them in its soft, benevolent light. In that quiet clearing, surrounded by the gentle decay of autumn and the promise of spring, Marisol and Theo had finally spoken the language of their hearts, their shared vision for the future a beautiful tapestry woven from dreams, trust, and the quiet, enduring power of love. The path ahead, illuminated by the moonlight and their mutual aspirations, felt boundless, and she knew, with a certainty that settled deep in her soul, that they were finally walking it together.

Theo's voice, usually measured and thoughtful, now held a new resonance, a hopeful current that vibrated with a conviction Marisol hadn't heard before. It was as if the dam of his carefully constructed reservations had finally yielded to the persistent, gentle force of her affection, allowing a clearer, more expansive vision to flow. He wasn't just agreeing to a future; he was actively imagining it, painting it with strokes of quiet desire and steady intent. The library, a symbol of their shared endeavor, had become more than just a project; it had become a catalyst, a tangible proof that collaboration and shared passion could indeed build something lasting. And in its success, he saw not just the revitalization of a beloved town institution, but the potential for a richer, deeper connection between them.

"It's not about making promises that feel like cages, Marisol," he'd said, his hand still warm around hers as they continued their moonlit walk. "It's about acknowledging that certain things are worth building towards. That the steady rhythm of two lives moving in sync is a powerful thing. I've spent so much time guarding against the fall, against the inevitable disappointments that life throws our way. But you... you make me want to look up, to see the sky. To see what's possible when you're not constantly bracing for impact." He squeezed her hand, a silent testament to his evolving perspective. "The library project, seeing it come to life, seeing how much it meant to you, and how much we achieved together... it clarified things for me. It showed me that my own ambition isn't just about building structures or achieving professional milestones. It's also about building a life that has meaning, a life that's shared."

He paused, gathering his thoughts, the silence filled only by the distant murmur of the river and the soft crunch of leaves underfoot. "I used to think of permanence as a kind of stagnation, a surrender. But now... I see it differently. I see it as a foundation. A deep, strong foundation that allows for growth, for exploration, for genuine freedom. Because when you know you have that stability, that unwavering support, you're not afraid to take risks. You're not afraid to be vulnerable. You're not afraid to... to truly live."

Marisol listened, her heart swelling with a quiet joy that threatened to overflow. This was it. This was the evolution she had hoped for, the articulation of a future that felt not just safe, but vibrant and full of promise. Theo's words were a testament to his own growth, his willingness to shed old fears and embrace new possibilities. He wasn't just looking for comfort; he was actively seeking a partnership, a co-creation.

"I envision us," he continued, his voice growing softer, more intimate, "not just as individuals who happen to share a town, or a project. But as a unit. A partnership where our strengths complement each other. You have that incredible ability to see the big picture, to inspire, to bring people together. And I... I can help bring those visions into tangible reality. I can be the steady hand that guides the compass, ensuring we navigate any storms effectively. It's not about one person leading and the other following. It's about two people walking side-by-side, each with their own unique contribution, their own unique perspective, but with a shared destination in mind."

He turned to her, his eyes, usually so guarded, now reflecting the moonlight with a clear, unreserved warmth. "I see us continuing to learn from each other. I want to be challenged by your ideas, Marisol. I want to be inspired by your passion. And I hope that I can offer you a sense of groundedness, a quiet confidence that allows you to soar even higher. It's about mutual respect, mutual admiration, and a deep, abiding trust. Trust that we can weather whatever comes our way, because we'll be doing it together."

He paused, a thoughtful expression crossing his face. "And it's the small things, too. I don't just dream of grand achievements. I dream of the quiet moments. Of waking up to find you beside me, of sharing a cup of coffee before the world demands our attention. Of late-night conversations, debating books or life or anything that sparks our interest. Of building a home, a real home, filled with the echoes of our laughter, the scent of our shared meals, the quiet comfort of knowing we belong to each other. It's not about possessiveness; it's about belonging. About creating a sanctuary where we can both recharge, where we can both be unapologetically ourselves."

Marisol squeezed his hand in return, her own voice filled with emotion. "Theo, that's... that's beautiful. It's exactly what I hoped for. It's more than I even dared to articulate sometimes." She felt a profound sense of relief, a lifting of a weight she hadn't fully realized she'd been carrying. His willingness to articulate these desires, to embrace the concept of a shared future with such open conviction, was a powerful affirmation.

"I know I've been... cautious," he admitted, his gaze meeting hers directly. "My past experiences, my own nature, they've made me wary of commitments that felt like an endpoint. But with you, it feels different. It feels like a beginning. Like a doorway opening to possibilities I hadn't even considered. You've shown me that building a life with someone doesn't mean sacrificing your own dreams. It means expanding them. It means finding someone who not only understands those dreams but actively wants to help you achieve them, and who has their own dreams you can help nurture in return."

He gestured vaguely towards the town lights twinkling in the distance. "This town, this community... it's important. And I'm committed to its future. But my commitment to our future, Marisol, that's something I'm realizing is even more profound. It's the bedrock upon which everything else can be built. If I have that certainty with you, then the challenges in the community, the projects, the inevitable setbacks... they become manageable. They become part of a larger narrative, a story we're writing together."

He pulled her a little closer, his arm encircling her waist. "I don't want to be afraid of forever anymore. I want to embrace it. Not as a sentence, but as a choice. A daily choice to continue building, to continue loving, to continue growing together. And with you, that choice feels not like a burden, but like the most natural, most exhilarating path forward. You have a way of making the ordinary feel extraordinary, Marisol. And I want to spend my life experiencing that."

The simple, heartfelt sincerity in his words washed over Marisol, a wave of pure, unadulterated joy. This wasn't just a romantic declaration; it was a fundamental shift in his perspective, a willingness to embrace permanence not out of obligation, but out of a deep-seated desire. He was choosing her, choosing them, with a clear mind and an open heart. The promises they were implicitly making weren't chains, but the strong, flexible ropes that would tie them together as they navigated the adventures ahead. It was a vision of a future built on mutual respect, shared dreams, and the quiet, powerful strength of a love that had found its footing and was ready to grow. And as they stood there, bathed in moonlight, Marisol knew that this emerging vision of Theo's was the most beautiful blueprint for their future she could have ever imagined.

The quiet understanding that had settled between them under the moonlit sky was a tender thing, a fragile bloom coaxed from the soil of shared vulnerability. Theo's words had painted a landscape of shared futures, a vision that Marisol had embraced with every fiber of her being. But as they walked back towards the soft glow of the town, a different kind of conversation began to unfold, one that delved into the deeper currents of Theo's past, not to rehash old wounds, but to illuminate the path they were now forging together.

"You asked once," Theo began, his voice a low murmur against the gentle night breeze, "if I was afraid of... of falling in love. And I was, and in many ways, I still am. But not in the way I used to be. It's not about the fear of the descent anymore, Marisol. It's about understanding the landscape I'm landing in, and knowing that it's worth the risk." He paused, his gaze fixed on the distant lights, his brow furrowed in thought. "My father. He was a good man, incredibly kind, but his life was... cut short. Unexpectedly. It was a shock that rippled through our family, and through me, in a way that left me feeling like the ground could shift beneath my feet at any moment."

He didn't elaborate on the details, and Marisol didn't press. She under-stood. The echoes of loss, especially from such a foundational figure, could be profound and lingering. It was the silence that followed, however, that spoke volumes. It wasn't a silence of avoidance, but one of careful consideration, as if he were sifting through memories to find the precise words to articulate their impact.

"After he passed," Theo continued, his voice gaining a steadier cadence, "I became acutely aware of fragility. Of how quickly things can change, how precious and precarious life is. And I think, subconsciously, I started to build walls. Not against grief, but against the possibility of experiencing that kind of profound loss again. I compartmentalized. I focused on my work, on building things that felt solid, tangible, things that wouldn't disappear overnight. And in a way, I was protecting myself. Protecting my heart from the potential devastation of losing someone I deeply cared about."

He turned to her then, his eyes holding a vulnerability that was both new and deeply compelling. "But what I've come to realize, especially over these past few months with you, is that in protecting myself from potential pain, I was also denying myself immense joy. I was so focused on preventing the fall that I never truly allowed myself to experience the exhilaration of flight. By keeping my heart guarded, by maintaining a certain emotional distance, I was inadvertently creating a different kind of loss – a loss of shared intimacy, a loss of the deep, resonant connection that makes life truly meaningful."

Marisol listened, her own heart aching with a sympathetic understanding. She had always sensed a certain reserve in Theo, a carefully cultivated composure. Now, she saw it not as a lack of feeling, but as a shield forged in the fires of past sorrow. His willingness to share this was a profound act of trust, a testament to the burgeoning intimacy between them.

"It's not about forgetting," he emphasized, his tone earnest. "The pain of losing my father is a part of me. It shaped me, it taught me invaluable lessons about resilience and the preciousness of time. But it doesn't have to dictate my present, or my future. I can honor his memory, I can carry the lessons he taught me, without allowing that past sorrow to overshadow the possibility of a bright and hopeful tomorrow. It's about integration, not erasure. Learning to carry the weight of the past without letting it crush the spirit of the present."

He squeezed her hand, a gentle pressure that conveyed a world of meaning. "You've helped me see that, Marisol. You've shown me that vulnerability isn't a weakness, but a conduit. That allowing yourself to be seen, truly seen, with all your imperfections and all your fears, is where the deepest connections are forged. I'd convinced myself that strong meant being stoic, being impenetrable. But that's a lonely kind of strength. The kind of strength I'm beginning to understand, the kind I see in you, is the strength to be open, to be brave enough to feel, to love, and to risk being hurt, because the reward of true connection is immeasurable."

He took a deep breath, as if shedding a long-held burden. "I used to think that emotional availability was a liability. That the more invested I became, the more vulnerable I made myself to disappointment. And that was true, in a sense. But what I didn't fully appreciate was the immense cost of that self-preservation. The cost of missed conversations, of unspoken affections, of shared moments that never happened because I was too afraid to let my guard down. It was a slow erosion, a quiet diminishment of my own capacity for joy."

"And with you," he continued, his voice softening, a warmth infusing his words, "it feels different. It feels like... like a homecoming. Like a part of me that I'd kept locked away for so long has finally found its way back. You don't just accept my past, Marisol; you help me understand how it has shaped me, and you encourage me to move beyond its limitations. You see the man I am now, and the man I aspire to be, and you embrace both with such unwavering grace."

He stopped walking for a moment, turning to face her fully. The moonlight cast a gentle glow on his features, highlighting the earnestness in his eyes. "It's like this library project. When we first started, I saw it as a challenge, a professional endeavor. And it was. But it became so much more. It became a testament to what we can build together, a tangible symbol of shared vision and collaborative effort. And in that process, I learned that building a life with someone isn't about sacrificing your own identity or your own goals. It's about finding someone who complements you, someone who inspires you to be your best self, and someone who is willing to walk alongside you, sharing in the triumphs and weathering the storms."

"My past," he mused, his gaze distant again, "it gave me a certain perspective on time. It taught me that life is finite, and that every moment counts. But it also instilled in me a fear of cherishing those moments too deeply, because of the inevitable pain of their passing. It's a paradox, I know. But you, Marisol, you've untangled it. You've shown me that the beauty of a moment isn't diminished by its impermanence, but amplified by the act of cherishing it. The joy of a shared laugh, the comfort of a quiet presence, the excitement of a new adventure – these are not things to be feared for their eventual end, but to be savored for their present beauty."

He reached out, his fingers tracing the curve of her cheekbone. "I was so afraid of being vulnerable, of being hurt, that I inadvertently built a fortress around my heart. And while it kept me safe from certain kinds of pain, it also kept me from experiencing the profound richness of true emotional connection. It was a lonely kind of safety, Marisol. And I wouldn't trade the possibility of a shared future with you for that kind of solitary security, not for anything in the world."

The sincerity in his voice was a balm to her soul. She had sensed the weight of his past, the subtle currents of a guarded heart. To hear him articulate it so openly, not as an excuse for his past reservations, but as a foundational understanding of his growth, was incredibly moving. It was the mark of a man who was not just looking forward, but actively choosing to build a future on the lessons of his past, integrating them without being defined by them.

"It's about acknowledging the lessons," Theo continued, his voice gaining a quiet strength, "and then consciously choosing to move forward. It's about understanding that the pain of past loss doesn't have to be a prophecy of future pain. It can be a teacher. And the lesson, for me, has been about the immense value of connection, of intimacy, of the shared journey. It's about recognizing that while I can't control the unpredictable nature of life, I can control how I choose to live within it, and who I choose to share that living with."

He looked at her, his gaze steady and full of a newfound confidence. "You've taught me that love isn't about erasing the past, but about building a future that is informed and enriched by it. It's about embracing vulnerability not as a weakness, but as the very essence of human connection. It's about choosing to believe in the possibility of enduring happiness, even when the shadows of past sorrow loom. And with you, Marisol, that belief feels not only possible, but inevitable."

The air between them hummed with a renewed sense of understanding, a deeper appreciation for the journey that had brought them to this point. Theo's willingness to share the vulnerability of his past, not to dwell in sorrow, but to illuminate his present choices, was a profound testament to his commitment. He was not trying to erase the scars, but to show how they had made him stronger, more capable of appreciating the present, and more determined to build a future filled with shared love and unwavering trust. This was not just about defining their future; it was about truly understanding the man who was helping her define it.

The gentle murmur of the river, a constant, soothing soundtrack to their lives in Havenwood, seemed to deepen its song as they continued their walk. The moonlight, once a soft caress, now painted their surroundings in a more dramatic chiaroscuro, highlighting the shadowed depths and luminous peaks of the night. Theo's words, raw and honest, had peeled back layers, revealing not just his fears but the profound understanding he had gained from confronting them. Marisol felt a profound sense of peace settle over her, a quiet recognition of the path they had navigated to reach this very moment.

It wasn't a sudden revelation, but a gradual unfolding, like the slow bloom of a desert flower after a rare rain. Theo hadn't arrived at this point of readiness overnight. His journey, marked by the shadows of past loss and the innate caution that had become his armor, was a testament to his resilience. And now, he was choosing, consciously, to lay down that armor, not because the threats had vanished, but because the possibility of what lay ahead – a life with her – was worth far more than the perceived safety of isolation.

"It's not about erasing the past, Marisol," Theo said again, his voice a low, steady rumble, the words weaving themselves into the tapestry of the night. "It's about honoring its lessons. My father's passing taught me the preciousness of every breath, every shared moment. For a long time, I interpreted that lesson as a reason to guard my heart, to avoid the intensity of deep connection because the potential for loss felt too overwhelming.

It was a form of self-protection, I suppose, a way to control the uncontrollable." He stopped, his hand finding hers, his thumb tracing small circles on her skin. "But as I've spent time with you, I've realized that true control isn't about building walls, but about choosing what you invite in. It's about recognizing that while life will always hold its share of pain and uncertainty, it also holds an immeasurable capacity for joy, for love, for a shared future that is richer and more vibrant than anything I could ever build alone."

Marisol squeezed his hand, her heart swelling with a tenderness that felt both familiar and exhilarating. She saw it in his eyes, in the subtle shift of his posture, in the way his gaze held hers with an unwavering warmth. This wasn't a fleeting emotion; it was a deep, abiding commitment, a choice made not out of impulse, but out of a profound understanding of what truly mattered. His declaration wasn't a grand, theatrical promise of forever, but something far more potent: a quiet, deliberate embrace of 'us.'

"You're right," she whispered, her voice thick with emotion. "It's about integration. About carrying the lessons, not letting them become burdens.

You've learned to see the fragility of life not as a reason to retreat, but as an impetus to cherish."

Theo's smile was a soft, genuine thing that lit up his face even in the dim light. "And you," he said, his voice laced with gratitude, "you've been the catalyst for that shift. You've shown me that vulnerability isn't a weakness to be hidden, but a doorway to authentic connection. You've accepted me, not just as I am now, but with all the layers of my past, and you've encouraged me to see that those layers don't define me, but shape me."

He gestured vaguely towards the town, its lights twinkling like fallen stars against the inky sky. "When I first came back to Havenwood, I thought I was just here for the library project, a professional obligation. I was so focused on the tangible, the measurable. I didn't anticipate the immeasurable impact of the people I would meet, of the life that would unfold around me. And you, Marisol, you are at the heart of that unfolding."

He paused, his gaze drifting towards the distant, moonlit surface of the river. "I used to think that building a life meant building a solid structure, something impervious to the storms of life. But I'm starting to understand that a life built with someone else isn't about creating an unbreachable fortress, but about cultivating a garden. A space where shared dreams can take root, where love can flourish, and where we can weather the storms together, supporting each other, finding strength in our shared vulnerability."

Marisol found herself nodding, the metaphor resonating deeply within her. It wasn't about imposing their will on the world, but about nurturing something beautiful, something that required care, attention, and a shared commitment. "A garden," she echoed softly. "One that we tend together."

"Exactly," Theo affirmed, his grip on her hand tightening slightly, a silent testament to the unspoken understanding that now flowed between them. "It's not about grand pronouncements, Marisol. It's about the daily choices. The choice to be present, to listen, to support. The choice to share the mundane moments and the extraordinary ones. The choice to believe in the possibility of a future, even when the past whispers its doubts."

He turned to her fully, his eyes reflecting the starlight, filled with a quiet resolve. "My commitment to you, Marisol, isn't a sudden leap into the unknown. It's a conscious, deliberate step forward. It's a promise to continue to grow, to continue to learn, and to continue to choose you, every single day. It's about building a life, brick by brick, moment by moment, with you. It's about the library, yes, but it's also about the quiet mornings, the shared laughter, the dreams we'll whisper into the night. It's about our 'us.'"

The simplicity of his words, devoid of flourish or pretense, struck Marisol with profound force. It was Theo, in his quiet, grounded way, offering her his whole heart, not with a flourish of a hero's vow, but with the steady certainty of a man who had finally found his true north. She saw the man who had wrestled with his past, who had learned the cost of emotional self-preservation, and who had emerged not unscathed, but stronger, wiser, and more capable of embracing the fullness of love.

"And I choose us too, Theo," she said, her voice clear and unwavering. "I choose the garden we're tending. I choose the quiet mornings and the shared dreams. I choose you."

A genuine, unadulterated smile spread across his face, erasing any lingering shadows. It was a smile that held a lifetime of unspoken affection, a quiet joy that radiated from within. He raised her hand to his lips, pressing a soft kiss to her knuckles. It was a gesture of respect, of tenderness, of profound love.

"Then let's continue to tend it," he said, his gaze holding hers. "Together."

They stood in comfortable silence for a moment, the river's song a constant reminder of the flow of time, of the journey they were on. It wasn't a river that rushed or churned, but one that moved with a steady, determined grace, carving its path through the landscape with quiet persistence. And in that moment, Marisol knew, with a certainty that settled deep in her soul, that their journey together would be much the same. It would be built on the solid foundation of shared understanding, nurtured by mutual respect, and strengthened by a love that was as deep and enduring as the river itself.

The conversation hadn't been about making grand promises or drawing up definitive blueprints. It had been about a mutual recognition, a shared acknowledgment that their individual paths had converged, and that from this point forward, their journey would be taken as 'us.' Theo's commitment wasn't a sudden pronouncement; it was an evolution, a natural progression of the genuine affection and deep respect that had bloomed between them. He wasn't offering a fairytale ending, but something far more precious: a partnership built on presence, on action, and on the quiet, unwavering promise of shared dreams.

Marisol accepted this, understanding the profound weight of Theo's declaration. It wasn't spoken in grand pronouncements, but in the quiet sincerity of his words, the unwavering gaze of his eyes, and the gentle firmness of his hand holding hers. It was a testament to his growth, a visible manifestation of the man who had learned to integrate his past without being defined by it, and who was now choosing to build a future on the bedrock of love and shared vulnerability.

He didn't speak of guarantees or a future devoid of challenges. Instead, he spoke of the act of choosing, repeatedly and intentionally, to face those challenges together. He spoke of the library, yes, the tangible project that had brought them together, but more importantly, he spoke of the intangible – the shared glances, the comforting silences, the quiet understanding that had become their unspoken language. He was offering not just his love, but his partnership, his willingness to build a life alongside her, a life that would be richer for their shared experiences.

"I've spent so long afraid of the 'what ifs'," Theo confessed, his voice barely above a whisper, as if sharing a secret with the night. "Afraid of what might go wrong, what could be lost. But being with you, Marisol, has shifted my perspective. Now, I'm more curious about the 'what if' of joy, the 'what if' of shared laughter, the 'what if' of a future where we build something beautiful together. It's a different kind of risk, isn't it? A risk of immense happiness."

Marisol leaned her head against his shoulder, the steady rhythm of his heartbeat a soothing balm. "It's the only risk worth taking, Theo," she replied, her voice filled with a quiet certainty. "The risk of finding a love that makes you feel truly seen, truly understood, and truly home."

He turned his head, his lips brushing against her temple, a tender gesture that spoke volumes. "Home," he repeated, the word carrying a profound sense of arrival. "Yes, Marisol. You've made me feel like I've finally found my way home."

The river continued its gentle, persistent flow, mirroring the steady progression of their relationship. It was a journey not of sudden leaps, but of deliberate, loving steps. The moonlight illuminated their path, a soft, guiding light for the future they were now choosing to build, together. The quiet understanding that had settled between them was no longer fragile, but had solidified into a beautiful, resilient bond, a testament to their shared journey and the profound choice for 'us.' They had navigated the currents of their individual pasts, and now, they were ready to sail into the future, hand in hand, their hearts beating in sync with the timeless rhythm of the river.

Chapter Ten: Building Forever

The air in The Bound Page, usually redolent with the comforting aroma of aged paper and a hint of lavender, now seemed to carry an additional layer of anticipation. It was a scent Marisol had come to associate with possibility, with the quiet hum of a life that was expanding, growing richer with each passing day. Theo's hand, warm and steady, rested on her shoulder as they stood amidst the towering shelves, the soft afternoon light filtering through the arched windows, illuminating dust motes dancing like tiny, captured stars. Their conversation, which had begun with the quiet intimacy of their moonlit walk by the river, had naturally drifted towards the tangible, the steps they could take to solidify the profound connection that had blossomed between them.

"So," Marisol began, turning to face him, a hopeful smile playing on her lips, "the library project is officially nearing completion. And your carpentry business is thriving. It feels like... like we're standing at the edge of something new, doesn't it?"

Theo's eyes, the color of warm, polished oak, met hers, a reflection of the same sentiment. He chuckled, a low, contented sound. "It does. And it feels good. For so long, I was so focused on completing tasks, on seeing projects through from start to finish, that I almost forgot about the living, breathing part of it all. The part that involves sharing the fruits of that labor, of building something that isn't just a structure, but a life." He stepped closer, his gaze softening. "And you, Marisol, you've shown me that the most important projects are the ones built together."

The idea had been a seed, planted during their earlier, more profound conversations, now ready to sprout. It wasn't about erasing their individual identities, but about weaving them together, creating a tapestry that was stronger and more beautiful because of its intricate patterns. Marisol's heart swelled at the thought. The Bound Page, her sanctuary, her lifelong dream, felt ready for this evolution. And Theo's steady, skilled hands, capable of shaping wood into art, felt like the perfect complement to her vision.

"I've been thinking a lot about this," Marisol continued, her voice gaining a touch of excitement. "About how we can make 'us' more than just a beautiful sentiment. How we can make it a tangible part of our lives, and our work." She gestured around the bookstore, her fingers tracing the spine of a well-loved novel. "The Bound Page... it's more than just a business to me, Theo. It's my heart. And your carpentry, your skill, the way you create with your hands... it's so much more than just a job to you. It's your passion, your artistry."

Theo nodded, his thumb absently stroking her arm. "It is. And I've always admired how you've poured so much of yourself into this place. The way you curate the books, the way you foster a sense of community here. It's inspiring." He paused, a thoughtful expression on his face. "I've been thinking about how my workshop, my tools, my expertise... they could integrate with this space in a meaningful way. Not just in terms of building bookshelves, though that's certainly a possibility," he added with a smile, "but in a more holistic sense."

This was it. The conversation they had both been waiting for, the one that would take their relationship from a blossoming romance to a fully realized partnership. The scent of paper and ink in the bookstore, once a solitary comfort, now felt like the prelude to a shared symphony of creativity and commerce. The old wooden counter, polished smooth by countless transactions, seemed to gleam with a new promise, a promise of shared futures.

"Exactly!" Marisol exclaimed, the word buoyant with enthusiasm. "Imagine it, Theo. We could create a small corner here, a dedicated space for your custom woodworking. Perhaps we could feature your pieces – handmade journals, carved bookends, bespoke furniture designed to complement the books. It would add another dimension to The Bound Page, something truly unique for Havenwood." She could already picture it: the warm glow of lamps illuminating handcrafted wooden treasures, nestled amongst the literary wonders.

Theo's eyes lit up. "I love that idea, Marisol. It feels... natural. Like it was meant to be. We could even host workshops together. You could do readings or author events, and I could offer classes on simple woodworking or bookbinding techniques. It would create a synergy, a reason for people to come here for more than just a book." He was already envisioning the logistics, the possibilities of combining their talents. His hands, usually busy with planes and chisels, were now sketching out ideas in the air. "We could brand it something like 'The Bound Page & Workshop' or 'Havenwood Creations by Theo & Marisol.'"

Marisol laughed, a clear, joyful sound that echoed through the quiet store. "Oh, I like that! It has a lovely ring to it. 'Havenwood Creations.' It feels grounded, authentic." She walked over to a sun-drenched alcove, usually reserved for displaying new releases. "We could set up a small display table here. Perhaps some of your smaller pieces – elegant letter openers carved from local wood, or perhaps beautifully crafted wooden bookmarks that customers could purchase along with their books."

"And I could build you that custom reading nook you've always wanted," Theo offered, his gaze sweeping over the cozy corners of the store. "A perfect spot for patrons to lose themselves in a story, surrounded by the warmth of natural wood. It would make this place even more inviting, more of a destination." He pictured the rich grain of walnut or cherry, the smooth, inviting finish. He could already feel the weight of a well-crafted chair, the comfort of a sturdy, beautifully designed table.

The prospect of merging their professional lives felt both exhilarating and a little daunting, but mostly, it felt right. It was a tangible manifestation of the commitment they had forged, a way to intertwine their passions and build a shared legacy. The familiar scent of paper, usually a comforting presence, now seemed to carry the subtle, earthy undertones of possibility, of wood shavings and linseed oil, a scent that spoke of shared endeavors and a future built with their own hands.

"That reading nook," Marisol sighed contentedly, her eyes shining, "would be a dream come true. And it's more than just furniture, isn't it? It's about creating an experience. About making this place a haven in every sense of the word." She walked back to Theo, reaching out to take his hands. His palms were calloused, a testament to his craftsmanship, but his touch was incredibly gentle. "We're not just merging businesses, Theo. We're merging our lives, our dreams. This is about building something substantial, something that lasts."

Theo's grip tightened reassuringly. "Exactly. It's about building a future, brick by brick, plank by plank, with you. This bookstore, it's been your world. And my workshop, it's been mine. Now, we get to create a shared world. A world where creativity flows freely, where both our passions are celebrated, and where we can build something extraordinary together." He looked around the store, his gaze lingering on the worn leather armchairs, the sturdy oak tables, the meticulously organized shelves. "This place has so much character, Marisol. And I want to contribute to that, to enhance it, to make it even more of a reflection of you, and now, of us."

The practicalities of such a merger would undoubtedly require careful planning and discussion. There would be new signage to consider, new marketing strategies, and undoubtedly, hours spent poring over blueprints and inventory lists. But for the first time, the prospect of such work felt less like a chore and more like an exciting adventure. It was the kind of work that was done with shared purpose, with mutual respect, and with the underlying knowledge that every decision was a step towards solidifying their 'us.'

"We could start small," Marisol suggested, her mind already racing with possibilities. "Maybe just a dedicated display for your smaller items, like those beautiful carved boxes you showed me. And we could have a small section of books on woodworking, craft, and design. It would tie in perfectly."

"And I could design and build custom display units for the books," Theo added, his enthusiasm infectious. "Shelving that's not just functional, but also beautiful. Think of the elegance of hand-carved details, the warmth of sustainably sourced wood. It would elevate the entire aesthetic of the store. It would make it feel even more like a curated collection, not just of books, but of art and craftsmanship."

The idea of integrating Theo's craft directly into the physical space of The Bound Page felt particularly significant. It was a visual representation of their union, a constant reminder of their shared commitment. The scent of wood, previously an external presence from Theo's workshop, would now be an integral part of the bookstore's atmosphere, mingling with the familiar scent of paper and ink to create a truly unique sensory experience. It would be a space that told their story, a story of two distinct individuals coming together to create something new and beautiful.

"I can see it now," Marisol mused, her gaze distant, lost in a daydream of their future. "Patrons browsing the shelves, their fingers brushing against the smooth wood of your craftsmanship, discovering not just a new story, but a new appreciation for the art of creation. And when they come to the counter to pay, they'll see us, working side by side, a testament to what we've built together."

Theo smiled, a deep, contented smile that reached his eyes. "It's a beautiful vision, Marisol. And it's one we can make real. I'm not just investing in a business, I'm investing in us. In our future. And that's the most valuable investment I could ever make." He gently squeezed her hands. "The Bound Page and Theo's Carpentry. They're not separate entities anymore. They're becoming one. A single, beautiful entity, built on love, partnership, and a shared passion for creating something meaningful."

The familiar comfort of the bookstore, the quiet haven that had always been her own, was now expanding to encompass Theo. It was a profound shift, a gentle unfolding that felt as natural as the turning of a page. The scent of old paper, once a solitary comfort, now mingled with the promise of fresh wood, of creation, of a future that was being built together, piece by carefully considered piece. The partnership felt less like a business arrangement and more like the natural evolution of their love, a way to weave their individual dreams into a shared reality.

"We'll need to sit down and really map out the details," Marisol said, her practical nature kicking in, but without any of the apprehension she might have felt before. "Think about the branding, the logistics of space, how we'll manage inventory and customer flow. It's a big step."

"And we'll do it together," Theo assured her, his voice steady and confident. "Every step of the way. I've learned from you, Marisol, that building something lasting isn't about rushing. It's about intention. It's about careful consideration, about nurturing each element, and about ensuring that every decision is made with our shared future in mind." He gestured to a sturdy, antique oak desk in the corner, where Marisol often did her administrative work. "We can use that desk as our planning hub. We'll spread out the maps, the ideas, the dreams, and we'll build our blueprint, together."

Marisol's heart swelled with a profound sense of gratitude and excitement. This was more than just a business merger; it was a commitment, a declaration of their intention to build a life, not just alongside each other, but intertwined. The scent of paper and wood, now a comforting blend, seemed to whisper promises of shared success, of long evenings spent planning, of vibrant days filled with creation and connection.

"I can't wait," she breathed, a genuine smile illuminating her face. "I can't wait to see what we create, Theo. Not just the physical space, but the life we build within it." She leaned in, pressing a soft kiss to his cheek. "This feels like the beginning of a whole new chapter."

Theo's arms wrapped around her, holding her close. "It is," he murmured against her hair. "A brand new chapter. And I'm so incredibly happy to be writing it with you." The gentle rustle of pages in the background, the faint scent of aged paper, and the subtle, earthy fragrance of wood – it was the scent of their shared future, a future that was just beginning to unfold, full of promise and the quiet strength of a love that was ready to build forever.

The bookstore, once a testament to her solitary dreams, was now a symbol of their shared aspirations, a beacon of their commitment to one another, and to the life they were so eagerly constructing, side by side. The familiar comfort of The Bound Page had expanded, embracing Theo's presence, transforming it into something even richer, a space where individual passions converged to create a unified vision. The scent of paper, once a solitary comfort, now mingled with the robust, grounding aroma of wood, a harmonious blend that spoke of their intertwined futures. It was a scent that promised not just growth, but a deeply rooted, enduring partnership, forged in the crucible of shared dreams and a mutual dedication to building something truly lasting.

The scent of freshly cut pine and the whisper of sawdust, usually confined to the controlled environment of his workshop, began to subtly infuse the air of The Bound Page. It was a new layer, a fragrant testament to the evolution taking place within the beloved bookstore. Theo, his brow furrowed in concentration, was sketching on a large sheet of paper spread across the antique oak desk, the very same desk that had become their planning hub. Marisol watched him, a soft smile playing on her lips, her heart a warm, contented hum. The charcoal pencil moved with a practiced grace, translating the intricate visions in his mind onto the page. This wasn't just any project; it was a declaration, a tangible manifestation of his promise to build a life, a future, with her.

"I've been thinking a lot about how we can best showcase your curated collections, Marisol," Theo began, his voice a low rumble that resonated with a quiet confidence. He looked up, his eyes, the color of rich earth after a spring rain, meeting hers. "Not just the books, but the way you present them. And of course, a place for my own creations to live within this space. So, I've started sketching out a design for a new display shelf. Something substantial, something that speaks to both our crafts."

He turned the sketch towards her. It was a beautiful thing, even in its nascent form. The lines were clean yet elegant, hinting at a structure that would be both functional and aesthetically pleasing. It wasn't just a shelf; it was a testament to their unity, designed to house not only the literary treasures of The Bound Page but also to serve as a proud platform for his handcrafted pieces. He had chosen a specific wood, one that held a deep significance for him.

"I've been leaning towards cherry wood for this," he explained, his finger tracing a curved detail on the drawing. "It's known for its durability, of course, but it also has this incredible warmth to it. And it ages so beautifully, developing this rich patina over time. Much like our relationship, wouldn't you say?" He gave her a playful, knowing look. "It's a wood that signifies longevity, strength, and a beauty that deepens with age. It feels like the right material to represent what we're building here."

Marisol's gaze softened as she absorbed his words and the artistry before her. The cherry wood. It was more than just a choice of material; it was a deliberate, loving statement. She saw the dedication in his focused expression, the care he was already pouring into this endeavor. It was a promise sculpted from wood, a future built with his own two hands, a testament to the depth of his commitment.

"It's gorgeous, Theo," she breathed, her voice tinged with emotion. "You've captured it perfectly. The way it flows, the integration of your work and my books... it's exactly what I envisioned, but even better." She ran her fingers over the smooth, rendered lines of the drawing. "And cherry wood... that's such a thoughtful choice. It's so fitting." She looked at him, her eyes shining. "It feels like a physical embodiment of your promise to me, doesn't it? A constant reminder of what we're creating together."

Theo's smile widened, a slow, genuine unfolding that crinkled the corners of his eyes. "That's exactly what I was hoping for," he admitted. "This isn't just about adding more shelving, Marisol. It's about marking this moment, about creating something that will stand here as a symbol of our partnership. Every joint, every curve, every sanded edge will be made with the intention of building a lasting life with you." He tapped the drawing gently. "I want it to be strong enough to hold centuries of stories, and beautiful enough to be a work of art in its own right. A piece that tells our story."

He spoke of the design with an architect's precision and a lover's passion. He described the carefully planned dimensions, ensuring it would fit seamlessly into the existing aesthetic of The Bound Page while also introducing a new element of bespoke craftsmanship. He envisioned sections dedicated to showcasing his handcrafted journals, perhaps nestled alongside poetry collections, or a dedicated space for his intricately carved wooden bookends, each a miniature sculpture in its own right. He even planned for a few smaller, more accessible shelves at a lower height, perfect for children's books, making the entire piece welcoming to all patrons.

"I want it to have a sense of history, even though it will be brand new," he continued, his voice gaining a lyrical quality. "The lines will be classic, almost timeless. But there will be subtle details, small carvings perhaps, that hint at the stories held within the books it displays, or the nature that inspired my own craft. It will be a piece that invites closer inspection, that rewards curiosity." He paused, his gaze distant for a moment, as if seeing the finished piece in its rightful place within the bookstore. "Imagine it, Marisol. The rich, deep color of the cherry wood catching the light, the smooth, inviting surface... and then, nestled within its embrace, your carefully curated selection of books. And beside them, my wooden creations, each one whispering tales of passion and dedication."

Marisol leaned in, captivated by his vision. She could already picture it, a magnificent centerpiece that would draw the eye and spark conversation. It would be a visible testament to their intertwined lives, a piece of furniture that was more than just wood and nails; it was a piece of their shared soul.

"It will be the heart of the store, Theo," she murmured, her hand finding his, her fingers intertwining with his rough, calloused ones. His touch, usually so capable and strong when wielding tools, was incredibly tender now. "A beautiful, physical representation of everything we're building. It's more than just furniture; it's a promise made tangible." She squeezed his hand. "Thank you. For seeing this, for envisioning this, for putting so much of yourself into it. It means the world to me."

He turned his hand, lacing his fingers with hers, his thumb gently stroking the back of her hand. "It's not just my promise, Marisol. It's ours. This shelf, this bookstore, this life we're creating... it's all ours. And this piece of furniture," he gestured to the sketch again, his expression earnest, "is just the first of many tangible expressions of that. It's a symbol of the foundation we're laying, strong and true, built on love and shared purpose." He met her gaze, his eyes holding a depth of emotion that made her breath catch. "I want to build a life with you that is as enduring and as beautiful as this cherry wood. A life that is solid, reliable, and filled with the warmth of shared moments. This shelf is just the beginning."

The practicalities of such a creation would be immense. Theo would spend countless hours in his workshop, carefully selecting the wood, meticulously shaping each piece, ensuring every detail was perfect. There would be the aroma of sanding and finishing, the quiet hum of saws, the satisfying thud of expertly joined pieces. But for Theo, it was a labor of love, a form of devotion. He saw the process as an extension of his courtship, a way to physically demonstrate the depth of his feelings and his commitment to their future.

He began to describe the joinery techniques he planned to use – dovetails, mortise and tenons – explaining how these traditional methods ensured not only strength but also an undeniable beauty, a testament to the enduring quality of well-crafted work. He spoke of the finish, a multi-layered approach that would enhance the natural grain of the cherry wood, giving it a lustrous sheen that would invite touch.

He even considered the hardware, contemplating custom-made brass fittings for any drawers or doors he might incorporate, ensuring every element, no matter how small, would be a reflection of their shared vision for quality and artistry.

"I'm thinking of incorporating a few hidden compartments too," he added, a mischievous glint in his eye. "Little surprises. Maybe a secret drawer for you to keep your favorite, most precious first editions, or a small, carved niche for a love letter or two. Little treasures, tucked away, just for us." He chuckled softly. "It'll be like a hidden chapter within the shelf itself, a private story only we know."

Marisol laughed, a sound as bright and cheerful as the sunlight streaming through the bookstore window. "Oh, Theo! That's so you. Always thinking of the details, the little touches that make something truly special." She was touched by his imagination, by the way he wove romance and sentiment into even the most practical of creations. "It will be perfect. A shelf that not only holds our past and present but also our little secrets and future dreams."

He picked up a small notebook from the desk, flipping through its pages until he found a blank one. With renewed vigor, he began sketching again, this time detailing some of the smaller elements he'd mentioned. "And for the top, I'm envisioning a slightly thicker slab, maybe with a subtly rounded edge, so that when you're standing here, perhaps reaching for a book, your hand can rest on it comfortably. It's about ergonomics, about making the space as welcoming and as functional as possible." He looked up again, his gaze earnest. "Every element has a purpose, Marisol, not just in terms of utility, but in terms of how it makes you feel. I want this piece to feel welcoming, to feel like a hug made of wood."

The anticipation for the finished piece began to build within Marisol. She could already see it in her mind's eye, a majestic structure that would anchor their joint venture, a beautiful, silent testament to their love and commitment. It was a tangible promise, forged in the heart of Theo's workshop and destined to become a beloved feature of The Bound Page. It was more than just a shelf; it was a piece of their future, lovingly crafted, ready to hold the stories of their lives, together.

"It sounds absolutely perfect," she said, her voice filled with a deep sense of contentment. "A piece of furniture that embodies our journey. Strong, beautiful, and full of hidden depths. It will be the perfect introduction to our combined endeavors." She squeezed his hand one last time, a silent acknowledgment of the profound gift he was offering. "I can't wait to see it come to life. And I can't wait to see our names, our vision, represented so beautifully in your work."

Theo's smile was a deep, resonant thing, a reflection of the happiness that bloomed within him at her words. "It will be a proud moment for both of us," he said, his voice resonating with emotion. "And it's just the beginning. This shelf is a promise, yes, but it's also an invitation. An invitation to fill it with our shared story, with the books you love, and the creations that come from my hands. It's an invitation to continue building, together, for years to come." He leaned in, pressing a gentle kiss to her temple. "This cherry wood promise. It's for you, and for us."

Marisol's gaze drifted from Theo's sketch, out the large front window of The Bound Page, and over the quiet, sun-drenched street of Cedar Ridge. The gentle hum of the town, a familiar and comforting symphony of distant lawnmowers, children's laughter, and the occasional passing car, seemed to underscore the profound peace settling within her. Theo's words, about building a life as enduring and beautiful as cherry wood, resonated deeply, but her mind was already expanding, weaving his tangible promise into a broader tapestry of their shared future. It wasn't just about a beautiful shelf, or even the bookstore itself. It was about the legacy they were meticulously, lovingly, crafting, not just for themselves, but for this town, this community they were so fortunate to call home.

"You know," she began, her voice soft but laced with a burgeoning excitement that she couldn't quite contain, "when I first dreamed of The Bound Page, I saw it as a sanctuary for stories. A place where words could breathe and readers could find solace. But I never truly envisioned it becoming... this. This blend. This convergence of narratives and artistry." She turned back to Theo, her eyes alight with a vision he was just beginning to sketch. "This shelf, this cherry wood promise you're building, it's the perfect embodiment of that. It's where your hands and my passion for books will physically meet, a constant reminder that our endeavors are intertwined."

She gestured broadly, encompassing not just the sketch on the desk, but the entire space around them, and beyond. "I imagine this place becoming so much more than just a bookstore. I see it as a hub, Theo. A place where people come not just for a well-loved novel or a rare poetry collection, but also for something unique, something crafted with soul. Imagine a corner dedicated to your wooden creations, each piece telling its own silent story, nestled right beside the authors who weave tales with words. Think of the synergy, the way one form of creativity can inspire and elevate another."

Her excitement was a tangible thing, warming the air between them. "We can curate not just books, but experiences. Perhaps we could host 'Meet the Maker' events, where local artisans, woodworkers, sculptors, even jewelers, could showcase their talents. Imagine, a space where the scent of aged paper and ink mingles with the subtle aroma of beeswax polish or the earthy scent of clay. A place that celebrates the breadth of human creativity. Cedar Ridge has such a rich artistic undercurrent, so many talented people whose work often goes unseen. We could provide a platform for them, a visible testament to the talent that thrives here."

She pictured it vividly: the warm glow of the cherry wood shelf, illuminated by carefully placed track lighting, showcasing not only Marisol's carefully chosen literary gems but also Theo's intricately carved boxes, perhaps a set of his unique chess pieces, or even a delicate wooden sculpture he might create. She envisioned patrons browsing, picking up a book and then, drawn by the craftsmanship of a nearby object, discovering a new appreciation for tangible artistry. It would be a destination, a place that offered something beyond the ordinary, something that spoke to the soul on multiple levels.

"It's about creating a legacy, Theo," she continued, her voice gaining a lyrical quality that echoed the rhythm of his own passion. "A legacy of stories, yes, but also a legacy of craftsmanship, of dedication, of passion poured into something beautiful and lasting. We can contribute to the vibrant tapestry of Cedar Ridge in a way that's uniquely ours. We're not just selling books or selling wooden objects; we're fostering connection, sparking inspiration, and celebrating the very essence of creativity."

She walked over to a shelf filled with her most treasured children's books, their colorful spines a cheerful contrast to the muted tones of the older volumes. "Even here, with the children's section, we can do more. Imagine a small, handcrafted wooden toy, a perfectly carved spinning top, or a set of stacking blocks made from sustainable wood, placed alongside Where the Wild Things Are or The Secret Garden. It's about adding another layer of wonder, of tactile engagement, for the youngest minds. It's about showing them that stories can be held, can be touched, can be created with their own hands, just as easily as they can be read."

Theo watched her, his sketching paused, his eyes following her movements, absorbing the depth of her vision. He saw the passion in her gaze, the way her hands moved as she spoke, painting mental pictures that were as intricate and compelling as any he could render on paper. Her ability to weave such grand, overarching ideas from the simple act of designing a shelf was extraordinary, and it fueled his own creative fire. He understood now that this wasn't just about building a piece of furniture; it was about building a shared future, a joint venture that would resonate far beyond the walls of the bookstore.

"I see it," he said, his voice a low, affirming rumble. "A place where the written word and the crafted object are given equal reverence. Where a reader can lose themselves in a novel and then, a moment later, be captivated by the smooth finish of a wooden bowl or the intricate details of a hand-carved bird. It's a holistic approach to art and literature, isn't it? Recognizing that they both spring from the same wellspring of human imagination and expression."

Marisol nodded enthusiastically. "Exactly! And Cedar Ridge is the perfect place for it. It's a town that appreciates authenticity, that values community, and that has a quiet strength that's so often overlooked. We can be a focal point, a place that draws people in, not just from Cedar Ridge, but from surrounding towns too. A destination for those who seek out beauty, who appreciate craftsmanship, and who understand the profound power of a well-told story, whether it's bound in paper or carved from wood."

She walked back to the desk, her fingers tracing the lines of his sketch again. "This shelf you're designing, Theo, it's not just a piece of furniture. It's a statement. It's the first tangible manifestation of our commitment to this blended vision. It's the foundation, literally and figuratively. It will hold our past – the stories you've shared with me, the books that have shaped my life – and it will hold our future, the new stories we'll create together, the new art that will emerge from this partnership."

She looked at him, her expression earnest and full of love. "Think about the impact. We can provide a space for emerging artists, a place for them to gain exposure, to connect with a receptive audience. We can host workshops, teaching skills in both bookbinding and woodworking, for example. Imagine a father and son coming in, the son wanting to learn how to make a simple wooden toy, and the father wanting to discover a new author. They could both find inspiration and guidance here. It's about enriching the lives of those in our community, fostering creativity, and building connections that last."

Theo picked up his charcoal pencil, a new energy coursing through him. He began to add details to the sketch, not just structural elements, but suggestions for how certain sections could be adapted for display. He envisioned a small, recessed area, perfectly sized for a single, striking wooden sculpture, bathed in a soft, focused light. He imagined a series of shallow drawers, each expertly fitted, for showcasing smaller handcrafted items like delicate wooden pens or intricately designed bookmarks.

"You're right," he said, his voice filled with a newfound purpose. "This shelf can be more than just a display unit. It can be a dynamic piece, adaptable to showcase a variety of works. We can even design interchangeable panels, perhaps carved with different motifs that can be swapped out seasonally, or to complement specific literary themes or artistic exhibitions." He looked at her, a smile playing on his lips. "This 'cherry wood promise' is evolving, just like us. It's becoming a canvas for our shared aspirations."

Marisol clapped her hands softly, a gesture of pure delight. "Oh, Theo, that's brilliant! Interchangeable panels! Imagine one panel carved with oak leaves and acorns for a fall poetry collection, and another with delicate cherry blossoms for a spring romance. It adds another layer of artistry, another conversation starter. It makes the shelf itself a work of art, constantly evolving and reflecting the life within the store."

She then moved to a corner where a stack of antique leather-bound books sat, their pages brittle with age and wisdom. "And these," she whispered, running a reverent finger over a worn cover, "these are the stories that whisper of endurance, of a legacy that transcends time. We can honor them too. Perhaps a dedicated section for local history books, alongside photographs and artifacts donated by long-time Cedar Ridge residents. We can become custodians of the town's narrative, preserving its past while celebrating its present and future through our combined creative endeavors."

"We can create a true sense of place," Theo mused, his pencil now moving with a fluid, inspired grace. "A bookstore that is intrinsically tied to Cedar Ridge, that reflects its unique character and its people. Not just a generic shop, but a place with a soul, a place that tells a story of its own. And that story will be written in wood and ink, in shared laughter and quiet contemplation, in the enduring beauty of well-crafted objects and the timeless power of words."

He paused, looking at the sketch with a new appreciation. It was no longer just a design for a shelf; it was a blueprint for their shared legacy. "This is what building forever looks like, Marisol. It's not just about the grand gestures, but about the thoughtful integration of our passions, the creation of something beautiful and meaningful that will stand the test of time. It's about weaving ourselves into the fabric of this town, leaving an imprint that is both strong and gentle, just like the cherry wood."

Marisol leaned against his shoulder, feeling the steady beat of his heart against her cheek. The scent of sawdust and pine was no longer just a reminder of his craft; it was the aroma of their shared future, a fragrance that promised growth, beauty, and an enduring connection. The hum of Cedar Ridge outside seemed to agree, a gentle affirmation of the vibrant life they were choosing to build, together, within its embrace. "A shared legacy," she whispered, her voice filled with a profound sense of joy and purpose. "I love that, Theo. I love us building that, together."

The hum of Cedar Ridge had faded, replaced by the soft, intimate symphony of their shared life. The lingering scent of Marisol's favorite lavender, a fragrance that had become synonymous with comfort and peace for Theo, still clung to the air in their bedroom. It was a subtle olfactory signature of their home, a quiet testament to the life they were meticulously, lovingly, weaving together. Tonight, the quiet held a different kind of resonance, a stillness that wasn't just the absence of noise, but the presence of something profound and deeply felt.

Marisol was curled up on the sofa in their living room, a worn copy of a classic novel open on her lap, though her eyes weren't on the page. They were fixed on Theo, who was meticulously polishing a small, intricately carved wooden bird, its wings poised as if for flight. The late afternoon sun cast long shadows across the room, bathing the scene in a warm, golden light that seemed to soften the edges of the world, leaving only the two of them, suspended in a moment of quiet contentment.

"You know," Marisol began, her voice a low murmur that barely disturbed the peaceful silence, "sometimes I just look at you, and I'm still amazed. Not just at your talent, though that's breathtaking, but at... you. At the man you are." She let the sentence hang in the air, a gentle invitation for him to meet her gaze.

Theo paused his work, the rhythmic sound of the polishing cloth ceasing. He looked up, his eyes, usually so focused on the grain of the wood, now held a warmth that mirrored the setting sun. "Amazed at what?" he asked, his voice a soft rumble, tinged with a curiosity that felt more like an embrace.

A soft smile played on Marisol's lips. "At how you see things. How you can take something as simple as a piece of wood, and see the story within it, the potential for beauty. It's like you have a secret language with creation." She shifted, tucking her feet beneath her. "And you bring that same quiet appreciation to everything. To me. To us."

He set the wooden bird down on the coffee table, its delicate form catching the light. He moved to the sofa, settling beside her, their shoulders brushing. The casual intimacy of their proximity was a language all its own, a silent affirmation of their bond. He reached out, his thumb gently tracing the curve of her jawline, a touch that spoke volumes more than words ever could.

"And I'm amazed at you, Marisol," he said, his voice low and earnest. "At how you can see the potential for a whole universe in a single story. How you can nurture a dream until it blooms into something real, something that enriches everyone it touches." He cupped her cheek, his gaze holding hers. "You see the world with such a vibrant heart. You make everything brighter, just by being in it."

The words, simple and unadorned, landed with a weight that was both profound and comforting. They weren't grand pronouncements or passionate declarations, but quiet affirmations, the kind that settled deep into the soul and resonated for a lifetime. These were the building blocks,

Marisol thought, not the flashy edifice, but the sturdy, unseen foundation that would hold their forever.

"I love how you say 'us'," she confessed, her voice a whisper against his thumb. "It's become my favorite word. 'Us.' It feels... complete. Like a puzzle piece clicking into place."

Theo chuckled softly, a warm sound that filled the quiet space between them. "It feels that way for me too. Like every piece I was looking for, every shape I was trying to carve, was leading me to 'us.'" He leaned in, pressing a gentle kiss to her forehead. "It's not just about the bookstore, or the town, or even the things we create. It's about the quiet moments, the shared breath, the knowledge that you're there, and I'm here, and we're... together."

He pulled her closer, wrapping an arm around her. She rested her head on his chest, listening to the steady rhythm of his heartbeat. It was a grounding sound, a constant reminder of his presence, of their shared journey. The lavender-scented air seemed to deepen their sense of intimacy, wrapping them in a fragrant cocoon of shared peace.

"Remember that first day I walked into The Bound Page?" she asked, her voice muffled against his shirt. "I was so nervous, so worried about whether this dream of mine was too... much. Too ambitious for a small town."

Theo tightened his embrace. "I remember. You were like a startled bird, beautiful but hesitant. And then you started talking about books, and your eyes lit up, and I knew you were exactly where you were supposed to be." He paused, a thoughtful smile in his voice. "And I knew I was supposed to be there too. Even if I didn't know it yet."

"And now," Marisol continued, her voice thick with emotion, "we're building something here, aren't we? Not just a business, but... a life. A real, tangible, beautiful life." She pulled back slightly, looking up at him, her eyes shining. "And I wouldn't trade our quiet declarations for anything.

The way you'll just reach for my hand when we're walking, or the way you'll leave me little notes tucked into my books. Those are the things that make me feel so deeply loved."

He kissed her then, a slow, tender kiss that spoke of shared history and an unfolding future. It was a kiss that said, I see you, I cherish you, I choose you. It was a kiss that held all the unspoken promises, all the quiet assurances that had become the bedrock of their relationship. When they broke apart, they were both breathing a little faster, the air between them charged with a gentle, potent energy.

"And the way you'll hum when you're reading," Theo added, his voice husky. "Or the way you'll leave little flour handprints on the kitchen counter when you're baking. Those are the things that make my world feel so much richer." He brushed a stray strand of hair from her face. "It's not just about the grand gestures, Marisol. It's about these small, consistent moments of grace. The everyday expressions of affection that weave us together, stronger with each passing day."

He stood up, extending a hand to her. "Come here," he said, his voice laced with a quiet command that she always happily obeyed. She took his hand, and he led her to the large window overlooking the darkening street. The lights of Cedar Ridge twinkled below, a constellation of shared lives.

"Look at that," Theo murmured, his arm around her waist, drawing her close against him. "All those homes, all those stories unfolding behind closed doors. And we have our own little story unfolding right here. One that's built on the quiet belief in each other, on the simple, profound act of choosing to build forever, piece by piece, word by word, touch by touch."

Marisol leaned her head against his shoulder, a sigh of pure contentment escaping her lips. The lavender, the warm lamplight, the steady presence of Theo beside her – it all coalesced into a feeling of profound belonging. They weren't just building a life together; they were creating a sanctuary, a space where their love could grow and flourish, nurtured by the quiet, consistent declarations that made their bond so uniquely theirs. This, she knew with absolute certainty, was the very essence of forever.

The quiet understanding that had settled between Theo and Marisol was more than just a comfortable silence; it was the palpable thrum of a trust meticulously built, brick by invisible brick. It wasn't a sudden revelation, but a slow, organic growth, like the roots of an ancient oak, deepening and strengthening with every shared season.

Theo found himself looking at Marisol, at the way her brow furrowed in concentration when she was engrossed in a new manuscript, or the way her eyes sparkled when she spoke about a particularly moving passage, and a profound sense of security would wash over him. He trusted her innate goodness, the unwavering compass of her heart that always pointed towards kindness and empathy.

He trusted her capacity for understanding, her ability to see past his sometimes gruff exterior to the softer, more vulnerable core that he often kept guarded. This was a trust that had been tested, not by dramatic upheavals, but by the subtle negotiations of everyday life, by moments of differing opinions or unspoken anxieties, and each time, Marisol's grace and understanding had only solidified his faith in her. He knew, with a certainty that resonated deep within his bones, that she would always see him, truly see him, and accept him, flaws and all.

Marisol, in turn, felt a similar bedrock of trust in Theo. It was in the way he anticipated her needs before she voiced them, the way he would bring her a cup of tea without being asked when he saw her shivering slightly, or the way he'd quietly rearrange his workshop schedule to be present for a rare evening out. This wasn't just attentiveness; it was a testament to his dedication, to his quiet, unwavering commitment to their shared life.

She trusted his word, knowing that when Theo gave his promise, it was as solid as the oak he so expertly carved. His evolving commitment, too, was a source of deep trust. She had seen him shed old reservations, slowly but surely, opening himself up to the vulnerability that love demanded. She trusted that the love she saw in his eyes, the gentle concern in his touch, was genuine and enduring. He had learned to lean on her, to share his burdens, and that willingness to be open, to allow her into the intricate landscape of his inner world, was a profound act of trust that she cherished.

This mutual reliance, this quiet faith in each other's intentions and affections, was the fertile ground upon which their future was being sown.

This deep-seated trust allowed them to navigate the inevitable currents of their differences with a remarkable degree of grace. They were, after all, two distinct individuals with their own histories, their own perspectives, and their own ways of seeing the world. Theo, grounded and methodical, sometimes found Marisol's more spontaneous flights of fancy a little disorienting, while Marisol, with her open heart and tendency to embrace new ideas, occasionally found Theo's cautious pragmatism a bit stifling.

Yet, their trust acted as an invisible bridge, allowing them to meet in the middle, to understand that their differences weren't obstacles, but rather complementary facets that enriched their lives. When disagreements arose, they no longer felt like battles to be won, but conversations to be had, opportunities to learn from each other. They had learned to listen not just to the words spoken, but to the emotions underlying them, to the unspoken needs that often lay beneath the surface.

Theo trusted Marisol's intention to communicate, to bridge any gaps, and Marisol trusted Theo's underlying desire for harmony and resolution, even when his initial response might have been silence or a terse observation. This willingness to engage, to truly hear one another, was a testament to the strength of their bond, a clear indication that their commitment to "us" superseded any fleeting disagreement.

The security that this mutual trust provided was a quiet, constant hum beneath the surface of their lives in Cedar Ridge. It was the assurance that no matter what challenges the future might hold, they had a shared foundation strong enough to withstand any storm. They understood, with a clarity that bypassed abstract theory and settled into the marrow of their beings, that true permanence wasn't about the absence of difficulties. Life, by its very nature, was a series of unpredictable turns and unexpected detours. Instead, their permanence was rooted in their unwavering commitment to face those challenges together, hand in hand, their individual strengths amplified by their shared purpose.

They had built something real, something tangible in the heart of Cedar Ridge, a life that was more than just a collection of shared possessions or a joint bank account. It was a sanctuary, a haven built on the unwavering belief in each other, a place where their love could not only survive but flourish.

Theo often found himself reflecting on the journey that had brought them to this point. He remembered the early days, the hesitant steps, the moments of doubt, the internal wrestling matches he'd had with his own ingrained reservations about commitment. Marisol's patient presence, her unwavering belief in him even when he struggled to believe in himself, had been the gentle force that had chipped away at his defenses.

He trusted that her love wasn't conditional, that it wasn't a fleeting emotion that would evaporate with the first sign of trouble. It was a steady flame, a reliable warmth that had finally thawed the last vestiges of his fear. This trust wasn't born of blind faith, but of witnessed actions, of countless small gestures of unwavering support and profound understanding. He trusted that she saw the best in him, not as a naive idealist, but as a grounded observer who recognized the inherent worth and potential for growth.

Marisol, too, had her own quiet moments of contemplation, where the sheer depth of her trust in Theo would settle upon her like a warm cloak. She had seen him evolve, not into someone he wasn't, but into a more fully realized version of himself, a process she had been privileged to witness and, in her own way, encourage. She trusted his integrity, his inherent desire to do the right thing, even when it was the harder path.

There were times when the demands of the bookstore, coupled with the quiet complexities of their personal lives, could feel overwhelming. In those moments, Theo's steady presence, his quiet strength, was an anchor. She trusted that he would not falter, that he would stand beside her, offering not just practical solutions but the invaluable comfort of his unwavering support. Her trust in his commitment was not a passive acceptance of his love, but an active recognition of his dedication, his consistent effort to nurture and sustain their bond.

This mutual understanding extended beyond their immediate relationship to their place within Cedar Ridge. They were no longer just individuals living in the town; they were a unit, a part of its fabric. Their trust in each other meant that when they presented a united front, whether it was supporting a local initiative or simply navigating the complexities of small-town gossip, their voice carried a weight and authenticity that resonated.

They had learned to rely on each other's judgment, to trust each other's instincts, and this made their decisions, both personal and communal, more considered and confident. Cedar Ridge, with its intimate pace and interconnected lives, had a way of magnifying the strengths and weaknesses of any relationship. For Theo and Marisol, their foundation of trust was the sturdy bedrock that allowed them to not only survive but thrive within its embrace.

They understood that building a forever wasn't about creating an impenetrable fortress against the outside world, but about cultivating a space within that world where their love could be nurtured, protected, and allowed to grow, unhindered by doubt or fear. Their trust in each other, and in the life they were building together in this cherished small town, was the most enduring and beautiful monument of all. It was the silent promise whispered in the rustling leaves of the oak trees, in the gentle flow of the nearby creek, and in the warm glow of their shared hearth – a promise of a forever built not on chance, but on choice, on understanding, and on a love that had weathered every season and emerged, stronger and more radiant, with each passing year.

The foundation was laid, not with grand pronouncements, but with a thousand tiny acts of faith, a testament to the enduring power of two hearts finding their truest home in each other, right here in the heart of Cedar Ridge.

Chapter Eleven: A Cedar Ridge Celebration

The decision for a wedding wasn't a sudden, impulsive spark, but rather the gentle, inevitable blossoming of a deep and abiding love. It arrived not with a thunderclap of pronouncements, but with a shared glance, a quiet sigh of contentment that spoke volumes. For Theo and Marisol, their journey had already been one of profound connection, a tapestry woven with shared moments, unspoken understandings, and the unwavering support they offered each other.

Their commitment had solidified organically, like the sturdy growth of the ancient oak that stood sentinel on the edge of town, its branches reaching towards the sky in a silent testament to time and resilience. The idea of marriage, when it finally surfaced, felt less like a new beginning and more like a natural, joyful affirmation of everything they had already built.

Marisol, curled on the worn leather sofa in Theo's workshop, the scent of sawdust and aged wood a comforting balm, was the first to articulate the unspoken thought that had been fluttering between them like a captured butterfly. Theo was meticulously sanding a small wooden bird, his brow furrowed in concentration, the afternoon sun catching the silver threads beginning to appear at his temples. She watched him, the quiet rhythm of his work, the steady competence of his hands, and a wave of overwhelming gratitude washed over her.

It was in these quiet moments, when the world outside faded away, that their love felt most potent, most real. She reached out, her fingers tracing the grain of the unfinished bird on his workbench, and then, with a gentle smile, she turned to him. "Theo," she began, her voice soft but clear, "have you ever thought about... us? About making it all official?"

Theo paused, his hand hovering over the wood. He looked up, his blue eyes, usually so steady, held a flicker of something akin to surprise, yet also a deep, inherent understanding. He met her gaze, and in that shared moment, a silent conversation passed between them, a reaffirmation of all the trust and tenderness they had cultivated. He understood instantly what she meant. It wasn't a question of doubt, but of desire, a longing to publicly declare what their hearts already knew.

A slow smile spread across his face, crinkling the corners of his eyes. He set the bird down carefully, then reached for her hand, his calloused fingers closing around hers. "Marisol," he said, his voice a low rumble, filled with a warmth that chased away any lingering shadows. "If you're asking what I think you're asking... then yes. I've thought about it. More than you know."

The confirmation, so simple, so direct, hung in the air between them, imbued with the weight of unspoken promises and future dreams. It was a mutual acknowledgment, a shared breath of exhilaration. There was no hesitation, no second-guessing. The decision was made, not in a grand, dramatic gesture, but in the quiet intimacy of shared understanding, a testament to the profound depth of their connection. The idea of a wedding, of a celebration, felt like a natural, joyous progression, a way to honor the journey that had brought them to this point and to embrace the boundless future stretching before them.

"A wedding," Marisol whispered, the word tasting sweet on her tongue. She squeezed his hand, her heart soaring. "It feels... right, doesn't it?"

"More than right," Theo agreed, his thumb gently stroking the back of her hand. "It feels like the only thing that makes sense. Like the next chapter we've been writing all along." He pulled her closer, her head resting against his shoulder, the familiar scent of cedar and him filling her senses. "We've built something strong here, Marisol. Something real. And I want to celebrate that. I want everyone to know."

The anticipation that settled over them was palpable, a sweet, fragrant scent that seemed to emanate from the very heart of Cedar Ridge. It wasn't just about the two of them; it was about sharing their joy, about acknowledging the community that had, in its own quiet way, played a role in their story. From Mrs. Gable at the bakery, who always had a knowing smile and an extra scone for Marisol when Theo was around, to Mr. Henderson at the hardware store, who offered Theo quiet nods of approval whenever he saw them together, the town had witnessed their burgeoning love.

They had seen the hesitations melt away, the guarded smiles transform into open laughter, the tentative steps evolve into confident strides. The town of Cedar Ridge was more than just a backdrop; it was an integral part of their narrative, a witness to the quiet miracle of their connection.

Marisol imagined the delight on her sister's face when she shared the news, the excited chatter that would undoubtedly ripple through the bookstore. She pictured Theo's quiet pride, the way his eyes would soften when he spoke of their plans. The decision to marry wasn't just a personal one; it was a catalyst that would send ripples of warmth and happiness throughout their small world. The air itself seemed to hum with possibility, as sweet and pervasive as the honeysuckle that climbed the trellis outside the workshop window.

It was the scent of a future being eagerly embraced, a celebration of a love that had found its true home in the heart of Cedar Ridge. This was more than just a wedding; it was a Cedar Ridge celebration, a testament to the enduring power of love in a town that knew how to cherish its own.

The news of Theo and Marisol's impending union spread through Cedar Ridge like wildfire, not with a frantic, gossip-fueled blaze, but with a warm, steady glow of shared joy. It was the kind of news that made the heart of a small town swell with pride, a collective acknowledgment that one of their own, and the beloved newcomer who had woven herself so seamlessly into their lives, were embarking on a new chapter. The sentiment was immediate and unanimous: this was not just a wedding; it was a Cedar Ridge celebration, a testament to the enduring power of love and community.

Almost as soon as the whisper of an engagement began to solidify into a confirmed plan, the offers of help started to pour in, each one a warm embrace from the town itself. It began, as many things did in Cedar Ridge, with Aunt Clara. Her kitchen, a legendary hub of culinary artistry, was already abuzz with the anticipation of a grand baking project. Clara, a woman whose hands seemed to possess a magical ability to coax perfection out of flour, sugar, and butter, declared with a twinkle in her eye and a decisive nod, "A wedding cake for Theo and Marisol? It shall be my honor. And it won't be just a cake, mind you. It will be the cake. The one they remember for a lifetime."

Her vision was already taking shape: layers of delicate vanilla bean sponge, filled with a raspberry coulis that tasted of summer sun, all enrobed in a silken Swiss meringue buttercream. She spoke of intricate sugar flowers, their petals impossibly thin, mirroring the wild roses that bloomed along the riverbanks, and a cascade of edible pearls, each one a tiny symbol of good fortune. The mere thought of Clara's cake sent a ripple of delicious anticipation through the town, and it became an immediate talking point at the general store and over fences. Marisol, upon hearing this, felt a wave of gratitude so profound it brought tears to her eyes. Clara's baking was more than just food; it was an expression of love, a tangible manifestation of her deep affection for her niece and the man she had chosen.

Then there was Mrs. Gable, the proprietor of "The Blooming Rose," Cedar Ridge's charmingly cluttered flower shop. Her fingers, perpetually dusted with pollen and scented with the sweet perfume of roses and lilies, had a way of transforming simple blooms into breathtaking arrangements that spoke of elegance and understated beauty. As soon as the wedding was on everyone's lips, Mrs. Gable appeared at Marisol's doorstep, a wicker basket brimming with fragrant lavender and sprigs of baby's breath. "Marisol, dear," she announced, her voice a gentle melody, "I've been thinking. Your wedding flowers will need to be something special.

Something that whispers of your love, not shouts it. I've got a vision… soft, romantic hues. Pale blush roses, creamy hydrangeas, and a touch of eucalyptus for that woodland touch. We'll make the chapel look like a dream. And for you, a bouquet that will make you feel like the most beautiful bride in the world." She described bouquets tied with silk ribbons, boutonnieres that were miniature works of art, and garlands of greenery that would drape from the eaves of the old chapel, their scent a fragrant welcome to guests. Marisol knew that Mrs. Gable's artistry would infuse their celebration with a natural, organic beauty that perfectly captured the spirit of Cedar Ridge and their own burgeoning romance.

Theo, ever the craftsman, found his own unique way to contribute to the tapestry of their wedding. While Marisol was immersed in the delicate details of flowers and cake flavors, Theo's mind turned to the structure, the foundation of their ceremony. He approached the task with his characteristic quiet determination, his hands itching to create something that would symbolize their union. "I've been thinking about the ceremony itself," he'd said to Marisol, his eyes alight with an idea. "I want to build something. An arbor. Something beautiful and strong, for you to walk through when we say our vows. Made of solid oak, perhaps, with a gentle curve, like an embrace.

We can weave ivy and roses around it, and it will stand long after the day is done, a reminder of this moment." He envisioned the wood weathered to a soft patina, the grain telling a story of strength and endurance. He spoke of crafting it with meticulous care, each joint seamless, each surface smooth to the touch. The arbor, he explained, would be more than just a decorative element; it would be a focal point, a silent witness to their promises, a permanent fixture that would become part of Cedar Ridge's landscape, imbued with the memory of their love.

The community's involvement extended far beyond these key contributions. Sarah Jenkins, who ran the local fabric shop, offered to help with any sewing needs, her nimble fingers capable of transforming bolts of cloth into elegant sashes or delicate trims. Young Timmy Peterson, eager to prove his worth and earn some pocket money, volunteered to be Theo's unofficial assistant for the arbor construction, his enthusiasm infectious.

Even gruff old Mr. Henderson from the hardware store, who rarely showed much outward emotion, was seen meticulously selecting the sturdiest nails and best quality wood for Theo's project, offering quiet nods of approval and unsolicited, yet surprisingly helpful, advice. The town council, in a rare display of unified enthusiasm, readily approved the use of the village green for the reception, promising to organize the setting up of tables and chairs. The local band, "The Cedar Ridge Ramblers," a group of seasoned musicians who had played at every town event for the past twenty years, immediately volunteered their services, their lively bluegrass tunes promising to fill the evening air with joy and merriment.

The preparations for the wedding became a reflection of Marisol and Theo's integration into the heart of Cedar Ridge. What could have been a daunting and overwhelming process for the couple transformed into a joyous, communal undertaking. Each offer of help, each suggestion, each shared moment of planning, was a thread in the rich tapestry of their relationship, woven with the warmth and affection of their new community.

Marisol found herself spending more time at the bakery, not just for the scent of fresh bread, but for the shared laughter and whispered confidences with Clara and Mrs. Gable. She would sit with them, sipping tea, while they sketched out designs, their enthusiasm mirroring her own. Theo, in turn, would find himself drawn into impromptu discussions with other men in town about woodworking techniques, about the best ways to age wood, or the merits of different types of varnish. These interactions, seemingly small and insignificant, were profound affirmations of his belonging.

The collective energy that surrounded their wedding was palpable. It wasn't just about celebrating Theo and Marisol; it was about celebrating Cedar Ridge itself, its ability to nurture love, to support its residents, and to come together in moments of shared happiness. The wedding was becoming a symbol of the town's vibrant spirit, a testament to the fact that in a world that often felt fragmented and impersonal, here, in this small corner of the world, connection and genuine care still thrived. Marisol often found herself watching Theo, his hands covered in sawdust, a happy weariness in his eyes as he discussed the arbor plans with Mr. Henderson, and a profound sense of belonging would wash over her.

This was more than just a wedding; it was a testament to the life they were building, a life intertwined with the very fabric of Cedar Ridge, a life that was, in every sense of the word, a community involvement. The anticipation of the day itself was now intertwined with the anticipation of the shared experience, the collective joy that would make their wedding not just a personal milestone, but a cherished memory for the entire town. The preparations, far from being a burden, had become an integral part of their love story, a beautiful, collaborative effort that spoke volumes about the depth of the bonds they had formed.

Theo's Vows of Enduring Love

The rhythmic rasp of sandpaper against aged oak was Theo's lullaby these past few weeks. His workshop, usually a sanctuary of quiet focus, had taken on a new aroma, one of anticipation mingled with the rich, earthy scent of linseed oil and freshly planed wood. He'd been meticulously finishing the arbor for Marisol's walk, each stroke of the cloth, each gentle buffing, an unspoken vow. The wood, salvaged from an old barn on the edge of Cedar Ridge, possessed a character all its own, its grain telling stories of seasons past. He'd treated it with a reverence that mirrored how he felt about Marisol, wanting to bring out its inherent beauty, to preserve its strength, to ensure it would stand as a testament to their commitment.

Now, with the arbor standing proud and adorned with the delicate blush roses Mrs. Gable had so artfully woven into its structure, his thoughts turned inward, to the words he would speak. The formal wedding invitations, penned in elegant calligraphy, lay on his workbench, a stark contrast to the rough, sawdust-covered surface. He'd stared at them for hours, the weight of the occasion settling upon him. He wasn't a man of grand pronouncements, his language usually as direct and unadorned as the furniture he built. But for Marisol, for this moment, he needed to find a voice that could capture the immensity of what he felt.

He remembered the early days, the quiet apprehension that had shadowed his heart. He'd carried a certain fear of imperfection, of the fragility of happiness, a lingering echo from past disappointments. But Marisol. She had a way of dissolving those shadows, of bathing everything in a warm, unwavering light. Her presence was not a fleeting flicker; it was a steady flame, a beacon that guided him home. His vows wouldn't be about grand promises he couldn't guarantee, about forevers etched in stone that might crumble. They would be about his presence. His unwavering, constant presence.

He picked up a piece of scrap oak, its surface smooth beneath his fingertips. He imagined Marisol's hand in his, the warmth, the gentle pressure that spoke of so much more than words could convey. "I don't promise you a life without storms, Marisol," he thought, the words forming in the silent space of his mind. "But I promise you that I will be your shelter. I will be the steady hand that steers our boat through the roughest waves. I will be the anchor that holds you fast when the winds rage." This was the core of it, wasn't it? Not avoiding the difficulties, but facing them together, hand in hand, heart to heart.

His thoughts drifted to the life they were building, not in abstract terms, but in the tangible details that made up their days. The way she hummed a soft tune when she was lost in thought, the way her eyes crinkled at the corners when she laughed, the quiet comfort of her presence beside him as he worked in his shop, even when she was simply reading a book. These were the bricks and mortar of their future, the small, precious moments that he intended to cherish and protect.

He pictured their home, the one they were slowly transforming, piece by piece. He saw himself adding another beam, reinforcing a wall, all with the intention of making it a sanctuary for them. "I promise to build our life with you," he would say, the words taking shape in his mind. "Not just a house, but a home. A place of peace, of laughter, of unwavering love. Each day, I will add another stone, strengthen another foundation, not out of obligation, but out of a joy that is deeper and more profound than I ever imagined possible."

He thought of Cedar Ridge, the town that had so readily embraced them, the community that had showered them with such warmth and generosity. The arbor, standing as a symbol of their union, was rooted in this very soil, a testament to the life they were weaving into the fabric of this place. He felt a profound sense of belonging, a feeling that had once seemed an impossible dream. Marisol had brought him here, not just to a place, but to a feeling of coming home. "You showed me what it means to be truly seen, Marisol," he'd whisper to himself, running his thumb over the polished wood. "You saw past the rough edges, the quiet exterior, and found the man who yearned for connection, for a love that was as honest and as real as the grain of this wood. For that, my gratitude is boundless."

He envisioned their future, not as a distant horizon, but as the unfolding of each new day. He saw the seasons changing in Cedar Ridge, the snow melting to reveal the first green shoots, the long, lazy days of summer giving way to the fiery hues of autumn, and then the quiet stillness of winter. He wanted to experience it all with her. "I promise to walk with you through every season," he'd formulate in his mind, the words gaining a quiet power. "To share in the joy of the bloom, the abundance of the harvest, and the quiet introspection of winter. I want to learn from you, to grow with you, to be the man you deserve, not by trying to be someone I'm not, but by becoming the best version of myself, with you by my side."

He paused, the scent of wood filling his lungs. He had always been a man of few words, his emotions often buried beneath a layer of quiet stoicism. But Marisol had unlocked something within him, a wellspring of deep, abiding affection. He wanted his vows to be a reflection of that unearthed emotion, raw and true. He wouldn't talk of conquering mountains or taming dragons. He would talk of the quiet strength he found in her gaze, the steadfastness he felt in her hand, the profound peace that settled over him whenever she was near.

He picked up a worn leather-bound journal, one he'd kept for years, filled with sketches and notes on his woodworking projects. He began to write, his hand steady now, his heart full. The words flowed, not like a torrent, but like a gentle, persistent stream, carving its path through the landscape of his soul. He wrote of the fear he'd once carried, the self-imposed isolation, and how her love had been the key that had unlocked him. He wrote of the simple beauty of their shared moments, the quiet understanding that passed between them without a word. He wrote of his commitment to nurturing their love, to tending it like he tended his beloved trees, with patience, with care, and with an unwavering dedication to its flourishing.

"Marisol," he would begin, the name itself a soft caress on his tongue. "I stand here today, not as a man who believes in perfect promises, but as a man who believes in the unwavering strength of my devotion to you. I've spent years building things, solid things, things meant to last. And now, I stand before you, ready to build the most important thing of all: our life together." He paused, picturing her face, the soft light catching her eyes. "You have a way of seeing the beauty in everything, of finding light even in the darkest corners.

You've shown me that beauty, and you've shown me the light within myself. My promise to you is not to eliminate hardship, but to face it with you. To be your constant, your steady hand, your unwavering support. I promise to be present, truly present, in every moment we share. To listen, to understand, and to love you with an honesty that mirrors the very grain of the wood I work with."

He continued, his voice growing stronger in his mind, resonating with the quiet conviction of a man who had found his truth. "I promise to nurture our love, to tend to it with the same care and dedication I give to my craft. I will build our life together, brick by brick, day by day, with patience, with kindness, and with a joy that fills my entire being. I choose you, Marisol. I choose this life with you, in Cedar Ridge, surrounded by the community that has shown us such love.

You are my home, my heart, and my forever." The scent of polished wood seemed to deepen, to infuse the air with a subtle, enduring fragrance, a silent testament to the vows he was crafting, vows of enduring love.

Marisol's heart felt as if it were expanding, a radiant bloom unfurling beneath the gentle weight of Theo's words. His vows, honest and as solid as the wood he shaped, had resonated deep within her, a melody that harmonized with the very beat of her soul. Now, as she prepared to speak her own promises, the world seemed to tilt and settle, framing them perfectly, a shared breath in the hushed reverence of the moment. The cedar arbor, a testament to Theo's skill and their burgeoning love, stood beside them, a silent witness to the vows they were about to exchange, rooted in the very earth of Cedar Ridge.

"Theo," she began, her voice soft but clear, carrying a warmth that seemed to fill the space between them, a tangible thread weaving their two souls together. "My dearest Theo." The sound of his name, spoken with such profound love, felt like a blessing, a sweet acknowledgment of the journey that had led them here. "When I first came to Cedar Ridge, I was seeking a quiet place, a respite. I found that, and so much more. I found you."

A gentle smile touched her lips, a silent echo of the first tentative sparks that had ignited between them, so unexpected and so utterly life-altering. "You walked into my life not with thunder and lightning, but with the quiet strength of an old oak, a steady presence that rooted me and made me feel safe. You saw me, Theo, truly saw me, and in your eyes, I found a reflection of a woman I was still learning to be."

She took a deep, steadying breath, the scent of roses and pine a comforting perfume around them. "My promise to you today is not one of grand, impossible feats, but of a love that is lived, a love that is actively cherished, moment by precious moment. I promise to be your partner in every sense of the word. I promise to celebrate your triumphs, big and small, to bask in the glow of your successes, and to always remind you of the incredible man you are, even when the world outside forgets."

Her gaze met his, unwavering and filled with a profound depth of emotion.

"When the inevitable challenges arise, and they will, for life is a tapestry woven with both joy and sorrow, I promise to face them with you. Not by your side, but intertwined, our hands clasped, our hearts beating as one. We will navigate the storms together, Theo, not as individuals weathering separate tempests, but as a unified force, drawing strength from each other, our love a beacon guiding us through the darkness."

Marisol's thoughts drifted to the countless small moments that had come to define their relationship, the quiet intimacy that had blossomed between them. "I promise to cherish the ordinary days just as much as the extraordinary ones. The shared silences in your workshop, the sound of your laughter echoing through our home, the way you instinctively reach for my hand when we walk, the simple comfort of falling asleep next to you.

These are the threads that will form the rich fabric of our life together, and I promise to weave them with intention, with gratitude, and with an abundance of love. I will always make time for us, Theo, for the conversations that matter, for the quiet moments of connection, for the silly jokes that only we understand. Our love will be a garden we tend, Theo, not one we leave to chance. I will water it with kindness, nourish it with understanding, and weed out any doubts or fears that might try to take root."

She felt a swell of exhilaration at the thought of their shared future, a future built brick by deliberate brick, not just a house, but a home, a sanctuary of their own making. "I promise to continue to build our life with you, with joy and with purpose. To explore the hidden corners of this beautiful town together, to discover new dreams, and to always encourage each other to grow. I want to be the person who inspires you to create, who supports your wildest ambitions, and who grounds you when you need it most. Our home, the one we're already filling with memories, will be a testament to our shared journey, a place where laughter rings freely and where peace resides. It will be a haven, a reflection of the love that has brought us here."

Her optimism, a trait she had always held dear, now felt amplified, a powerful force propelling them forward. "My promise is also one of constant discovery. I promise to never stop learning about you, Theo. To be curious about your thoughts, your dreams, your evolving spirit. I believe that love is not a destination, but a continuous journey, a beautiful, unfolding adventure, and I am so incredibly excited to embark on every single step of this path with you.

I promise to approach our life together with an open heart, a willingness to learn, and an unwavering faith in the strength and resilience of our union. I believe in us, Theo, with every fiber of my being."

Tears welled in her eyes, not of sadness, but of overwhelming joy and profound gratitude. "You have given me a gift, Theo, a gift of a love that is both comforting and exhilarating, a love that feels like coming home. My promise is to honor that gift, to reciprocate it with all that I am, and to love you faithfully, fiercely, and forever. You are my heart's truest north, my constant companion, my greatest love. Today, I choose you, I choose us, and I choose this beautiful, shared life we are creating together, here in Cedar Ridge, and for all the tomorrows to come." The words hung in the air, a testament to her enduring spirit, her vibrant love, and the promise of a shared journey that was only just beginning to unfold.

The air, still cool from the lingering night, carried the crisp scent of pine and damp earth as Marisol and Theo made their way to the banks of the Cedar River. It was a place etched in their hearts, the very spot where tentative hopes had bloomed into a love as sturdy and as true as the ancient cedars that lined its course. Now, under the nascent blush of a Cedar Ridge dawn, it would be the sacred ground for the beginning of their married life.

The sky, a canvas of soft grays and pearlescent pinks, was just beginning to awaken, mirroring the new dawn breaking within their souls.

Theo's hand, strong and warm, was a steady anchor in Marisol's, a silent reassurance that grounded her in the profound beauty of the moment. Around them, a small gathering of their dearest friends and family had assembled, their faces illuminated by the soft glow of a few strategically placed lanterns, casting a warm, intimate circle against the encroaching daylight. There were no grand pronouncements, no ostentatious displays, only the quiet hum of shared anticipation, a collective breath held in reverence. The gentle, melodic rush of the Cedar River provided a natural soundtrack, a constant, soothing murmur that spoke of timelessness and the unwavering flow of life. It was a symphony orchestrated by nature itself, a prelude to the vows they were about to exchange.

As the first rays of sunlight began to pierce the horizon, painting the eastern sky with strokes of molten gold and fiery orange, a profound sense of hope settled over the riverside clearing. The rising sun, a potent symbol of new beginnings, seemed to bless their union, casting a warm, ethereal glow that embraced them, weaving threads of light into the fabric of their shared future. The light touched their faces, chasing away the last vestiges of shadow, promising clarity and warmth for the journey ahead. It was as if the very dawn was celebrating their commitment, its golden hues a testament to the radiant love that had brought them to this point.

Marisol's gaze met Theo's, and in his eyes, she saw not just her beloved, but a partner, a confidante, a steady presence who had transformed her world. The quiet intimacy of the setting, the soft lapping of the water, the hushed reverence of their loved ones – it all conspired to create a moment so deeply personal, so profoundly moving, that it felt as if the entire world had shrunk to encompass just the two of them. Yet, the presence of their community, those who had witnessed their journey, added another layer of richness, a collective blessing that made their vows feel all the more significant, all the more enduring.

They stood before a simple arrangement of river stones and wildflowers, a natural altar crafted by the very landscape that had captured their hearts. There was no need for elaborate decorations; the raw beauty of Cedar Ridge was the most breathtaking backdrop imaginable. The river, their constant companion, whispered secrets of continuity and resilience, its gentle flow a reminder that life, like love, is a continuous, evolving journey. Each ripple, each gentle eddy, seemed to echo the steady pulse of their shared heartbeats, a testament to the deep, abiding connection that had taken root and flourished.

Theo cleared his throat, his voice a low rumble that resonated with emotion. "Marisol," he began, his gaze unwavering, "the sun rises on a new day, and for us, it rises on a new life. Standing here, with the river as our witness and our loved ones near, I feel a peace I never thought possible. You are the dawn in my life, Marisol. You chased away the shadows and brought a light so pure, so steady, that it illuminates every corner of my existence.

You are my home, my haven, and my greatest adventure. Today, I pledge myself to you, not just for this beautiful beginning, but for every sunrise and sunset that follows. I promise to love you fiercely, to cherish you deeply, and to build a life with you that is as strong and as beautiful as this river, as enduring as these ancient trees. I promise to be your steadfast companion, your truest friend, and your devoted husband, through all seasons of our lives."

Marisol's breath hitched, a tremor of pure joy running through her. Her own vows, spoken with a clarity born of unwavering conviction, felt like a natural extension of his, a harmonic melody in the symphony of their shared commitment. The river's gentle murmur seemed to amplify her words, carrying them out into the vastness of the dawning day, a promise whispered to the world and to each other. The rising sun, now a brilliant orb peeking over the distant hills, cast a warm, golden hue across their faces, a benediction upon their union. The warmth on her skin felt like a tangible embrace, a divine affirmation of the love that bound them.

She looked around at the faces of their families and friends, each one a testament to the love and support that had nurtured their relationship. There were smiles, tears of happiness, and the quiet acknowledgment of a shared journey reaching a beautiful, significant milestone.

The simplicity of the ceremony, stripped of all pretense, allowed the raw emotion of the moment to shine through, creating a profound sense of connection not only between her and Theo, but also with the community that surrounded them. It was a celebration of love in its purest form, grounded in authenticity and shared experience.

The river, with its ceaseless, flowing energy, felt like a metaphor for their love – a force that was both gentle and powerful, constant and ever-changing. It had witnessed their conversations, their laughter, their dreams, and now, it was bearing witness to their most sacred promises. The water, reflecting the burgeoning light of the sun, shimmered with an almost magical quality, as if holding the very essence of their joy and hope. The rustling leaves of the surrounding trees, stirred by a gentle breeze, seemed to whisper their blessings, their ancient wisdom adding to the solemnity and beauty of the occasion.

As they exchanged rings, simple bands of polished silver that felt weighty and significant in their hands, the light of the new day fully broke, bathing the scene in a warm, golden radiance. The transition from twilight to full daylight was a mirroring of their own journey, moving from uncertainty and tentative beginnings to a bright, assured future. The symbolism was not lost on them; this was not just a ceremony, but a profound testament to the power of love to transform, to illuminate, and to create something entirely new and beautiful.

Theo gently cupped Marisol's face, his thumbs tracing the curve of her cheekbones. "You are my forever, Marisol," he murmured, his voice thick with emotion. "My sunrise, my steady ground, my heart."

Marisol leaned into his touch, her eyes shining with unshed tears. "And you are mine, Theo," she whispered back, her voice barely audible above the gentle rush of the river. "My everything."

The official pronouncement, delivered by their officiant, a close family friend whose presence added another layer of warmth and intimacy, felt like a formal embrace from the universe itself. And then, with a kiss that sealed their promises and declared their union to the world, they were married. The soft cheer that rose from their assembled loved ones was not boisterous, but heartfelt, a wave of joy that washed over them, a testament to the shared happiness of this momentous occasion.

As they turned, hand in hand, to face their gathered friends and family, the sun was now fully above the horizon, its light streaming through the trees, dappling the ground with patterns of gold. The Cedar River flowed on, a silent, constant witness to their love, and in the embrace of this breathtaking Cedar Ridge dawn, they knew their life together had begun, bathed in the promise of a new day and a love that would forever be their guiding light. The air was alive with a sense of renewal, a quiet exultation that settled deep within their souls. This was more than just a wedding; it was the sacred inauguration of their shared existence, a moment forever imprinted on the landscape of their hearts, as enduring and as beautiful as the very river that flowed beside them.

Chapter Twelve: The Earned Ever After

The world outside the windows of "The Bound Page & Hearth" might have been bathed in the soft hues of a Cedar Ridge morning, but inside, a different kind of light had settled – the warm, comforting glow of a shared life. Marisol, now officially Mrs. Hart-Vega, felt it in the easy way Theo's hand found hers as they stood behind the counter, the familiar scent of old paper and brewing coffee mingling with the faint, sweet aroma of the wildflowers still adorning their kitchen table from the wedding. The ink on their marriage certificate was barely dry, yet it felt as though this partnership, this quiet merging of their souls, had been in the making for a lifetime.

"Morning, Mrs. Hart-Vega," Theo's voice was a low rumble, a melody that still sent a delightful shiver down her spine. He leaned in, his lips brushing against her temple, a gesture so tender it made her heart swell. "Ready for another day of conquering the literary world, one book at a time?"

Marisol chuckled, the sound light and airy. "Always, Mr. Hart-Vega. Especially when I have you by my side. Though I think our conquering might involve a bit more restocking than battling dragons today." She gestured to the overflowing shelves, a familiar, comforting chaos that was now their shared domain.

Their home, a cozy haven nestled just a few blocks from the bookstore, had also transformed, not in its physical structure, but in its very essence. It was no longer just Marisol's sanctuary or Theo's quiet retreat; it was theirs. The worn armchair by the fireplace, where Theo used to lose himself in his own reading, now often held them both, legs tangled, a shared blanket a testament to evenings spent in comfortable silence or hushed conversation.

Marisol's collection of antique teacups, once a solitary pleasure, now found their place on the coffee table during shared breakfasts, their delicate clinking a soft accompaniment to the morning news or their whispered plans for the day.

The integration of their lives hadn't been a sudden, jarring shift, but a gentle, organic weaving, like two strong threads becoming one. The trust they had built, brick by painstaking brick, through the challenges and triumphs of their courtship, now formed the bedrock of their married life. There were no grand pronouncements needed, no elaborate displays of affection. Instead, it was in the small, almost unconscious gestures that their love manifested. It was Theo remembering to buy her favorite dark roast coffee beans, knowing she'd be too engrossed in a new shipment to stop herself. It was Marisol leaving a small, encouraging note tucked into Theo's lunch bag, a silent reminder that even in the mundane, he was cherished.

Mornings had taken on a new ritual, a symphony of domestic harmony. The alarm would chime, and before the sun had fully committed to rising, they'd be in the kitchen. Theo, ever the early riser, was usually the first to stir, the quiet hum of the coffee maker his morning serenade. Marisol would often emerge to find him already dressed, a newspaper open on the table, his brow furrowed in concentration. But the moment he saw her, his face would soften, a warm smile spreading across his lips.

"Morning, love," he'd say, his voice still rough with sleep, and then he'd be up, crossing the small kitchen to pull her into a morning hug that smelled of sleep and possibility.

Then, the dance would begin. Theo would pour the coffee, the rich, dark aroma filling the air. Marisol would often be the one to prepare their breakfast, a simple affair of toast and fruit, or sometimes, on particularly indulgent mornings, scrambled eggs and a side of bacon. They'd eat together, often without much conversation, comfortable in the shared silence, each appreciating the other's presence. Sometimes, Theo would read aloud a particularly interesting article from the paper, his voice a steady cadence that Marisol found soothing. Other times, they'd discuss the day ahead, the books they hoped to sell, the customers they were looking forward to seeing.

"Did Mrs. Gable call about that rare poetry collection yet?" Marisol might ask, her voice still a little sleepy, as she sipped her coffee.

"Not yet," Theo would reply, folding the newspaper. "But I put a hold on it for her. I have a feeling she'll be in later this morning, eager to get her hands on it."

The bookstore, 'The Bound Page & Hearth,' was more than just their place of employment; it was a tangible manifestation of their shared dream. It had been Marisol's passion, her legacy, and now, it was their shared enterprise. The integration had been seamless, a testament to their mutual respect and understanding. Theo, with his keen business acumen and his genuine love for people, had brought a new level of organization and customer engagement to the establishment. He wasn't just selling books; he was building relationships, fostering a community around their shared love for literature.

Marisol, with her encyclopedic knowledge of authors and genres, her innate ability to recommend the perfect read, continued to be the heart and soul of the bookstore. But now, she had a partner, a sounding board, someone who understood the quiet satisfaction of a perfectly curated shelf, the thrill of discovering a hidden gem, the challenges of keeping a small business afloat in a changing world.

The 'Hearth' part of their bookstore's name had taken on a new significance. It was no longer just about the cozy atmosphere they cultivated within its walls. It was about the warmth they brought into each other's lives, the feeling of belonging and security that permeated their days. The familiar scent of coffee, once a solitary comfort for Marisol, now signified a shared start to each day, a symbol of their enduring partnership. It was the aroma that greeted them as they unlocked the doors each morning, the scent that lingered in the air as they discussed sales figures, and the fragrance that accompanied their contented sighs as they locked up for the night, knowing they were heading home, together.

Their customers noticed the change, of course. There was a new energy in 'The Bound Page & Hearth,' a palpable sense of joy and shared purpose that radiated from Marisol and Theo. Mrs. Gable, a frequent visitor and a staunch supporter of the bookstore, had commented just the other day, "You two, you're like two peas in a pod, but better. Like two perfectly bound volumes, each enhancing the other."

The sentiment was echoed by many. The easy laughter that now punctuated their interactions behind the counter, the stolen glances of affection, the way they instinctively anticipated each other's needs – it all painted a picture of a love that was not only passionate but also deeply comfortable, profoundly settled. It was the kind of love that didn't need grand gestures to prove itself, but was instead evidenced in the everyday, in the quiet rhythm of their lives together.

Evenings were a blend of shared responsibilities and stolen moments of pure connection. After closing the bookstore, they'd often walk home hand-in-hand, the setting sun casting long shadows across Cedar Ridge's charming main street. The conversation would flow easily, recounting the day's triumphs and minor mishaps, or simply sharing observations about the changing seasons. Back at their little house, the scent of whatever Marisol was cooking for dinner would fill the air, often with Theo right beside her, chopping vegetables or offering a taste of the sauce.

"Needs a little more garlic, don't you think?" he'd venture, and Marisol, trusting his palate, would add another clove, a smile playing on her lips.

Dinner was a sacred time, a pause in the day where they could truly connect. They'd talk about their families, their friends, the books they were reading, the dreams they were still nurturing. The integration of their lives wasn't about erasing their individual identities, but about enriching them, about expanding their worlds to encompass each other's.

One evening, as they were clearing the dinner plates, Marisol paused, looking at Theo, his face softened by the warm glow of the kitchen light. "You know," she said, her voice quiet but firm, "sometimes I still can't believe this is real. That we're... us. Mr. and Mrs. Hart-Vega."

Theo's eyes, the same deep, warm brown that had captivated her from the beginning, met hers. He set down the plate he was holding and stepped closer, his hands finding her waist. "It's real, Marisol," he said, his voice a low, resonant tone that always managed to calm her. "It's the most real thing I've ever known. And it's just the beginning." He pulled her close, his lips meeting hers in a kiss that was both tender and possessive, a silent promise of all the days, all the dawns, that lay ahead.

The integration of their lives extended beyond their home and the bookstore. It was in the way they now navigated Cedar Ridge together, a united front. When Theo was at a town council meeting, Marisol was often there, a quiet, supportive presence in the back row. When Marisol was at a literary festival planning session, Theo would be by her side, offering practical advice and unwavering encouragement. They were a team, partners in every sense of the word, their individual strengths complementing each other, their shared vision guiding their every step.

The scent of coffee, once a solitary pleasure for Marisol, now served as a constant, comforting reminder of their shared journey. It was the first thing she smelled in the morning, a warm embrace that signaled the start of a new day, a day spent with the man she loved. It was the scent that filled 'The Bound Page & Hearth,' a subtle but persistent testament to the warmth and intimacy that had become the hallmark of their lives together.

It was the aroma that lingered in their home, a comforting presence that spoke of shared meals, whispered secrets, and a love that was as deeply ingrained and as beautifully aromatic as the finest blend. Life as Mr. and Mrs. Hart-Vega was not just a title; it was a feeling, a state of being, a harmonious melody played out in the heart of Cedar Ridge, with the enduring scent of coffee as their constant, sweet refrain.

The chime of the bell above the door of 'The Bound Page & Hearth' had become more than just an indicator of a customer entering; it was a gentle overture to the shared world Marisol and Theo had meticulously built. Each time it sang its sweet, melodic tune, it announced a new arrival into a space that was now a vibrant tapestry woven from threads of literature, craftsmanship, and a love that had found its permanent anchor. The bookstore, once Marisol's solitary haven, had blossomed under their joint stewardship into something far richer, far more resonant. It was no longer just a place to purchase books; it was a destination, a reflection of their unified lives and a testament to the enduring power of shared dreams in the heart of Cedar Ridge.

Theo's contribution had transformed the very essence of the store's physical presence. His workshop, a space once relegated to the quiet hours after closing or the early mornings before opening, had begun to spill its creative output into the public realm of the bookstore. The sturdy, elegantly crafted wooden shelves that now lined the walls, each one a testament to his meticulous attention to detail and his innate understanding of wood's inherent beauty, were more than mere storage.

They were works of art in themselves, warm and inviting, their smooth surfaces inviting a lingering touch. He had designed and built custom display tables, their surfaces polished to a soft sheen, perfect for showcasing new releases or the prized antique editions Marisol so adored. These pieces weren't just functional; they were imbued with Theo's quiet strength and his passion for creating things that were both beautiful and enduring. They stood as silent, yet powerful, partners to the stories contained within the pages of the books they held.

The integration of his furniture into the bookstore's landscape had been a gradual, yet profound, evolution. It had begun with a single, exquisitely carved reading chair, placed strategically by the sun-drenched front window, a silent invitation for patrons to linger. Marisol had watched, her heart swelling with pride, as customers gravitated towards it, drawn by its comfort and the undeniable artistry. Soon, the chair was rarely empty, a silent testament to Theo's ability to create spaces that fostered connection and contemplation.

Then came the small side tables, perfect for resting a teacup or a well-loved paperback, followed by the larger display units, each one a masterpiece of joinery and design. The rich, warm tones of the oak and maple wood created a visual dialogue with the diverse spines of the books, adding a layer of tactile and aesthetic appeal that had previously been absent.

"It's like the store grew a whole new set of limbs," Mrs. Gable had remarked one afternoon, running a hand over the smooth surface of a new display shelf. "Strong, sturdy, and beautiful. You two, you just... you make everything better."

Her observation was more profound than she knew. The furniture wasn't merely decorative; it was an extension of Theo's personality and his commitment to Marisol and their shared venture. He had poured his skill, his patience, and his quiet love into every piece, and the result was a bookstore that felt not only curated but also deeply rooted, grounded in the tangible reality of craftsmanship. It was a physical manifestation of their partnership, a space where Marisol's literary world and Theo's material artistry were not just coexisting but harmoniously intertwined. The scent of freshly planed wood, a subtle counterpoint to the ever-present aroma of coffee and aged paper, now permeated the air, adding another layer to the sensory experience of 'The Bound Page & Hearth'.

The success of their joint venture was undeniable, a tangible outcome of their unwavering belief in each other and their shared vision. The bookstore had become a bustling hub, a place where the community felt not only welcome but also a sense of belonging. The gentle chime of the shop door was now an invitation into their shared world, a world where the boundaries between their individual passions had blurred, creating something richer, something more vibrant.

Customers, drawn by the unique atmosphere, the exceptional selection of books, and the warm, genuine hospitality of its proprietors, were returning with greater frequency. They found not just a good read, but an experience, a place where they could escape the everyday and immerse themselves in a haven of literature and thoughtful design.

Marisol found immense joy in observing this transformation. She watched as Theo, with his innate ability to connect with people, would engage customers in conversations not just about books, but about the furniture, its origins, its craftsmanship.

He spoke with a quiet pride about the wood, its grain, the techniques he'd employed, and in doing so, he introduced a new dimension to the bookstore experience. It was no longer just about the stories bound within pages; it was also about the stories embedded in the very structure of the place, the stories of creation and dedication. He had a knack for understanding what customers were looking for, not just in a book but in their environment, and he had, with his hands and his heart, provided it.

"This table," a young woman had said, tracing the intricate inlay on a small reading table, "it makes me want to curl up with a good book and never leave."

Theo would simply smile, a quiet warmth in his eyes, and Marisol would feel that familiar surge of pride and affection. He had a gift for creating spaces that invited stillness, that encouraged introspection, and that ultimately, fostered a deeper connection with the very act of reading. He had taken her literary sanctuary and infused it with his own quiet artistry, creating a space that felt both intellectually stimulating and deeply comforting. The combination was potent, irresistible.

The bookstore had become a symbol of their earned ever after. It was a physical manifestation of their commitment, not just to each other, but to the town of Cedar Ridge itself. They were invested, not just financially, but emotionally. They had poured their energy, their dreams, and their love into this endeavor, and the flourishing success of 'The Bound Page & Hearth' was a direct reflection of that dedication. It was a place where the tangible and the intangible converged, where the solid craftsmanship of Theo's furniture met the boundless imagination of Marisol's literary world, all under the watchful, nurturing gaze of their shared love.

The aisles, once solely dedicated to the orderly procession of books, now offered a more dynamic experience. Customers could browse fiction, then pause to admire a handcrafted bookshelf, or perhaps find the perfect gift in a set of Theo's beautifully bound journals, each one destined to be filled with thoughts and dreams. The synergy was palpable. Marisol, in her role as curator of literature, found her recommendations often complemented by Theo's pieces.

A historical romance might be displayed on a sturdy oak table, its rich grain echoing the timeless quality of the story, while a collection of poignant poetry might rest on a delicate, elegantly carved side table, its slender form mirroring the lyrical beauty of the verse.

They had created a holistic experience. It was a place where one could find a novel to transport them to another time and place, and in the same breath, find a handcrafted wooden pen that felt perfect in the hand, ready to capture their own reflections. The customers responded to this authentic blend, this genuine fusion of passions. They saw not just a store, but a vision brought to life, a testament to a partnership built on mutual respect, shared values, and a deep, abiding love.

The chime of the door became a welcoming note, an invitation into a space that was not just filled with books and furniture, but with the very essence of their shared journey, a journey that was still unfolding, chapter by beautiful chapter. The bookstore, in its entirety, was now a living, breathing embodiment of their commitment, a testament to the enduring power of love to create something truly extraordinary, something that resonated with the very soul of Cedar Ridge. It was a place where stories, both written and crafted, found their perfect home, and where two hearts, once separate, had found their eternal hearth.

Theo moved through his workshop, the air thick with the comforting, earthy scent of freshly planed wood. Sawdust, fine as confectioner's sugar, dusted his worn jeans and settled on the shoulders of his favorite flannel shirt. Each curl of wood that peeled away from the workbench was more than just shavings; it was a tangible piece of a dream being coaxed into reality. This space, once a sanctuary of solitary creation, now hummed with a different kind of energy, a quiet yet potent confidence that radiated from him like the warmth of a well-used hearth. He no longer saw the potential for loss in every commitment, but rather the profound strength that lay in embracing permanence.

The ghosts of his past, the ache of what had been taken from him, were still a part of his story, etched into the very grain of his being, but they no longer held the reins of his future. Instead, they served as a gentle reminder of the preciousness of what he now held, a silent testament to the depth of his gratitude.

He was building more than just furniture these days. He was constructing a life. With every joint he meticulously fitted, every surface he sanded smooth, he was reinforcing the foundation of his future with Marisol. The vulnerability he had once shielded himself from, the raw exposure of his heart, had been met with an unwavering tenderness that had allowed him to blossom. It was a quiet bravery, a conscious choice to open himself fully, to trust that the love he was nurturing was sturdy enough to withstand any storm. And it was. He felt it in the steady rhythm of his hammer, in the sure grip of his tools, in the unshakeable certainty that settled deep within his soul.

The new commission—a custom-built window seat for the Cedar Ridge community center, a place where young and old would gather, where stories would be shared and laughter would echo—was a perfect reflection of this evolved perspective. It wasn't just about showcasing his skill; it was about creating a space for connection, a place where shared experiences could take root. He pictured the sunlight streaming through the large windows, warming the polished oak of the seat, warming the people who would settle there, a silent testament to the interconnectedness of their small town. He found a deep satisfaction in this tangible expression of his love, a love that was no longer confined to hushed confessions and stolen glances, but was now an open, celebrated facet of their lives.

Marisol's joy, her radiant happiness that seemed to emanate from her like the very light that filled the bookstore, was the most potent fuel for his quiet confidence. He saw it in the way her eyes sparkled when she spoke of their shared future, in the way her hand instinctively sought his when they were amidst the gentle bustle of the shop. She had seen him, truly seen him, not just the craftsman, but the man beneath, and had loved him not in spite of his past, but with a profound understanding that embraced every part of him. This acceptance, this unwavering belief, had been the catalyst, freeing him from the shadows of his former fear and allowing him to step fully into the light of their shared present.

He remembered the early days, the hesitant steps, the constant hum of anxiety that had underscored his every interaction with her. The fear of imperfection, the dread of his own perceived inadequacies, had been a constant companion. He had been so afraid of not being enough, of his love not being enough to fill the void left by tragedy. But Marisol had a way of seeing past the surface, of recognizing the enduring strength beneath the veneer of his reserve. She had coaxed it out, nurtured it, and in doing so, had helped him understand that his past loss, while deeply painful, did not define his capacity for future joy. It had, in fact, made him more acutely aware of its value.

His woodworking had always been an outlet, a way to channel his thoughts and his emotions. But now, it was more. It was a language of love, a consistent, tangible expression of his commitment. He would spend hours in his workshop, the rhythmic rasp of sandpaper and the steady tap of his hammer a soundtrack to his devotion. He would often find himself sketching designs, not just for commissioned pieces, but for small, personal gifts for Marisol—a delicate wooden bookmark inlaid with a tiny sprig of lavender, a sturdy but elegant frame for a photograph of them laughing by the lake. These were not grand gestures, but they were imbued with a deep sincerity, a silent promise whispered through the grain of the wood.

One afternoon, while working on a set of custom shelving for a new children's section in the bookstore, he paused, a piece of cherry wood held loosely in his hand. The rich, reddish hue seemed to glow in the dappled sunlight filtering through the workshop window. He ran his thumb over the impossibly smooth surface, imagining the small hands that would reach for books from these shelves, the eager minds that would be ignited by the stories they held.

This was the essence of their shared dream, a synergy of his craft and Marisol's passion for literature, creating a space that nurtured both imagination and a sense of belonging. The bookstore, 'The Bound Page & Hearth,' had become a physical manifestation of their love, a place where every detail, from the carefully chosen books to the sturdy, beautiful furniture, spoke of their shared commitment.

He thought about the fear he used to harbor, the gnawing apprehension that any happiness he found was fleeting, destined to be snatched away. It was a heavy burden, one he had carried for so long that it had become almost a part of his identity. But Marisol had helped him shed that weight, piece by painstaking piece. Her unwavering belief in their shared future had chipped away at his doubts, revealing the solid core of hope that had always been there, waiting to be rediscovered. He found a quiet exhilaration in this newfound freedom, a sense of peace that settled deep within his bones.

He was no longer afraid of permanence. In fact, he craved it. He craved the steady rhythm of waking up next to Marisol, the comforting routine of shared meals, the silent understanding that passed between them with a mere glance. He found a profound sense of fulfillment in the predictable beauty of their everyday lives, a beauty that was earned, not stumbled upon. His past loss was a scar, a reminder of a pain he would never forget, but it was no longer an open wound. It was a part of his history, a testament to his resilience, and a quiet motivator to cherish every moment of joy he now possessed.

The scent of wood shavings was more than just a fragrance; it was the scent of purpose, the scent of a future being meticulously crafted. He would catch Marisol sniffing the air when she visited his workshop, a soft smile gracing her lips. "It smells like your love, Theo," she'd said once, her voice warm and laced with affection. And he knew she was right. Every piece he created, every project he undertook, was infused with the quiet, steady current of his love for her. It was a love that was expressed not in grand pronouncements, but in the consistent presence, the intentional actions, the unwavering commitment to building a life together, brick by carefully placed brick, board by perfectly joined board.

He picked up a chisel, its smooth wooden handle a familiar weight in his palm. He was about to start carving the decorative motif for the community center's window seat, a subtle pattern of interwoven leaves and branches, a symbol of growth and interconnectedness. It was a small detail, easily overlooked, but to Theo, it was as significant as the sturdy frame of the piece itself. It was another layer of his love, another whispered promise to Marisol, a promise of a life deeply rooted, beautifully crafted, and eternally shared. The quiet confidence that had taken root within him was not a boastful pride, but a deep, abiding peace, the peace of a man who had found his hearth, and knew, with absolute certainty, that he was home.

He no longer feared the unknown future, for he was building it, together, with the woman who had shown him the true meaning of an earned ever after. The scent of wood shavings, the steady rhythm of his work, the quiet hum of purpose—these were the new anthems of his life, songs of love, commitment, and a happiness that was as solid and enduring as the oak he so expertly shaped. His past was a chapter closed, not forgotten, but no longer defining.

His present was a vibrant, unfolding story, written in the language of shared dreams and the quiet confidence of a heart finally at rest, nestled within the warmth of a love that was as real and tangible as the furniture he built.

Marisol moved through the bookstore, the familiar scent of aged paper and brewing tea a comforting balm to her soul. Each turn of a page, each hushed conversation between a browsing customer and herself, was a thread woven into the rich tapestry of her life. It was a life she had once only dared to dream of, a life built on the solid, unwavering foundation of Theo's love. The hollow ache of uncertainty, the gnawing question of whether her quiet desires for a love acknowledged and returned would ever be truly met, had faded into a distant echo. Now, it was replaced by a profound sense of peace, a deep-seated contentment that settled in her bones like the warmth of the hearth in their shared living room.

She no longer felt the need to chase fleeting moments of affection or to constantly seek validation; Theo's steady presence, his quiet devotion manifested in a thousand small gestures, had spoken louder than any grand declaration.

The window seat Theo was building for the community center was more than just a piece of furniture; it was a symbol of their shared commitment to Cedar Ridge, a tangible representation of the roots they were digging deeper into this welcoming town. She'd visited his workshop a few days prior, drawn by the rhythmic cadence of his tools and the earthy scent that always clung to him. He'd been engrossed in his work, his brow furrowed in concentration as he sanded a curved piece of oak, the late afternoon sun casting a warm glow on his strong profile.

When he'd looked up and met her gaze, his eyes, usually so reserved, had held a profound tenderness, a silent acknowledgment of the journey they had traversed together. He'd simply smiled, a soft, genuine smile that reached his eyes, and for a moment, the world outside the workshop had ceased to exist. In that shared glance, she saw not just the craftsman, but the man who had bravely offered her his heart, the man who had learned to trust again, and the man who had chosen her, fully and without reservation.

"It's coming along beautifully," she had said, her voice barely a whisper, running a hand over the smooth, unvarnished wood.

"Almost ready for its homecoming," Theo had replied, his voice a low rumble that resonated deep within her. He'd reached out, his calloused fingers brushing hers as he guided her hand to a section of intricate carving. "Little acorns," he'd explained, his thumb tracing the delicate lines. "For new beginnings. And for strength. Like us."

Marisol had felt a tremor of emotion run through her. Acorns. New beginnings. Strength. It was all there, in his quiet language of wood and craftsmanship. He didn't need to articulate every fear he had overcome, every doubt he had banished. She knew. She felt it in the way he held her hand, in the way his arm instinctively wrapped around her waist when they walked through town, in the way he looked at her when he thought she wasn't watching. Their love wasn't a fragile seedling requiring constant watering and protection; it was a sturdy oak, its roots intertwined, weathering storms and basking in the sun, growing stronger with each passing season.

The bookstore, 'The Bound Page & Hearth,' was a testament to this earned permanence. It was more than just a business; it was their shared sanctuary, a place where Marisol's passion for literature and Theo's appreciation for solid craftsmanship merged seamlessly. The custom-built bookshelves, the sturdy reading chairs, the warm, inviting hearth that gave the store its name – each element was a reflection of their partnership.

She remembered the initial trepidation when they'd decided to combine their visions, the quiet fear that their individual dreams might clash. But Theo, with his innate understanding of balance and form, had seamlessly integrated his skills into her established world, enhancing it, enriching it, making it even more beautiful than she could have imagined. He hadn't just built shelves; he had built a more complete version of her dream.

She found herself pausing by the children's section, a smile playing on her lips as she watched a young boy excitedly pull a brightly colored book from one of the shelves Theo had meticulously crafted. The wood was smooth, the edges rounded, perfect for little hands. It was a small detail, but it spoke volumes about Theo's thoughtfulness, his innate understanding of the people who would use the space he created.

He had even carved tiny, whimsical animals hidden amongst the decorative trim, a secret delight for those who looked closely. These were the elements that made their shared life so rich, the quiet expressions of love that permeated every aspect of their days.

Her optimism, once a tentative flicker, now burned with a steady, unwavering flame. Cedar Ridge had welcomed her, and more importantly, it had embraced Theo, allowing him to shed the lingering shadows of his past and step fully into the light of their present. She had seen the subtle shift in him, the gradual unfurling of his spirit as he realized that love, once lost, could indeed be found again, and that permanence wasn't a trap, but a sanctuary. Her own yearning for a love that was both spoken and lived, for a relationship where her heart was not just accepted but cherished, had been answered in the most beautiful way imaginable. Theo's actions had spoken volumes, painting a picture of a future filled with shared joys and unwavering support.

She remembered the initial conversations, the hesitant confessions, the moments when she had felt her own vulnerability laid bare. Theo, who had once guarded his emotions so fiercely, had met her openness with a tenderness that had disarmed her completely. He had shown her that true strength wasn't in building walls, but in allowing someone to see past them. He had shared his own past, not with regret or self-pity, but with a quiet dignity that spoke of resilience and a hard-won understanding of life's complexities. And in sharing, he had invited her to be a part of his healing, to be a witness to his emergence from the darkness.

Now, as she tidied a shelf of poetry, her fingers brushing against the spines of familiar verses, she felt a surge of profound gratitude. Gratitude for the quiet strength of Cedar Ridge, gratitude for the vibrant community they were now a part of, and above all, gratitude for Theo. He was her anchor, her confidante, her greatest supporter. Their conversations were no longer about navigating the uncertainties of burgeoning feelings, but about shared dreams, about the practicalities of building a life together, about the little joys that peppered their days. They talked about expanding the bookstore, about hosting more community events, about the simple pleasure of a quiet evening spent reading side-by-side.

She paused, picking up a worn copy of Emily Dickinson. "We learned to live outdoors," she murmured, the words resonating with her current state of being. Yes, they had learned to live outdoors, metaphorically speaking, their hearts exposed and unafraid in the open air of their shared love. The fear of loss, the specter of grief that had once loomed so large, had receded, replaced by an appreciation for the preciousness of each shared moment. Every sunrise they witnessed together, every shared laugh, every quiet evening walk, was a treasure, savored and held close.

Marisol often found herself reflecting on the journey that had led them here. It hadn't been a straight path, but a winding one, filled with un-expected detours and quiet moments of introspection. She had learned that love wasn't just about passion and grand gestures, but about the quiet, consistent effort to understand, to support, and to cherish. Theo embodied this understanding. He was a man of few words, but his actions were a symphony of devotion. He fixed the squeaky hinge on her favorite reading chair without being asked, he always made sure her teacup was refilled before it was empty, he remembered the small details of her day and asked about them with genuine interest. These were the threads that wove their lives together, creating a fabric of enduring love.

She thought about the future, not with the anxious anticipation of her past, but with a calm certainty. The future was not a daunting unknown, but an unfolding adventure, a path they would walk together, hand in hand. She envisioned their lives in Cedar Ridge, filled with the comfortable rhythm of community, the quiet satisfaction of meaningful work, and the deep, abiding love that had become the bedrock of their existence.

The bookstore, 'The Bound Page & Hearth,' would continue to be a hub of connection, a place where stories were shared and lives were enriched. Theo's woodworking would continue to bring beauty and functionality to their town, his creations a testament to his skill and his generous spirit.

As she straightened a display of new releases, her gaze drifted towards the window. The late afternoon sun cast long shadows across the cobblestone street, painting the familiar landscape in hues of gold and amber. A sense of profound peace washed over her.

She was home. Not just in Cedar Ridge, but in herself, in her relationship, in the life they had so carefully and lovingly built. The yearning she had once carried had been transformed into a quiet strength, a deep-seated knowledge that she was loved, fully and unconditionally. Her chosen permanence, once a hopeful aspiration, was now a beautiful, vibrant reality, a testament to the power of honest communication, unwavering support, and a love that had weathered storms and emerged stronger, brighter, and more beautiful than she could have ever imagined.

She exhaled slowly, a soft smile gracing her lips, her heart brimming with a contentment that felt as solid and enduring as the very foundations of Cedar Ridge itself.

The air in Cedar Ridge carried a different kind of scent these days, a blend of freshly baked bread from Mrs. Gable's bakery, the earthy aroma of Theo's workshop, and the crisp, clean fragrance of pine from the surrounding hills. It was a perfume of belonging, a subtle yet powerful testament to the lives that had taken root and flourished within its embrace. Marisol felt it every time she stepped out of 'The Bound Page & Hearth,' her bookstore, a space that was no longer just her own haven but a vibrant extension of their shared existence. It was a life woven from countless small moments, each one imbued with the quiet strength of their commitment, a tapestry whose threads were as strong and resilient as the ancient oaks that dotted the landscape.

Her story, and Theo's, had become more than just a personal narrative; it was a story that resonated with the very heart of Cedar Ridge. It was a tale of two souls, each carrying their own history of shadows and uncertainties, who had found solace and unwavering support in each other's presence. Marisol remembered the initial hesitant steps, the careful dance around unspoken fears, the tentative confessions that had paved the way for a deeper understanding.

Theo, with his quiet stoicism and his profound capacity for tenderness, had shown her that vulnerability was not a weakness but an invitation, a bridge built between two hearts. He had met her deepest insecurities not with judgment or indifference, but with a steady hand and a reassuring gaze, creating a safe harbor where she could finally let down her guard.

Their commitment wasn't forged in grand pronouncements, but in the steady rhythm of everyday life. It was in the way Theo would pause his work at the workshop, the sawdust clinging to his clothes, just to watch her greet a customer with a warm smile. It was in the way Marisol would instinctively reach for his hand as they walked through the town square, a silent declaration of their unspoken bond. These were the quiet affirmations, the constant reassurances that their love was not a fragile bloom, but a sturdy, deeply rooted tree, capable of weathering any storm. Cedar Ridge, with its inherent sense of community and its gentle pace, had provided the fertile ground for their love to grow, free from the anxieties and pressures of the outside world.

The community center, a project that had brought them closer than ever, was a tangible symbol of their shared vision for Cedar Ridge. The window seat Theo had meticulously crafted, adorned with the delicate carvings of acorns, was now a beloved fixture, a place where children's stories were read aloud and quiet conversations unfolded. Marisol often saw couples sitting there, their hands clasped, their faces relaxed as they absorbed the warmth of the afternoon sun.

Each time she witnessed it, a gentle smile would grace her lips, a quiet acknowledgment of the love that bloomed in this town, a love that their own story had helped to inspire. Theo's craftsmanship, his ability to imbue wood with so much warmth and character, had become a hallmark of Cedar Ridge, his creations gracing homes and public spaces alike, each piece a testament to his skill and his generous spirit.

He had a unique way of communicating his affection, a language spoken through his hands and his creations. The custom-built bookshelves in 'The Bound Page & Hearth' were more than just storage; they were an art form, each shelf perfectly spaced, the wood smoothed and finished to perfection.

He had even incorporated hidden nooks and crannies, places where Marisol could tuck away special editions or personal notes, small surprises that made her heart sing. It was this thoughtfulness, this deep understanding of her needs and desires, that had solidified their bond. He didn't just see her; he understood her, and he built their life together with that understanding at its core.

The bakery, once a symbol of her solitary ambition, was now a place of shared dreams. Marisol recalled the early days, the scent of yeast and sugar filling the air as she poured her heart into her creations. Now, Theo often joined her, his strong hands skillfully shaping dough, his presence a comforting balm to her soul. They'd work side-by-side, their movements synchronized, their conversations flowing effortlessly, a gentle murmur of shared plans and quiet affirmations.

The customers, once familiar faces, had become friends, their lives interwoven with Marisol and Theo's. They celebrated their milestones, offered comfort in times of sadness, and cheered them on as they navigated the everyday joys and challenges of building a life together.

One crisp autumn afternoon, as Marisol was arranging a display of pumpkin-spiced biscotti, Mrs. Gable, her face etched with a lifetime of laughter and kindness, leaned against the counter. "You know, Marisol," she said, her voice warm and full of affection, "you and Theo... you're like the heart of this town now. Your love story, it's become a part of Cedar Ridge's own story. It reminds us all that even after the hardest winters, spring always comes."

Marisol felt a blush creep up her neck, but her heart swelled with gratitude. She looked over at Theo, who was carefully stacking a new shipment of artisanal flours, his brow furrowed in concentration. He caught her eye and offered a small, knowing smile, a silent acknowledgment of Mrs. Gable's words and the truth they held. Their love had blossomed here, nurtured by the kindness of this community and the unwavering devotion they shared. It was an earned happiness, a testament to their courage in opening their hearts and their willingness to build a future together, brick by steady brick, word by quiet word.

The children's section of the bookstore, with its sturdy, handcrafted shelves and the whimsical carved animals peeking out from the edges, was a particular source of joy for Marisol. She'd often watch as young children, their faces alight with wonder, discovered the hidden creatures, their squeals of delight echoing through the quiet space. It was a testament to Theo's vision, his ability to see beyond the utilitarian and infuse his creations with a touch of magic. He had a way of making everything he touched feel special, imbued with a sense of warmth and personality.

Their conversations had evolved from hesitant explorations of feeling to robust discussions about their future. They spoke of expanding the bookstore, of hosting author readings and poetry nights that would further cement its place as a cultural hub for Cedar Ridge. They discussed Theo's dream of creating a small woodworking cooperative, a space where he could mentor young apprentices, passing on his skills and his passion for craftsmanship. These were not just abstract ideas; they were plans, concrete steps they were taking together, their shared vision for their lives unfolding with a quiet certainty.

Marisol often found herself reflecting on the contrast between her past anxieties and her present contentment. The gnawing fear of inadequacy, the persistent whisper of doubt that had once shadowed her, had receded into a distant memory. Theo's unwavering belief in her, his consistent support, had been the antidote to those lingering insecurities. He had never asked her to be anyone other than herself, and in doing so, he had given her the greatest gift of all: the freedom to simply be, to love and be loved for who she truly was.

The town square, once a place of fleeting encounters, was now a landscape of shared memories. The bench where they'd had their first real conversation, the café where they'd celebrated small victories, the park where they'd watched the leaves turn vibrant shades of red and gold – each location held a special significance. Their journey had been marked by these milestones, each one a stepping stone on the path to their enduring happiness. They hadn't rushed into anything; instead, they had allowed their love to unfold organically, nurtured by shared experiences and a growing understanding of each other's hearts.

Even the smallest gestures held profound meaning. The way Theo would leave a single, perfect rose on her pillow, the way Marisol would bake his favorite apple pie on a dreary Tuesday, the way they'd instinctively reach for each other's hands during a quiet moment – these were the threads that strengthened their bond, weaving a tapestry of love that was both beautiful and unbreakable. Cedar Ridge had provided them with a backdrop of peace and acceptance, a community that celebrated their union and embraced them as one of their own.

One evening, as they sat by the hearth in their cozy living room, the fire casting a warm glow on their faces, Marisol leaned her head on Theo's shoulder. "Sometimes," she murmured, her voice soft with contentment, "I can't believe how lucky we are."

Theo wrapped an arm around her, his calloused hand gently stroking her hair. "It's not luck, Marisol," he said, his voice a low rumble that resonated deep within her. "It's choosing. It's building. It's loving. And it's you."

His words, simple and direct, held a profound truth. Their love story wasn't a fairytale born of chance; it was a masterpiece meticulously crafted through shared effort, unwavering commitment, and a deep, abiding love that had found its permanent home in the heart of Cedar Ridge. The gentle rhythm of the town continued, now graced by the enduring melody of their earned ever after, a testament to the power of love to transform, to heal, and to last a lifetime.

Glossary

The Bound Page & Hearth: Marisol's beloved bookstore, which also serves as a warm, inviting community gathering space.

Cedar Ridge: The picturesque small town where Marisol and Theo's love story unfolds.

Artisanal Flours: High-quality, often specialty flours used in baking, suggesting a focus on craft and quality within the bakery.

Pumpkin-spiced biscotti: A popular seasonal baked good, indicative of the cozy, autumnal atmosphere of Cedar Ridge.

Woodworking Cooperative: A collaborative workshop where artisans share tools, space, and knowledge, a vision Theo holds for his craft.

www.ingramcontent.com/pod-product-compliance
Lightning Source LLC
Chambersburg PA
CBHW030151310726
48970CB00005B/1681